The GILDER

The GILDER

KATHRYN KAY

KENSINGTON BOOKS
www.kensingtonbooks.com

KENSINGTON BOOKS are published by

Kensington Publishing Corp.
119 West 40th Street
New York, NY 10018

All Kensington titles, imprints, and distributed lines are available at special quantity discounts for bulk purchases for sales promotion, premiums, fund-raising, educational, or institutional use.

Special book excerpts or customized printings can also be created to fit specific needs. For details, write or phone the office of the Kensington Special Sales Manager: Kensington Publishing Corp., 119 West 40th Street, New York, NY 10018. Attn. Special Sales Department. Phone: 1-800-221-2647.

Kensington and the K logo Reg. U.S. Pat. & TM Off.

ISBN-13: 978-0-7582-6322-3
ISBN-10: 0-7582-6322-8

First Kensington Trade Paperback Printing: January 2012
10 9 8 7 6 5 4 3 2 1

Printed in the United States of America

For mothers and daughters everywhere

ACKNOWLEDGMENTS

I am deeply grateful to:

My agent, Meg Ruley; my editor, John Scognamiglio; and everyone at Kensington Books who worked on bringing this book to fruition.

Nancy Thayer, for introducing me to Meg and for her continued support and wisdom.

The members of my Nantucket writing group, for listening to this story as it evolved, and for their ongoing encouragement.

My workshop students, who inspire me with their honesty and courage.

Ariel, for being the best daughter a mother could have, and for being my first and most faithful reader.

Ted, for his invaluable technical support and for his part in creating my darling Elsie.

Tyler and Blakney, for showing me just how wide a heart can open.

Robert, for having faith that I would one day finish this book, and for loving me in spite of how long it took.

The Gilder

Hudson River Valley, 1993

It wasn't unusual for soccer practice to run late, but Marina couldn't shake the sense of uneasiness that had hovered all day. From the window, the road was all but invisible under a canopy of gold and russet oaks. Marina strained to see beyond the end of the drive, as if she could conjure Zoe's appearance, but all she saw were leaves spiraling down and tumbling across the lawn into the thorny arms of a rosebush. She checked her watch again and then turned away to stoke the wood stove.

Slipping her hand into the ragged, patchwork oven mitt, she grasped the iron handle on the front of the stove, turned it smartly to the right, then dropped the mitt.

"Shit," she muttered, shaking out her hand. She then folded the cloth in two and tried again. Thin as it was, she didn't have the heart to throw the mitt away. It had been a birthday gift from Zoe, one of her first attempts at sewing. At age nine, her daughter had come to the realization that knocking boys down on the soccer field was not the best way to gain their friendship or affection, and had turned her attention briefly to the more feminine pursuits of cooking and sewing before realizing that her heart belonged to soccer and not to the boys. Now, at fifteen, Zoe was still passionate about soccer, but boys seemed to be ever more evident on the periphery. Time would tell.

Where was Zoe? Why was she feeling so damn anxious?

Marina leaned away from the heat of the glowing embers as she wedged two pieces of split oak into the cast-iron box. It had taken a couple of winters to get the hang of heating the studio she'd set up in the small, white clapboard chapel adjacent to her house. Before mastering the art of stoking and airflow, she'd worked layered in sweatshirts or stripped down to nearly nothing. Today, she wore a light cotton shirt and blue jeans under her coverall. Sitting back on her heels, she gazed into the flames, their smoky scent evoking thoughts of pumpkin pie and mulled cider, reminding her that Thanksgiving was just around the corner.

Marina straightened up, pressing her thumbs into her low back, and after a quick glance out the window, made herself return to her workbench. Her muscles protested as she bent to examine a corner of the massive frame. Although she'd designed the workbench to raise and lower, a certain amount of bending was unavoidable. She'd tried sitting on a stool, but it limited her range of motion and inhibited her rhythm. Besides, she was hard-pressed to make improvements on anything she'd learned during her apprenticeship in Florence all those years ago. She brought her face closer to the freshly gilded area and squinted. No, not a rip in the gold leaf, just a trick of the light. This stage of gilding was a welcome relief after the many hours of painstaking repairs, surface preparation, and application of the gold leaf. She picked up an agate-tipped burnishing tool and began to move it in a circular motion across the surface of the frame, her mind relaxing as the gilded leaves melded into a smooth surface, concealing any signs of the damage beneath.

At the sound of a car door, Marina hurried back to the window. Down at the bottom of the drive, her soccer cleats slung over one shoulder, Zoe waved to the Volvo station wagon just leaving the driveway. Marina lifted her hand to wave, but Zoe headed for the house without so much as a glance toward her mother's studio. Marina sighed and turned back to her work. Granted, teenage girls could be moody, but Zoe had done nothing but sulk since Marina told her that, no, she could not accompany her to Florence, where she was to give a lecture on restoration. She'd cited missing school as the reason, but in truth, she didn't know how she was going to cope with returning to the place she'd run away from all those years ago, and taking Zoe along would only complicate things. When she'd received the invitation to make a presentation at the conference, her immediate reaction had been to decline, but an event hosted by the Uffizi Gallery was not one to be passed over lightly, and in the end, prestige had won out over her reluctance to revisit Florence and the memories it held.

The click of the gate latch, followed by footsteps on slate, penetrated Marina's thoughts. She looked up but kept her hand in motion as Zoe entered through the arched doorway at the far end of the studio. She had a sandwich in her hand.

"How'd practice go? How come you are so late?" Marina asked.

"It went good," Zoe replied through a mouthful.

"*Well*. It went well."

"Whatever." Zoe pulled a stool out from under the bench and slipped onto it as Marina turned the frame a few degrees and continued working. Zoe finished her sandwich in silence.

"You know, Mom, I've been thinking." She paused, and then rushed to the end of the sentence. "You really *should* take me with you to Florence."

Marina's hand faltered for a second as she continued burnishing the gilt. Without looking up, she said, "You have school."

"I know, but you said you'd take me to Florence one day."

Marina put down the tool. "And I will, sweetie. But *not* this time."

Zoe's voice dropped to almost a whisper. "I have to go with you. I *need* to know more . . . more about my dad."

Marina looked at Zoe, who was studying a glob of dried gesso on the workbench, picking at it with her thumbnail. "What, exactly, do you want to know, Zoe?" She tried to keep her voice neutral, but her constricting heart gave it an inevitable edge.

"Just stuff. I want to see where you guys lived, your special picnic spot, stuff like that."

Marina gripped the edge of the table. "I've already told you everything."

Zoe lifted her head; her gray eyes, so like her father's, sparked against her mother's blue. "No, Mom, you *haven't*. You never really tell me *anything!*"

Marina pushed her hair off her face with one hand. "Look, Zoe, it's hard for me. . . ."

"Hard for you? What about me?" The stool wobbled as Zoe stood up abruptly.

"Zoe, I . . ."

"You try not having a father. See how you like it!" Zoe spat the words at Marina and spun on her heel.

"Zoe, wait!" Marina called after her as Zoe ran the length of the workshop, yanked open the door, and disappeared into the dusky light.

Marina sank onto her stool, following the sound of her daughter's feet across the paving stones to the house. The back door slammed. It had been so much easier when Zoe was little. She'd answered the tell-me-about-Daddy question with: "Your daddy liked to take pictures of people," or "Sometimes I helped Daddy with his pictures," or "Daddy is watching you from heaven. He loves you very much." As Zoe got a little older, these platitudes became: "Your father was a well-known portrait photographer," or "Sometimes I modeled for your father or helped him in the darkroom," or "It was a terrible motor scooter accident." The year Zoe turned twelve, her curiosity faded, seemingly displaced by nascent adolescence, but evidently it had merely lain dormant in her psyche, waiting to resurface.

The question now was how much of that story to share with Zoe. How much did Zoe really need to know about Thomas? He was her father, he was dead; couldn't they just leave it at that? And then there was Sarah. It was impossible to talk about Thomas without talking about Sarah. Zoe already knew that Sarah had been her mother's closest friend during that year in Florence; did she need to know more than that? Did she need the whole truth? After so many years of denial and lies, Marina wasn't sure she even knew what the truth was, let alone how to explain it to her daughter.

Part One

FLORENCE, 1977

CHAPTER 1

Marina felt the train ride in every limb as she hefted her backpack onto one shoulder and headed down the deserted platform. It was close to midnight. The tears she'd fought earlier that day blurred her vision as she headed for the exit in search of a taxi. Her plan of arriving in the safety of daylight had gone awry when she boarded the wrong train in Milan and, instead of arriving in Florence, had ended up in a tiny station somewhere on the coast. Her dream—of speeding through flat fields dotted with whitewashed farmhouses and cypress trees, of turreted towers and terra-cotta roofs in the distance, the red dome of the cathedral rising from their midst—had been reduced to a black nightscape dotted with blurred pinpoints of light.

She scanned the sole cab at the curb with a practiced eye honed by years of hair-raising Yellow Cab rides, and decided that the middle-aged man in a sweater-vest and tie looked harmless enough, more like a college professor than a cabbie. She pushed her pack into the backseat of the Fiat and climbed in. He waited patiently as she pulled a crumpled paper from her pocket and read the words, "Pensione Alberto," but before she could read the street address, he put the car in gear and said, *"Sì, sì, andiamo,"* and pulled away from the curb. After a few twists and turns down narrow, cobblestoned streets, she let go of any attempt at tracking their route. Besides, there were no discernable markers, only a sheer façade of shuttered buildings, dim streetlights, and shadowed doorways. Suddenly, they broke free from the tight tangle of streets and turned onto a wider road that ran along the river. She leaned forward with a rush of excitement at the sight of the Arno River and, yes, there up ahead was the Ponte Vecchio spanning the river as it had for centuries. She was here. It had taken years of dreaming and persistence, but she'd finally made it! A few minutes later, the cab turned again and stopped at the curb.

Marina awoke the next morning to ripples of sunlight playing across her face. Peering over the edge of the coverlet, she took in the wardrobe, beautifully carved with cherubs and vines, that the night before had appeared dark and hulking, and in the corner, her discarded sweater and jeans looked quite at home where she'd flung them on the threadbare armchair.

On her arrival the night before, she had attempted to apologize for the late hour, but the woman who received her in a sagging cardigan, nightgown, and leather slippers was interested only in getting back to her bed as quickly as possible. She took Marina's passport, indicated where to sign the thick guest register, then delivered her to the top floor in an elevator the size of a telephone booth, unlocked a room, handed over the key, and pointed out a bathroom at the end of the hall.

Now as she lay staring at the shuttered window, part of her wanted to leap out of bed, throw open the sash, and shout, "I'm here! I'm here!" but another part of her hesitated. It had been eight years since she'd happened across the pictures of Florence, eight years of dreaming of this moment, and she wasn't sure she was quite ready for the dream to become a reality.

Her fourteen-year-old world had been hazy, flat, tasteless, filled with irritations: her parents, her friends, school; even the Rolling Stones were getting on her nerves. It was a Saturday afternoon and her parents were out, her mother at the gallery, her father at his chess club. She was supposed to be working on a term paper for social studies but had yet to come up with a topic that would fulfill the assignment to write about an international catastrophe. From her point of view, the entire world was one big catastrophe. As she often did when she was bored and alone in the house, she wandered into her father's study in search of a distraction. Sitting at his desk with her eyes closed, she tried to imagine her thoughts as groups of numbers the way her father, a mathematician, once told her he saw his, but all that appeared behind her closed eyelids were fluorescent squiggles. She opened her eyes and studied the collection of Victorian glass paperweights that were lined up along the back edge of the desk. One by one, she picked them up, allowing their cool, smooth, blue-green heft to fill her hands as she stared into their depths, admiring the fissures and imperfections. As always, when she was done, she replaced them as she had found them, equidistant, one from the other. Inevitably, her restlessness led to the bookshelves where her mother's novels and art books shared space with her father's tomes on math and science. She already had *Lady Chatterley's Lover* hidden under her pillow, and she'd read the dirty parts of *Goldfinger* and *From Russia with Love* when she was twelve, so it wasn't sex she was looking for that day.

A stack of coffee table books on the window seat caught her eye. She sat down and pulled the top book onto her lap and ran her fingers across the raised gold letters printed across a panoramic view of the city. *Florence: Art and Architecture*. Turning the pages, she found photographs of paintings that were nothing like the ones her mother hung in her cavernous, white gallery, with their splashes and slashes of color that pretended to be something they were not. Although she tried hard to see what her mother saw in this artwork, she found neither recognizable objects nor beauty. However, in the paintings of the Renaissance, she discovered a world revitalized. There was love in cherubic faces, peace in the eyes of a Madonna, pain and devastation in chaotic battle scenes. Even the folds of a robe made sense to her. In the photographs of the city itself, the light and color drew her in, inviting exploration. She sat for hours that afternoon wandering the streets of Florence, imagining herself a lady in a long, flowing gown, or a painter in a spattered smock.

That night, her mother told her about the flood that had devastated Florence a few years earlier when the river overflowed, leaving the city underwater to depths as much as fifteen feet in places and priceless works of art buried in the mud once the waters retreated. She told her about the "mud angels," young people from all over the world who had gone to Florence to help retrieve and restore the artwork. She gave Marina the issue of *Life* magazine that covered the catastrophe, and suggested she might consider the flood as a topic for her term paper.

For weeks, as Marina researched and wrote her paper, she begged her mother to take her to Florence. "Maybe we can help," she pleaded. When that did not work, she resorted to accusations. "I thought you cared about art. Or is it only the art that makes you money?" Finally, her mother told her that if she still wanted to go to Florence when she graduated from high school, she would take her. High school came and went, as did college, and invariably, her mother always had a show to hang, an opening to arrange, or an artist in crisis.

Marina stared at the stains on the ceiling and tried not to feel bitter. Hadn't she been lucky to have parents with interesting careers, to be treated like an adult, to meet famous people and get to stay up late? So what if no one was ever home after school? In the face of envious friends who begged to be invited to gallery openings, she pretended to be that lucky girl, but she would have exchanged their mundane lives for hers in a second. While she never doubted that her parents loved her and had basked in their praise of her self-sufficiency, their distraction often left her lonely and longing.

But she wasn't fourteen anymore, she was twenty-two and she was in *Firenze!* When she'd told her mother she was planning to take the long-awaited trip on her own, her mother had simply said, "Of course you are, you're an artist." In that respect, Marina was profoundly grateful for her mother's unwavering support and encouragement of her interest in art. Preoccupied as she might have been, her mother had recognized her daughter's talent early on and had spared no expense when it came to art classes. It was the one area where Marina might have rebelled, and there had been times during her adolescence when Marina had feigned disinterest, but it was always short-lived.

Unable to wait another minute, Marina pushed back the covers, crossed the room, and unlatched the window. As she parted the shutters, she saw in her mind's eye every panoramic view of the city—with its domes, spires, and towers—that she had ever seen in a book or on film. However, all she saw now was a jumble of red-tiled rooftops, TV antennas, and clotheslines hung with washing, but surprisingly, it was enough. It was perfect.

Dressed in clean jeans and a fresh sweater, Marina slung her leather satchel across her chest, covering it with a woven poncho. Unsure how to work the elevator, she took the wide, faded runner down the stone staircase to the ground floor, hoping she would not run into the woman from the night before. Grateful to find the foyer deserted, she made her escape into the day.

As she stepped from the building, the noise of cars and motorbikes funneled down the narrow street, pushing her back against the building, as if by a physical force. The air smelled of exhaust and damp stone. She stood for a moment, her heart pounding. Which way should she go? In her excitement, she had not bothered to look at the map or make a plan. But wasn't that why she was here, to dive into a new life and see where it led? Maybe her mother was right. *You can't always plan everything, Marina; sometimes you just have to let life unfold and trust that it will be all right.*

Across the street, a man was cranking an awning out over three sidewalk tables in front of a small café. Marina hesitated a moment, then surrendered to the scent of freshly baked pastries. She managed to order her breakfast by saying, "Cappuccino," and pointing to a pastry in the glass case, adding *"Per favore,"* then *"Grazie,"* which she had learned from a cassette tape before leaving New York. The woman behind the counter smiled and nodded encouragingly when Marina indicated she would like to sit outside. The early-morning air was still crisp, but the patch of sun splashing the face of the buildings opposite held a promise of midday warmth, and Marina congratulated herself on skipping out on New York's cold March winds.

But what to see first? The coffee coursed through her veins, flooding her mind with a thousand thoughts: the Uffizi or the Duomo, the Bargello or the Pitti Palace, make a list or just wander? She dug in her bag for the guidebook and a pen. On the inside of the front cover was a list of every site she wanted to visit. At the bottom of the list, in capital letters, she had written, *FIND APARTMENT* and *LANGUAGE SCHOOL.* Now she put a star by *LANGUAGE SCHOOL.* She would need that right away if she was going to understand anything in the gilding course she had signed up for. Her art history professor at NYU, Teresa Campione, had convinced her that the gilding course would satisfy her thirst for history as well as her need to do something with her hands. "I've seen your drawings and your sculpture, and I've talked to the studio faculty. You've got the touch, trust me."

She advised that an "immersion" class in Italian was the thing to look for and would be easy enough to find, and that the American Consulate might possibly have leads on an apartment. Marina made a mental note to send her very first postcard to Teresa with thanks for all her help in planning the trip and an apology for what must have seemed like a stalking during the months preceding her departure.

Marina knew she couldn't present herself at the consulate in jeans, so that would have to wait. Besides, she wanted to give herself a few days to explore the city and soak it all in before getting down to business, the business of making a life here. She consulted the map at the front of the book and fixed a short route in her mind so she would not have to walk along clutching her guidebook like a tourist, then drained her cup, licked the sweet crumbs from her fingers, and set out toward the Duomo.

She didn't know if it was the coffee, jet lag, or culture shock, but as she made her way along the street, it was as if her consciousness had split in two, part of it floating above her body, observing her progress along the street. She watched herself look in a store window, push her hair back off her face, and hook it behind her ears. Yes, there she was, an ordinary-looking girl, average height and weight, chin-length brown hair, blue eyes, but she definitely looked like someone who knew what she was doing and where she was going. Embracing this confidence, she continued along the wide street to the next corner, where she turned and then stopped abruptly. Although she was still two blocks away, she found herself in the shadow of the cathedral, the church of Santa Maria del Fiore, otherwise known as the Duomo, which sat like a too-large toy in a make-believe village. Only a giant's hand reaching down from above to lift off the dome for a peek inside could possibly put it into perspective. Cars, tiny by comparison, buzzed around the base of the massive structure, while the ground swarmed with an ant-sized public.

She felt herself jostled by people on their way to work, running errands, keeping appointments, citizens who passed this masterpiece of engineering every day without giving it a thought. She had an urge to grab them, stop them, and make them look. Moving forward, she looked every inch the tourist—head tipped back, mouth slightly open—as her dreams became her reality.

CHAPTER 2

By the end of the first week, Marina knew her way around the center of town, had located all the sights on her list, and had given each at least a cursory visit. She even managed to pick up a little Italian along the way, how to ask for directions (although she rarely understood the answers) and the names of the pastries she pointed to every morning in the little café across from her hotel. Now it was time to focus on the sites with gilded carvings, the church of Santa Croce being the first on her list.

The interior of the dim church was chilly, belying the signs of spring that flourished outside. Pulling her poncho tightly around her, she moved slowly into the gray stillness, walking as quietly as possible across the stone floor, but it was as if the silence inhaled the scrape of her leather-soled boots and the tap of their heels, breathing it back at her like a reprimand.

She made her way toward the front of the church, her eyes on the altar, her brain working to reconcile images in her mind from books and magazines with the one coming into focus. It had been like that all week, the split sense of being in the dream and living it at the same time. Then, unexpectedly, her foot struck an uneven part of the floor and her ankle buckled, bringing her down onto all fours.

"Shit," she muttered, pushing herself back into a squatting position, rubbing her knees.

"That was a rather sudden genuflection." The voice from overhead had an American accent. A pale hand reached into her line of vision. He was tall, at least six feet, his tweed jacket and corduroy pants hung on a thin frame, his face showed concern. She took his hand, cold in hers, and allowed him to help her to her feet.

"Look. You've stepped on the face of a Medici."

Marina withdrew her hand and looked down at the stark white face that pressed up from within the marble floor. Taking a step back she saw that it was attached to a life-sized bas-relief of a nobleman dressed in a long robe.

"Oh, sorry. I didn't see it. I was looking at the altar."

He shrugged. "It's nothing to me, but these old priests don't take kindly to young women throwing themselves onto their revered countrymen." He held out his hand again. "I'm Thomas."

Marina gave it a quick shake. "Marina. Thanks for your help." She turned away, moving toward the center nave.

Thomas moved with her. "Is this your first time in Santa Croce?"

Getting picked up was the last thing she wanted right now. Every day she had been hassled by men in the streets who did not seem to understand either the shaken head or the word no. She'd even resorted to giving one of them the finger, only to receive his fisted version in return. But Thomas did not seem to fit into that category. He spoke softly, as if he, too, respected the silence. She took in his wide-set gray eyes, long narrow nose, and the soft, rosebud mouth that saved his face from its harsh angles. Salt-and-pepper hair curled across his forehead and around his shirt collar. He looked harmless enough. She told him, yes, she had been in Florence a week, that she was here now to see the altar.

Thomas nodded. "You should have seen it after the flood. It was a mess." He touched her elbow lightly to stop her progress, then raised his arm and pointed at a line high up on the wall at the back of the church. "See the water mark? That's how high the floodwaters rose in here. This side of town was the hardest hit." He paused as if picturing it. "Isn't it wild to stand here and imagine all this under water? It'll give you a different perspective when you look at the restoration that's been done on the altar."

Marina looked around, trying to imagine water creeping up the walls, submerging everything. It wasn't hard. Hadn't she lived and breathed that catastrophe in the self-imposed exile of her teenage bedroom as she pored over tattered articles and magazines, crying about paintings and sculptures by artists she had never heard of? But still, she hadn't felt the enormity of it in the way she could now, standing in the actual spot. Her mother had told her that someone mistakenly opened the floodgates upriver too soon, causing the worst flood in the history of art, but Marina wasn't sure if that was true. She'd never come across that fact in any of her reading.

She was about to ask Thomas if there was any truth to the story when he said, "After you're done here, go through that doorway and you'll see photographs of the damage." Then he turned and walked away.

From behind the velvet rope, a few feet from the altar, Marina lost herself in the gilding as her eyes transmitted to her fingers the smooth surfaces and graceful curves they were not allowed to touch. She imagined the tools—carving knives, awls, and brushes—in the hands of an artisan, an old man or his young apprentice. In the glinting twists and burnished edges, she saw herself bent over a workbench, a magnificent frame or candlestick in some stage of repair, her hands moving with confidence.

When she surfaced from her reverie, Thomas was gone. She followed his advice, finding the photographs of the flood in a corridor that connected the basilica to the Pazzi Chapel.

There were aerial shots of the area under water, nearly two stories deep in the Piazza Santa Croce, and heartbreaking pictures of cars, pieces of furniture, and art buried under mud and debris. It was hard to imagine that one person's error in judgment could have such far-reaching consequences.

Marina found her way out onto an airy portico that led to the cloisters. From there, she headed back toward the piazza.

"Hey, Marina!" Thomas waved from a table in front of a café across the street.

She waved back but kept going.

"Hey, wait." Thomas jogged across the street toward her. "Come join me for a coffee."

"Thanks, but I have to see about an apartment."

"That's great. Where is it?"

"I'm going to the American Consulate. I don't know yet where, or if, there's an apartment."

Thomas grinned. "Oh, I see. Well then, good luck. Maybe we'll meet again."

She wasn't sure what he thought he saw. Maybe he thought it was all a line, that she was giving him the brush-off, but she really didn't care. She had an apartment to find and a future to get on with.

As it turned out, the consulate had no leads on apartments. The man behind the highly polished desk under the Stars and Stripes suggested Marina ask at the American school on the other side of the river. They might know of something. If all else failed, she could try one of the local rental agencies, but he warned that the prices would be exorbitant. The elation that had carried her from Santa Croce to the consulate ebbed. She'd already scrutinized the rental ads posted in agency windows, and while she fantasized about alfresco meals on rooftop terraces and leisurely soaks in marble baths, they were all beyond her price range. He also suggested she might check at the university, but she was not anxious to jump back into student life, with its late nights and sloppy habits. Besides, she wanted to live alone, simply. One room with a hot plate would do, as long as she had space for a workbench. She wanted a real life, an artisan's life, not some rehashed student life. Nor did she want to fall in with a community of transplanted Americans. That was not why she had come to Florence.

The next morning, as soon as it was light, Marina put on the same black turtleneck sweater and beige corduroys she'd worn to the consulate, hoping she looked presentable enough, in spite of the wrinkles, for her appearance at the American school. But first there was something she had to do.

The streets were quiet as she made her way across town, only the occasional buzz of a taxi or three-wheeled truck disturbing the stillness. She passed block after block of the blank metal shutters and decorative grills that rolled down at night, sealing the storefronts. About halfway across town, she came upon a coffee bar that had its shutter raised enough to see chair and table legs, an occasional pair of shoes going about the morning preparations, and to let escape the scent of fresh coffee and pastries just out of the oven. But breakfast would have to wait. She'd woken at dawn with the gilded altar on her mind, and she needed to see it again before the day was set in motion.

Piazza Santa Croce was empty except for the ubiquitous flock of pigeons. Marina stopped on the far side of the square and considered the church's geometric, pink and green marble façade, not unlike that of the Duomo, more austere, but pretty. On impulse, she lifted her arms, flapping them as she ran down the center of the square, scattering the birds. At the top of the church steps, three massive wooden doors rose two stories high across the front of the church. She stopped there, panting, and composed herself before entering through a smaller door cut into one of the larger.

She stopped just inside the little door, giving her eyes a moment to adjust to the dusky light. The silence pressed on her. Quietly, she removed her boots and began her walk to the front of the church, the floor icy even through thick socks. When she reached the velvet rope, she put down her boots and fixed her eyes on the altar. Looking around and seeing no one, she stepped over the barrier.

Even at this proximity, the intricacies of shape and texture under her fingers informed her far better than her eyes. Closing them, she let her fingers take her back, and for the first time, she knew without a doubt that she'd been right all along. Right to petition her high school's board to allow her swap out of Domestic Sciences and into a boys-only woodworking course. Right to stick it out, ignoring the stares and sniggers, cherishing the feeling of completeness when she used a carving knife. She'd been right about it all: leaving home, coming to Florence, learning Italian, the gilding course. Now all she needed was a place to live.

Following the directions she'd obtained from the consulate, Marina caught a bus up to Bellosguardo, where the American school sat on a hill overlooking the city. The gray-haired secretary, in a twin-set and pearls, somehow managed to look down at Marina from her seat behind the desk, informing her that she couldn't "just appear" during school hours without an appointment, and that the school was not "in the habit" of providing real estate leads to transients. Marina tried to explain that she was not a transient, that she had moved to Florence and would be studying and then working here, but the woman only pursed her lips tighter and invited Marina to "vacate the premises."

After standing at the bus stop for fifteen minutes, Marina decided to walk back to the center of town. Scuffing the heels of her boots along the pavement, she thought of all the things she should have said to the bitch in pearls, but it didn't help. Her early-morning conviction began to wane. Perhaps she'd made a big fat mistake in coming to Florence. Her words, "moved to Florence" and "working here," dogged her footsteps. Did she really have any idea what she was doing? Was she a fool for not going to graduate school or getting a teaching job at some prep school? But she didn't want to teach. She wanted to work with her hands. Sure, she'd stumbled onto the idea of gilding, but she knew it was right from the first time Professor Campione mentioned it. It fit with everything she loved—art, history, the feel of a tool in her hand, the way wood yielded, curling into the blade of her carving knife—and the idea of restoration, of taking something that was damaged and restoring its beauty, thrilled her. Was there any better place for her to be right now? Her steps lengthened to a stride as she reached the bottom of the hill and started back along the river toward the town center. She *would* find an apartment, if not today, then tomorrow. Today, she vowed, she would eat a proper meal, on her own, in a restaurant, something she had thus far avoided by eating piecemeal from coffee bars and cafeterias.

She crossed the river at the Ponte Vecchio, taking her time, perusing the windows of the jewelry stores that lined both sides of the bridge. The shops, cantilevered out over the river, were barely large enough to hold two or three people. One shop had a large selection of cameos in the window. As a child, she had coveted her grandmother's cameo that lay buried in her mother's jewelry box under the cool, clean lines of modern pieces. She remembered with Braille-like accuracy the lines of the patrician profile, the delicate filigree frame. It reminded her that she should call her parents on the off chance they were wondering how she was doing. That wasn't fair. Of course they'd be wondering how she was doing. Although, her mother's initial reaction to her proposed trip had been matter-of-fact and she'd never acknowledged that she'd broken her promise to Marina, her encouragement had been unwavering, and as the plans unfolded, her excitement had been genuine. Marina's father, too, had come out of his study long enough on a number of occasions to listen and murmur appreciatively.

Long ago, when her parents weren't looking, and they weren't, she had created a life for herself within the shadow of their lives and had grown accustomed to her own company. In retrospect, she considered herself lucky to have been naturally suited to a solitary life; had she been a needy child, she might not have survived so well. She understood that her parents' attention spans for anything outside their worlds of contemporary art or mathematical equations was limited, and had mastered the art of condensing her needs into as few words as possible for fear of losing their focus before she was finished. Yes, she must call them.

At the center of the bridge, Marina stopped to watch a street artist draw caricatures for a group of giggling French girls. Then she proceeded through the loggia of the Uffizi Gallery, turning once again toward Santa Croce, where she remembered seeing a number of small restaurants in the warren of streets around the piazza. She'd look there for something small and cozy.

Walking down a narrow alley away from the tourist shops, Marina followed the scent of wine, garlic, and olive oil to the door of a small restaurant with a sign over the door: Trattoria Anita. The menu was posted in a small glass case on the wall to the right of the door. She scrutinized the list, knitting her eyebrows as she read the obvious words: spaghetti, ravioli, tortellini, and vino. The rest was a mystery. Good. No English, no tourists.

"Stepped on any Medici today?"

The voice, close to her ear, startled her. She turned. "Oh, hi. Thomas, right? I was just checking out the menu."

"About ready to devour it, don't you think?" Thomas addressed the woman at his side.

"Hmmm, yes, just about to take a bite, I'd say," replied the woman, who, like Thomas, had an American accent. She smiled at Marina. "Shall we save her from a nasty paper cut and take her in with us?"

The woman had deep green eyes set in a pale oval face, and the most remarkable head of hair. Long, the color of rust flecked with gold, strands of it curling out beyond her shoulders as if exploring the atmosphere.

"Yes, that's just what I was thinking," said Thomas. He took Marina's arm and ushered her through the doorway.

Inside, a woman who couldn't have been more than five feet tall, if that, came out from behind a counter to hug Thomas and his companion. He said something to her, possibly about the clumsy American girl he'd rescued from the floor of Santa Croce. Whatever it was made her chuckle, then smile and nod at Marina. As she led them to a table, Marina looked around, trying to get a sense of where she had landed. The smell was so familiar she might have been down in the Village at Mario's, with its red-checked tablecloths and wax-covered Chianti bottles. Here, though, the decor was simple, if not ascetic: white walls and ceiling, simple overhead lighting, and a tiled floor made of gray and white terrazzo. High up on the walls, a narrow shelf overflowed with bottles of wine, while square tables with white cloths and butcher paper filled the room.

Once seated, Thomas's companion extended her hand toward Marina with a smile. "I'm Sarah." She had long graceful fingers and a firm clasp. "And I gather you're the woman who stepped on the face of a Medici."

Marina rolled her eyes. "I can see I'm never going to live that one down. Thomas came to my rescue, then told me a bit of history about the flood."

"Yes," said Sarah, shaking her hair off her face. "You have to watch out for this one." She indicated Thomas with a lift of her chin. "He'll give you a full-blown history lesson if you aren't careful. But you know"—she lowered her voice and leaned toward Marina—"what he's really good at are all the juicy bits, the things that most people don't know. Who was

cheating on whom, artists stealing each other's patrons, murder, treason. It's fascinating, a bit of a medieval soap opera."

Marina glanced at Thomas to find him looking at her intently. She blushed and turned back to Sarah.

Sarah laid her hand on his forearm and said, "Honestly,
Thomas, take off the lens and join us for lunch." Turning
once again toward Marina, she continued, "Did Thomas tell
you that he's a photographer?"

"No." Marina shook her head, then pushed her hair off
her face, hooking it behind her ears, aware that it was not
nearly as elegant a gesture as Sarah's shudder, which seemed
to put every coppery strand in just the right place.

"Sometimes, when he's struck by an image, he virtually
turns into a camera. I can see the look in his eyes, as if they're
actually responding to aperture settings and focal points."

Thomas blinked. "Sorry, I don't mean to stare, but . . .
your eyes, that fine ring of dark blue at the edge of your iris,
it's as if it's holding in that pool of pale blue. Amazing. And
the shape of your face—"

Sarah laughed. "Thomas, stop. You're making her blush."
She turned to Marina. "And did I say that he's a terrible
flirt?"

Was there something in her tone, an undercurrent of warning? Marina looked from one to the other but wasn't sure.

Thomas scowled and picked up his menu. "Let's order."

Sarah translated the menu, describing their favorite dishes
while Thomas slouched in his chair and picked at his fingernails. After they ordered, Sarah put her elbows on the table
and leaned toward Marina. "So, tell us what you're doing
here in Florence."

Marina was not sure if it was nerves or so many days without a good conversation, but she ended up telling them her
life story—how she had grown up in New York an art brat,
then fallen in love with Florence as an adolescent, eventually
giving up on her mother's promise to bring her to Italy and
funding the trip herself by working as a waitress. Laughing,

she told them about ending up at the seaside by mistake and her middle-of-the-night arrival. She'd found a language class that was about to start, and was registered for a gilding and restoration course. Now the only thing missing was an apartment.

Marina took a breath, then realized the food had arrived and Sarah and Thomas were well into their tortellini. Her own fork was in her hand, so she stopped talking and twirled it in the nest of angel-hair pasta that was dressed in a pink sauce laced with mushrooms and pancetta.

Sarah put down her fork and wiped her mouth, leaving a smear of peachy lipstick on the white napkin. "It sounds to me like you plan to stay on here after the gilding course is finished."

Marina nodded her head emphatically as she chewed, then swallowed. "That's my plan. I'm hoping to find an artisan who will take me on as an apprentice."

Sarah and Thomas exchanged glances. Thomas, who hadn't said a word through dinner, put down his fork and leaned back in his chair, clasping his hands behind his head. "I don't know if you're aware of this, and I don't want to rain on your parade, but I've been in Florence a long time and I've never seen a female apprentice anywhere."

Thomas's statement lay on the table between them like a deflated balloon, but Marina just shrugged, dipped her fork back into the pasta, and, with more conviction than she felt, said, "Then, I guess I'll have to be the first."

Marina spent the next few days immersed in the collection of gilded furniture and objets d'art at the Pitti Palace. The palace, commissioned by a Florentine banker in an attempt to outshine the Medici family, was an exercise in excess, every inch of its interior embellished with gold, frescos, mosaic, or tapestries, a grandiosity that distracted her from the furniture and frames she wanted to study. Adding to this frustration were the velvet ropes that, once again, kept her at a distance from the details she wanted to experience first-hand, forcing her instead to consult the catalogues for details she'd rather touch. Her fingertips ached for the burnished surfaces, but she knew it would be foolish to attempt an escapade like the one in Santa Croce.

Typically, after two or three hours, sensory overload set in and Marina would head for the palace garden feeling light-headed and slightly nauseated, as if she'd eaten too many sweets. In the Boboli Gardens, a potentially overwhelming eleven acres of manicured flowerbeds, hedgerows, fountains, statues, and even an amphitheatre, Marina managed to find a stone bench in the crook of a lush pathway. She sat there, taking deep breaths as if surfacing from a long dive. The spring sun warmed crisp shadows and carried the scent of apple blossoms across the plump heads of tulips and daffodils. She couldn't believe how lucky she was to be able to spend her time among such treasures, things she had only read about, fantasized about working on. It seemed too good to be true, and she wished she had someone to talk to, someone to affirm her good fortune, to confirm that she deserved it, to reflect her joy. Turning her face to the sun, she inhaled the sweet air, then once replenished, plunged back into her gilded world.

A few days after their first meeting, Marina found a note from Sarah and Thomas waiting for her at the *pensione*.

Meet us for dinner tomorrow at Anita's. S&T

She had not seen Sarah and Thomas since their lunch together, although she'd kept an eye out for them in the streets, hoping she might run into them as she walked from her *pensione* to the Pitti Palace. The note had not said at what time to meet and she had no way of getting in touch with them. Dinner, she knew, was a late affair, with people often sitting down to eat as late as ten o'clock. While she appreciated the leisurely rhythm of the city, the long lunch hour followed by an afternoon siesta and then the reluctant resurgence in late afternoon as the shopkeepers lifted metal gates and shutters for the last few hours of business, she wasn't sure she could wait that late to eat. She would just have to guess at a time and hope she wouldn't look stupid hanging around outside the restaurant. In the end, she decided on eight thirty and was saved from potential embarrassment when she saw Sarah and Thomas disappearing through the doorway of the restaurant just as she rounded the corner.

Sarah greeted her with an enthusiastic embrace and Thomas kissed her on both cheeks.

"I've found you an apartment!" Sarah announced as they settled at the table, her eyes sparkling. "It's on our side of town, in Via Luna. Moon Street, isn't that lovely? It belongs to my friend's parents. Marcello says you can see it tomorrow."

Thomas was enthusiastic. "It's on the ground floor in what used to be a workshop. The whole street was workshops at one time, but I think almost all of them have been converted to apartments. It's a tiny little street, a dead end. No traffic."

Marina looked from one to the other. She hardly knew these people. She had not even started her classes yet. The words "Moon Street," "workshops," "no traffic" echoed in her head. "Wow, I don't know what to say."

Sarah reached over and squeezed Marina's hand. "It sounds great. Marcello says it has two rooms, so maybe you could set one up as a workroom and the other as a bedroom/sitting room. And, of course, it has a kitchen and bath."

"I think it may have a garden as well," Thomas added.

He ordered a bottle of wine, and Marina allowed them to sweep her up in the celebration. They ate gnocchi in a creamy Gorgonzola sauce, followed by veal scallops cooked in butter and lemon, and at Thomas's insistence, the three of them shared a plate of tiramisu to finish.

They wanted to hear about everything Marina had done

since their lunch together, each of them volleying questions at her in a way that came to feel a bit like they were verbally elbowing each other out of the way, vying for her attention. When dinner arrived, Thomas engaged her in a lengthy conversation about photography, which Marina knew something about, having been the photographer for her high school paper. But by the second course, Sarah had turned the conversation back to Marina's life, and the two women chatted easily as if they'd been friends for years while Thomas grew quiet, seemingly absorbed in his meal, although she caught him staring at her more than once.

She agreed to meet them the next morning at their apartment, from where they would proceed to Via Luna to see the apartment. When they parted, Sarah hugged Marina tightly and kissed her on both cheeks, her excitement palpable. Marina wondered if she was always this friendly but couldn't help feeling flattered. Thomas stood off to the side, watching, then gave her a lingering embrace that seemed to include the press of his hips, but she couldn't be sure. He had one final instruction on finding their apartment. "It's the bottom bell. There's no name."

Marina found their street adjacent to the church of Santa Croce. A narrow sidewalk ran along the base of the tall, shuttered apartment buildings, but it was easier to walk in the street. If the buildings had been brownstones, with leafy trees planted at regular intervals, it could have been Greenwich Village. Joey's Bakery would be up ahead, and Elsa would be sitting on a stoop, smoothing her collection of fabric scraps, her shopping cart heaped with rags. Marina passed a small *latteria* that sold milk and cheese, and a tiny bar with a clientele of toothless, white-haired men who sat on rickety chairs heatedly debating some topic. Out of nowhere, a wave of homesickness swept over her, and she blinked back the sting of tears. "You are in Florence," she admonished herself. "This is your dream. Get a grip!" It wasn't so much a longing for home as it was apprehension. Having the dream was one thing, but having it manifest was another, and things seemed to be moving quickly. She'd met her first friends and they seemed genuinely interested in her, her language course was about to start, and she was going to look at an apartment to rent. But what if she'd dreamed the wrong dream? Taken the wrong path? How would she know?

She found the number Sarah had given her and stood on the sidewalk looking up at the building, a sheer façade of gray stone with skinny windows. Larger than those surrounding it, it was without balconies or decorative elements of any kind. The entrance was a set of doors painted poppy red, each with a heavy iron handle. To the right of the doorway, set into the stone, was a highly polished brass plate with seven bells, running from top to bottom. Each bell had a name alongside it except the bottom one. Marina pushed the button. A moment later, the buzzer sounded and the latch released. Stepping through the doorway, Marina found herself in a cool, dark vestibule. A set of wide stone steps with a wrought iron handrail was dimly lit by light filtering down from a skylight on the top floor. As Marina looked up, she heard Sarah's voice echo down the stairwell.

"Come up. We're on the second floor."

Marina climbed to the landing where Sarah stood like a flower blooming in a cracked pavement against the backdrop of gray stone and drab walls. The ankle-length Indian dress reminded Marina of the hippies at NYU, except this dress, with its heavy celadon skirt and multicolored woven bodice, had an air of authenticity. Sarah's hair was caught up in a bright silk scarf fringed with tiny mirrored discs, and enameled earrings hung from her ears like miniature chandeliers. In her jeans, boots, and sweater, Marina felt as dull as the stone floor, but at least she had on her Guatemalan sweater, which she hoped counted for something, if not style, a progressive attitude or something to that effect.

Sarah took her hand and pulled her into the apartment as

if she were a reluctant child on the first day of kindergarten, which was actually not far off, since Marina had been wrestling with doubts the whole way there. After all, she didn't know these people, and while she was intrigued and attracted, if for no other reason than they were interested in her, she had sworn not to get sucked into the ex-pat scene. But she was here, and the room in which they now stood was amazing. She hadn't known what to expect, but it certainly wasn't this. The room was at least forty feet long, with a high ceiling and two sets of French doors that opened onto a terrace. Oriental rugs were scattered like stepping-stones across the tiled floor, and large abstract paintings and framed black-and-white photographs covered the walls. At the far end of the room, a bed was partially visible through an archway draped with a red velvet swag.

Marina turned in a circle. "Wow. This is beautiful. I didn't realize there'd be so much light. From the street it looks like the building hardly has any windows."

Sarah's earrings jingled. "I know. Everyone's surprised. But this was a convent at one time. I guess the nuns didn't want the outside world peeping into their holy space. Most of the windows face the courtyard."

Marina followed Sarah onto the terrace.

"This is great." Marina took in the terrace's wide expanse, the iron railing covered in vines, large pots of geraniums, mismatched metal and wooden garden furniture.

"It's a bit of a mess right now." Sarah waved her hand across the air in front of her. "I'm behind with my gardening. Thomas has a show coming up, he's at his studio now, and it's taking up all my time. Between organizing the invitations, food, and flowers, I haven't had a second. Honestly, I can't figure out why we give the gallery such a large percentage when all they do is provide the space." She sighed, pinched a dried geranium head from its bright green stalk, then touched Marina's shoulder. "We should go. Marcello will be waiting for us."

The two women walked along the street, where every few blocks Sarah greeted someone with a wave and smile, or a few words, all the while keeping up a running commentary about the people they passed. "That's our neighbor's daughter. She's about to have twins, but her husband still chases anything in a skirt. Then he runs home to Mama when they fight about it." She pointed out her favorite shops and the bar where she had coffee.

Marina nodded, murmuring her interest, but most of her attention was on Sarah, who had the air of a benevolent queen surveying her kingdom, and she half expected a shower of flower petals to rain down on them from above. It was as if light seeped from Sarah's pores, illuminating the air around her. Was this what people meant when they talked about a person's aura? Marina walked beside her, a lady-in-waiting, entranced by the ease with which Sarah seemed to traverse her world. She wasn't sure, but she judged Sarah to be about thirty and Thomas closing in on forty, and while she'd often been on friendly terms with older clients of her mother's, she'd never had older friends of her own; she matched her stride to Sarah's with a renewed sense of confidence and burgeoning sophistication.

"Watch out!" Sarah grabbed Marina's arm, saving her from a mound of ripe dog droppings. Linking her arm through Marina's, she said, "They don't believe in curbing their dogs over here. You've got to train your senses to be on poop patrol at all times. It becomes an automatic-pilot thing after a while."

Sarah felt more solid than she looked in her diaphanous dress, hair floating in all directions. While Marina had admired the elegant couplings of Italian women walking arm-in-arm, she found proximity to Sarah and her lavender-scented aura made her clumsy, and she was at a loss to match her step.

After a few twists and turns, they came into a square where rows of small kiosks with tin roofs were barely visible under mounds of junk: dented copper pots, rusted light fixtures, shabby furniture, and old toys. Sarah explained this was known as the flea market, and it was possible, if one dug deep enough, to find a rare treasure every now and then.

When Sarah released her arm, Marina felt both relieved and momentarily adrift.

"I found this here," Sarah said, holding out her left hand.

On her ring finger, she wore a silver band with an oddly shaped blob overlaid on the top. Marina took Sarah's hand and brought it up to her face. The blob was, in fact, a tiny crucifix so worn down as to be barely discernable. It was odd and slightly creepy.

Sarah withdrew her hand and held it at arm's length, considering the ring. "It's not a religious thing, but Thomas liked it and it was a perfect fit."

"Is it your wedding band?"

Sarah turned and began to walk. "Thomas doesn't believe in wedding rings. When we got married, he said we didn't need rings to tell the world what was between us. But I like wearing this. It reminds me that I belong to him."

Marina followed Sarah onto a busy street where they walked single file along the sidewalk, threading their way around shoppers carrying baskets or string bags bulging with fruits and vegetables. Sarah explained, over her shoulder, that there was a market nearby, not as large as the Central Market in San Lorenzo, but without the tacky souvenir stands. Marina's mind was still on the strange ring. If it wasn't a religious thing, why wear the image of Christ on your finger? And she couldn't imagine Sarah "belonging" to anyone, Christ or Thomas.

"Almost there," Sarah said as they approached a wide boulevard lush with flowering shrubs and passed under a stone archway that in medieval times had been one of the gates to the city.

On the other side of the boulevard, the streets were wider and the shops less elegant than in the historic center, but there seemed to be everything one might need for everyday life. Sarah pointed out a small department store, a supermarket, bakery, pharmacy, and greengrocer, as well as a clothing store with underwear and woolen tights in the window. Marina turned her head from side to side, trying to take it all in. In the middle of the third block, Sarah stopped suddenly and took hold of Marina's arm.

"This is it."

The façade of shops gave way to an arched tunnel through the building. "See?" Sarah pointed to a white enameled sign fixed to the wall, with the words in blue: Via Luna.

They followed the road, barely wide enough for a small car, through the tunnel and around behind the buildings where it came to a dead end at a high stucco wall. A young man leaning against the wall waved and called out a greeting when he saw them. Marina's heart knocked in her chest as they walked the length of the street, but the sun on her face and the reassuring sounds of lunch preparations coming from open windows overhead served as a calming balm.

Marcello was only slightly taller than the two women, very thin, and possibly the most beautiful man Marina had ever seen. His skin was flawless, the color of honey. His lustrous chestnut hair was pulled back into a ponytail. Dark eyes regarded her through lashes so thick they created a heavy line, as if drawn by an eye pencil. He wore tight jeans tucked into soft leather boots, and his fitted white shirt pressed against hard nipples. For the second time that day, she felt large and clumsy in her heavy boots and chunky sweater. Marina glanced at his crotch, at the same faded spot she'd noticed on so many young Florentine men. It was hard not to notice the contrast of dark denim to light, as if they rubbed themselves day in and day out. Sarah made the introductions as Marina shook Marcello's hand, which lay limply in hers, as if waiting to be kissed. He smiled at her, then said something to Sarah, motioning toward a doorway.

Marina took a deep breath and followed them into a small kitchen, whitewashed with light from the open door. Against one wall, a tiny stove with four gas burners and an oven looked like something she had played with as a child. Next to it stood its twin, a pint-sized refrigerator. A deep enameled sink and draining board hung on the wall under a window that looked out into the alley, while a Formica-topped table and two chairs filled the remaining floor space. She followed Sarah and Marcello through a doorway into a windowless room lit solely by light filtering in from the kitchen in the front and a room at the back. Where were the French doors, the high ceilings, the expansive terrace?

Sarah was talking. "This is perfect. You could have a sitting room/bedroom here, and set up a workroom in the back."

The back room looked out onto a garden, its tall window guarded from the outside by an ornate grill. Marcello gestured toward the window as he said something to Sarah.

Sarah turned to Marina. "Marcello is apologizing that you can't use the garden, there's no access from here. It belongs to the apartment next door."

Marina cast a regretful glance into the shady garden and forced a smile. "That's okay, it's enough to have the light."

"It's perfect for a workroom. Good light, ventilation." Sarah looked at Marina. "Don't you think?"

"I guess so . . ."

"I know, it's not very big, but let's go see how much his parents want for it."

Sarah and Marcello chatted away as Marina followed them back to the main street and down the block, where they entered a butcher shop. A taller, heavier version of Marcello wore a bloodstained apron and stood behind a glass case filled with organs glistening reddish black under fluorescent lights. He had salt-and-pepper hair and brown eyes that drooped down at the corners, a sad comment on an otherwise happy face. Marcello greeted him with a quiet, "Ciao, *Papà*," then without waiting for a reply, slipped behind the counter and through a doorway hung with wooden beads. As soon as Marcello's father finished with his customer, he turned to Sarah with a jovial greeting and a wink for Marina. His eyes sparkled for that moment, but went flat when Marcello returned. The woman who followed Marcello from behind the curtain might have been his twin sister, with the same silky hair and smooth skin, but Sarah introduced her as his mother, Antonella. She was dressed in a slim tweed skirt, silk blouse, and tall, high-heeled boots. She and Sarah had a quick conversation while Marcello fidgeted at his mother's side. Marina was trying not to look at the carcasses strung up along the wall when Marcello's father began to mutter and then to shout, throwing his arms up as if talking to heaven, then holding them out beseechingly. Antonella waved him off as if he was saying something of little consequence, something they already knew, something they had heard a thousand times. Marcello responded loudly, jutting out his chin, but did not move from his mother's side. Sarah and Antonella finished their conversation in hushed tones while Marcello's father muttered from behind the counter until another customer entered, transforming him back into the jolly butcher.

Once they were back on the street and had said good-bye to Marcello, who sped off on a shiny red Vespa, Marina turned to Sarah. "What was that all about?"

Sarah grinned. "The loud part was about Marcello's father not approving of his son's lifestyle, and the quiet part was about getting you the apartment."

"What do you mean, his lifestyle?"

Sarah hooked her arm through Marina's. "I'll tell you another time. Right now, let's find Thomas and celebrate!"

The following morning, Marina woke to a dark sky and torrential rain. Seeing no reason to get up, she burrowed under the covers. She had slept fitfully, dreaming of cavernous rooms with murky corners, windows that opened onto brick walls, and staircases that led nowhere. Was she really going to set up house and make a life here? She thought back to the apartment she'd rented with two girlfriends during her last year at NYU, and the sublet with a different set of friends this past year. There had always been someone around, someone to share in the cooking and shopping, or to call the landlord if problems arose. But alone? She lay very still, taking shallow breaths under a blanket of panic, until Sarah's voice came back to her. *They will let you take the apartment on a monthly basis to start, but at some point you'll have to decide whether you're staying, and then they'll want you to sign a year's lease.* When Marina had hesitated, Sarah said, *You have nothing to lose. It's a steal, and so much cheaper than staying in the* pensione. *This way, you'll be set with an apartment if you decide to stay.*

Marina relaxed as she thought about setting up a workspace in the back room and cooking at the tiny stove with the kitchen door open onto the sunny alley. When she woke again, the rain was still coming down, but her mood had lifted enough to prompt a step toward permanence—she would buy an umbrella, not a travel-sized one, but a big black one, the kind that was kept next to the front door.

She made her way to the department store in the Piazza della Repubblica, only to find the umbrella selection thoroughly picked over. The only type left had pictures of the *David* on them, and while she was tempted for a moment by the thought of a naked man protecting her from the elements, she didn't want to end up looking like a pathetic tourist. Besides, the rain had stopped; the umbrella could wait. Now it was time to call home with the good news.

Marina departed the central post office after waiting thirty minutes for an international phone booth for a ten-minute conversation that seemed to take only seconds. Her parents had been suitably enthusiastic about the apartment, encouraging her to get settled before her Italian class started the fol-

lowing week, and had made vague promises about coming to
visit in the fall. She stared down at the water-stained tips of
her boots as she made her way to Sarah's, dodging dripping
overhangs and the spray from careless drivers. Did her parents really have that much faith in her? Shouldn't they be
worried about her making a life so far from home? But neither of them had ever been that sort of parent, had they? If
they had perfect faith in her, then so would she.

She found Sarah at her desk going over a list of things that
still needed to be done before Thomas's show opened that
weekend, and was disappointed when she said she was too
busy to help her make the final arrangements for taking the
apartment.

"You'll be fine," Sarah assured her. "I'll call Antonella and
let her know. All you have to do is go to the shop with a
month's rent and she'll give you the key." Sarah kissed Marina on both cheeks and pushed an invitation into her hand.
"Seven o'clock, Saturday. See you then."

Two days later, Marina managed the negotiation for the
key by handing Antonella a stack of lire and smiling and
nodding at everything she said. She might well have been saying, "You look like a big fat cow in that baggy sweater," as
Marina bobbed her head in agreement. Her husband was
busy behind the counter, but he gave her a wave between customers. Marina left the shop with the key in her hand, feeling
a little more secure—even though they could not understand
each other, at least someone she knew, and who knew her,
was just around the corner.

The sun was just beginning its slide up over the rooftops as
Marina entered Via Luna for the second time. In another
hour, it would tumble into the little street, evaporating the
puddles she now skirted. When she reached the end of the
alley, she noticed, for the first time, a white tile with a blue
number twenty-eight just to the left of the door. She stared at
it, key in hand, and wondered if she could get her money

back. It had only been a few minutes. The money wouldn't be in the bank yet. She would say she'd changed her mind. It wasn't too late to apply for graduate school in the fall, and she could live at home for a while, then find an apartment with friends. In two years, she'd be teaching art history and maybe a woodcarving class in some cushy prep school in New England. She looked back down the street for a moment, then inserted the key, and stepped inside.

CHAPTER 3

From the middle of the crowded room, Marina let the vibrations of language and gesture wash over her. The opening had been in full swing when she arrived. Thomas and Sarah were occupied, she as hostess, he as man of the hour, so Marina managed to slip in unnoticed. This gave her time to look at the show and take in the crowd. There was a familiar feel to the gathering: the warm crush of people, animated conversation, sharp light reflected off white walls, so much like the openings she had grown up attending. As a toddler, she'd been carried to the openings held at her mother's gallery, there as the token child, at first darling, then precocious. As an adolescent, when she'd just as soon have stayed home watching *Gilligan's Island* or *The Man from U.N.C.L.E.*, coercion was needed to get her to an opening, but as she matured and her interest in art grew, she attended them eagerly.

She had memories of big faces, red lips, and lots of talking teeth, all set against a backdrop of stark walls and black clothing. Here in Florence, no one dressed in black, at least not completely in black, but the cigarette smoke was the same, if not worse. Marina recalled her mother's exasperation with her artists, all of whom, she said, seemed to feel the need to smoke and drink themselves to death. She had also complained bitterly about the unkempt appearance of some of her favorite protégés, and would have appreciated the fashionable crowd that now milled around her daughter.

Marina worked her way along one wall of large black-and-white portraits. It was an art form she appreciated. She had studied photography again in college and had seen more than her share of both good and bad over the years. This show was called *I Zingari*, a word she couldn't pronounce or define. The subjects of the pictures looked like homeless people, but she had yet to see anyone sleeping in the streets here, unless the city confined them to certain areas. She'd have to ask Thomas. There were craggy-faced old men with missing teeth, dirty children, and women dressed in voluminous rags. The photographs themselves were beautiful, large and grainy, but something felt missing, a certain connection between the subject and the photographer. She couldn't quite put her finger on it. At first she thought it was because none of the subjects were looking at the camera, but she'd seen many portraits where the face was directed down or away from the camera without losing that feeling of collaboration. Then she saw what it was—only the subject was in focus; everything else was a blur. The pictures must have been taken from a distance, with a zoom lens. What she was looking at were "stolen moments."

Intrigued, Marina turned away and considered the best way to navigate to the photos on the wall opposite. She looked toward the back of the room where, earlier, she'd seen Thomas talking to a tall, blond woman. He was still there, the woman at his side. She seemed to be entertaining the group gathered around them with an anecdote that involved touching Thomas every few words. Marina had a clear view for a moment and stood watching. The woman was as tall as Thomas and had long, ash-blond hair that fell in one sheer drop down her back, and while it was hard to judge her age from a distance, she had the sense that the woman was a number of years older than Thomas. Just then, he turned his head and she caught his eye for a moment before quickly turning her head away. She cursed herself. Couldn't she have just smiled and waved like a grown-up instead of acting like a silly schoolgirl?

She scanned the other end of the room, where Sarah was at the door greeting new arrivals, directing them toward the bar set up in an alcove. As she watched, Antonella entered, looking svelte in a tight skirt and slinky blouse, although her makeup looked surprisingly heavy and overdone. But the two women who accompanied her had a similar look, so maybe it was just the fashion. What did she know; her expertise in that area went as far as mascara and lip gloss. Maybe it was part of letting loose, sloughing off the butcher's shop, enjoying a little time with the girls. Marina didn't see how she could possibly get through the crowd to Sarah's post at the door, so she continued across the room to the grouping of smaller photographs.

Again, the photographs were black and white, but now she recognized the subject. They were gypsies. *Zingari*. She had seen them begging around town, mostly near tourist attractions. Walking slowly down the row, she examined the photographs of a gypsy girl in the process of picking pockets. At first glance, it looked like the girl was just begging, but closer inspection brought her true intent into focus. In some of the shots, she was holding what Marina assumed was a baby, but the infant itself was not visible; there might have been anything in the cloth sling she wore across her chest. One picture showed her bending over a young woman sitting on a bench, a map spread out on her lap, her day pack open on the bench beside her. The gypsy was pushing her baby bundle into the woman's face, effectively pinning her to the seat while she pleaded her case and rummaged the woman's pack for valuables. Obviously Thomas had followed the girl on more than one occasion. But why? How? How had he tracked her for hours, perhaps days, taking her picture with-

out her knowing? Marina could tell he had not used a tele-
photo lens for these shots. Others were taken indoors. She
recognized the interior of the central post office, the train station, and various galleries. It was uncanny how he had captured her, over and over again, in the act. In one picture, it
almost seemed as if she was looking at the camera.

"I guess that's what you'd call the light-fingered side of
life."

Marina turned at Thomas's voice, accepted his embrace,
and said, "I'm intrigued. It's almost as if the two of you were
in cahoots."

Standing next to him, the blond woman blew a stream of
smoke through her nostrils. "Ah, yes. Thomas. He takes a little walk on the dark side."

Marina wasn't sure what to make of the comment, and
Thomas acted like he hadn't heard her. Up close, the woman
was clearly a good ten years older than Thomas, and her
makeup, heavy black eyeliner and frosty pink lipstick, was
about that many years behind the times. Still, she was striking in a white silk blouse, tight velvet jeans, and enough gold
jewelry for three people.

Thomas turned to the woman and said, "Contessa, let me
introduce our new friend, Marina, the one I was telling you
about."

"Yes, my dear." The contessa spoke with the air of a
mother whose child has just shown her his new toy. She
flashed a row of tiny, pointed teeth. "You are the girl Thomas
rescued in our Santa Croce."

At least she hadn't said "stepped on the face of a Medici."
Marina was trying to think of a clever response when Sarah
appeared.

"Marina! How did you get in here without me seeing you?
Have you been here long?"

"A while. I've been admiring the photographs and just enjoying the scene. This is quite a turnout. I saw Marcello's
mother come in with her girlfriends, but I haven't seen him

yet. Is he here? I'd like to thank him for his help with the apartment."

The contessa said something to Thomas that made them both laugh, but Sarah was not amused.

She took Marina's arm. "He's here somewhere. We'll find him later." She turned to Thomas and the contessa. "You don't mind if I steal her, do you?" And without waiting for a reply, she pulled Marina away. They had not gone more than a few steps when she said under her breath, "I can't stand that woman."

Marina said, "The contessa?" Although it was clear whom she meant.

"She's the damn Ice Queen, but I'm not allowed to call her that in front of Thomas."

They reached a pair of French doors that led onto a small balcony. The night was chilly, but Marina was relieved to be in the clear air, out of the smoke and noise. Sarah sat down on a stone bench and patted the space next to her.

"So what's the deal?" Marina asked. "Does she own the gallery?"

"No, but she thinks she owns Thomas."

"What do you mean? Is she a patron or something?"

"Something like that. She introduces Thomas to a lot of people and helps him with his career. Thomas has known her forever. When he and I first met, he took me to meet her. I don't think I've ever seen him that nervous. You'd have thought he was taking me home to meet his parents."

"Did she approve?"

"She was nice enough. Thomas said she thought I was 'suitable.' Whatever that means. But it's clear she's only interested in Thomas."

Marina raised her eyebrows. "You mean romantically?"

"No, I don't think so, but for a long time I did think that, and it drove me crazy. Thomas and I had big fights about it. In the end, I just let it go. It's clear she's in his life to stay, and she's important. I don't believe it's just about his career, but I don't know what it is. I try and ignore it." Sarah stood up. "But I really didn't come out here to talk about her. I just wanted to have a few minutes with you, and a break from my duties. Tell me you'll stay and come to Anita's for dinner with us after we're done here."

Marina hesitated. She wasn't sure if she was prepared to sit down to dinner and make intelligent conversation with the gallery owner, patrons, and other cultural glitterati.

As if reading her mind, Sarah said, "It'll just be Thomas and me. I know it goes against the tradition of dining with the patrons, but he's always insisted on a quiet dinner after an opening. He can only take so much social stimulation."

"I don't want to impose."

"No, not at all. We both want you to come."

Marina was flattered. "Of course, that sounds great."

As they stepped back into the room, Marina pointed. "Look, there's Antonella, but I don't see Marcello."

"That's not his . . ." Sarah hesitated, then smiled. "Come on, you'll have to see for yourself."

Marina couldn't see Marcello, but she followed Sarah through the crowd toward where Antonella was laughing with her friends. As they closed in on the group, the women greeted Sarah with exclamations and embraces, then Sarah turned to Marina with a grin and said, "These are Marcello's friends, Giorgio and Paolo."

George? Paul? Marina looked from one to the other, speechless as she struggled to reconcile the masculine voices with the pretty faces of the women, no, men, she shook hands with. Transvestites! The makeup was a bit heavy, but the result was quite stunning. She checked the expression on her face to make sure her mouth wasn't gaping or her eyes popping, then turned to Antonella, only to find herself staring into Marcello's beautiful face.

Sarah was saying, "Marcello says that he's happy he could be of help, and that his parents are pleased to have you in the apartment."

*   *   *

"Why didn't you tell me he was transvestite?" They had just ordered dinner at Anita's, and Thomas and Sarah were laughing at her. Marina laughed along with them, happy to share in the joke, even if it had been at her expense.

"What if I'd made a fool of myself or embarrassed Marcello?" Marina's attempt at indignation dissolved in her giggles.

"I know," said Sarah, "but I had complete faith that you would carry it off as elegantly as you did. I meant to tell you at some point, I really did, it just never came up. Besides, Marcello likes it when people don't know beforehand. He may be shy, but he has a flair for the dramatic."

"Well, that was pretty dramatic." Marina relaxed back in her chair, savoring the word "elegant."

She and Sarah had slipped out of the reception when the crowd thinned, leaving Thomas to talk to the last few people. As they walked to Anita's, Sarah explained that Florence was well known for its transvestites, that most of them took it very seriously, priding themselves on their ability to pass as women. Some were straight men, even married men, who got their kicks from dressing up, some were gay men who got a different kick, and some were men who lived as women and hoped some day to change gender. Sarah was not sure about his friends, but Marcello was bisexual, and it was anyone's guess how things would turn out for him. Marina listened and nodded, afraid to let on how bewildered she felt. Of course she knew about gay men, the baths, drag queens. How could she not, growing up in Greenwich Village? But somehow the complex world of transvestites had escaped her notice.

Thomas had joined them a little while after they were seated, long enough for the two of them to put a significant dent in the bottle of wine. The food arrived as Sarah began to giggle again.

Marina smiled. "It's not funny."

"You're right, it's not. It's hilarious!"

"Weird, is more like it." Thomas poured them each a glass of wine.

"Oh, Thomas." Sarah turned to Marina and whispered loud enough for Thomas to hear, "His masculinity is threatened."

Thomas turned his attention to Marina and said, "A man is either into women or he's not. All this in between, dressing-up stuff is just self-indulgent theatrics."

After they had eaten in silence for a few minutes, Sarah leaned in to Thomas. "What do you say we take a walk when we're finished and show Marina the ladies of the night?"

Thomas rolled his eyes and shrugged.

They strolled toward the Piazza della Signoria, where the Palazzo Vecchio functioned as the city hall, its turreted tower rising high above the square. In the restaurants and cafés along the perimeter of the piazza, waiters were putting chairs up on tables and calling *buona notte* to their departing clientele.

They crossed the piazza and headed down a dark side street, the damp, musty scent of centuries leading the way.

"There's always someone along this stretch," Thomas said in a low voice. "Look in the doorways."

Sarah and Thomas chatted about the opening, the sales, the gossip, while Marina peered into the shadows. Sure enough, in the next block, she spotted a figure in a doorway, an attractive woman dressed in an elegant suit with a fur collar and cuffs. Her eyes flicked over Marina and then settled on Thomas. She called out something in a low singsong voice, to which Thomas responded in a gruff tone. The woman laughed.

"You are not going to tell me that was a man," Marina said.

"Yes, I am," he said. "The real women, the *puttane,* are selling their wares down around the train station."

Marina couldn't put her finger on exactly what she found

intriguing. The subtlety, perhaps, the absence of the in-your-face flamboyance that drag queens had. Still, she wasn't quite sure she understood it. So, these were men who dressed up as women to be with men? So they were gay, right? But did they want to be with straight men or gay men? Who wanted to be with them? And how come Thomas seemed to know so much about them?

CHAPTER 4

Two weeks into the Italian class, Marina decided that "crash course" was a far more accurate description than "immersion," which had led her to believe she would pass her days floating in the Italian language, lulled by its undulating rhythms. In actuality, it was more like boot camp, with the constant drills in verb conjugations and vocabulary. The class was composed of a couple of students, a handful of bored housewives, and a few antiques dealers. Fortunately, she caught on quickly. She loved that the rules of pronunciation made sense and that she was able to roll the letter *r* off her tongue with relative ease. The class met for four hours every morning followed by afternoon outings where they put their language to use. They learned how to shop and open bank accounts, visited museums, and even went to the movies. After the second week of outings, Marina decided her afternoon hours might be better spent with the English-Italian dictionary, making lists of words and phrases she would need for her gilding class. Although she was unable to find many of the technical terms in her pocket dictionary, she practiced phrases like: "I don't understand," "Please explain again," and "Would you demonstrate that for me?"

The apartment was beginning to take shape. In the back room, she'd fashioned a workbench out of a piece of plywood and two sawhorses, and created shelving with plastic crates she'd found in the street one night on her way home from dinner with Thomas and Sarah. Marcello's father had brought over a double bed, which she set up in the middle room, where it doubled as a couch, and Sarah had given her an old coffee table, some throw cushions, and the bare bones of a kitchen.

At first, Marina had to force herself out into the neighborhood and into the shops, where she practiced her Italian, laying out the words one by one, like newly minted coins, onto the counter at the bakery, the cheese shop, the pharmacy. She felt conspicuous in her new locale in a way she had not in the tourist-packed center of town. Now she truly was the stranger in the Italian word for foreigner—*straniero*. However, she soon discovered that people were charmed by her efforts to communicate, and gradually she grew less intimidated by the loud voices and wild gesticulations. She had yet to eat solo in one of the local restaurants, but every morning for breakfast, she went to the coffee bar on the corner of Via Luna, where she was greeted as *"la Signorina Americana."*

Often during the siesta after lunch, Sarah stopped by to help Marina with her Italian. She was a good instructor, patient, entertaining, creative. Along with the basic vocabulary for buying the necessities and navigating her new life, she taught Marina all the profanities she would ever need, including the appropriate gesture for each one. When they grew tired of verb conjugations or laughing too hard, they moved from the kitchen table to the living room and lounged on the bed, the only place to sit, and little by little, shared their life stories.

One afternoon, as Sarah lay sprawled across the bed, her head propped up on a pillow, her multicolored skirt draped over her legs like a quilt, she told Marina that her parents had been killed in a car accident when she was eighteen, and how instead of going right to college, she had gone on a tour of Europe with her Aunt Eileen and fallen in love with Florence, and how with her aunt's blessing, she had taken the life insurance money, moved to Florence, and enrolled at the Accademia di Belle Arti. It was there at the art institute that she'd met Thomas, who occasionally modeled for her life drawing class.

Marina sat at the foot of the bed, her knees pulled up to her chest. She wanted to stretch out alongside Sarah, head to foot, and relax into the story, but remained immobilized as if by some magnetic force. All through college, she'd lounged around in dorm rooms with roommates and friends, often in various states of undress, and she'd never thought twice about it. What made this any different? True, Sarah was older and more sophisticated than any friend she'd ever had, but they'd grown close, seeing each other most every day, and she felt sure Sarah valued their friendship as much as she. Why couldn't she just relax?

Sarah stared at the ceiling as if a film of her past were projected there, and twirled a lock of hair around her index finger as she spoke. "I'd been here about a year when Thomas walked into the class one morning and everyone started whispering. I didn't know what the buzz was about, but it turned out he had a reputation at the school for being able to hold unusually difficult poses for a great length of time. Plus, he was really good-looking."

"Was he a photographer then?" asked Marina in an effort to let go of her internal struggle and engage with Sarah's story.

"He was just starting to be successful, but he still modeled for some of his favorite professors, the ones who had helped him along the way. Anyway, he came in, stripped off his clothes just like that"—she snapped her fingers—"and then did some incredibly difficult poses, holding them forever. At the end, he walked around and looked at our work. I was mortified, of course. When he got to my easel, he stopped and flipped through my sketches."

Sarah sat up suddenly and leaned toward Marina, her face glowing. "I thought he was terribly arrogant. I wanted to slap his hand away, but I just stood there. You won't believe what he said."

"What?" asked Marina, captured as much by the proximity of the freckles dusting the bridge of Sarah's nose as by her story.

"I'd done all these drawings of his hands. He just stared at me with those cool gray eyes and said, 'I guess you liked my hands better than my balls.' "

"You're kidding!" Marina opened her eyes wide, both in astonishment and to better study Sarah's face, the crinkle at the corners of her eyes, the twitch of her lips as she suppressed a smile. "What did you say?"

Sarah shrugged. "I don't know, something about liking hands. I was just trying not to die of embarrassment. I know my face was bright red. Then he turned and walked away. Oh, and I forgot." She laid her hand on Marina's forearm. "All he had on was his jeans, no shirt or anything. After he finished the pose, he just pulled on his jeans, right in front of everyone, no underwear."

Marina couldn't sit still another moment and, pulling her arm gently from under Sarah's hand, got off the bed. "I need some water. Want some?"

Sarah shook her head.

"So then what? How did you get together?" Marina called from the kitchen, letting the water run at the kitchen sink until it ran cold. She drank half the glass, then refilled it before returning to the living room.

Sarah was now propped up against the wall, her legs tucked up under her skirt. "Wouldn't you know it, he was waiting downstairs when I left. Supposedly wanting to apologize for embarrassing me. It was just a ploy to get my attention." She looked at Marina and shrugged. "I guess it worked."

Marina stood in the doorway and leaned against the doorjamb. "But what about your work, did you finish the program? Do you still draw?"

"I finished the degree, but I got involved with Thomas right away and just got wrapped up in his life, I guess." Sarah was quiet for a moment. "Actually, I always wanted to be a sculptor."

The gilding course was held in a crumbling palazzo on the other side of the river, the Oltrarno district, near Piazza Santo Spirito. A makeshift workshop with several large tables had been set up in the grand salon where large sections of the frescoed walls and ceiling had fallen away, giving the effect of a giant paint-by-numbers canvas waiting to be finished. Large, south-facing windows provided not only light, but also, on sunny days, a modicum of heat.

Marina found herself in a panic the first few days of class, when all she understood was a word or two in each sentence. However, she quickly realized that she could learn as much from watching as from anything that was said. The teacher, Sauro, was a local artisan, a third-generation master gilder who worked with his father in his grandfather's workshop. This much she gleaned from the brochure that Sarah helped her translate. He was a round man with a cherubic face and gentle manner and seemed to understand that she was serious about her work, so he explained things slowly, checked her work closely, and made sure she followed his instructions. Marina hadn't realized that the gilding course would emphasize restoration to such an extent but was pleased to be learning two skills for the price of one. She was intrigued by how well damage, even that which seemed irreparable, could be concealed beneath a fresh layer of gold. Because the other students were hobbyists or antiques shop owners who wanted to learn a few quick tricks, she imagined that the course would only scratch the surface of this fascinating art, and she was determined to learn as much as she could. She shared her workbench with two English girls who were simply fulfilling a requirement in their study-abroad semester and were more interested in chattering nonstop about their sex lives than learning how to mix rabbit glue, and a middle-aged Italian man who came to class impeccably dressed in a crisp shirt, cashmere sweater, pressed trousers, and gleaming loafers, and never wanted to get his hands dirty.

Toward the end of her first month in the course, Marina got up her nerve to ask Sauro if she could take home the small box she was gilding. She'd been trying to think of a way to accelerate her learning and figured that if she started working on her projects at home at night, she might get twice the work done. He was surprised by her request but, after a moment's consideration, gave her permission to take the needed supplies. When she returned on Monday with the repair completed, she could tell he was not quite sure what to make of her. He took his time looking over her work, then nodded his head approvingly. *"Bravissima!"* he said, patting her back.

As the weeks went by, Marina saw that Sauro was impressed with the skills she'd brought with her—a steady hand with a carving knife and a solid understanding of design. He continued to take her seriously and gave her increasingly difficult moldings to duplicate, suggested carving knives she hadn't considered, and corrected her technique.

"Practice, practice, practice, the gold can only hide so much," he said again and again in a way that made it sound like a nursery rhyme. One day, after watching her unpack a carving that she'd taken home to work on overnight, he took her aside and showed her an intricately carved frame that was in desperate condition, and suggested she make it a separate, extracurricular project she could keep at home. That way, he explained, she wouldn't have to carry her in-class project back and forth every day. "When you are finished," he instructed her, "you must bring it to my studio and meet my teachers."

*   *   *

Marina had left the front door ajar for Sarah while she worked at her bench in the back room, and when she heard the gentle rap, she called out, "I'm back here."

A moment later, she was startled to see Thomas in the doorway.

"Hey, the place looks great." He stood in the doorway, his hands in the pockets of his jeans.

Marina put down her burnishing tool and straightened up. "Hi. I thought you were Sarah."

"Marcello needed to talk to her about something, so I thought I'd come see where she's been disappearing to all the time."

Marina flushed. "Would you like something to drink? A coffee? Come in the kitchen, I'll make us one."

Thomas stepped into the room. "Sure, but first I want to see what you're working on. Sarah's been bragging about your progress."

Marina hesitated, then stepped out of the way as Thomas approached the workbench.

"Let's see what you have here," he said, looking at her rather than the workbench.

"It's no big deal." Marina pointed to a spot on the frame. "You see here? This piece was missing. I had to carve a piece to match, glue it in, and then regild the area."

"Impressive." Thomas nodded, although he didn't seem particularly interested, scanning the room as if searching for something.

Marina moved to the door. "I'll make that coffee."

She could sense him pause in the living room before he followed her into the kitchen. Again he stood in the doorway. She filled the coffeepot with water and measured out the rich, dark grounds.

Marina glanced at him and, surprising herself, wondered if he had on any underwear. She turned away and picked up an already clean mug from the draining board and gave it a rinse. "Sit down. This'll just take a second," she said over her shoulder.

She had spent a fair amount of time around Thomas, mostly over dinners at Anita's with Sarah, but had been unable to develop a comfortable rapport with him. She always had the sense he was watching her, even when he appeared not to be. With Sarah present, she had been able to shrug it off as a photographer's quirk, but alone with Thomas, it felt implacable.

She stood with her back to him, washing the cup as if her life depended on getting every last germ, when suddenly Thomas stepped toward the front door and opened it.

"Look, I brought you something. Come see."

Marina dried her hands and followed him into the alley, where a blue bicycle leaned against the wall. It had been well used—the paint was worn and the beginnings of rust showed on the handlebars—but the tires looked new and the chain glistened with grease.

Thomas looked pleased with himself. "I've done a little work on it. I think it rides pretty well. Don't worry"—he chuckled—"I didn't find it in the street. A friend gave it to me. Why don't you give it a try?"

Marina knew Thomas often wandered the streets at night when he couldn't sleep, reappearing at first light with all sorts of things people had put out on the street for the rubbish men, things Thomas considered treasure, but Sarah considered junk. Marina hesitated a moment, then mounted the bike and pedaled down the alley and around the corner toward the main street. She hadn't been on a bike in years, but it felt glorious, and it would make the trek to the other side of the river so much faster. She made a tight turn at the end of the tunnel and headed back toward Thomas, ringing the bell.

"This is great!" The brakes squealed a little as she came to a stop next to him. "Thank you so much. It's just what I need."

Thomas smiled. "I know. Sarah told me that your class is over near my studio in Santo Spirito. That's quite a hike from here. You should stop by some time when you're in the neighborhood. It's not fair for Sarah to have all the fun."

Sauro's workshop was located in a warren of streets behind Santa Croce, where it appeared that every ground-floor space was some sort of workshop. Some had glass windows so grimy Marina couldn't see inside, and from all of them came either the hum of machinery or the softer vibrations of handheld saws and hammers. She moved down the street, searching for the number Sauro had given her. She was excited to see his workshop and show him the completed frame. Arriving at a wide wooden door that stood open to the street, she paused, then stepped over the threshold. It was dark, and only the muted chatter of a radio announcer came from the shadows. As her eyes adjusted, she saw three heavy wooden workbenches with built-in adjustable vises, each lighted by a goosenecked lamp. Three men were at work. At the bench nearest the door, a stooped, old man with thin, white hair stirred something on a Bunsen burner. At the next, an older version of Sauro with salt-and-pepper hair was engrossed in carving a large frame. Toward the back of the workshop, she saw Sauro stacking boxes against the wall.

She took another step and stopped. The old man looked up, but Marina could not tell if he saw her, since he bowed his head again and continued to stir. Sauro's father nodded at her and called to Sauro, who stopped what he was doing and came to greet her. He shook her hand and, indicating the old man who was now muttering into his pot, said, "That's my grandfather," but he didn't take her close enough for a personal introduction. Instead, he turned to introduce her to his father as his *"studentessa Americana."* Sauro's father shook her hand, then folded his arms across his chest as if to say, "I'll believe it when I see it." Thomas had warned her that she would not be taken seriously, but the fact that Sauro had invited her to his grandfather's workshop confirmed that at least *he* had faith in her ability and dedication. She didn't think the grandfather would be much of an obstacle, as he seemed already to have one foot in another world. But Sauro's father, that was a different story. She would just have to do her best and let him see she was serious about the work. He looked her up and down, and it occurred to her that perhaps he thought she was after his son, which was a ridiculous notion, since Sauro was married with two children, too old, and definitely too chubby. But she'd have to take care not to inadvertently cross any boundaries.

Sauro touched her elbow and she followed him to his bench in front of a set of double doors that opened out onto a courtyard, which had probably been beautiful in its day, but now, with several other workshops opening onto it, was littered with piles of discarded metal, plastic containers, broken bottles, and wood scraps.

"I like to have natural light and some fresh air when I work, but we must keep the doors closed when any of us is working with the gold. You know how this is."

Marina nodded. She knew that the slightest draft could interfere with applying the tissue-thin gold leaves. She still held her breath when she worked with it, while Sauro, she noticed, had mastered some way to breathe without disturbing the air around him.

Sauro indicated the massive frame on his bench, pointing out several places where it had needed extensive repairs. He shuffled through a pile of papers and produced several Polaroid pictures that showed the original damage as well as the various stages of restoration. As Marina's admiration grew, her self-confidence dwindled. How could she ever hope to reach this level of expertise? Sauro had grown up in this workshop, probably gilding his building blocks at age three and carving by five. For all she knew, it was in his damn genes. She tried to think of some excuse to leave, to escape before he asked to see her work, but before she could come up with anything, he moved his things aside and said, "Show me what you have done."

Marina opened her pack and pulled out the frame, which, in the shadow of his masterpiece, seemed but a glorified piece of junk. She handed it to him but looked away as he turned it in his hands.

"*Brava,*" he said, nodding his head.

His father had stopped working and was watching from the other bench. Sauro said something to him that Marina didn't catch, and gestured with the frame. His father put down his brush and came over to examine the piece. After a moment, he nodded, then, without a word, handed it back and returned to his bench.

"He agrees with me. This is good, but let me show you the places that need more work."

By the time she left his workshop, she was feeling a little better. Sauro said she was ready for something more challenging and had given her an intricately carved candlestick with a number of deep gouges, nearly a third of the base missing, and almost all of the gold leaf worn off. She wondered where he found these things. Maybe he wandered the streets, like Thomas, looking for objects his students could repair, although she imagined even Thomas might pass up the candlestick Sauro proffered.

Over the following weeks, under Sauro's tutelage Marina duplicated the candlestick's missing pieces, the most arduous part of the reconstruction. This required studying the piece from every angle, sketching her interpretation of what was missing, deciding which carving knives had the right blade to duplicate a tight curve or a sweeping one, then carving an experimental piece. Once the repairs were complete, she applied a layer of gesso to the entire candlestick in preparation for laying the gold leaf. Even though this was one of her extracurricular projects, Sauro had asked her to bring it into class for gilding and had promised to let her use the real thing, twenty-three-karat gold leaf, instead of the sixteen karat she'd been practicing with.

CHAPTER 5

Sweat trickled between her breasts, but her hand was steady as she floated the gold leaf into place with the gilder's tip. Then she let out her breath, relaxed her shoulders, and put the brush down, shaking the cramp from her fingers. She took a deep breath and blew it out slowly.

"*Calmati,*" Sauro said, patting her back, urging her to relax.

Marina nodded and picked up the gilder's tip, a thin, flat, squirrel-hair brush used for lifting and laying the gold leaf.

As promised, Sauro had brought in a small packet of twenty-three-karat gold for her to use. Each leaf, about the size of a business card and thinner than a Kleenex, was pressed between individual pages of waxed paper into a miniature booklet. After sanding the gesso with fine sandpaper, Sauro helped Marina prepare the bole—red clay mixed with rabbit glue—that was applied to create a smooth surface for gilding. Red, in addition to warming the patina, would help hide any faults that occurred in the application of the gold. Once the leaf was in place and dry, she would burnish the entire piece with a smooth agate, rendering the seams invisible.

Marina stroked the brush lightly over her forearm, picking

up enough oil from her skin to lift a sheet of gold and carry it to the candlestick. She repeated the painstaking process until the entire candlestick was covered with overlapping squares, ragged edges drifting like golden seaweed on the surrounding air currents. She stood back and admired her work, marveling at how a thin veneer of gold could conceal so much damage.

Marina was elated as she stepped from the cool shadows of the stone building after class. She had used her first high-karat gold, practically solid gold! She took off her sweater, letting the sun caress her bare arms and neck. Behind her, the two English girls clattered down the stairs, urging her to join them for lunch.

Jocelyn, a tall, buxom blonde with a gap-toothed smile, elaborated. "There's the greatest little trattoria over near Santo Spirito. Dead cheap, but good."

"And the blokes are dishy," added Felicity, her cap of dark curls bouncing against flushed cheeks.

Marina accepted and pushed her bike along as they filled her in on their lives, which seemed to revolve around sleeping with as many men as possible before their time in Florence was up. She was a little envious as she listened to their stories, not that she was interested in sleeping around, but a little sex might be nice. After all, it was spring, and she hadn't slept with anyone since her misguided-by-alcohol and very forgettable New Year's Eve date with the friend of a friend of a friend.

She wasn't familiar with Santo Spirito, other than having visited the church during her first week there, but knew that students, drug addicts, and dealers frequented the piazza. The streets were narrow and claustrophobic with the smell of rotting vegetables. They walked single file for a few blocks until Jocelyn stopped and said, "You can lock your bike up here. Best lock it to something or someone will just lift it up and carry it off."

Marina locked the bike to a signpost and followed her

classmates down a stairway and into a large room lined with long tables flanked by benches. The place was packed with students and workmen, some still wearing their dark blue *grembiulini*, the workingman's version of a lab coat. Loud conversation filled the space, and a thin layer of smoke clung to the ceiling. They found a spot at one end of a table when several people moved over. A grubby plastic-coated menu was passed down to them, and Marina ordered *spaghetti alla puttanesca* and a side serving of spinach.

During the meal, which was simple and fresh, an unending stream of young men passed the table, stopping to greet Felicity and Jocelyn, who spent more time squealing and kissing cheeks than eating. It seemed the Persian students were their favorites. During a lull in all the attention, the girls explained to Marina that there was a large community of Persian students studying at the university, mainly in the school of architecture, and evidently they both had slept with most of the group at one time or another before settling on their steady boyfriends. "You should come to one of our parties. They'd love you. They're hot for Americans." Felicity leered at Marina and elbowed Jocelyn. "Don't you think, Jo?"

Marina was about to ask about these parties when she felt warm hands on her shoulders. Startled, she turned. "Thomas!"

"This is the last place I'd expect to see you," Thomas said.

"This is my first time. I love it! What about you?" Her voice was loud, whether from too much red wine and twenty-three-karat gold, or being recognized by an older, handsome man in front of her friends, she didn't know and didn't care.

Thomas smiled at her. "I'm here almost every day. My studio is around the corner."

Marina did her best to gather her composure. "Yes, right, Santo Spirito."

"Come and see. Are you finished?" He gave Felicity and Jocelyn a nod. "I'll wait for you outside."

Marina turned back to her friends as Thomas left the restaurant. Felicity leaned forward and raised her eyebrows up and down. "So, an older man, and a dishy one, too. You've been holding out on us."

Marina blushed and explained that he was just a friend, but that she had to go, she was going to see his studio.

"Ah. Going to see his etchings, are you?"

Marina waved dismissively, turning her back on their lecherous cackling.

The simplicity of Thomas's studio, with its whitewashed walls, tiled floor, and vaulted ceiling, was unexpected, as was the feeling of relief she felt standing in the clean, open space. Florence had saturated her senses with the ocher and sienna of stucco and terra-cotta, the green scent of virgin olive oil, and the clatter of hooves and high heels across stone, leaving the taste of centuries thick in her throat. But here, bathed in the cool northern light from the massive windows, all the turmoil and excitement of the past three months settled quietly at her feet.

She was surprised, too, to discover that Thomas had an orderly side. She had assumed from his unruly hair, shabby clothes, and dented Vespa that organization was not a part of his makeup, imagining it was Sarah who kept their lives together. Along one wall, metal shelving was filled with neatly arranged photography equipment: camera bags, film canisters, tripods, a collection of lenses, floodlights, and darkroom supplies. At the far end of the long, narrow studio, Thomas had built a darkroom, leaving the center of the studio clear to accommodate sets and lighting, although he explained that he rarely did studio photography. In one corner, out of the way, two armchairs sat next to a velvet-covered daybed that Thomas said he had inherited with the studio.

On one wall, photographs of varying sizes held in place by tape or thumbtacks were layered, one on top of the other like a collage. Over this, as if it were wallpaper, hung framed photographs. This was his early work, mainly nudes, many of Sarah.

"Sarah told me she'd modeled for you," Marina murmured, her eyes following the curve of Sarah's back. "I know it's a cliché, but her skin looks like alabaster."

"You're right, it does. It was the autumn light, very warm and soft. Would you like to see the darkroom?"

Marina nodded, reluctant to take her eyes off the photographs, but turned and walked to the center of the room.

"What a great space. How did you find it?"

"The contessa. It belonged to a painter friend of hers."

"Really?"

"Yes. She found our apartment as well. I was already living there when Sarah and I met, but it was a dump until she moved in."

Marina moved to the shelves, admiring the collection of cameras and lenses. With her back to Thomas, she said, "Seems like the contessa is a pretty handy friend to have."

"I wouldn't be where I am today without her. I owe her a lot." Thomas crossed to where Marina was standing and picked up a camera. "Sarah had a hard time with her at first, said she controlled my life too much. I think she was just jealous, even though I told her there was nothing to be jealous of."

Marina could smell the garlic and wine on his breath. Not unpleasant, but too close. She moved along the shelf. "And now?"

"She's okay with her now."

Yeah, right, thought Marina. "Okay, so show me the darkroom."

"Only if you let me take your picture."

Marina turned, her hand on her chest. "Me? Why me?"

Thomas laughed. "Don't be coy. I told you I wanted to photograph you."

An angry flush burned her cheeks. When had she ever been coy? "I just don't like having my picture taken, that's all." She moved toward the darkroom door.

"Come on, you'll be great. You've got wonderful cheekbones and a lovely long neck." He reached in front of her to open the door, his arm brushing her breast. Marina glanced at him, but he appeared unaware. Had she imagined it? "I'd like to do a study in black and white to get the angles of your face. Then do a little color, too. I want to see if I can capture your eyes." His face was very close to hers. She could feel the heat from his body. She moved away, toward the cluster of furniture, feigning interest in a large wooden trunk with a padlock that served as an end table.

"So what's in the trunk? Treasure?"

"No, nothing like that. Just some whips, leather straps, the usual props." Thomas wiggled his eyebrows up and down.

Marina laughed. "So how come you don't use Sarah as a model anymore?"

"I think she got tired of me bossing her around." He grinned, then disappeared into the darkroom, only to return a minute later with a bottle of wine and two glasses. He filled both glasses and handed one to Marina. "So what do you say? How about a couple of shots?"

Marina was reluctant. She really did not like having her picture taken. She always looked washed-out and her nose was too pointy. But part of her wanted to be that woman Thomas saw, the one with the high cheekbones and lovely neck. Had he said beautiful? Before she could answer, Thomas grabbed her hand and led her to the center of the room, where he stopped and put a hand on her shoulder. "Okay, stand here." Then he moved to the shelves and pulled out a large leather bag. He rummaged around for a minute, finding a camera and then a lens.

"Okay, now come over to the window."

Marina did as she was told. He brought over a tall stool

and instructed her to sit on it. She sat tentatively on the edge of the stool with both feet on the floor, gripping her wine-glass with both hands. She expected Thomas to give her a hard time about being stiff and awkward, but it was almost as if he was ignoring her. He talked while he set up a tripod but did not look at her. She sipped the wine and answered his questions about her classes, Sauro, and what she was work-ing on. He moved back and forth between the tripod and the shelves, adding or exchanging equipment. Marina was so en-grossed in talking about her work that she scarcely noticed when he started shooting. Every now and then he gave her an instruction. "Put down your glass. Look at me. Turn your head. Lick your lips." She complied, then continued talking, describing the intricacies of her work. When Thomas finally put down the camera, Marina was shocked to see that nearly an hour had passed and that the wine bottle was empty. The light outside the window had shifted to gold, and in the street below, the shopkeepers were opening for evening hours.

As Marina made her way home in the twilight, she consid-ered stopping for a shot of espresso to clear the wine from her head but didn't want to forfeit the high she was on from her modeling session. Never had she experienced herself in the way she had that afternoon in Thomas's studio: confi-dent, carefree, beautiful.

When she arrived at her apartment, she found a note tacked to her door.

Marina, Where are you? Birthday picnic on Saturday.
I'll do food, you bring wine. My place 11:00 sharp.
XO, Sarah

Marina had completely forgotten that her twenty-third birthday was less than a week away. Her intention had been to keep it to herself, let the day pass quietly as she went about her business, celebrating her new life rather than the passing of another year. But Sarah, who had a fascination for astrology, had once asked when her birthday was, and apparently she hadn't forgotten.

By midmorning, it was hot. Marina hurried toward Sarah, who waited in front of her building.

"Sorry I'm late. I forgot the wine and had to go back."

"That's okay. I just came down."

Sarah wore a Mexican peasant blouse tied at the waist with an embroidered sash over a long, red, tiered skirt with black trim at the edge of each layer. Only her coloring and the garment's immaculate condition might keep her from being mistaken for a gypsy. She slung her market basket into the crook of one arm and linked the other with Marina.

"We'll catch the number seven bus in San Marco. It'll take us up to Fiesole." Sarah squeezed Marina's arm. "That's where my special picnic spot is."

The orange city bus was packed with tourists, predominantly German and French, who pointed and exclaimed, turning their heads from side to side as the bus wound its way up into the hills. Marina found a seat by a window and kept her eyes fixed on the dwindling city, Brunelleschi's dome refusing to shrink.

When they arrived in the town's ancient piazza, Sarah took Marina's hand and led her through the crowd of waiting tourists to a narrow street that led out of the village. The dusty road was lined with towering cypress trees that rose up like candlewicks and cast long shadows across their path. Along one side of the road, a tall stucco wall was periodically interrupted by the wrought iron gates of hillside villas, and on the other, a low, stone wall bordered an olive grove terraced into the hillside. After half a mile, they reached an opening in the wall.

Sarah motioned and said, "This way."

Marina followed her deep into the grove, until Sarah stopped and put her basket down in the shade of a gnarled olive tree.

"Here, give me a hand." Sarah pulled a faded Indian bedspread from her basket and handed one end to Marina. Together, they shook it out onto the ground.

Sarah flopped down on to her back. "Isn't this heavenly?" She sighed, looking up through the tree branches. "I love it here; look at the green leaves against the blue sky. Who would think to put those colors together?"

Marina sat down on the edge of the blanket. The air around them, redolent with the heady fragrance of olives, was still and quiet. She wondered if this was just Sarah's special place or if Thomas came here, too. In either case, she was pleased that Sarah had chosen to share it with her. Across the olive grove, on the backside of Fiesole just below the town, an Etruscan amphitheater was carved into the side of the hill. Tiers of massive stone blocks formed a perfect semicircle of seats around a stone platform. She could just make out a few people wandering through the ruins.

Sarah sat up. "They do performances there in the summertime, usually music. We could go sometime." She began unpacking her basket: coarse Tuscan bread; mascarpone cheese; tiny, shriveled black olives; two apples; a chocolate bar. She held up the candy. "I didn't think a cake would travel well, so I got us this."

Marina smiled and fished the bottle of Chianti from her satchel. "I hope you brought a corkscrew; I forgot to loosen the cork."

Sarah reached into the basket. "*Ecco la,* here you go, but I forgot glasses. We'll just have to drink from the bottle."

Marina pulled the cork and held out the bottle. "Here, you first, since this picnic was your brilliant idea."

"No, no, you're the birthday girl."

They sipped the wine, passing the bottle back and forth, silence settling between them, a silence that wasn't exactly awkward for Marina but not completely comfortable either. They'd spent a great deal of their free time together in the past months, much of it sprawled across Marina's bed sharing intimacies. She'd heard Sarah's life story and told Sarah hers. They were both only children, but that's where the similarities ended. Sarah had grown up under the rule of Bible-thumping, fundamentalist parents who didn't believe in sparing the rod, while Marina managed to find her way under the benign neglect of a bohemian mother and eccentric father, both of whom were completely absorbed in their careers. They'd shared stories from childhood and adolescence both serious and silly, but somehow, sitting in this peaceful orchard sharing a bottle of wine, the silence felt more intimate than anything Marina could remember. She took a long pull on the bottle and broke the silence. "Did Thomas tell you he ran into me the other day and showed me his studio?"

"Yes, he did, and he sent you something." Sarah drew a scuffed manila envelope out of her basket and handed it to Marina. "Go on, open it."

Marina undid the clasp and pulled out a stack of photographs. "Oh, my God!" She stared down at herself, sitting on the high stool in her jeans and boots, her heels hooked on the rungs of the stool, knees spread wide. She was leaning forward on her hands, resting them on the stool between her legs. Her arms squeezed her breasts, and she could see her nipples through the thin cotton tank top. "Jesus. I don't remember doing that." She looked up at Sarah, afraid she might be angry, but her friend was grinning.

"Look at the rest of them. They're great." Sarah leaned her head close and removed the top picture. The next one, a closeup of Marina's face turned toward the light, captured her lost in thought. There was another of her face, her eyes half closed and her tongue peeking out between moist lips. How much of that bottle of wine had she had that day? The remainder of the pictures caught her in motion, her arms up-lifted as if she had been demonstrating something.

"I didn't realize. . . ." She was at a loss for words.

"He's good, isn't he?"

"Amazing! You'd never know I hate having my picture taken."

"That's what makes him so good. He has a way of being there without seeming to be. At least, people seem to forget he's there."

Or don't know it in the first place, thought Marina, re-membering the stolen-moment portraits at his show. She shuffled through the photographs. What she didn't say was how good she thought she looked, not washed-out at all, and even in profile, she liked her nose.

"You know, you should consider working with Thomas." Sarah was spreading cheese on a piece of bread. "He some-times needs help in the studio. You know your way around a darkroom, don't you?"

"Somewhat." Marina put down the pictures and picked up an olive.

"You could help with that. Sometimes he needs a model. He'd like to shoot you again, I know that."

Marina hesitated. "I don't know. Maybe I could help in the studio, but I'm not really model material."

"Maybe not in the classic sense, but clearly the camera likes you." Sarah reached out and ran her finger down Ma-rina's bare arm. "You've got beautiful skin, very peaches and cream."

Goosebumps rose on her flesh. "I don't know. Maybe."

"That's good enough." Sarah brushed the crumbs from her lap and got up on her knees. "Okay, now let's have a look at your feet."

"My feet?"

"Yes, let's see what you've got under those heavy boots of yours." Sarah reached for Marina's nearest foot.

Marina laughed and squirmed away. "Wait. Why do you want to see my feet?"

Sarah sat back down and unfolded her legs. She had taken off her espadrilles. Her toes were painted pink. "It's a sign of beauty. Beautiful feet, beautiful face. See?" She wiggled her toes.

Marina considered them. "Yeah, they're okay," she teased.

"Okay! What do you mean okay?" With that, Sarah pushed her down on the blanket and straddled her, sitting on her hips. She held Marina's arms down over her head and repeated in a threatening voice, "Okay, you say? Just okay?" Then she let go of Marina's arms and began tickling her ribs.

Marina shrieked and writhed under Sarah's weight. "I was only kidding! They're gorgeous, gorgeous!"

Sarah stopped tickling and put her hands on her hips. "That's better." She slid down Marina's legs. "Now yours."

Marina sat up, laughing, and pushed her gently out of the way. "Here, I'll do it myself." She pulled off her boots and socks and thrust her feet out. "There, are you satisfied now?"

Sarah lifted one foot and cradled it in her hands. "They're warm." She turned the foot from side to side and took each toe between her fingers as if she were doing "This Little Piggy." "And quite pretty, too. But you need some polish. I'll paint them for you sometime."

Marina tried to pull her foot away, but Sarah held on and told her to lie back on the blanket. "It's your birthday. I'll give you a foot rub. Ever had one?"

"No, not really." Marina shook her head. "But, no tickling!"

"Don't worry, you're safe in my hands. Relax."

By the time Sarah put her foot gently on the blanket and lifted the other one into her hands, Marina felt as if she were sinking into the earth, its molecules rearranging themselves, creating space for bone and muscle, supporting every inch of her with its warmth. She opened her eyes a crack and peeked at Sarah, who sat cross-legged, head bowed over her task. Never having been ministered to quite so intimately, she wasn't quite sure what to make of it. Was Sarah just being friendly, or was she flirting with her? She'd never had a woman come on to her, so she didn't know what the signs might be, surely something more obvious. Besides, Sarah was happily married and devoted to Thomas. She brought her attention back to her foot and allowed herself to sink into the sensation.

CHAPTER 6

With summer in full swing and tourists swarming the city, Marina found herself on the defensive, a denizen whose turf was under attack. It became "us" and "them," with Marina now firmly in the "us" camp. She was glad at the end of the day to cross the boulevard and return to her neighborhood, where the invaders might wander only by chance.

Her workday was divided between the classroom and either her workroom or Sauro's workshop, where he now allowed her to help him on his projects. The grandfather smiled and nodded in her direction but rarely spoke, while Sauro's father occasionally gave her work his grudging stamp of approval.

She and Sarah continued to share the siesta hours, sometimes lazing on the banks of the Arno or, if it was cool enough, riding bikes in the Cascina Park. When the heat became too much, they retreated to Marina's apartment, where Sarah might paint Marina's toes or brush her hair. Marina was caught off guard the first time Sarah asked if she could brush her hair. She hadn't had her hair brushed by anyone since her mother's cursory strokes when she was young.

"Come on, you'll love it." Sarah sat down on the edge of

the bed and pointed to the floor in front of her. "Go get your brush and sit here."

Marina rarely said no to anything Sarah wanted to do, no matter how odd, like on the scorching day she insisted they strip to their underwear and lie on the stone floor of her living room in an effort to cool off. She retrieved her brush from the bathroom and sat on the floor between Sarah's knees. A shiver ran down her spine as Sarah pulled her fingers slowly through her hair from her forehead to the base of her skull, scratching her scalp lightly with her nails. She repeated this motion twice more, and Marina couldn't help but let out a little moan.

"Now, just breathe and relax. I'm going to try for a hundred strokes, just like Renaissance women, only their hair was three times as long as yours." Sarah gave the hair a few long, firm strokes from the crown down to the tips, where it brushed Marina's shoulders. "It's beautiful hair, so silky. You should grow it."

"Mmmm," was all Marina had to say as she tipped her head to one side in anticipation of the next stroke.

The odd thing was that Sarah would never let her return the favor. Marina had offered to paint her toes and brush her hair, but Sarah had simply shaken her head and said, "I'm too ticklish." She wasn't sure how to take Sarah's rebuff. Wasn't she good enough? It made her feel a bit like a plaything, a doll that Sarah could do with what she wanted.

Most evenings, she joined Thomas and Sarah for dinner, usually at Anita's, but on occasion, a languid night might take them to a restaurant upriver, where they would sit outside admiring the city, its lights multiplied on the still surface of the water. On one such night, they asked if she would look after their apartment while they spent the month of August in the country with Thomas's agent, Stefano.

"One of the contessa's cronies," Sarah told her later. "Actually he's not bad, and his wife's a sweetheart and a fabulous cook. So I'll be as fat as a pig when you see me in September."

Marina was thrilled to finally be able to do something for Sarah and spent most of their last evening together reassuring the two of them that she would be all right on her own for the month. "I have so much to do, you wouldn't believe it. Sauro has left two pieces for me to work on while he's away. It took me a while to convince him that I wasn't going on vacation. You'd think it was against the law not to take August off."

"I think it is. You'll see. The tourists will be the only ones left in the city," said Thomas.

"That's good, I'll need them."

He looked at her quizzically.

"I'm going to work for Sauro's brother at his leather stall in Santa Croce."

"What?" Sarah put down her fork. "Why didn't you tell me?"

"It just happened today. The German girl he had ran off with the Spaniard who worked at the stall next to his."

Thomas frowned. "If I'd known you needed work, I would have taken you on. I could use some help."

"No, no. I don't need work. I have enough money to keep me going for a while. This just came along, and I thought, what the hell. My gilding class will be over, Sauro's away until September, and it's something different."

"Okay, but swear to me that you'll help me out this fall. *And* do some modeling."

Marina laughed and held up both hands, palms out. "Okay, okay, I promise."

Sarah reached across the table and covered Marina's hand with hers. In mock seriousness, she said, "And promise me that you won't kill my plants."

Thomas's forecast was correct. As the summer heat increased, the citizens left, heading for cooler air at seaside resorts or country houses. For every one that left, two tourists arrived. The city became a different place, barely recognizable, and not one Marina would have stayed in had she arrived at the height of summer. She watched groups of foreigners led by flag-toting guides roam the streets around her stall like herds of cattle, taxis and city buses waiting patiently for them to move out of the way. But the tourists gave Marina a sense of belonging, as if the city were hers to protect, and rather than fend off the invaders, she welcomed them and did her best to guide and educate them. After making a sale of a leather bag, belt, or wallet, she'd asked her customers what they had seen, suggesting sights they might have missed. She wanted to share the city, her city, to have them love it as much as she did. She directed them to museums, churches, galleries, and to Vivoli, just around the corner, for "the best gelato in the world."

The week following Thomas and Sarah's departure, Marina let herself into their apartment with the key Sarah had given her. It was eerily quiet, the bright rugs and tapestry throw pillows not nearly as cheerful as when Sarah was there. She had the feeling that at any moment, Sarah would call to her from the bedroom, or she would turn around and find Thomas sitting on the couch reading the paper. She opened the terrace doors to the sun and busied herself watering the large pots of geraniums before coming inside to tend to the houseplants. Sarah had instructed her, with all seriousness, to talk to the plants so they knew they were loved, "just like children." Marina thought it was silly, but she'd promised.

"Hello, Mr. Tree. Are you thirsty? Here, have a drink." She felt like an idiot, but after the third or fourth plant, she found herself addressing a small African violet with some feeling. "Here you go, sweetie. Don't worry, Sarah will be back soon." By the time she was finished, she was sure the apartment felt friendlier.

Crossing back toward the kitchen with the watering can in

hand, she noticed an ivy plant high up on the bookshelves. Finding a stool in the bedroom, she stood on tiptoe to reach the plant. "Here you go, honey, I almost missed you." Next to the plant lay a large portfolio with the words *Sarah Drawings* written in faded script on the binding. Marina climbed down with the watering can, then back up to retrieve the folder. She carried it to the couch and laid it carefully on the coffee table.

The folder, marbleized cardboard with reinforced leather corners, was tied with black string and covered in a thick layer of dust. Marina undid the knot and turned back the cover. The first drawing was a charcoal rendering of a hand, palm upturned, fingers gently curved. It looked so real Marina imagined she could drop something into the palm, something delicate, a speckled robin's egg or a dandelion head. She slid the drawing to the side and found more hands on the next few sheets of paper. The detail was remarkable, the folds along the joints, the crosshatching of lines on the skin, veins pushing up from within. It was as if she could see the blood pulsing through them. Then came drawings of two different models: a slim, small-breasted girl and an old man with a creased face. Sketches of their hands followed, his gnarled and laced with veins, hers plump and unlined.

The last few drawings were of Thomas. He knelt on a small padded mat in the center of a dais; a narrow wooden pole about the size of a broom handle rested horizontally on his shoulders, behind his neck. His arms were draped over it, the pole in the crook of his elbows, his forearms hanging down in front. His head was bowed. The muscles in his shoulders and thighs were accentuated by the pose, and his hands, pendent at the ends of his arms, presented themselves for the taking. There was only one drawing of his entire body, and Marina stared at it for quite a while. Looking at a picture of Thomas naked, she couldn't decide how she felt exactly—voyeuristic, naughty, titillated? His genitalia were in shadow, but she never would have suspected that under his baggy jeans and sweaters lay a well-developed, finely muscled body. The remaining drawings were studies of his hands. Marina turned each one over carefully until she came to the end, then leaned back on the couch and stared up at the ceiling. Why didn't Sarah ever talk about her work? She had talent, and there was a definite intensity about the hand thing. Marina shook her head. Thomas had never mentioned it either. She sat for a moment longer wondering if she should leave the folder out on the table, so Sarah would know she had seen it, but then she closed the cover, tied the string, and returned it to its place on the bookcase.

Occasionally, Jocelyn and Felicity came by the leather stall to invite Marina to parties, which she never attended, but when their boyfriends rented a house in the country, Marina relented and accepted an invitation to a weekend house party. The heat was getting to her and she was lonely. Jocelyn arranged a ride for Marina with a few of the Persian students. "You can have your pick. We've already got our guys. Reza and Parvis are really cute and sweet, but Amir has the best bod, and he's a great dancer." When Marina said that she'd just as soon take the bus, Jocelyn told her she had already made the arrangements for her to be picked up on Friday at noon. Marina did not relish the thought of a long drive with three guys she didn't know, and contemplated not answering the door when they came, but in the end, the appeal of escaping the city for a couple of days won out.

The three young men who appeared at her door were not only perfect gentlemen, fighting over who would carry her bag, but handsome as well. Parvis turned out to be tall and thin, with long curly hair and a mustache. Amir was not quite as tall, but was more muscular and had large brown eyes fringed with thick lashes. Reza, the slightest of the three, was clearly the one in charge, the one with the car. Marina ended up in the back of the tiny Fiat with Parvis, who took great pains not to jostle against her as they flew down the

Autostrada in the shimmering midday heat. Amir spoke English well, talking easily with her from the front seat. He told her about the design project he was working on for the completion of his architecture degree, and about returning to Iran to take care of his elderly parents when he was finished.

By the time they bumped to a stop in front of the ramshackle farmhouse, Marina's reservations had drained away— she was ready to let loose and have some fun. As she squeezed herself from the car, Felicity and Jocelyn, in short shorts and bikini tops and pink with sunburn, burst from the front door. They kissed and hugged everyone, then ushered Marina into the house.

The cool, dark interior was a welcome relief from the white heat outside.

"It's been so bloody hot," said Jocelyn, "we keep the shutters closed most of the time, only opening them at night. Even then, it's stifling." The girls led Marina up the stone staircase to her room at the end of the hall. "This is Amir's room," said Felicity, "but he's giving it to you for the weekend. He'll share with Parvis. Take a minute to freshen up. Then come down for drinks."

In the dusky, shuttered light, Marina made out a beamed ceiling draped with cobwebs and a double bed that appeared to be freshly made up. She put down her bag, picked up a thin towel from the end of the bed, and made her way to the bathroom, where she splashed cold water on her face. Her eyes seemed bluer than normal against her flushed cheeks. She ran wet fingers through her hair and spoke sternly to her image in the mirror: "Have fun!"

Downstairs, she found Felicity in the kitchen mixing a large pot of sangria, orange slices floating on the surface like tiny life rafts.

"Here, help me ladle this out." Felicity directed her to some glasses set out on the table. "Everyone is out on the terrace."

It was still hot, but bearable, under the shade of a large

tree, where Jocelyn introduced Marina to Mohamed and Henry. A flurry of clinking glasses followed and someone produced a fat cigarette laced with hashish. When it reached her, Marina took a drag, not anticipating its strength. Once she finished coughing and wiping her eyes, Amir said, "It is strong, no?"

"No shit," gasped Marina, taking a sip of wine.

There was a great deal of laughter, followed by chatter between the men in Farsi. After a while, Jocelyn leaned over and said to Marina, "I know it seems rude for them to carry on like this, but we've gotten used to it. If we get bored, we interrupt and make them speak English."

Marina shrugged. She was happy just floating in a haze of wine and hashish.

After a while, someone suggested a swim before supper. They made their way down a narrow path, through the heady scent of honeysuckle, to a small lake. It was almost dark and the air had cooled to lukewarm. The men stripped off their clothes and ran splashing into the water, calling for the women to follow. Marina didn't hesitate, the combination of dusk and drugs having stripped her of any self-consciousness. The water, warm and silky, was like slipping into a perfectly fitted garment. Sleek. Caressing. Marina couldn't remember ever feeling anything so wonderful. Amir swam over to her. At some point, it seemed to have been decided that she was his to pursue. She giggled to herself, wondering if they had drawn straws or played some Persian betting game. Whatever the case, she was glad that Amir had come out on top.

"Allow me to show you something," he said, instructing her to lie on her back as he slipped his arm under her shoulder blades, the other behind her thighs just below her buttocks. "Now relax. I support you," he said.

Still lucid enough to appreciate the discreet placement of his hands, Marina relaxed and let her eyes drift across the sky, where the first stars of the night were beginning to appear. After a moment, Amir whispered, "Later I will show you the full heavens." She might have laughed had his tone not been so earnest, and for all she knew, it might have been a direct translation from the Prophet or some other exotic poet.

That night Marina dreamed about Sarah. They were picnicking in the olive grove when the grove changed into a river, in that inexplicable way things in dreams change from one form to another. At first they floated, holding hands and talking, but then the current became stronger and they had trouble keeping hold of each other. Marina was sucked under, but in the midst of her panic, she found that she could breathe underwater. She surfaced, calling to Sarah that it was all right to let go, that she, too, would be able to breathe. But the raging waters were too loud, and Sarah could not hear her. She called again and again as the water swept Sarah away.

Marina woke with a start and the overwhelming feeling that she had failed her friend somehow. Beside her, Amir snored softly, his lips pursed like a child's, long dark lashes curled against his cheeks. He'd been a lovely lover, soft touch, soft voice, soft hands, and she'd happily floated by his side throughout the evening and into the night. She hadn't realized how much tension and yearning Sarah's titillating and confusing attentions had left her with. Amir had released it all, easily and effortlessly, and she hadn't even had to ask for a condom. It simply appeared when it was supposed to. She wondered what Sarah was doing at that very moment. Was she snuggled up against Thomas? Had they made love in the night? She tried to envision this, but couldn't. Usually she had an easy time imagining people in bed together, even unlikely couples where one was much taller or larger than the other. Not that she thought Thomas and Sarah were unlikely. Did she?

* * *

She hadn't gone to the apartment with the intention of dressing up in Sarah's clothes, but a flash of color from the closet had caught her eye, and she'd reached for the embroidered dress without thinking. She held it up, hugging it to her body, turning this way and that in front of the large mirror that leaned against the wall at the foot of Thomas and Sarah's bed. Before she knew what she was doing, she was out of her clothes and stepping into the dress, her T-shirt and shorts crumpled on the floor.

She hummed to herself as she watered Sarah's plants. She liked how the dress felt, how it floated around her, the celadon skirt creating a pocket of air that caressed her legs. Since her weekend with Amir, she'd felt deliciously carefree and somehow emboldened, otherwise she never would have tried on Sarah's clothes without permission.

"There you go, you little green thing, drink up." That was the last of the houseplants. Now for the geraniums on the terrace. She crossed the living room and was about to step through the French doors when she heard something that stopped her. The unmistakable scratch of a key finding its way into a lock. Before she could move, the front door swung open and Marcello stepped in, shutting it behind him, but when he saw her, he froze, and for a moment, the two of them stood like gunslingers, each eyeing the other.

"*Dio mio!* Marina!" Marcello clasped the envelopes he was carrying to his chest and let out a dramatic sigh.

Marina smiled apologetically, holding up the watering can.

"*Sì, sì,*" he said, and held up the mail.

They chatted for a few moments about nothing of consequence but enough for him to compliment her on her Italian, all the while glancing at the dress. Before leaving, he arranged the mail on the desk, eyed her one more time, then departed with a small wave.

Marina wondered if he'd recognized Sarah's dress. Of course he had. Would he tell on her? He was never anything other than sweet to Marina when their paths crossed, but she worried that he might tattle if he had any inclination toward disrupting her relationship with Sarah. After all, he'd been her closest friend before Marina showed up. Not long after Marina moved into Via Luna, the three of them had met for lunch, but the language barrier and the fact that Sarah turned out to be the only thing they had in common had made it awkward, and Sarah hadn't suggested it again. She knew that he and Sarah still spent time together, but Sarah was forever saying that he felt neglected and she needed to spend more time with him.

Marina put away the watering can and walked into the bedroom. She stood in front of the mirror again, cocking her head to one side. The dress felt nice, but somehow it didn't look quite right on her. The way it looked on Sarah, feminine and exotic, didn't translate to her, any more than her mother's clothes had when she was a little girl standing in front of the hall mirror, in lipstick and too-large high heels, trying to imagine the woman she would one day become. Her mother's knack for understated elegance and bohemian chic was not a trait Marina seemed to have inherited, at least it hadn't surfaced yet, so she relied on the trends, following the herd, playing it safe. No one would ever accuse her of making a statement in her Levi's, Frye boots, and shapeless sweaters. She sighed at her image in the mirror, hoping that someday she'd find a style all her own and stop looking in other people's closets for her identity.

CHAPTER 7

The summer heat seemed to go on forever, and by the time Sarah and Thomas returned in early September, it still showed no signs of letting up. Marina aired out their apartment and had a cold supper of antipasti, cheese, and salad waiting for them when they returned on the evening train from Siena. They seemed pleased to see her, and while they ate supper, Thomas regaled her with humorous anecdotes about their hosts and fellow houseguests. Sarah was reserved, presumably tired from the journey, and it wasn't until Thomas had talked nonstop through most of dinner that Marina realized he and Sarah were not speaking to each other. After dinner Thomas went off to check on his studio and she finally had an opportunity to ask Sarah what was going on. Sarah told her how the contessa had swooped down in the middle of their vacation and carried Thomas off to Rome on the pretext of meeting some important client.

"That bitch didn't even have the decency to apologize for interrupting our holiday." She began to cry.

"What did you do? Did you ask him not to go?"

"I told Thomas not to bother coming back if he went with

her. He told me I was acting like a fool, that there was nothing to worry about. That he had to go. It was business."

"So he just went?"

Sarah nodded and sniffed. "He was gone for five days. He never called, and then when he came back, he acted as if nothing had happened. I don't know what got into him. He hasn't done anything like that in a long time."

"What do you think is going on?" Marina hesitated. "Are they having an affair?"

"Nothing's going on. It's not like that. It's just that it makes me so mad when he lets her do as she pleases, with no regard for me or my feelings."

It seemed pretty clear to Marina that something was going on and probably had been for a long time, but Sarah seemed exhausted, so she let it go.

The glut of tourists continued along with the heat, and Marina decided to stay on at the leather stall working half days as long as she was needed. She and Sarah fell back into their pattern of spending the lunch and siesta hours together, most often at Marina's apartment, since Sarah was still angry with Thomas and avoided him as much as possible. They taught themselves how to macramé, and when they tired of making jute and bead plant hangers, they read aloud to one another. Marina was enthralled with *The Agony and the Ecstasy*, following Michelangelo's footsteps through the streets of Florence on a map she tacked to the kitchen wall. Sometimes, after too much wine with lunch, they lay head to foot on the bed and dozed, and while Marina was still unsure what to make of Sarah's attentions, she had decided to stop overexamining Sarah's motives, to relax and accept the friendship she offered.

One day, as they lay on the bed, they talked about trips around Italy they might take together. Marina wanted to experience some of the countryside, and Sarah said she'd love to see all the great sculpture she could, especially any of children.

"Florence is full of Donatello's putti, and I adore them, but I've seen enough babies with wings to last me a lifetime, and most of the paintings you see around here have children in them who look like miniature adults." Sarah waved her hand across the ceiling as if she were painting them herself. "I'd like to see someone do children who look like children."

Sarah often talked about children in relation to art, but she never mentioned why she and Thomas didn't have any of their own, and although Marina wondered about it, she sensed the topic was off-limits. Instead, she engaged Sarah in talking about which cities to visit in order of importance, but when she pressed her to make a definitive plan, Sarah balked. "I don't think Thomas would like it if I went off without him."

Marina poked Sarah's shoulder with her foot. "So what! Doesn't he go off with the contessa at the drop of a hat?"

"Yes, but if I went off, it would just make the situation worse."

"What do you mean?"

Sarah paused before replying. "It would just give her more opportunity to be with him."

Marina propped herself up on her elbows and looked at Sarah. "You can't stay here and guard him. What about *your* dreams, *your* life?"

"My life is with Thomas."

"But at what cost?" Marina knew she was pushing the point, but it made her crazy that Sarah allowed everything to be about Thomas. "What about your work? I saw your portfolio. You're good."

"That was years ago. Besides, one artist in the family is enough."

Marina flopped back onto her back in a huff. "I suppose Thomas said that."

Sarah sat up. "What is going on with you, Marina? And when did you see my portfolio?"

"When you were away, I found it on the bookshelf." Marina stared at the ceiling, remembering the hands. "Your drawings are beautiful. Why did you stop?"

"Oh, I don't know." Sarah flicked her hand dismissively. "Thomas's career was taking off. He needed my help. Then . . ." Sarah stopped.

"Then what?"

"Nothing. I just got over it." She lifted her hair off her neck, tying it in a knot at the back of her head. "Look, Marina, you don't know what it takes to be married. It's a compromise." She swung her legs off the bed and stood up, indicating the end of the conversation.

In the late afternoon, Marina always went faithfully to Sauro's workshop, where he allowed her to help him prepare pieces for gilding and advised her on projects of her own, small frames and boxes that she bought inexpensively at the flea market and restored lovingly with thoughts of Christmas and her parents' birthdays in mind.

Most nights she and Sarah had dinner together at Anita's, and each night, Anita would ask for Thomas, only to be met with a shrug from Sarah.

"She thinks she's being crafty," said Sarah. "She's only asking about Thomas to see if I'm still mad at him."

Finally, Marina felt obliged to ask the question she'd been avoiding. She tore off a piece of crust and began to chew. The truth was she liked it that she had Sarah's undivided attention and didn't want to bring Thomas into their world, preferring to believe that he'd vanished, run off with the contessa, leaving the two of them to carry on happily on their own. But she was afraid that she might have been too critical of their marriage and wanted to at least appear supportive. "So, how *are* you feeling about Thomas?"

"Oh, I don't know. I'm getting a little tired of all this avoidance. He creeps into bed at dawn and I scurry out of the house as soon as I hear him stirring in the morning." Her earrings shivered as she shook her head. "It's silly, and it never seems to get me anywhere. Thomas can out-stubborn me any day."

Marina felt the flush of jealousy on her cheeks as she sensed Sarah slipping away from her, but she managed to keep her tone neutral. "So, what will you do?"

Sarah sipped her wine. "All I have to do is be home more, then everything will go back to the way it was."

"Is that what you want? For things to go back the way they were?"

Sarah shrugged. "What choice do I have? Some things never change."

But you could change things, Marina thought as she looked down at the tangled mass of spaghetti on her plate and realized she'd lost her appetite.

The next day, Sarah did not appear at lunchtime, and Marina didn't think too much of it until there was no sign of her at dinnertime either. She hadn't expected Sarah to switch her affection back to Thomas quite so quickly, and to avoid further disappointment, didn't go home at midday for the rest of the week.

On Saturday she found a note on her door.

Meet us for dinner at nine. Bring Amir if you like. S & T.

Following the weekend in the country, Marina had enjoyed a number of dinner dates with Amir, as well as an occasional night at his apartment, but since Sarah's return, she hadn't paid him much attention, declining his invitations with one excuse or another. But she didn't want to have dinner with Sarah and Thomas on her own, to be the third wheel again, so she screwed up her courage to call Amir and was pleased when he agreed to come along.

It was just as Sarah had predicted—everything appeared to have returned to normal between Thomas and her. Thomas seemed especially pleased to see Marina and spent most of the evening talking to her about his work, trying to persuade her to come help him in his studio once her stint at the leather stall was up. Marina had been anxious about seeing Sarah after the silence of the past week, afraid she might be upset about her criticism of their marriage. But Sarah seemed relaxed and included Marina easily in her conversation about Iran with Amir. While Marina was flattered by Thomas's attention and relieved that Sarah showed no signs of being upset with her, she understood that a shift had taken place. She was once again the odd man out. That night she went home with Amir, but his tender ministrations were not enough to fill the place vacated by Sarah's undivided attention.

With the summer now behind them, the crowds thinned, and Marina's time at the leather stall came to an end. When Thomas heard that she was available again, he asked her to make good on her promise to help him with his work, and Marina saw no reason to refuse. She'd get a little extra income, which would come in handy with Christmas approaching, plus she'd be learning more about photography.

For the first two weeks, while Thomas scouted for stonework and statuary he might want to shoot, Marina followed him around town. In addition to carrying his extra camera bag, he had her mark the locations he liked on a map and make corresponding notes in a small notebook. At any given site, he might take ten to twenty quick shots using his 35mm Leica. He said there was plenty of time for more exacting shots once he knew what he wanted. The most crucial piece of information he had her record was the time of day. That way, he explained, he'd be able to return to the site at the same hour if he liked what he saw in the proofs, or try another time of day for a different effect. She knew that he was working toward a new show, but whenever she asked him what exactly he was looking for, he put his finger to his lips and said, "Watch and learn." His response irritated her, reminding her of her parents, who'd so often left her questions unanswered, but she let it go and dutifully followed his directions.

They worked from the early morning, a few times starting at dawn, until midday, when they'd find their way to Anita's and join Sarah for lunch. Following the meal, Thomas disappeared to his studio to look at the morning's work, while Marina either returned home if she was working on something, or followed Sarah back to her apartment and collapsed on the couch.

"Thomas says you've been a big help." Sarah was ironing shirts while Marina lay on the couch flipping through a magazine.

"What he has me doing isn't exactly brain surgery." Marina had come to the conclusion that Thomas didn't really need her help at all. He could easily have done the things he had her doing, but for some reason he wanted her around, and she was flattered.

"Maybe not, but he says it's helping him. Anyway, it's good for him to have the company. I worry that he spends too much time alone."

"Honestly, you shouldn't worry about him. We can't go two blocks without someone stopping him for a chat." Marina watched Sarah pick up another shirt from the basket and wondered why Thomas always looked so crumpled.

"I know," Sarah replied. "He's got that street life, but . . ."

"He's an artist. They're all loners. You know that."

"I suppose so. Are you having any fun or is it just tedious?"

Marina put the magazine down and sat up. "So far, it isn't very exciting, but I'm enjoying it. Thomas said I can help him in the darkroom next, and it'll be interesting to see the finished product. But it's been fun being out in the streets with someone who knows so much about the city. He seems to have stories about every place we go and almost everyone we run into."

Sarah smiled. "Yes, he's quite the storyteller. I'm glad you're enjoying it. I know Thomas is, too."

It seemed important to Sarah that her friend was happy working with Thomas, and it suddenly occurred to Marina that perhaps Sarah wanted her to keep an eye on Thomas. Maybe Sarah thought that if she worked with Thomas every day, he'd be less likely to spend time with the contessa. It seemed a bit extreme, but at the same time, it made sense. She lay back on the couch and closed her eyes. She'd have to be careful not to get sucked into Thomas and Sarah's drama. She wasn't the damn babysitter.

When Thomas was ready for her to work in the darkroom with him, she had to rearrange her schedule to work on her own projects in the mornings instead of the afternoons, which was when Thomas did his darkroom work. Marina had assumed that Thomas took a siesta after lunch, perhaps on the velvet daybed in the corner of his studio, but that wasn't the case at all. He went right back to work, and expected her to do the same. Now she followed him up the stairs, eager to see what the darkroom had in store for her. Darkroom work intrigued her more than any other aspect of photography. She loved the way an image slowly came to life, seemingly out of nowhere, spreading itself into sharper and sharper focus across a blank sheet of paper. It was nothing short of magic.

As near as she could tell, the studio hadn't changed. It was still bright and empty.

Thomas pointed to the back corner. "Put your stuff on the daybed and I'll give you a tour of the darkroom."

Marina put her coat and bag on the bed and followed Thomas into the darkroom. The dim light and sulfurous smell transported her instantly back to her high school darkroom and her first kiss. She'd always maintained that that first kiss from her lab partner, a boy named Dan Star, might have led to more had their teacher not become wise to the budding romance and split them up.

Thomas indicated a shelf over the deep sink. "I'm not sure how much you know, but this is pretty much your typical darkroom. I keep the chemicals there." He pointed with his first two fingers as if he were shooting the items off the shelf. "Developer, stop bath, fixer."

Marina nodded. "I remember the basics."

"Good. Then you remember to keep the basins separate. They're under the counter there, one for each chemical. Tongs are with the basins. I keep the paper in the studio."

The darkroom was smaller than Marina had imagined, but once they started working, she adapted easily to Thomas's rhythm and economy of movement. Over the next week, they worked side by side on prints that were overdue for delivery to a gallery in Rome. Thomas was anxious to get them out of the way so he could focus on the work for his show.

Marina lifted the contact sheet out of the pan, letting it drip for a minute before she pegged it to the line. Thomas reached over her shoulder and adjusted the clip. "Like that. So it doesn't leave a smudge."

Working in the confined space, Marina had grown accustomed to his body touching hers, lingering at times, fleeting at others. None of it seemed intentional. In fact, he seemed oblivious to the contact, so she decided not to read anything into it. As the days went by, his scent—a blend of coffee, tobacco, and sweat—became as much a part of her landscape as the vast, light-filled studio and the insular darkroom.

In contrast to the time they'd spent out in the streets, Thomas was talkative and more than willing to have a conversation. In response to her questions, he told her about meeting Sarah, how interested she'd been in his work, and how she had offered to model for him. He laughed. "I didn't even have to ask her to take off her clothes, she just put herself there in front of me."

Marina wondered where the truth lay. According to Sarah, she had resisted his pursuit.

One afternoon, as he slipped a contact sheet into the basin in front of Marina, he said, "I suppose Sarah's told you about her first marriage?"

Marina shook her head. *First marriage?* They'd been close friends for the better part of a year. Why hadn't she told her?

Thomas continued, "It's not a secret or anything. She just doesn't like to talk about it. I think it embarrasses her. She was married off at seventeen to some old geezer from her parents' church group. Brainwashed, if you ask me. They were real holy rollers—tent meetings, speaking in tongues, the whole nine yards."

Marina put down the tongs and stared at Thomas. *Brainwashing, speaking in tongues!* What was he talking about?

"Evidently, the guy turned out to be a real control freak, wouldn't let her have a job or go to college. So she spent all her time in the library reading about art. And she drew a lot, pretty much in secret. Evidently, he thought art was the devil's work or something. So one day the husband gets run over by a truck, and before her parents can say, 'Lord have mercy,' she takes the life insurance money and runs. Just disappears. She ended up here and hasn't seen her parents since."

Why had Sarah said that her parents were killed in a car accident? She didn't know if she was angrier with Sarah for not telling her the whole story, or with Thomas for knowing something about Sarah that she didn't. Either way, she felt like a fool.

The following weekend, Sarah suggested one last picnic before the season turned definitively toward winter, and while Marina still felt slighted by Sarah's deception, she missed her terribly, and the prospect of some time together won out over her anger. Perhaps Sarah had a good reason for lying to her.

However, when Marina saw Sarah at the bus stop, she felt her anger anew, and in spite of Sarah's warm greeting, she rode the bus in sulky silence, clutching the remnants of her pique. The fall air was cool, but the sun burned hot in a cloudless sky as Marina followed Sarah to their favorite olive tree. Sarah spread her quilt in the dappled shade, then without a word, Marina flopped down on her back and covered her eyes with one arm while Sarah opened a bottle of wine and lifted her face to the sun, seemingly oblivious to her friend's mood.

"We better enjoy this weather. Pretty soon it'll be raining every other day, then it'll be Christmas."

"What about snow?" asked Marina in a flat tone from beneath her arm.

Sarah plucked a stray leaf from Marina's shoulder. "It snows some in the hills, but I've only seen snow in the city once. It was the funniest thing. Everyone walked around with umbrellas as if it was raining."

"So it's just cold and rainy, and foul all winter. That's what I have to look forward to?" Marina removed her arm and stared up at the branches. She knew she was being a brat, but she couldn't help it.

Sarah chuckled. "It's not *that* bad. I didn't say 'foul.' Anyway, you have Amir to keep you warm."

Marina shrugged and replied without emotion. "He'll be gone by Christmas. His semester's over in two weeks and he's going home."

"That's it?"

"That's it." Marina shrugged again. "It's not like I'm in love with him or anything."

"Well then"—Sarah poked Marina's arm—"I guess there's always spending time with me."

Marina turned her head and looked up at Sarah, who smiled down at her with a goofy, just-little-old-me smile on her face.

"Why didn't you tell me that you were married before?" There was no mistaking the accusation in her tone.

Sarah's smile vanished and she turned her face away. When she spoke, it was as if to the orchard. "Because I try to forget it ever happened. Because I'm ashamed to admit that I was once that passive, that I allowed myself to be bullied into a marriage arranged by my parents to a man I didn't love." She paused for a moment. "I suppose Thomas told you that my parents are still alive." She didn't look at Marina for confirmation. "As far as I'm concerned, they're as dead as that bastard."

The anguish in Sarah's voice made Marina's anger seem small and petty. She sat up and touched Sarah gently on her shoulder. "I'm sorry. I didn't know."

Sarah shook her head as if to say, "You couldn't have known," or "You wouldn't understand," or perhaps she meant, "Leave me alone." Marina wasn't sure, and a thread of panic squeezed in her chest. Sarah bent her head, letting a curtain of red curls fall between them. In her lap, her fingers were busy snapping a twig into tiny pieces. Then, in almost a whisper, she said, "If it hadn't been for that truck, I'd probably be dead by now."

Marina didn't know if she meant figuratively or literally, and remained silent. When she heard Sarah sniff, she reached out and lifted her hair, settling it behind her shoulder, smoothing it across her back. The harder Sarah cried, the more confident Marina became, and after a moment, she took Sarah into her arms and rocked her until her sobs subsided.

A while later, Marina lay on her side watching Sarah sleep. She had dozed a little herself, but the combination of wine and emotion seemed to have knocked Sarah right out. Marina traced Sarah's profile with her eyes: the high brow, sculpted cheekbones, narrow patrician nose, and the delicate chin separated by full lips. Lips she had never really noticed before, not like this. She had the urge to reach out and touch them lightly with her finger . . . with her lips. Marina held her breath. Her heart knocked. She looked at the lips again. Yes, they definitely looked kissable. She rolled onto her back and closed her eyes. *Where had that come from?* She'd never had a thought like that before, not about any woman, ever. She lay motionless, afraid of what might happen next. What did this mean? Was she mistaken about Sarah's intentions? Did Sarah feel this way, too?

"You know what we'll do?"

Sarah's voice startled her. Marina turned and looked at her friend, who still had her eyes closed.

Sarah continued, "When the weather gets too cold to picnic, we'll still come up here, but we'll go to that little pizzeria in the square. You know, the one that's like a cave, with the long tables."

The weather turned chilly in mid-November, and by early December, the city lay under a steely sky, the days dawning with frost and ending with drizzle. The arrival of Advent, however, brought a sparkle to the city as colorful toys, brightly wrapped packages, and boxes of panettone and torrone filled shop windows. Even in New York, Marina had never seen a display as stunning as the Christmas windows at Gilli, the elegant café in Piazza della Repubblica where a piece of cake and a coffee cost as much as a two-course lunch at Anita's. Every day on her return from Thomas's studio, she walked out of her way just so she could stop and lose herself in the winter fairyland that shimmered in Gilli's windows. Exquisite animals made entirely of colored sugar frolicked in a chocolate and marzipan forest while gilded angels with spun-sugar hair graced another window. Draped with tinsel, the market stalls overflowed, resplendent with produce pyramids, and small forests of bundled Christmas trees sprouted up in parking lots and on street corners.

Aside from the windows at Gilli, Marina barely had time

to notice the brewing festivities or the weather. Thomas gave her some time off while he went back out into the streets to shoot for his show, something he preferred doing solo, but Sauro had projects he needed help finishing before the holidays, and she had her own Christmas gifts to make. Time was short and the pressure was on, but her conflicted feelings for Sarah fueled her work pace. In the days and weeks following their picnic, Marina had watched Sarah closely for signs that her hugs meant more than friendship, or that an intimacy exchanged held a deeper meaning, but she was at a loss to decipher Sarah's intent. She'd had many girlfriends over the years, some very close, but Marina had never felt the sort of nervous excitement she now felt around Sarah. Was she in love? Was she reading too much into nothing? Was she gay? She thought of those girls in college with their boyish haircuts, leather jackets, and combat boots, and couldn't imagine herself marching for Gay Liberation or raising her fist at anti-imperialist political rallies. Besides, she still enjoyed sex with Amir, so she couldn't be gay. She'd had a serious boyfriend in high school, Bob Prince, with whom she'd discovered sex on Saturday afternoons in the third-floor bedroom of his family home in Gramercy Park. It was an exciting, hot, sweaty time, and she'd been sure it was love but, in looking back, knew she'd been more in love with the thrill of discovery than with Bob himself. Her college trysts had been just that, brief assignations that never blossomed into fullblown relationships. There was some good sex, some fun, but she'd never experienced the connection or intimacy she had with Sarah. Was it some inexplicable chemistry or an attraction born of loneliness? Had she suddenly become needy? She fluctuated wildly between desire and fear, seeking out Sarah, then making excuses to leave as soon as she arrived. Her pulse ran high, she worked late into the nights, and then slept restlessly.

CHAPTER 8

Something tickled Marina's cheek. She brushed it away, not ready to wake up. The tickle persisted. She brushed at her face again and this time came away with something tangled in her fingers. Opening one eye, she saw a silver thread. A piece of tinsel from the Christmas tree. She closed her eye and drifted, savoring the fresh memories of her first Christmas away from home. She had been heartsick when her parents canceled their trip, but Sarah helped her see that just because her mother was having a crisis with one of her artists it didn't mean Marina had to have one herself. She had a wonderful new life, and damn them if they weren't interested. Marina's parents had sent a substantial check in their stead, and Sarah suggested she spend every penny of it on herself. They decided to make Marina over into a new woman, one that reflected her new life. She had her hair layered into the shaggy style that was all the rage and, with Sarah's guidance, invested in new boots and a few outfits. The previous night, Christmas Eve, she'd worn her new boots with the pale gray skirt that fell in soft folds to midcalf. She'd topped it with a slim, white cashmere sweater and cinched her waist with a burgundy suede belt. Thomas's wolf whistle upon her arrival was the best gift she could have received.

The thought of the boots made her open both eyes. From her vantage point on the floor, they were right at eye level. Made out of supple leather the color of buttercream frosting, they were knee high and had tan stitching across the vamp and up the sides. More than anything else, they made her feel that she truly had stepped into a new life.

She shifted onto her back and looked up through the branches of the Christmas tree.

"What on earth are you doing down there?" Sarah stood at the end of the couch where she and Thomas had left Marina bedded down the night before, after a champagne dinner and too many chocolates.

Marina began to slide out from under the tree.

"No. Don't move! I have to get a picture of this. You look adorable." Sarah retrieved Thomas's camera from the dining table and snapped a couple of shots.

"Whatever possessed you to sleep under the tree? Were you there all night?"

Marina nodded and wiggled herself off the cushions she'd put down for a bed.

"I read about it once, in a story, when I was little, sleeping under the Christmas tree, and I've always wanted to try it."

"I love it." Sarah gave her a hug. "Merry Christmas. Thomas is still asleep. I'm going to make us some coffee."

Marina was stretched out on the couch with her feet in Sarah's lap, her eyes closed, her mind drifting to the previous night and Thomas's whispered comment as he leaned over to refill her glass. "You look good enough to eat." She'd been flattered in spite of the slimy residue the compliment left in its wake. She still wasn't sure what to make of Thomas. Sometimes he seemed to genuinely enjoy her company, but at other times he was withdrawn and taciturn, making her feel that she was in the way. Sarah's sigh drew her back into the moment. Opening her eyes, she asked, "What's the matter?"

Sarah looked surprised. "Nothing. Why?"

"You're sighing."

"Am I?"

"Yes, you seem a little down."

Sarah waved her hand, a dismissive gesture. "Don't mind me. I sometimes get a little morose at Christmastime."

"Why, what's the matter?"

"I'll tell you another time. I don't want to spoil your Christmas."

"You couldn't possibly spoil this Christmas. It's been perfect." Marina sat up, pulled her feet off Sarah's lap, and hugged her knees to her chest. "What is it? Tell me."

Sarah sighed again. "It's just that Christmas always makes me think about children."

"You mean having them?"

"Yeah. Wanting them, having them, the whole thing. It's silly."

"It's not silly. I didn't know you wanted them. You've never said. What about Thomas?"

"It doesn't matter. I had a bad abortion. Now I can't have them."

"When? Are you all right?"

"I'm fine. It was years ago, when I was first with Thomas."

"Was something wrong with it? With you?"

Sarah shook her head. "Thomas said that it wasn't the right time, that we would have kids later, when his career was up and running."

Marina's good cheer began to fade, as if good old St. Nick had put it back in his sack and taken it with him up the chimney.

"I didn't want to do it. I even thought about leaving, having it by myself. But we were so happy. He told me everything would be all right."

"And it wasn't." Marina's voice was as flat as the statement.

Again, Sarah shook her head. "Abortion is illegal here. But there was this underground doctor, someone in the Radical party. He had a good reputation, safe and clean . . . but something went wrong. I still don't understand what, exactly. It was such a mess. I ended up in the hospital, where I was interrogated by the police and prayed over by the nuns. It was a nightmare."

"How awful for you." *What an awful man you're married to,* was what she wanted to say.

"Afterward, I went to three different doctors, and they all said the same thing, that there was too much scar tissue, that I'd never be able to conceive." She glanced toward the bedroom where Thomas was still asleep. "I think Thomas was relieved, not that he wanted me to go through all that, but I know now that he never would have wanted children. His life is all about his work."

Marina brought Sarah a fresh cup of coffee and sat with her until she heard Thomas begin to stir. To escape the apartment before Thomas got out of bed, she used the excuse of needing to shower and a change of clothes. The streets were deserted as she made her way to Via Luna. *Thomas!* How could he have done that to Sarah? It made her so furious she didn't know how to think about it. And Sarah, how could she stay with him after that? The two of them! They *deserved* each other. The intensity of her anger made her want to cry, and that made her even angrier. It was Christmas and she wanted to be happy. She turned toward the river—perhaps a walk and some fresh air would clear her head.

The river was swollen, gray, and churning. Marina leaned over the wall and dropped a stick into the roiling waters, watching as it was sucked in and spun around. She dropped a few more sticks, which distracted her for a while, then climbed up onto the wall and let her feet dangle over the raging river. She thought about how lovely their Christmas Eve had been, the three of them opening their gifts. She'd given Sarah a gilded frame that had required extensive repairs and regilding, and Thomas a small box with gilded edges. She reached for her bag and took out the gifts they'd given her. Sarah's was a silver necklace with a small alabaster heart, and Thomas had given her one of the photographs he'd taken of her last spring, one where she was sitting on the stool, the sexiest one. He'd enlarged it to eight-by-ten and put it in a pewter frame. She felt like throwing it in the river, and the little pink heart after it. What was she doing with these people? Hadn't she said that she wasn't going to hang out with the ex-pats? Now her life was so intertwined with Thomas and Sarah's she didn't see how she could extricate herself. She had no one else. Felicity and Jocelyn were long gone and Amir had returned to his family in Tehran. He'd been a nice distraction while it lasted, but she knew that even if he'd stayed, they wouldn't have had anything more than a superficial relationship, not with her conflicted feelings about Sarah.

She got off the wall and headed toward the street. There were a few people out walking, mostly parents with children trying to run off the sugar-high from two days of feasting. She felt a drop of rain and thought of New York blanketed in snow. Her parents would now have been up for a while and were probably on their way out to brunch with friends. She wondered if they'd made popovers, a family tradition since she could remember. She put her hands in her pockets and scuffed her feet along the gravel path. When she'd called them the day before, she had not asked what their plans were. She hadn't wanted to know that Christmas as she'd always known it might be going on without her. Still, maybe she'd try them again later today.

As she walked back to her apartment, she congratulated herself on surviving her first Christmas alone. Well, not alone, but away from home, away from her family, and she'd been fine. Grudgingly, she acknowledged that this had been due to Thomas and Sarah's generosity in sharing the entire holiday with her. Perhaps she shouldn't be so quick to judge them. She tried looking at Sarah's story from a different angle. What if Thomas had been right? What if it had been the wrong time to have a baby? But how did people decide that? She turned down Via Luna, wondering if Sarah ever looked at children in the street and thought, *My child would be doing that by now.* Without a doubt, Thomas's career, if not Thomas himself, had become her child, and as much as Marina didn't understand it, as much as she wanted to think that there was another, happier life for Sarah, she really wasn't sure. Could Sarah survive, thrive, without Thomas, and Thomas without Sarah?

In January Sauro's father had a heart attack. When it became clear that he would not be returning to work for a while, Sauro invited Marina to join him as a full-time apprentice. At first she couldn't believe she'd heard him correctly and made him repeat himself twice before she was convinced she had the job. She wouldn't be paid much to start, but it was thrilling to be formally invited into the time-honored tradition of master and apprentice, and she had no illusions about the pressure she would be under to prove her worth. Contrary to what Thomas believed, there were women restoring paintings at the Pitti Palace, both students and professionals. Also, she knew of a woman, a friend of her mother's, who had studied in Rome and then set up her own restoration studio in Chicago. Progress was being made, and now she would stretch it a little further.

That afternoon Marina went to Thomas's studio to tell him the good news about Sauro's offer and break the news that she would not be able to work with him on his new shots as he had requested. When there was no answer, Marina took out the key he'd given her back in November and let herself in. She was surprised to find that Thomas had drawn the heavy draperies that separated the front door and vestibule from the main studio, and when she parted the drapes, she was met with yet another surprise. A large, red Oriental rug covered the floor in the center of the studio, with lights set up at each corner of the rug. Marina walked onto the carpet and looked around. What was going on? She'd never known Thomas to shoot indoors. She called out, but there was no answer, so she decided to leave him a note. As she moved toward the small desk in the corner by the daybed, she noticed that the wooden trunk that was usually padlocked was open. She peered inside but couldn't believe what she was looking at. Thomas hadn't been kidding when he'd said on her first visit to the studio that it was full of whips and chains. There were also velvet cords, leather cuffs of some sort, whips, and a riding crop. At the bottom of the trunk, there was a jumble of things, but she didn't dare move anything to get a better look. Just then she heard his key in the lock and scurried back to the carpet. A moment later, he came through the curtain carrying some packages. On seeing Marina, he looked shocked, then angry.

"Marina! What are you doing here?"

"Hi, sorry I scared you. I just got here a minute ago."

Marina saw his eyes dart to the open chest and then back at her. She kept her back to it and did her best to look innocent.

Thomas's face began to close down as he composed himself. "I thought we agreed you weren't working today." He walked over to the shelving and stowed the boxes.

"We did, but I had some exciting news I wanted to share with you. But what's all this about?" she asked, gesturing toward the lights.

Thomas shrugged. "Just fooling around, experimenting. So, what's your news?"

Marina knew better than to press Thomas for more information, which she wasn't sure she wanted anyway. She told him about Sauro's offer, and while he seemed genuinely pleased for her, it was clear that he was anxious for her to leave.

As she walked back toward the center of town, she remembered other times when she'd arrived at the studio and noticed things out of place, equipment moved, furniture slightly askew, as if Thomas had been working on something during the night, then packed it away. She didn't have the nerve to question Thomas about what he did in his own studio, and when she asked Sarah if Thomas ever worked at night, she'd just laughed and said, "God only knows what he gets up to at night. I'd rather not think about it."

The first weeks of the new year were unseasonably warm and dry, but by month's end heavy rains arrived, creating puddles, streams, then small rivers in the streets. The skies thundered overhead and a sulfurous odor leached from the sewers, but Marina scarcely noticed. She appeared at Sauro's workshop every morning, eagerly pulled on her blue *grembiulino,* and threw herself blissfully into the day. There was a great deal of work to be done. Sauro's father, whose recovery was taking longer than expected, was unlikely to return before spring, and while his grandfather came to the workshop every day, he had lost some of his vitality and spent a great deal of the time dozing in an armchair by the heater. Marina tried not to be grateful for their misfortune and worked as hard as she could to merit her own good fortune.

Sauro's workshop was close to Sarah and Thomas's apartment, and Marina often went there at midday, picking up a chunk of cheese or a loaf of bread on the way to supplement the bottomless pot of soup that bubbled on their stove. Thomas usually joined them for lunch but rarely stayed long.

"Doesn't he ever rest?" Marina asked one afternoon. While she had once jealously coveted her time alone with Sarah, she found herself wishing that Thomas would linger after lunch. Having him around diffused the anxiety she increasingly felt when she was alone with Sarah. She avoided physical contact as much as possible, declining Sarah's offers to rub her feet or brush her hair, hoping that a little distance might help her to better understand the situation. If Sarah noticed Marina's withdrawal, she didn't let on and was as warm and attentive as ever.

Sarah shrugged. "I don't know. He has more energy than he knows what to do with. Plus he's working on a new idea for his show."

When Marina asked what the idea was, Sarah smiled mysteriously but would only say that it involved Marina modeling for Thomas again and that he would tell her himself once he had all the details sorted out in his mind.

As she walked back to Sauro's after lunch, Marina was irritated as much by Sarah's secretiveness as by the relentless rain. Why was she always left out of the loop? She knew it was unreasonable to think that Thomas would confide in her just because she'd helped him with a few projects, but did Sarah have to go along with everything he did? She kicked a stone out of her path; maybe she'd refuse to model for him when he asked.

When Marina entered Sauro's shop, she found him engaged in a conversation with a gray-haired man she'd never seen before. He wore an elegant camel-hair overcoat and was speaking fairly good Italian, but with a terrible American accent. They were examining one of the altarpieces she'd been working on for the past week. Sauro waved her over and introduced her to Josh Stevens, explaining that he had his own restoration studio in New York but always stopped to see him when he was passing through Florence on business.

The man bowed slightly as he shook Marina's hand, then winked and said, "Actually, I come to steal his secrets."

Sauro laughed and clapped Josh on the back, then excused himself when his grandfather called to him from the other side of the room.

Josh switched to English. "This is beautiful work you're doing, very impressive."

Marina smiled at him. "I have a great teacher."

"That you do. I met Sauro at a conference in Rome years ago, and I've never known anyone with his sense of integrity about preserving the traditions of his trade. It restores my faith every time I come here. You're a lucky young woman."

"Yes, I'm very fortunate."

He reached into his coat pocket. "Here, take my card. If you ever find yourself in New York, look me up. I'd be pleased to see you."

She couldn't imagine ever going home but tucked the card in her pocket.

Thomas revealed the new idea for his show a few days later when he asked her to accompany him to Santa Croce after lunch. All he would say was that he had something to show her in the church, something that would be the center-piece of his new show.

"Why are you being so mysterious?" Marina demanded, irritated all over again.

"Trust me, you have to see it to understand it."

They entered the church by the side door, their breath crys-tallizing in the gloom. She followed him to the center aisle, where Thomas stopped in front of the bas-relief figure in the floor, the spot where they had first met. He gripped her arm and whispered, "I've been looking at these for years. I knew there was something I wanted to do with them, but I didn't know what."

Marina looked down at the robed figure carved into a slab of white marble set in the floor. It looked as if the figure were pushing up through the marble, trying to escape.

"And now you know what you want to do?" she whis-pered.

"Yes. I'm going to do you in marble for my show, *Flesh in Stone*."

"What do you mean? Make me into a fake statue?"

"No. Yes, sort of. I'm going to make you into one of these." Thomas's voice rose as he gestured toward the marble figure staring up at them from the floor.

"Shhh." Marina pulled on his arm. "Come on, let's go back outside. It's freezing in here."

The air outside seemed balmy by comparison as they emerged from the church and crossed over to the café on the corner. The barman greeted them with a nod, grunting in response to their request for *caffè con panna*. Thomas was still talking and waving his hands around as they settled at a table. He was saying something about shutter speeds, diffused lighting, and ways to make the water white.

"What do you mean, make it white? What water?" Marina asked, stirring the sweetened whipped cream into her shot of espresso.

"The water in the tub."

"What tub?"

"Have you heard anything I've said?" Thomas scowled at her.

"Sorry. I was cold. Tell me now."

"I'm talking about the tub you're going to be lying in."

"What makes you think I'm going to lie in a bathtub full of water and let you photograph me?"

Thomas looked surprised. "Why not? If it turns out like I think, it's going to be spectacular."

Marina sipped her coffee and willed the blush to leave her cheeks.

"Don't worry, you're going to be all covered up by the white water."

"What makes the water white?" She wasn't going to immerse herself in any sort of paint.

"I'm not sure yet. I'll have to do some experiments. Maybe

soap. Maybe milk. Hopefully, I can make it close to the color of your skin, at least, so it reads that way in black and white. Then when you rise out of the water, it will look like you and the water are one and the same. Like the statue in the floor."

"I thought I was going to be all covered up."

"You will. Just your face and torso will stick out. Your breasts will be covered by your hands. If we do it right, it might look like someone else's hands are grasping you from behind." As he described the scene, he arched his back, thrusting his chest forward, clasped his chest with his hands, keeping his elbows tucked against his ribs, and then tipped his head back. "See?"

Two weeks passed before Marina had time to model for Thomas; Sauro was swamped with work from a private collection, and her assistance was indispensable in prepping furniture, frames, and objects for gilding. Finally he declared they were far enough along to take a weekend off. "If I don't, my wife will kill me."

It was Sarah who persuaded Marina to model for Thomas in the bathtub. She, too, was convinced that if it worked out the way Thomas thought, it would be a stellar photograph.

"Why don't *you* model for him?" Marina wanted to know.

Sarah snorted and shook her head. "My modeling days are long over. It's not good for our relationship. Besides, he's in love with your neck."

Marina blushed. "My neck?"

"Yeah, I think it's part of the arching thing, you need a long neck to get the effect he wants. Anyway, you'll be fine. If he gets fresh, just give a shout, I'll be right here in the living room."

When the day came, though, Thomas decided to use the bathroom in his studio, which had the light he wanted, and Sarah declined to come along, saying that she'd just be in the way. Marina was nervous but did as Thomas directed and filled the old claw-footed bathtub with hot water and enough soap flakes to turn the water milky white while he removed the muslin curtain from the tall, narrow window.

"Are you going to be warm enough?" asked Thomas.

"I'm fine." Marina pulled the terrycloth robe a little tighter and hugged it to her.

"I'll get my cameras. You get in the tub. I'll be right back." Thomas shut the door behind him.

She had never been naked in front of any man unless they'd been about to get into bed together, and it felt more than a little strange. She'd considered begging Sarah to come but decided against it. This was work, she needed to be professional, and that meant not behaving like an innocent in need of a chaperone. For her part, Sarah seemed easy about the arrangement and more concerned that Marina not catch a cold in the drafty studio than about her stripping down in front of Thomas.

Thomas knocked on the door. "Don't get in yet. I've got something for you."

Thomas handed her a glass of red wine. "This will help keep you warm." Holding her gaze, he clinked his glass against hers. "To my beautiful statue."

Marina blushed and looked away as she brought the glass to her lips.

"Call me when you're in," he instructed.

Marina nodded. "Sure." She shut the door, leaned her back against it, and drained the glass. It was now or never.

She set the wineglass on the edge of the sink, slipped out of her robe, and stepped into the tub, easing herself into the warm water, her body disappearing into its whiteness. When the water reached her neck, she rested her head at the end of the tub.

"You in?" Thomas called from the other side of the door.

Marina hesitated and then replied, "All set, let's do it."

Thomas closed the door behind him. He had two 35mm cameras strung around his neck, the Nikon and the Leica. He set the precious Hasselblad on a folded towel on the bidet. Then he stood very still and looked down at Marina. Anyone who didn't know him might have wondered at the vacant look that came over his face, the blank flatness of his eyes, but Marina knew this look—he was hard at work.

"This is going to be great. Your skin is the same color as the water. Okay, now slide down farther. Let your hair get wet. Slick it back. That's it, that's great." Thomas spoke from behind the camera.

"Now arch your back so your breasts come out of the water. Great. Now cover them with your hands. Yes, but tuck your elbows in."

Suddenly Marina's head slid under the water. She sat up coughing, laughing. "Ahhg, I got water up my nose," she sputtered, shaking her head and clasping her nostrils between thumb and forefinger.

Thomas handed her a hand towel for her face. "Okay, let me think for a minute." He let the camera rest against his chest as he refilled her wineglass and handed it to her.

Sitting up as she was, Marina was exposed from the waist up. She pulled her knees up to cover her chest as she reached for the glass.

"Let's try it again. This time rest on your elbows so you can prop yourself up and still clasp your breasts."

Marina gulped the wine, then lay back once again.

"That's it, head back, more, more, perfect, don't move." Thomas's voice sounded a long way off as she relaxed into the pose, breathing slowly and carefully through her nose, willing her heart back to a steady beat. With her eyes closed, she was able to forget for a moment that Thomas was there, her awareness resting in the water as if suspended in time and space. She felt the edges of the water caress her face, and a gentle current drift through her hair and between her legs. After a while, she heard the distant command, "Okay, take a break."

She sat up once again, but this time after she'd reached for her wineglass, she leaned back against the end of the tub and rested her elbows on either side. The water played around her breasts, gently lapping her nipples. She liked how she felt. Thomas gazed at her, shifting his eyes to her breasts, then back to her eyes. "You have no idea how beautiful you look."

Marina smiled. Now this she understood. Thomas admired her, she felt beautiful—it made sense. What a relief to not be confused about her feelings.

Thomas turned away. "Why don't you add some more hot water while I change the film."

When he returned, Thomas refilled both glasses, then sat down on the edge of the tub. Marina sipped her wine as Thomas reached out and ran his finger very lightly across her collarbone, over her shoulder, and down the front of her arm to the wrist. His eyes followed his finger as he spoke. "I really appreciate you doing this, Marina. It's going to be fantastic, I can tell already."

Marina didn't know what to say; her nipples were hard as her breasts lifted from the water.

Thomas stood up. "You look just like marble, like you're imprisoned in the stone. Your hands look like they belong to someone else, like someone is holding you down."

Marina slid deeper into the water. "Let's keep going. Before I turn into a prune."

Once again wrapped in the robe, Marina sat on the daybed and nestled into the red and gold velvet cushions like a dove in a nest of feathers.

"Hang on a sec and I'll set up the heater for you," said Thomas from the darkroom.

"I'm fine, take your time." Marina tucked her legs up underneath her and closed her eyes. She felt as if she were floating, her body weightless.

"Here you go." Thomas placed a small gas tank on the floor just outside the circle of chairs. He looked at Marina.

"For a second there, in that robe, with the towel on your head, you looked just like Sarah used to look."

"Well, don't get too bossy or I might have to quit modeling for you, too."

Thomas grinned at her as he snaked a narrow black hose between two chairs and set the heater as near to the daybed as was safe. He turned the valve on the gas tank and flicked a blue plastic lighter in front of the element, bringing the heater to life with a gentle pop. The air around her warmed instantly.

"You get cozy, I'll finish unloading the film."

Marina drifted in a haze of wine and warmth as the afternoon drizzle increased to a steady downpour, turning the room from white to lavender, then gray. She imagined Sarah modeling for Thomas, pictured her in the middle of the studio, her alabaster body shimmering, her hair longer than it was now, curling down her back, teasing the curve above her buttocks. Thomas circled her, a camera to his face, then the camera was gone and he was running his hands over Sarah's body. He said something to her, perhaps told her not to move while he explored with palm and fingertip. In her half-dream state, Marina welcomed the hands, imagining Sarah's lips on her face, neck, her breasts. She arched her back, inviting the soft hands to her belly, her thighs, and felt herself lifted higher, again and again until she let go, spiraling into blackness.

When Marina woke, the studio was dark. She was naked, tangled in the velvet spread. Her throat was dry. Her head ached. Muted sounds came from the direction of the darkroom. She listened, trying to remember why she was there, what she had done, when suddenly it all came into sharp focus. She clutched at the spread and covered her body, praying it had been a dream. Then she heard footsteps crossing to where she lay.

Thomas stood looking down at her for a moment before he spoke. Marina couldn't make out his face in the shadows, but his words, though quiet, were final.

"Sarah doesn't need to know about this."

Part Two

Hudson River Valley, 1993

CHAPTER 9

The night was quiet. From where Marina sat huddled in the armchair in her darkened studio, she could see an occasional set of headlights flickering through the trees. Even the frogs in the pond out back were silent, a sure sign that winter was on its way. After Zoe had stormed out of the studio, Marina took her time finishing the section of the frame she was working on, hoping that Zoe might cool off by dinnertime. Usually, given some space, Zoe recovered from her piques fairly quickly, but lately a wash of sullen moodiness, not unlike the glazes Marina used to dirty a brilliant surface, obscured her daughter's usual lighthearted and loving personality. Tonight when Marina had returned to the house to make dinner, Zoe had refused to come out of her room, and even the scent of bacon frying for her favorite spaghetti al carbonara failed to lure her downstairs. Later, when Marina knocked on her bedroom door to tell her that she was returning to the studio for a while and that there was food on the stove, Zoe's response had been to turn her music up a few decibels.

Marina shifted her position under the cashmere throw so

that her head rested on the back of the armchair. In the shadows overhead, she could just make out where the slender beams met at the peak of the high ceiling. During the day, with Ella or Etta crooning while she worked, Marina rarely thought about the studio's previous incarnation as a chapel, which for eighty years had served the farming community, with its white clapboard siding, slate roof, and cupola. Now shrouded in silence, she imagined the hallowed space filled with well-scrubbed folk in neatly mended clothes, sitting in rows of simple pews with hands clasped and heads bowed. After the larger brick church was built in town, the county sold the small chapel, along with the adjacent house and an acre of land, to the first in a long line of absentee owners who never seemed to know what to do with it. Finally, it had come to rest with her parents, who fixed it up as a weekend retreat long before the area became fashionable and "going upstate" was a trendy thing for Manhattanites to do. But by the time she went off to college, her parents had begun to lose interest in the country life, and upon her return from Florence, in spite of their concerns about the safety and sanity of her being pregnant and all alone so far from the city, Marina convinced them to let her move to the property. Eventually, after Zoe was born and Marina's business was up and running, she worked out an arrangement with them to buy the house over time at a greatly reduced price.

Marina shut her eyes and allowed the silence to close in around her, quieting her mind, granting her a moment's relief before the problem insisted its way back into her psyche—how was she to deal with Zoe's questions about her father? She cursed herself for agreeing to speak at the conference in Florence. How naïve she'd been to think that Zoe wouldn't react to the mere mention of that city, that it wouldn't bring on a flood of questions, questions she thought had been laid to rest long ago. She pulled the old Bakelite telephone onto her lap and moved her hand back and forth across the cool, hard receiver as if conjuring a genie from a bottle. Lydia would know what to do, she always did, and besides, she was the only one who knew the whole of Marina's story.

Lydia's friendship was the windfall that had come with Zoe's birth. They'd met scarcely an hour after Zoe's relatively quick (but still painful) entrance into the world as Marina lay in her semiprivate room in the county hospital studying the plaster patch on the ceiling above her bed.

The doctor had told her to rest, but adrenaline continued to pump through her veins, making her legs twitch as her mind scrambled to make sense of this new reality. *A baby.* She had a baby. The patch on the ceiling looked like the profile of a Renaissance man, like so many paintings of that period, with their high brows and thin hooked noses. No, she would not think about Florence. She willed her awareness back to the stillness of the pond she'd learned to visualize in childbirth classes. If only she could lie there indefinitely, floating peacefully on the surface, with no thought to the future—of running a business, creating a home, and raising a child, all of it—alone. In the scramble of the last six months since she'd fled Florence, Marina had not had the time or inclination to connect with old friends or make new ones. She had Rachel, her midwife, who would come daily to help with the baby for the first two weeks, her parents would be up for a couple of days as soon as she gave them the green light, and Josh would want to come and pay homage to "the littlest gilder." But then what? Her parents might visit more often with the lure of a grandchild, and Josh would certainly be by to drop off frames and have a cup of tea, but that was the extent of her support system. If Josh hadn't come into Sauro's that day and given her his card, she wouldn't even have him. A tear ran along her jaw to her neck. She dragged her focus back to the pond, willing her mind to look neither forward nor back, but within seconds, it drifted again, this time back to that final push, the feeling of the tiny torso, arms, and legs falling out of her like a bundle of giant, overcooked spaghetti—then the words, "It's a girl." She was surprised at the overwhelming sense of relief that came with those words—at the very least, she'd be able to relate to this little creature's anatomy.

"You're awfully quiet over there. Are you okay?" The voice startled Marina from her reverie. She hadn't given any thought to the fact that there might be someone on the other side of the curtain that was drawn between the two beds.

"I'm fine." Marina hesitated. "I didn't realize there was anyone there. Were you asleep?"

"No, just resting, following orders. I thought I'd give you a little time to yourself." A rustling of sheets accompanied the voice as the curtain drew back to reveal a massive bouquet of white lilies on the nightstand. A blond head appeared from behind the flowers. "I'm Lydia. Sorry about these flowers. I hope the scent isn't overpowering. They're not really the right thing for a shared room, but they're my favorites." The woman's hair was pulled back in a ponytail and her large brown eyes were set in a round face. She had a crooked mouth that hiked up on one side, giving the effect of perpetual mirth. "Is this your first?"

Marina nodded.

"Me, too. It's mind-blowing, don't you think? What did you have?"

"A girl."

"I had a girl, too. Have you named yours?"

"Her name is Zoe." The words took Marina's breath. *Not just a name, a person.*

Lydia pushed the flower arrangement out of the way and lay back on her pillows. "Zoe. That's nice. You don't often hear that name." When Marina didn't say anything, she continued, "For us, it was a toss-up between Lorna and Sasha."

After a moment, Marina found her voice. "Which did you choose?"

"Sasha."

"That's a beautiful name. It makes me think of a Russian princess."

"Well, maybe she is. June's father is part Russian. We chose it in his honor."

Before Marina could ask who June was, the door opened, and a small boy hurled himself onto the side of Lydia's bed.

Lydia laughed. "Easy, Ben," she said and pulled him onto her lap, kissing his chubby cheek. Over his head, she looked toward the door, where a petite, dark-haired woman stood with a pink-swaddled bundle in her arms, and said, "June, sweetheart."

The woman crossed the room, seemingly caught in Lydia's gaze. When she reached the bed, she whispered in a choked voice, "She's so beautiful. I can't believe she looks so much like Ben."

Lydia whispered into the little boy's ear, "Look, sweetie, it's your new baby sister, Sasha." Ben nodded solemnly. Lydia turned to Marina. "This is my son, Ben, and his mother, June."

Marina nodded although she didn't understand at all. If Ben was Lydia's son, how could June be his mother?

Marina smiled at the memory as she unfolded her legs and repositioned the phone on her lap. After June and Ben left that day, Lydia had explained to Marina how much she and June had wanted children and how difficult it had been to find the right man to donate his sperm. They needed someone they knew well enough to ascertain that he was intelligent, in good health, and of sound mind. But it couldn't be a friend. It had to be someone willing to give up any claim to or involvement with the child. In the end, they'd settled on an acquaintance of June's from medical school, a fellow doctor who was conveniently married to his research and had no interest in children. Everything had gone smoothly. June gave birth to Ben, and when he turned three, she and Lydia decided it was the right time for Lydia to get pregnant. Even though sperm banks had become more prevalent and single women were beginning to be considered by adoption agencies, they wanted their children to have the same father if at all possible—which it had been. Marina had never heard of such a thing but was so profoundly touched by Lydia's story that she burst into tears. Lydia's attempts to console her were no match for the bitter taste of irony that rose in Marina's throat. How often during her pregnancy had she fantasized about raising this child with Sarah, about creating a life together?

Marina shook her head, remembering her naïve fantasies about a life with Sarah and the baby, flights of fancy that kept the reality of her lonely predicament at bay and nurtured her denial about what she'd done. In some scenarios she told Sarah about the baby as soon as she realized she was pregnant, and the prospect of a child in her life was enough to lure Sarah away from Thomas. As her fantasy went, sometimes they stayed in Florence and Thomas floated benignly on the periphery of their life; at other times, she imagined them disappearing to a stone farmhouse hidden somewhere in the hills of Tuscany. Alternately, she had fantasized about returning to Florence after her baby was born and using it to lure Sarah back to the States, where they would set up a life somewhere Thomas would never find them. For some reason, perhaps her youth, careening hormones, or stress, her flights of imagination had always been tritely cinematic, down to the hooded cape she wore as she emerged from the shadows holding her child, and the golden glow that surrounded the images of her with Sarah working blissfully in a shared workshop.

Now Marina had the urge to laugh out loud at that girl she'd been so long ago, but the prospect of facing Sarah again after so many years of lies sobered her. She had a fleeting thought about going to Florence without seeing Sarah, but she couldn't imagine it. Florence without Sarah didn't exist. First, though, she must deal with Zoe. She lifted the receiver and dialed Lydia's number as fact and fiction swirled through her mind like eddies in a ferocious tide that threatened to drag her down.

"Mom, come on, let me in. I'm going to be late."

Marina opened the bathroom door and stood back as Zoe pushed past her with sharp shoulders and jutting chin. That morning she'd been relieved to find Zoe at the kitchen table eating cereal and took it as a good sign in spite of the traces of anger that crackled around her daughter like heat lightning. Now, she stood in the doorway watching Zoe ignore her as she fussed with her hair, and inexplicably, her heart expanded, pushing despair aside for a moment. How she loved this child.

Zoe glanced at her. "Mom, stop staring. You look really scary when you do that," she said, pushing past Marina again. "I'm going to be late. What am I going to do about lunch?"

Marina followed on her heels. "Take a couple of dollars from my purse."

An emphatic honking came from the road. "The bus is here, sweetie."

"Tell them I'm coming." Zoe rummaged through a pile of magazines on the coffee table. "I can't find my French report."

Marina gave a wave from the front door to encourage the bus driver to be patient. Zoe snatched up some papers, rushed past her mother without looking at her, and jogged down the driveway. Marina waited on the front porch until the bus pulled away, her inaudible "Bye" dissolving in a frosty puff of breath.

At the kitchen window, a fresh mug of coffee in hand, Marina was surprised to see a delicate bloom of frost on the grass in the backyard. So fragile was this lacing of crystals, so tentative this first touch of winter, that the early-morning sun at the front of the house had removed any sign of it. The thought of winter reminded her that she still had the frame to finish, then crate, and ship before her trip. She checked the calendar on the wall next to the phone, where a gold star marked Zoe's fifteenth birthday on the first day of the month. She'd asked for dinner and a movie with a gang of friends (thankfully, no boys yet) and her first makeup, lip gloss and mascara. How could fifteen years have gone by so quickly? Marina shifted to the end of the month where the word "Florence" was written in red letters across the week following Thanksgiving. She counted the squares with her finger, only fourteen until Turkey Day. Each time she looked at the calendar, her feelings vacillated. One moment she imagined herself happily strolling by the Arno or sipping cappuccino at a sidewalk café, the next she was overwhelmed with a sense of remorse and confusion. If only she'd told Sarah the truth that day Sarah found her holed up in her apartment, red eyed and puffy faced.

It had been three days since the bathtub shoot with Thomas, and from where she lay curled on the bed breathing in the stale scent of her pillow, she could hear Sarah knocking and calling to her

"Marina, what's going on? Sauro says you haven't been to work in two days. If you don't open up, I'm getting the key from the butcher's shop."

The knocking stopped and a shadow moved across the kitchen window. Marina wanted to get up, knew she had to, but she couldn't stop hugging herself. No matter how tightly she squeezed, she couldn't feel herself wrapped in her own arms.

Sarah banged on the window, her voice shrill. "I'm not kidding, Marina! I'm going to get Marcello's father!"

From somewhere a sliver of self-preservation prodded Marina into action and shuffled her to the door, where she threw the bolt, then scurried back to her bed. Sarah opened the door and stepped inside, allowing a shaft of white sunlight to slice through the gloomy kitchen and into the living room, almost reaching the bed where she lay. Muffled sounds from the alley sounded at once familiar and alien.

"What is it? Are you sick?"

Marina nodded, hiding her face under one arm. She heard the rustle of Sarah's skirts and the tinkle of her bangles as she knelt by the bed. The scent of lavender caressed Marina's cheek as cool fingers found her forehead.

"You don't feel hot. Let me look at you." Gently, Sarah moved Marina's arm away from her face. "You do look a bit rough around the edges."

Based on how she felt, eyes swollen almost shut from crying, nose red, hair a tangled mess, Marina figured that "a bit rough" was an understatement. Her eyes filled again.

Sarah stood up. "Damn that Thomas! I knew this would happen."

Marina held her breath, her heart suspended between beats.

"He said everything went really well, that you were fabulous. And now look." Sarah waved her arms around as if gesturing to an audience. "He let you catch a chill. I'll bet he had you soaking in that tub for hours and then let you sit around in that cold studio. Honestly!" She reached for Marina. "Come on, sit up. I'll make you some tea, then I'll whip up my magic chicken soup and you'll be over this cold before you know it."

Marina sat down at the table and pushed Zoe's breakfast dishes aside as she recalled the agony of letting Sarah think she was sick, growing more morose and guilt-ridden as Sarah nurtured her. Every night she swore to herself that she would confess to Sarah the following day, but when the moment came, the pounding shame and the thought of losing her friend kept her silent. Now she put her head in her hands and tried to gather her thoughts. What had Lydia told her the night before? *Stay calm, everything will be fine. Remember to breathe.* Those had been her parting words before she'd hung up. Marina took a deep breath and let it out slowly, thinking back on their conversation.

"Zoe knows he's dead, right?"

"Yes, but I told her that he died in a scooter accident before she was born. I can't change the story now."

"Why not?"

"She'd hate me, that's why."

"She's never going to hate you. Besides, it's partly true. The scooter part."

"I should never have told her that Thomas was her father. I should have made someone up."

"No, Marina, you were right to tell her. You had to give her some of the truth."

"I suppose. But I've made up so much. All those things I did with Sarah, I told her I did them with Thomas. The picnics up in Fiesole, the walks we took, the meals at Anita's. I don't know what else I've told her, it's hard to remember."

"You were just trying to give her something to hold on to."

"I know, but it's gotten so complicated. This conference has stirred everything up. She wants to come with me, for God's sake!"

"I know this is tough, but it's going to be fine, trust me. Don't make yourself crazy. We'll see you for dinner on Saturday and help you sort this out. Okay?"

The slate floor was frigid through her thin socks. Marina rubbed one foot across the top of the other in an effort to warm them. She took another deep breath. Something smelled sour. Was it the breakfast dishes or was it her? Ever since Zoe's birth, she had days when, no matter how freshly showered or clothed she was, she couldn't shake the sense that she smelled, as if she had forgotten to put on deodorant or worn her jeans too long between washes. When she was pregnant, she'd read about the myriad physical changes that came with childbirth, but nowhere had she read anything about odor or, for that matter, *anything* that lingered for fifteen years. She sniffed the air around her, once, twice, then cleared the table, put the milk away, and made her way upstairs.

Before heading for the shower, she stopped in Zoe's room, where she had permission to open the window and pull back the bedding, nothing more. She crossed the floor gingerly, looking for a patch of carpet, some foothold in the jumble of discarded clothing, magazines, and missing homework. She raised the window, letting in crisp, apple-scented air, then swept back the duvet and, in doing so, bumped the bedside table, sending an avalanche of objects to the floor.

"Shit." Sitting on the edge of the bed, she bent over to retrieve the items from the floor: a miniature flashlight, half a pack of gum, a plastic cup, an amethyst crystal, and the framed photograph. Marina held the picture for a moment, recalling the day six years earlier when Zoe had found the photograph of Thomas. It had been a rainy Saturday afternoon when, tired of listening to Zoe complain that she was bored, Marina decided they should clean out the attic together.

They'd struggled up the narrow stairs with a heavy wooden stepladder, lifting it up and over the post at the top and onto the runner in the upstairs hall. A few dead spiders fell to the floor in a shower of dust and paint chips as the ladder bumped along the floor.

"Okay, help me open it up, right here under the hatch."

"Mom, do we have to do this today," Zoe moaned.

"Stop whining. You said you were bored and had nothing to do. Now you do."

"I wasn't that bored."

"Come on, we've already got the ladder up here. It'll be fun."

Zoe rolled her eyes. "Yeah, right, Mom, a lot of fun. Cleaning out the attic is just what every kid wants to do on a Saturday."

Marina started up the ladder, pushed the hatch aside, and

felt around for the light switch. "I'll just hand the stuff down to you. If it's too heavy, you can come up here and pass it down to me, okay?" Marina disappeared into the attic while Zoe stood at the base of the ladder, her arms crossed in front of her chest. The only sound coming from the attic was the scuffle of Marina's sneakers on the floorboards as she duck-walked under the low beams, then the sound of boxes being pushed toward the open hatch. Then silence. Suddenly, something soft bounced off Zoe's head. "Hey!" she shouted in surprise, raising her arms to protect herself as a torrent of stuffed animals showered from the hatch. By the time Marina's head appeared, Zoe was laughing and hugging a large penguin to her chest.

"Look, Mom. It's Opus!"

"I see. Do you think we can get rid of any of these?"

"Mom! This is my baby stuff. You can't get rid of it." She clutched it tighter.

"We'll see. Here are two empty boxes. The ones you can part with we'll give to June for the children's clinic, the rest we'll pack away to give to your children some day."

"I'm not having any children."

"Why not?"

"I don't know, I'm just not."

"You're only nine, you might change your mind."

"I won't."

"Well, do it anyway, in case I adopt myself some grandchildren." Zoe smiled and set about gathering up the toys. Marina returned to her task and periodically handed boxes down to Zoe to be sorted through later. After a while, Zoe called up to her.

"This is boring, Mom, can I come up there?"

"That's a great idea. My back is killing me and I've got a phone call to make. You come up here and move these last few boxes over to the hatch. I'm almost as far as the window at the end."

The one phone call led to another and then another, and

Marina was gone much longer than she had intended. When she reached the upstairs landing, there was no sign of Zoe.

She looked up at the hatch and called, "Sorry I took so long. Are you still up there, Zoe?"

There was no reply. All Marina could hear was the creaking and popping of the cast-iron radiator in the hallway.

"Zoe?"

"I'm here." Zoe's voice sounded very far away, as if from another world.

Marina climbed a few rungs of the ladder and looked into the attic gloom. Zoe sat cross-legged at the far end of the attic under a half-round window that looked out toward the river. She was studying a piece of paper.

"Zoe, what are you doing?" Marina asked, climbing the rest of the way into the attic.

"Is this my dad?" Zoe's voice was small, plaintive.

"What? What is that?" Marina shifted onto her hands and knees and crawled as quickly as she could toward Zoe, her heart pounding. She found Zoe holding two photographs.

"This one says 'Thomas and Sarah' on the back. Is it my dad?"

Marina cursed herself. An open box sat beside Zoe and a brown folder lay in her lap. Marina knelt next to her and put a hand on her shoulder as she looked at the black-and-white image of Sarah in her flowing gypsy garb standing with Thomas, who wore khaki shorts and a wrinkled white shirt. He had one camera slung around his neck and the Hasselblad in his hands. Zoe had stumbled upon one of two boxes Marina had packed away after Zoe was born and then promptly forgotten. She was relieved to see that there wasn't much else in the box other than a few Italian grammar books and some old T-shirts. She scanned the attic but didn't see the other box. It would turn up eventually, then she'd get rid of both of them once and for all.

"Yes, that's your father . . . and that's Sarah, my best friend. The one who sends you a birthday present every year."

"Yeah, the one that's always months late," Zoe said quietly.

"Right." Marina couldn't tell Zoe the truth about why it always arrived three months late. Instead, she'd turned it into a joke, one they rolled their eyes at each year. "Let's see the other picture."

In the second photograph, also black and white and obviously taken on the same day, Sarah and Marina were laughing, their arms around each other's shoulders, their heads touching.

"You look so young." Zoe sounded surprised.

"I *was* young," Marina replied, smiling at Zoe's incredulity. "I wasn't always old, you know."

"Aren't there any of you and my dad together?" asked Zoe, clearly disappointed.

"I don't think so, sweetie. Mostly he took the pictures. He didn't like to pose for them."

Zoe had asked if she could keep the two photographs, and now, sitting on the bed in Zoe's room, Marina looked down at the frame where her image lay next to the one of Thomas fiddling with his camera. Zoe had come to her that night and handed her the two leftover images of Sarah that she'd cut from the photographs, and said, "Here, I thought you might want these."

CHAPTER 10

Marina ran her hands along the large frame on the workbench, stopping occasionally to caress a high point in the carving, the oil from her fingertips providing the final highlights. It had taken all week to finish. As her fingers led the way, her mind revisited each stage of the repair: the carving, the applications of gesso and clay, the gold leaf, and finally the burnishing. The frame was in the Sansovino style, so named for the sixteenth-century Italian architect and sculptor Jacopo Sansovino, who was known for the complex ornamental detail in his designs. "A bitch to work on but a delight to get lost in," Josh had often said. Dear, sweet Josh. By some miracle, Marina had saved the business card he'd handed her that day as he was leaving Sauro's workshop, and when she found herself unemployed and pregnant in New York, she'd screwed up her courage and called him. He and his wife, Clara, who was a conservator of paintings on wood, had taken her under their wings, no questions asked. Josh put her to work gilding, letting her work on various restoration projects until shortly before Zoe's birth, and he was her biggest supporter when she set up her own gilding studio.

She turned the frame a quarter rotation and continued her

final inspection. All week as she worked, thoughts of Thomas had insinuated their way into what was typically a reflective and meditative time at the end of a challenging project. The pieced-together photograph on Zoe's bedside table that she'd managed to ignore for so many years had somehow unleashed Thomas from the depths of her psyche, where he'd been successfully submerged. Now he floated on the surface like a piece of flotsam, inexorably bumping against her conscience. Worse still, now every time she looked at Zoe, she saw his lanky build, the narrow nose, the unruly curls, and, of course, the gray eyes. Was it possible Zoe had grown into these features overnight? How had Marina not recognized them before? By the end of the week, it had gotten to the point where she dreaded the slam of the car door, the click of the gate latch, and was relieved when Zoe announced she was spending the weekend at Sasha's.

For Zoe's sake and perhaps to some extent to appease Thomas's specter, Marina had attempted to come up with some form of apology or explanation for not taking Zoe to Florence with her. All manner of civilized banalities came to mind. "I know you want to know more about your father, and I'll do what I can to answer your questions," or "I understand that you're feeling angry and confused right now, and I'm going to do whatever I can to help you sort things out," or, even worse, "I'm sorry I haven't taken the time to talk to you about your dad, but I'll try and do better from now on." One by one, she cast aside these vapid clichés as it became clear that rectitude led her to a place she'd rather not go— facing the truth. Nor was she convinced that honesty was the best policy with Zoe at this point; she was too young for the whole truth. In any case, Zoe hadn't asked any more questions since she'd slammed out of the studio, and Marina saw no point in stirring things up.

The sharp trill of the phone cut into her thoughts, saving her from further doubt and self-denigration. It was Lydia calling to tell her that June would not be joining them for dinner, something about helping Ben cram for a physics test. Marina picked up a small whisk broom and brushed off the area around the frame. Even the tiniest bit of debris accidentally picked up on a brush or rag could mar its perfect surface. She admired Lydia and June's relationship, and over the years had seen firsthand what went into building a nurturing and committed union, something far deeper and more mature than her infantile fantasies about a relationship with Sarah. She couldn't now fathom what had possessed her to cling to them even after Sarah had made it clear that day by the river that she wasn't interested in a life together.

They had taken a walk along the Arno one afternoon under tree branches weighted with the promise of spring, and settled themselves in the shelter of a stone parapet about a mile from the center of town. They'd seen little of each other since Sarah had nursed Marina through her "cold." Marina had made herself unavailable by burying herself in a restoration project for Sauro; Sarah was immersed in preparations for Thomas's show.

A light breeze ruffled the water as Marina tipped her face to the sun, the same sun that had welcomed her a year earlier. But instead of feeling pride in all she'd accomplished—her work with Sauro, her home in Via Luna, her friendship with Sarah and Thomas—she felt only confusion and despair as the life she'd created began to crumble. She needed to make a decision—to confess or not. Living in perpetual limbo was making her sick to her stomach. But would her friendship with Sarah survive the truth? And what, exactly, was the truth? That she'd had sex with Thomas, made love with Thomas, been seduced by Thomas? She sensed that the wine alone was not responsible for what had happened with Thomas, that in some strange way, her feelings for Sarah had drawn her into Thomas's seduction, but she couldn't quite make sense of it all. Yet, an unidentifiable force brewed inside her, pressing her to confess. But confess what? That she had feelings for Sarah? That she'd had sex with Thomas? Presented side by side, the two were incongruous—how could she have slept with Thomas if she loved Sarah?

In the weeks following the bathtub photo shoot, Marina had seen Thomas only once, when Sarah pressed her into joining them for dinner at Anita's, and she'd known that to decline an invitation yet again might raise questions. That evening Thomas had feigned nonchalance as he kissed Marina on both cheeks and bantered with Anita as usual. He'd talked about how great the show was going to be, the photos, the framing, the invitations; he'd talked nonstop as if he were afraid Marina might fill any lull in the conversation with an accusation or confession. For her, it had been an agonizing evening spent between rage and shame that rendered her numb and the meal tasteless.

Now Sarah was complaining about how much work she had to get done before the show opened, but Marina wasn't listening. The knot in her belly was becoming a cramp. Maybe, if she could get Sarah to go away with her like they'd always talked about, to have some time to themselves without Thomas around, they could work this thing through.

Without opening her eyes, she interrupted Sarah. "What would you think about taking a trip together after the show's up?"

"Where would we go?"

"I don't know, one of the places you've told me about. Cinque Terra, or even down to Amalfi."

"They're a bit far, we'd have to go for longer than a weekend."

Marina continued basking her face in the sun, her heart pounding. "I was thinking of a couple of weeks, or maybe a month. We could rent a place. You could do some drawing or even start sculpting."

"What about Thomas?"

"What about Thomas?" Marina hadn't meant it to sound as harsh as she felt.

Sarah didn't say anything for a few moments, so many moments that Marina began to think that she really had gone too far and offended her friend.

"Marina, there's something I need to ask you." Sarah's voice was soft.

Marina opened her eyes but didn't look at Sarah. Her life paused for a second—no thoughts, no heartbeat, no breath.

"Do you think you might be in love with me?"

Marina turned her head and stared at Sarah, for a split second elated, until she heard the rest of her statement.

"Thomas says that you are."

"What? When did Thomas say that?"

"He's said it a couple of times recently, mostly just teasing me, telling me to watch out for you, that you might steal me away. Silly really."

Marina felt nauseated. Her stomach cramped. She watched Sarah's lips move, seemingly out of sync with her voice. What was Thomas playing at? Hadn't he done enough damage? He'd already compromised her relationship with Sarah by seducing her, now he was stirring up more trouble. Maybe it wasn't silly, maybe he really was afraid that Sarah would leave him and run away with her. Was he simply jealous of their friendship? Her anger threatened to spill over into tears.

When she didn't respond, Sarah continued. "You've been such a good friend to me, the best friend I've ever had besides Marcello. The only girlfriend. And I do love you, but . . . not like that, not like Thomas said, and . . . I would never leave him, not for any reason. You must know that."

"I'm not asking you to leave him, I'm just suggesting a trip. It's not as if we haven't talked about it before." She tried but couldn't keep the anger out of her voice. Her months of speculation, confusion, hope, fear, and anguish had just been put into perspective—she *had* misread Sarah's signals. Perhaps there had been no signals at all, just her longing for more. She'd been so focused, first on school and then on getting to Florence, that she'd never really thought about what her life might look like beyond becoming a gilder, and this intense longing took her by surprise. But didn't she deserve to have someone for herself, someone to love, who loved her, someone to make a life with? Every cell in her body was telling her that she did and that Sarah was this someone.

At the time, Sarah's rejection had been a blow that Marina fended off with denial, at first, simply refusing to think about it, and later, creating fantasies where she and Sarah raised Zoe together. Eventually, though, time fulfilled its own cliché by healing that staggering loss as she became immersed in her career and motherhood.

Marina wrapped the frame in soft packing cloth and then bubble wrap. Moon Craters would be there in the morning to pick up the frame for crating and shipment. Now she could turn her full attention to the conference and the impending trip. She gave the bundled frame one final pat and made her way out of the studio and across the yard to the house. At barely five o'clock, it was already dark and the temperature had dropped considerably. The lights were on in the kitchen, the TV flickered across the living room ceiling, and the bass from Zoe's stereo pressed its obstinate rhythm against the antique panes of her bedroom window. Marina shivered in her thin denim shirt as she hurried onto the back porch and into the kitchen. Overhead, copper pots of every shape and size hung from the beamed ceiling, while underfoot a honey-colored, wide-plank pine floor stretched obliquely toward the back of the house. The long trestle table was strewn with the remnants of Zoe's snack: an open package of pita bread, a half-empty container of hummus, a pile of cucumber skin, the peeler, and a crusted table knife. Marina, who favored comfort foods—macaroni and cheese, mashed potatoes and gravy, in fact, anything with a sauce, the richer the better—marveled at Zoe's healthy eating habits. She did not have her mother's sweet tooth or her carnivorous cravings, most often eschewing red meat for fish or poultry. Consequently, Marina had fallen into the habit of cooking red meat only when Zoe was elsewhere. Now Marina's taste buds perked up at the culinary prospects of a weekend to herself, but at the same time, she felt a pang for the long lazy weekends she and Zoe had once shared baking, working in the garden, scouring yard sales along Route 9, or packing a picnic and taking a drive to nowhere. As tempting as it was with her studio right next door, she had always been strict about not working on the weekends, but with adolescence came a social life that had expanded Zoe's world beyond her mother's embrace, and now the studio was exactly where Marina ended up spending her weekends.

Finding the living room empty, she turned off the television and went into the hall, where she paused at the bottom of the stairs, then, realizing Zoe wouldn't hear her over the music, climbed up in search of her daughter. From Zoe's open door, Marina surveyed the room, what she could see of it under the wreckage of Zoe's wardrobe. Surely only a bomb in the laundry basket could have gotten the purple panties up on the curtain rod. Zoe was cramming a portion of the debris into her gym bag.

"Zoe," Marina called over the unrelenting beat as she rapped her knuckles on the doorjamb.

Zoe zipped up the bag, slung it over her shoulder, flipped off the stereo, and turned to face her mother. "June's on her way to pick me up."

"That's fine, but . . ." The rule was that Zoe had to pick up her room before she went on a sleepover, so that when she returned tired and cranky from too little sleep, her room was in some semblance of order, enough to get homework done and prepare for the next school day. Marina surveyed the room, weighing which battle to choose. She stepped into the hall and let Zoe pass, following her down the stairs. "You need to clean up your snack mess before you go."

"I was going to."

Right, thought Marina. "When will you be home? We need to organize ourselves for Thanksgiving."

Zoe dropped her bag on the kitchen floor and began clearing the table. "Are we going there or are they coming here?"

"We're going there. All we have to do are the pies. Lydia's doing the rest. I think Peter's helping her."

Zoe turned, her face bright. "Uncle Peter's coming? I thought he was going to his dumb girlfriend's."

"Zoe." Marina's reprimand was halfhearted. No one liked Peter's current flame, the most recent in a long line of unfortunate women he'd dated. Unfortunate not because there was anything intrinsically wrong with them, although this one was a bit of a dullard, but because Peter would never commit to any of them. Lydia claimed that her brother, the favorite uncle and primary male influence in her children's lives, chose women who were wrong for him on purpose so he wouldn't have to commit.

"That is soooo great." Zoe wiped the table, moving the crumbs from one spot to another. She wagged the sponge at her mother. "This is your chance, Mom. You should marry him before the next ditz gets her claws into him."

"I don't think . . ."

Zoe interrupted. "Come on, Mom, he likes you, you know he does."

"And I like him, I always have, but . . ."

"But, but, but. You're perfect for each other. He's waiting for you. You're just chicken."

"Zoe . . ." A horn honked in the driveway. "You go. I'll finish clearing up. Say hi to June for me."

Marina picked up the discarded sponge and rinsed it out in the sink. She wasn't afraid of dating, she just wasn't interested. Her life was busy. She had her work. She had Zoe. She opened the fridge and reached for the package of lamb chops, then gathered oil, garlic, tamari, and rosemary for a marinade. As she whisked the ingredients together, she thought about Peter. She definitely had a soft spot for him, and he for her, at least according to Lydia. But in all the years they'd known each other, shared holidays and children's birthdays, he'd never crossed the line of friendship, and neither had she—after all, he was practically family.

Lydia and June had opened their hearts and home to Marina and Zoe right from the beginning, providing a support system and a sense of family for which she was grateful. Although Lydia had a large circle of friends, few of them had children, and with June working the long hours of a pediatrician, one who still made house calls, she spent most of her time with Marina. Initially, the connection had been their baby girls, but in time they discovered common interests: art, history, music, and antiques. With Ben already in preschool and the babies in their Snuglis, the two women were free to explore the flea markets, auction houses, and galleries that the area from Hudson to Poughkeepsie had to offer. Before Ben was born, Lydia had worked as a freelance draftsman out of a small office over her garage, but she and June agreed that the children needed one full-time parent, so Lydia took on that role after Sasha was born, and when Marina began working again, Lydia offered to care for Zoe during the day. Over the years, Lydia, June, and their children became her extended family, along with Peter, who lived over his antiques shop in Hudson just a few miles away and was always available to lend a hand with the kids or tackle a project around the house.

Marina poured the marinade over the lamb chops, returned them to the refrigerator, and began tearing a loaf of three-day-old bread into bite-sized pieces for the *pappa col pomodoro,* a rustic tomato soup she would serve Lydia the following night. It was true that her dating track record was spotty, but she took exception to being called "chicken" by Zoe. She wasn't afraid to go to a party and have a good time—she just didn't have the patience for dating, with all its unspoken expectations and coy rules of seduction. During the first couple of years of their friendship, Lydia and June had tried fixing her up with a number of male friends, and when nothing developed in that arena, they invited her to a Halloween party hosted by the local Gay and Lesbian Alliance. *Just to test the waters,* Lydia had said one afternoon as they were sharing a cup of tea and watching Zoe, Sasha, and Ben tumble around on the grass, chubby limbs akimbo. When Marina asked what she meant, Lydia said, "I've listened to you talk about Sarah for two years, about how beautiful she was, about all the time you spent together, all the places you went, the things you did, Sarah this, and Sarah that. It seems pretty clear to me that you were in love with her."

Marina was quick to respond. "I wasn't in love with her."

"Then what was it?"

"A crush, maybe. Enamored maybe."

Lydia gave her a knowing look. "More than that, I think."

Marina shrugged. "Nothing like what you and June have."

"That's different, we've been together for years. I'm not saying that you're necessarily gay. Straight women often fall in love with their girlfriends." She paused. "Did you think about sex with her?"

"Lydia!"

"Oh, come on. Don't be such a prude."

"Well . . . I certainly had a lot of *feelings* as our friendship evolved, but I really didn't know what they were or how to deal with them. I know it sounds dumb, but I didn't know how to think about it. My head didn't go *there.* I'd never met a lesbian until I met you. I'd honestly never given any thought about women together sexually. I just imagined us *together.*"

Lydia grinned. "But not in the biblical sense?"

Marina swatted Lydia's arm and shouted to Zoe, "Get off of Sasha; you're going to hurt her."

"I'm not convinced you really know what you felt. How about you come to our party and check it out?"

"I don't know, maybe, I'll think about it."

"What's the matter? You afraid we'll feed you to our lesbian friends?"

Marina smiled. "Of course not, I love your friends."

"Well then, let's just see how much you love them. God knows you haven't been interested in any of the guys you've dated."

Marina had joined them reluctantly, and as they turned onto the gravel driveway, lights twinkling through the tendrils of the giant willows that lined the property, she wished she'd stuck to her guns and declined Lydia's invitation. After all, she had nothing to prove. A low, stone wall snaked along the drive toward a Victorian farmhouse with peaked windows and a deep, covered porch, its front walk lined with brown-paper-bag luminaries, the porch railing with leering jack-o'-lanterns. The minute they opened the car doors, they could hear the rhythmic beat of dance music pounding on doors and windows as if trying to escape.

Under a black night sky dotted with stars, Marina took a deep breath. The air smelled of frost. "I think I'll leave my coat in the car. It's crushing my wings." She closed the car door and turned her back to Lydia. "Would you straighten them for me?"

Lydia smoothed the lace of the small wings sewn to the back of Marina's yellow and black striped dress. A small gold crown perched on the top of her head and large glow-in-the-dark glasses on the bridge of her nose.

June pulled a camera from her bag. "Let me get a picture before we go in. You look adorable, Marina, the queen of all queen bees."

"Thanks. Whose house is this again?" Marina turned to face the twin aliens in silver suits and helmets, one tall, one short.

"It's Susan's. The editor, remember? You met her at June's

birthday party last summer," Lydia replied. "Don't be nervous, it's just a bunch of women in costumes."

"I'm not nervous."

The three women approached the house, navigated the porch's giant cobwebs, and slipped into the hot, pulsing rhythm of the party.

Two hours later, Marina stood with a bottle of beer, her sweat-soaked back to the icy panes of the French doors. She had danced with Cleopatra, Tinker Bell, Elvira, numerous aliens, and Alice from beyond the looking glass. She'd also danced on her own to avoid conversation. Now the music slowed and a liquid-hipped belly dancer beckoned, but Marina smiled, lifted her beer in salute, and looked away just as Lydia arrived at her side.

"Are you having fun?" asked Lydia, bumping hips with Marina. "You've been on the dance floor all night."

"The music's great." The song changed, and Marina had to shout to be heard.

"What's your favorite costume?"

"I love Alice; she looks like she just stepped out of the book, only she's the six-foot-tall version."

"That's Veronica. She's a model. She comes up from the city to party with us country folk. She used to date Susan."

"Who are all the women in jeans, flannel shirts, and vests? I've seen five or six. I don't get what they're supposed to be."

Lydia laughed. "They're just being themselves. No costumes."

Marina nodded as if she understood, then turned her attention back to the dance floor. The truth was she didn't understand anything, least of all what she was doing there.

The temperature had dropped, frosting the women's breath as they made their way back to the car under the three sisters in Orion's belt. It took June a few minutes to maneuver the car through the maze of small pick-up trucks and SUVs.

Lydia turned around, hooking her arm over the back of

the front seat. "There was quite a buzz going around tonight. Everyone wanted to know who the honeybee was."

Marina smiled. "They did not!"

"Oh, yes, they did," confirmed June, nodding her head.

"You created quite a stir," continued Lydia. "It always happens when there's a new girl on the block."

"I'm not the new girl on the block. Don't let people think that. I just came with you two to have some fun."

Lydia laughed. "Don't get your panties in a twist. Didn't you have fun?"

"Yes, it was great. I loved the dancing, and everyone was really nice, but . . . I didn't feel like I . . ."

"Like you what?"

"Like I belonged there."

"Did you actually have a conversation with anyone? You were a bit elusive, dancing all the time."

"I talked to people. But that's not what I mean. I just don't think I belong in . . . that world."

"You mean the lesbian world?"

"Yeah."

"Maybe not." Lydia rested her head on her arm and stared into the backseat. "Did it make you think about Sarah?"

"What do you mean?"

"Tonight, at the party, did you wish she was there? Is that why you didn't connect with anyone, because you were wanting to be with her?"

"Lydia!" June glanced at her partner.

"Okay, okay. Sorry. I just want to know what you thought."

Marina dropped her head onto the back of the seat and closed her eyes. "I have no idea what I thought."

CHAPTER 11

Dinner debris was scattered across the polished pine table-top, china, crystal, and silver glinting in the candlelight. The fire cast narrow ladder-back shadows up the wall and across the ceiling.

"This is one of my favorite things about you," Lydia said as she ran her finger around the rim of a green and gold Limoges bowl, then licked her finger clean. "We're eating a peasant's meal, basically—stale bread and mushed tomatoes—on china fit for a queen."

Marina smiled. "Are you implying I'm irreverent?"

Lydia nodded. "Irreverence is good. At least you use this china. I'd have it locked up in a cabinet gathering dust."

Marina fingered the silver dinner knife at the edge of her plate. Of course it should be used. That's what the craftsman intended. In any case, she didn't need to worry about it as an investment, having picked up most of her tableware for next to nothing at estate sales and thrift shops. She raised a delicate wineglass. "Here's to junk shops. My one indulgence and addiction."

Lydia snorted. "What about chocolate? And books? Not to mention your work. And . . ."

"Okay, okay. One of my *many* indulgences."

"Better you than me," said Lydia, raising her glass in salutation. "I'd hate hand washing all this stuff; I can't stand dishpan hands."

"I don't mind." Marina held out her hands, palms down. The skin was flecked with tiny scars; wrinkles pooled around her knuckles. "Mine are in rough shape anyway."

"I've always thought your hands were beautiful, very elegant."

"Very wrinkled, you mean."

"They've worked hard for you. They have history."

"Thanks a lot. You make them sound like ancient relics." Marina put her hands in her lap. "Now Zoe, she's the one with the beautiful hands. Even when she was a baby people remarked on how long and shapely her fingers were, remember?"

"I do. You once said she had her father's hands."

Marina stared down at her lap, then looked up at her friend. "What am I going to do with her?"

"She seemed fine last night at our house. Is she still asking a lot of questions?"

"No, she seems to have dropped it. But I know it's going to come up again with me going to Florence."

Lydia leaned back in her chair and nodded. "You're right, it probably will. After all, it's a part of who she is, a part of what places her in the world. Have you considered telling her the truth?"

"What! That I screwed my best friend's husband, got pregnant, and never told either of them about her?" Marina shook her head in disbelief at what Lydia was suggesting.

"No. But the thing is, she's fifteen and hardly knows more about her father than our children know about theirs, and we really *don't know* all that much about him."

"Does it still come up for Ben and Sasha?"

"Yes, of course, from time to time. It changes. As they get older, they want to know different things, and I hate it that I can't tell them more, but that's the way it is. Right or wrong, it's the path June and I chose, and now we have to honor it."

"So, you've told them that he was a doctor and that he wanted to help you two in the name of science."

Lydia laughed. "We don't say it quite like that, but that's pretty close to the truth." She hesitated and then said, "To tell the truth, I think he felt sorry for us. You know, saw us as disenfranchised and wanted to help. Maybe that's how he saw himself, a nerdy, reclusive scientist, outside the norm."

"What else do you tell them?" Marina began to stack the plates in front of her.

"Not his name, or where he lives, which we don't know anyway. He moved a long time ago. I suppose we could track him down if we needed to. . . ."

"You mean in the case of a medical emergency? If you need an organ or something?"

Lydia shuddered. "What a horrible thought. But, yes, I suppose we could." She gave a small shrug. "At the time, none of us thought that far ahead."

Both women were quiet for a moment, then Lydia smiled and went on. "We tell the kids that he is tall, handsome, smart, creative, and funny, which is really what you hope any child would want to think about his father. And it's not far from the truth."

"Would you do it any differently if you had to do it over?"

Lydia shook her head. "Maybe it's selfish, but I have to say no, I'd do it all over again. Besides, what choices did we have back then? Sperm banks were new and at the time seemed weird, adoption was not an option, and neither of us was about to go out and fuck some stranger. Ben and Sasha's lives are filled with love, and they're sorting it out as they go along. By the time they grow up, there will probably be support groups for kids with anonymous donor fathers."

Marina pushed her chair away from the table and began to clear the dishes, motioning Lydia to stay seated. "I don't know what to tell Zoe. I've made up so much."

"What, exactly, does she want to know?"

"I'm not sure. Maybe she just wants to talk about Thomas to fill the void created by not having a father. I don't blame her. It's just that I don't know how to do it. The truth always gets in my way."

Lydia brushed a few crumbs along the tablecloth. "Is it possible that you don't really want to face the truth?"

Marina let the dishes clatter on the countertop. Her face was flushed as she turned to face Lydia, her words measured. "You don't think I face the truth? Don't you think I look the truth in the face every day?"

Lydia looked Marina in the eye. "Maybe, but have you ever really dealt with it? You've hardly even talked to me about it."

"Yes, I have. I've told you the whole story!"

"Telling a story and *dealing* with the reality of it is not the same thing. People make mistakes. It's how you deal with them that makes the difference. Don't get me wrong, you've created a beautiful life with Zoe, but you've gilded the lily until it can't bear the weight of its own beauty any longer."

Marina smiled at the turn of phrase, and the tension between the two women eased.

"I don't even know where to begin." Marina opened the freezer, removed two cartons of ice cream, and held them out for Lydia's inspection.

Lydia nodded at both and said, "What if you begin by telling Sarah that you are coming to Florence and want to see her?"

"What's that going to accomplish? How does that help me with Zoe?"

"If you can bring yourself to be honest with Sarah about what happened, it might relieve some of your guilt, and that might give you a better perspective on what to tell Zoe."

"I don't know." Marina scooped ice cream into a fluted parfait glass and set it in front of Lydia.

"Aren't you having any?"

Marina shook her head, patting her belly, and put the cartons back in the freezer. "You know what I feel really guilty about? How I said that Thomas was dead for five years when he wasn't . . . and then he was. It's like I willed it to happen."

"That's ridiculous."

"Yeah, I know. It's just weird."

Lydia put a scoop of ice cream in her mouth, then pointed the spoon at Marina. "Sarah is the one you need to focus on right now."

"So, *now*, after all these years, you think I should tell her about Zoe?"

"What choice do you have? Do you want to keep living this lie?"

"I just can't imagine telling her. She'll be devastated."

"Possibly, but do you want to keep lying to her every time you write or send photos of Zoe? Just because she doesn't know what you're doing doesn't mean it isn't hurting her, or more importantly, you. This is about getting your life cleaned up so you can give Zoe what she needs."

Marina was silent.

"Just think, if you told her everything now, it would free you of all this for the rest of your life."

"It would mean the end of our friendship."

"You don't know that." Lydia scraped her spoon around the bottom of the dish. "But ask yourself this. What sort of a friendship do you have based on so much deception?"

After Lydia left, Marina sat at the table for a long while contemplating the ruins of their feast. Lydia had offered to help clean up, but Marina had shooed her out, saying it was late, that June would be waiting. Around her, the house was silent except for the occasional groan of a restless radiator. She didn't appreciate Lydia passing judgment on her friendship with Sarah, but maybe Lydia was right, maybe she should come clean with Sarah, maybe it was time. But how? There were so many lies to unravel. She hated to think of herself as a liar, but one lie had led to another and then another. The first lie had been by omission, in not telling Sarah what happened with Thomas at the photo shoot. This made the second deception unavoidable—how do you tell your best friend that you're pregnant by her husband when you neglected to tell her that you slept with him in the first place? The next fabrication had been the story about her father needing heart surgery, thus providing an excuse to go home. (She thanked God her father was still alive and well.)

When Marina fled to the States, she'd had every intention of having an abortion but for some reason kept putting it off—until it was too late. Not having any moral or religious reservations, she had never understood her procrastination until one day as she sat watching her ten-month-old daughter learn to walk. Zoe tottered, then fell, then pulled herself up, over and over again, without a tear. Marina had no doubt that this single-minded determination and indomitable spirit had been hard at work in the womb to assure her birth. About six weeks after leaving Italy, she had written a brief note to Sarah saying she'd gotten pregnant on a one-night fling during her first week home and had decided to keep the baby even though the father wanted nothing to do with it. After Zoe was born, in an effort to maintain the false timeline, Marina waited three months before writing a card to Sarah and Thomas announcing Zoe's birth. It had no birth date and implied that she'd just had the baby.

Marina and Sarah's correspondence remained steady through the first year after Zoe's birth. Marina wrote of her work and Zoe's progress, while Sarah wrote about Thomas's work and neighborhood gossip, and regularly asked for photographs. Marina was reluctant about sending photographs for fear Sarah might see a resemblance, although she herself saw none and eventually obliged with a slightly out-of-focus shot that had Zoe's face partly in shadow. Over the next few years as Marina's life became busier, the time between letters grew longer, until they were exchanging news but once a year in a Christmas letter.

Marina let the water out of the sink, chose a fresh dish-towel from an adjacent drawer, and picked up the first piece of silver. Her thoughts drifted to Thomas. Was it really so ridiculous to think that she was somehow culpable in his death? Not directly, of course, but in the grander scheme of things. When she was pregnant, she'd often wondered if Thomas suspected that her pregnancy was linked to him but always came to the same conclusion—that he was too ego-centric and selfish to give anyone's life more than perfunctory consideration and probably hadn't thought of her at all. And then he was dead. It had been nearly ten years, but she re-called that day, with its saccharine scent of honeysuckle and the sigh of soggy heat on her neck as she stood by the mail-box with the letter in her hand. She was surprised to see the envelope with its Italian stamps and Sarah's round, loopy script, and while she was curious about the reason for this deviation from their holiday correspondence, she was in no way prepared for the news of Thomas's death.

The newspaper clippings, three from the *International Herald Tribune*, filled in the gaps in Sarah's brief and some-what vague note. *I thought you'd want to know. They say it was an accident.* The first article, dated two months before the note, reported that the hit-and-run accident had hap-pened just after midnight on a narrow street near his studio, and the second article, written the following week, stated that no leads had been found. The third clipping, dated three weeks before Sarah's note, reported a break-in at Thomas's studio, in which nothing was stolen but the place had been ransacked. Marina hadn't known what to make of any of it. It was shocking to think of Thomas dead, really and truly dead, when she had thought of him as fictitiously dead for five years. But, who were "they," and why had she underlined the word "say"? Did Sarah not believe it was an accident? There was no way to reach her by phone, since Thomas had always maintained that if someone wanted to talk to them, they could come and find them, so Marina had no choice but

to write and wait for a response. When she didn't hear anything after a month, she wrote again, and then once a month,
until finally, well into the new year, Sarah replied.

Marina put the last dish away and blew out the candles on
the table. Sarah's letter had been a vague and rambling list of
all she'd had to contend with in the months since Thomas's
death. She made no further reference to the break-in or any
suspicions about the accident. After that, their correspondence resumed its original pattern, and for the first three
years after Thomas's death, Sarah's Christmas letters painted
a bleak existence. *I don't know where the days, weeks, and
months have gone. I try to do the things I've always done,
but when I go for my morning coffee I have nothing to say to
anyone, and the market no longer has any appeal, as I have
no one to cook for. I never realized how much of my life was
consumed with tending to Thomas's needs. Marcello has
been a dear, forcing me out once in a while, but I still cannot
bring myself to go to Anita's.*

Although she knew that Thomas hadn't wanted children
and Sarah couldn't have them, when Marina read these letters, a sense of dread seeped into her heart with the realization
that, by having Thomas's child, she had stolen something
that by all rights belonged to Sarah, something that might
have comforted her in these dark days. Her mind, now overwhelmed with guilt, imagined taking Zoe to Florence, where
she would present her to Sarah as some sort of consolation,
and Sarah, in her elation at finding a living piece of Thomas,
would forgive her.

On the third Christmas following Thomas's death, Marina
received a letter from Sarah that was completely different.
She wrote that she'd taken over Thomas's studio in Santo
Spirito, emptied it of his things, and set it up for herself. She
was drawing again and had started sculpting in clay, and
hoped to cast a bust in bronze before too long. Over the en-
suing seven years, her career as a portrait sculptor flourished.
She was now represented by a prestigious gallery in Milan,

and it seemed she made quite a good living from commissions. In addition, Marina suspected (from reading between the lines) a romantic relationship with the owner of the gallery, but never asked too many questions for fear of inviting questions in return.

The following morning Marina woke to the wallop of rain on the roof. She opened one eye, checked the clock on her nightstand, then burrowed back under the comforter. Thoughts and snippets of her conversation with Lydia the previous evening had churned all night, tossing her into choppy dreams she couldn't quite recall, beyond a sense of helplessness, leaving her with a scorching thirst. She had experienced this feeling before, as an adolescent, and always upon waking—a deep and abiding thirst that permeated her entire being with an unquenchable yearning, for what, she never knew. She threw the covers back, slid from the bed, and went in search of water.

Sitting on the edge of the tub with a second glass of water, her dream came flooding back, her mind blank one minute, then filled with Technicolor details the next. In the dream she was sitting in a bathtub filled with water holding an infant in her hands, supporting it as it floated and gazed up at her. Then without warning, the water began to drain, rapidly forming a whirlpool into which the baby, suddenly tiny, was sucked around and around. In a panic, she tried to catch it as it spiraled downward toward the drain, but her hands moved sluggishly, refusing her will, and then in the split second before the baby disappeared down the drain, she woke. Marina glanced at the drain, a tingle of fear scurrying up her spine.

Later that morning, Marina stood with her hands on her hips surveying her reflection in the full-length mirror on the backside of her bedroom door. It was the third outfit she'd tried on in an attempt to put together a wardrobe for her trip. She ran her fingers through her thick, wavy hair, twisting it up off her neck as she examined her face first from one side, then the other. Her jaw was still firm, her lips full, but the skin under her eyes was slightly puffy and crinkled at the corners even when she wasn't smiling. She hoped she would be able to squeeze in a haircut and facial before her departure the following week. She dropped her arms, letting her hair fall to her shoulders, and surveyed the outfit: black wool pants, black cashmere sweater, camel blazer, and black boots—a bit severe, perhaps, but professional. It would do for her presentation. She ran her hand around the inside of the waistband, which felt a bit snug, but it was too late to lose five pounds, especially with Thanksgiving just a few days away. She'd just have to leave the button undone under the sweater.

She turned back to the bed, which was heaped with clothing. "Less is more," she muttered to herself as she began picking and choosing, creating a smaller pile on the trunk at the end of the bed. She moved a skirt and sweater from the heap to the pile and then back again, exchanging them for jeans and a shirt. Would she wear jeans? Maybe, if she dressed them up with a nice jacket and her good boots. She'd lived in jeans that year in Florence, jeans and T-shirts in the summer, jeans and baggy, coarsely knit sweaters in winter, with the exception of the Christmas outfit Sarah had encouraged her to buy. She'd never worn the skirt again, but she'd resoled the beautiful boots twice and worn them until they looked too tired to take another step. Opening the closet door, she rooted around with her foot in the jumble of Reeboks, clogs, and boots, but not finding them, she dropped to her knees and crawled partway in until she located them at the back of her closet behind her boxes of rarely worn dress shoes. As she pulled them on, she half expected to be transported back in time, but all she felt was the stiff ridges of a crumpled innersole. She tried to recall what Sarah had worn for shoes, but all she remembered was her wild, rusty hair, voluminous skirts, and Indian jewelry. Sarah was now close to fifty, and the thought of her still swathed in her ethnic garb was depressing. Marina pulled the boots off, tossed them in the closet, and retrieved two pieces of luggage from under the bed. A small suitcase and good-sized tote bag would hold enough for five days.

After an attempt at filling the suitcase, only to change her mind and empty it again, Marina decided to abandon the project and head out to the studio to work on her presentation. She had decided to focus on fifteenth-century gilding techniques, which were the basic techniques she'd learned with Sauro and from which all modern practices came. Also, Josh was encouraging her to include an overview of the evolution of her career. There were increasing numbers of women entering the restoration field and, according to Josh, they would be well represented at the conference. Marina wasn't sure how inspirational her story would be, so much of her own good fortune had come from being in the right place at the right time, but she agreed to make a stab at it. She was aware, however, that in order to tell her story, she'd have to go back to the beginning—a direction the hands of fate seemed to be pushing her none too gently.

By midweek the notes for her presentation were in order and neatly stowed in a manila envelope. Marina sat at her desk, a trestle table she'd found under a heap of yellow newspapers in the back room of a junk shop and which now, after years of butcher's wax and elbow grease, shone as silky and sublime as a fine antique. She'd placed it against a wall in her studio under a niche that had probably once held a religious icon but now paid homage to a compact stereo system. She stared at her letter to Sarah. She'd used her business stationery, with her gold letterhead across the top. Under it, her black-inked script moved across the page in a stiff backward slant, as if each word were digging in its heels. Next to it, on a yellow legal pad, a scribbled draft of the letter filled the page with crossed-out words and deleted sentences. She exhaled hard through pursed lips. This would have to do. She couldn't take back the years of hastily scrawled Christmas greetings that shared little and hid much, nor could she begin to explain something she didn't completely understand herself. At this late date, all she could do was tell Sarah she was coming to Florence, where she was staying, and leave it to her to get in touch. Cowardly, perhaps, but it was the best she could do. Right now she needed to get it in the mail if it had any hope of arriving in Florence before she did. She should have seen to it at the beginning of the week, but she'd put it off in favor of fine-tuning her presentation, and now she was out of time. It was the day before Thanksgiving. Zoe had a half day of school, and Marina had promised to spend the afternoon making pies with her.

On Sunday Zoe had returned from Sasha's in good spirits and eager to talk about how many and which kinds of pies they should make. Evidently, June had bought a "humongous" turkey that wouldn't fit in the fridge and had been relegated to a cooler on the back porch. She confirmed, with zeal, that Peter was coming *alone,* and that he and Marina would once again be in charge of making the gravy. Over the years, a friendly rivalry had blossomed between Peter and Marina over who had the best gravy recipe, and they argued endlessly about milk versus water, whether to add the flour directly to the fat or make a roux first, and the ethics of adding canned gravy in order to extend the quantity. Marina was the purist, while Peter believed that more was better as long as it had flavor.

Zoe's eyes shone and her cheeks flushed as she described the place cards she and Sasha had made for the holiday table. While Marina was relieved to see Zoe focused on something other than her trip to Florence, she was wary of the high spirits. Lydia had called Sunday afternoon to report that Zoe seemed to be fine, that the two girls were shut in Sasha's room with the contents of the craft cupboard, but she wanted Marina to know that she'd overheard them discussing NED. NED was an acronym Zoe and Sasha had come up with a few years earlier that stood for Non-Existent

Dads, and they had been known to egg each other on in the quest for answers to unanswerable questions that invariably ended with one or both of them in tears. But so far Zoe hadn't broached the subject, seemingly content to plot their pie-making strategy.

Marina surveyed the damage: A coating of flour dusted every counter surface, the floor, and most of Zoe's face; flattened bits of pastry dotted the old floorboards like coins spilled from a purse; and the sink overflowed with bowls, measuring cups, and utensils. The Rolling Stones screamed about dissatisfaction from the living room stereo as Zoe finished crimping the last piecrust.

"That looks beautiful, sweetie. I think we're done. *Now,* can we please turn the music down?"

Part of their pie-making deal was that Zoe got to be in charge of the music and, as it turned out, the volume as well. Marina went along with it since Zoe had chosen her mother's favorite group, but enough was enough.

Zoe pursed her lips and spoke as if to an infant. "Ooh, is the music too much for Mommy-wommy's wittle ears?"

Marina laughed but gave her the I'm-the-parent-don't-push-me-too-far look, and Zoe complied, but not without blasting it at full volume for a moment before turning it down. She'd been in a good mood ever since her return from Sasha's, and Marina was grateful for the return of her sweet child, hoping that her surly, churlish counterpart had taken a permanent hike. Now if only they could get through the Thanksgiving holiday in peace, after which Marina would slip quietly away to Italy. While she was gone, Zoe would be staying with Lydia and June, and she'd have Sasha and Ben to distract her from any thoughts of what she might be missing in Florence.

"Come on, Mom, come dance with me. It's your favorite song!" Zoe yelled from the living room, turning up the volume again.

The two of them jumped and shimmied around the living room to "Brown Sugar" and then "Gloria," collapsing on the couch as the tape ended. It had been months since they'd danced together, something they'd once done regularly around the kitchen, the living room, even in the car, wiggling in their seats and shaking their shoulders when an irresistible tune came on the radio. Marina hadn't given it much thought, but now with the same breaths that savored the precious moments at hand, she lamented its loss. As Zoe got older, she supposed that moments like these would become fewer. Then she smacked Zoe gently on the thigh and said, "Up we go. Time to clean up our mess."

Marina cleaned the surfaces and swept the floor while Zoe did the dishes.

Zoe was humming to herself as she splashed in the water. "Mom, can Sasha spend the weekend here?"

"You just spent a weekend with her, Zoe. I thought maybe we'd go shopping and out for lunch." She didn't want to remind Zoe that this was the weekend before her trip.

"But we've got this project we're working on. Can't we go out some other time?"

"I don't know. What are you working on?"

"Just something. I'll show you when we're done."

Reluctantly, Marina agreed. At least she'd have Zoe around for the weekend. "Okay, but she has to go home Sunday evening."

"Duh, Mom. It's a school night."

Marina blinked under the glare of the overhead kitchen light, then fumbled for the dimmer, turning it down to something that more accurately replicated the slumber from which she'd woken. What had roused her from her bed? The doors were secure, the furnace was making its usual cacophony of burps and sighs, there was no wind rattling the windows. She shrugged mentally and eyed the pies that sat on cooling racks on the table—two pumpkin, one pecan, and one apple—perhaps *they'd* been calling to her. Crossing to the fridge, she took out a carton of milk, gathered a glass, plate, fork, and knife, and settled at the table in front of the pies, like a judge at a contest. The taut, glistening expanse of pumpkin custard beckoned. Her mouth watered. Maybe just a tiny sliver, surely no one would begrudge her that.

What could be better in the middle of the night than the soft, silky taste of nutmeg and cinnamon? Marina savored the slick filling against her tongue, remembering the fruitless search she and Sarah had embarked on for a can of pumpkin filling for her first, and as it turned out, only Thanksgiving in Florence. In the end, they'd settled for apple pie, and she'd had her mother send a can of pumpkin in time for Christmas. Her mind snagged on the calendar of that fateful year, and she watched the pages turn over, beyond that Christmas, into the new year, past the bathtub fiasco with Thomas to the day she discovered she was pregnant. Over the years, she'd come to understand that her assignation with Thomas was the result of too much wine, a seductive man, her misplaced feelings for Sarah, and a fair amount of naïveté. But now, sitting in the kitchen with a fifteen-year-old daughter asleep upstairs, she still couldn't believe it hadn't occurred to her afterward to wonder if Thomas had worn a condom. She'd been so wrapped up in her guilt and the fear of Sarah finding out that she hadn't given it a thought. She couldn't remember much about that day or the weeks that followed. It all seemed to hover perpetually out of reach, shrouded in a hazy mantle of denial. But she recalled perfectly the moment it dawned on her that she was pregnant. It happened a few days after her riverside talk with Sarah, as she was leaning over the toilet bowl vomiting for the third day in a row. She sat on the cold stone floor in her little bathroom in Via Luna, stunned at the realization. When she could move again, she scanned her small pocket calendar in search of the red dot that religiously marked the first day of every period. She found it two months back, just after Christmas. Her mind scurried to all sorts of reasons why she might have missed a period, the most logical being the emotional upheaval she was going through, but two days later, a kindly English doctor took her urine sample and confirmed her fears.

Marina put the kettle on and cut herself another piece of pie. She thought about lighting a fire but didn't want to get too invested in staying up. It was going to be a long day and a couple more hours of sleep would serve her well. The kettle began its whistle and she caught it up before it could reach a full-blown shriek, not that anything less than a bullhorn could penetrate Zoe's slumber.

Sleep. Sleep had been Marina's refuge those final weeks in Florence. Whether a defense mechanism, a psychological coping skill, or just the pregnancy itself, during the end of her time there, she'd slept more than she'd been awake. In her waking hours, she vacillated about whether or not to tell Sarah, to beg for her forgiveness, for her help. But help with what? Aborting her husband's child? She dreaded seeing Sarah, afraid that her condition would somehow be all too obvious even though she could see no signs of it herself. As it turned out, their first encounter was by happenstance and rife with other distractions. Marina had been in the Oltrarno running an errand for Sauro and had run into Sarah on her way back as she crossed over the Ponte Santa Trinita. When she saw Sarah coming toward her, she stopped and contemplated turning and running, but Sarah raised her hand and waved.

Sarah didn't seem to notice her hesitation and greeted her with an enthusiastic hug. "Hey, you! I've missed you. If I didn't know better, I'd think Thomas and Sauro were conspiring to keep us apart. Come on, let's have a coffee."

Without waiting for a response, she linked her arm through Marina's and pulled her into a corner bar. Every thought Marina had entertained about confessing, asking for forgiveness and help, evaporated in the hot breath of fear that scorched her neck and face. She stood immobilized as

Sarah ordered a cappuccino for each of them and began un-fastening the leather portfolio she'd been carrying under her arm.

"Wait 'til you see this. It's fabulous! You'll love it!" Sarah pulled out a sheet of heavy stock the size of a manila folder and held it up in front of her.

It took Marina a second to realize what she was looking at. After what had happened *that day,* she'd never seen even a proof of the bathtub photograph, but there it was, white tub, white skin, white water. Thomas had cropped the pic-ture to the inside of the tub, which created an arched frame for the torso arching out of the water. With her head tipped back, the focal point became her neck, then her hands clasp-ing her breasts, with her ribs and belly disappearing back into the water. She couldn't tell if Thomas had doctored it in any way in the darkroom other than to print it in sepia tones rather than black and white, but the effect was stunning, and it did look very much like stone.

"Takes your breath away, doesn't it? I was going to bring it by your place later so you could see it."

"It's beautiful," Marina replied, then hesitated. Thomas's name was at the top of the poster, and the name of the gallery and its address were printed at the bottom next to the dates the show would run. "You're not going to put them up, are you?"

Sarah looked at Marina. "Of course we're putting them up. It's a poster. That's the point. Didn't Thomas tell you?"

Marina shook her head. "He should have asked me if it was okay."

"Marina, it's art. The image belongs to Thomas. I thought you understood that. He can do what he likes with it. I as-sumed he'd told you. Maybe he wanted it to be a surprise. Don't you like it?"

It was a surprise all right. Her life seemed to be full of sur-prises these days. "I like the picture. It's amazing. I just don't like the idea of my naked body plastered all over town."

"No one will know it's you with your head tipped way back like that. Is this going to be a problem?"

Marina was taken aback by Sarah's businesslike tone. She hadn't known she even had one. "No . . . I suppose . . . I just wasn't expecting . . . this." She motioned toward the poster.

Outside the kitchen window, dawn was breaking with the faintest hint of pink. Marina pushed her empty plate away and leaned back in her chair, holding the mug of herbal tea between her palms, staring into the murky liquid as if a revelation might surface. After that encounter with Sarah, for some reason she couldn't now fathom—perhaps because of the poster, perhaps because she felt he owed her—she had decided that Thomas should be the one to help her. After all, he was the one who didn't want children; he should be happy to help her get rid of the evidence.

Not wanting to face Thomas in person, she had decided to leave a note for him at his studio during the night. A midwinter thaw in the mountains had sent a torrent of water downriver, carrying broken branches that snagged on the banks and under bridges catching all manner of debris in their tangled limbs. It was past midnight when she crossed the Ponte Vecchio on her bike, the note in her pocket. Her plan was to tape it to the darkroom door where he'd see it first thing in the morning. *I need your help.* But what if Thomas helped her right into a botched abortion like he had Sarah? The only alternative she had come up with was the British doctor, but when she'd broached the subject, he hadn't let her finish her sentence, holding up his hand like a traffic cop.

She left the tumbling waters behind and slipped into the shadows of a narrow street that came out near Thomas's studio in Piazza Santo Spirito. The piazza seemed to be deserted, but it was hard to tell, shrouded as it was by a canopy of twisted branches that cast distorted shapes against the buildings. The streetlight in front of Thomas's was out, and Marina had to feel for the lock on the front door. Once it was unlocked, she stepped quickly into the foyer, hit the light switch, and made her way quietly up the stone staircase, past silent apartments to the top floor. The second key slipped easily into the studio door, and she had it partway open before she heard the music. And voices. The velvet drapes to the studio were closed, creating a vestibule of pitch-black. She was about to leave her note on the floor and creep away when she heard a woman's laughter. Curiosity got the better of her. The music was loud enough to cover any slight noise on her part, so she closed the door, easing the latch into a whisper, and moved to the curtain, taking care not to disturb it. She put her eye to the sliver of light where the velvet panels met, then brought her hand to her mouth, silencing an audible intake of breath.

The studio was dimly lit except in the center, where portable lights illuminated the red Oriental rug. Thomas stood behind his tripod with his head bowed over his large-format camera, his back to the door. The contessa, dressed in jodhpurs, black riding boots, and a tight, crimson jacket, stood at one end of the carpet surveying the scene. She lifted the leather crop in her hand and pointed it. "Now mount her," she commanded. In the center of the carpet, a man thinly disguised as a woman knelt on all fours. The makeup was crude and there was no hiding his burly physique under the lace peignoir. Astride him, another man, wearing nothing but a black riding hat, riding boots, and a large erection, grinned with bared teeth.

"What do you think, darling?" The contessa directed her question at Thomas, who nodded his head without looking at her.

Marina recalled pedaling home through the streets that night as if the devil himself were chasing her, then not sleeping a wink as she turned the scene over and over in her mind. What were they up to? Was Thomas some sort of pervert or just a pawn in one of the contessa's sordid schemes? She'd only had a glimpse of him, but something in his stance, in the way he'd nodded, made her think of a bullied child. Did Sarah know? She thought back over all the conversations they'd ever had on the subject of Thomas and the contessa, but she couldn't decide. The fact that Sarah had been dishonest about other things gave Marina pause, and in the dark hours of night, her mind ran wild, imagining schemes and conspiracy. What if Thomas and Sarah had contrived to impregnate her and intended to keep the child for themselves? Even in her exhausted, confused state, she could see the absurdity of the idea, but she was unable to find a compelling reason in favor of telling Sarah about her pregnancy or Thomas's moonlighting. Perhaps she'd taken the coward's way out in telling Sarah that her father was ill and that she was needed at home. But what else could she have done?

CHAPTER 12

Peter and Marina stood hip to hip in front of Lydia's stove, where steam rose from pots of boiling vegetables, curling wisps of hair that had escaped Marina's brocade headband. June bustled into the kitchen carrying a stack of serving bowls and platters. "Marina, you look like a cherub with those curls around your face."

Marina rolled her eyes and Peter elbowed her. "She's our little gravy angel."

"Sure is," replied June. "Are we almost ready?"

"Not quite," Marina said in the same moment that Peter replied, "Yep, just about."

"It still needs to thicken, Peter. You put in too much water. Look." Marina tapped the edge of the pot with the whisk.

"Well, if you'd let me put in that can of gravy, it wouldn't have needed the water."

"It didn't need any . . ."

"Okay, you two," Lydia warned with a brandish of the corkscrew in her hand. "Let's not have the gravy crusades all over again. I thought you made a pact."

"We're still waiting to have it ratified by the Pope," Peter responded.

"Funny, very funny." Marina smiled into the rich, brown sauce that was finally beginning to show signs of thickening.

Marina glanced at Zoe, who sat at the island watching their antics with bright, eager eyes, and hoped she wasn't giving her daughter the wrong impression. She couldn't deny that she liked Peter immensely. He was easy to be with, funny, smart, sensitive, and attractive. With his red hair and freckles, he might easily be mistaken for a grad student rather than the well-respected antiques dealer that he was. But he was family, and she didn't want to mess with that. He stood close to her now, even though he'd clearly let her take over the gravy, and she could smell his aftershave—something spicy.

Marina moved away from him slightly and announced, "Okay, we're ready. Let's get this bird on the table."

Dinner was filled with laughter and a great clattering of plates and cutlery, seconds and even thirds for some, followed by a lull, during which the adults leaned back in their chairs with a groan, and told the children they were excused until dessert.

"Why is it that everyone always eats too much at a holiday dinner?" June asked no one in particular.

"Is this a riddle?" asked Peter.

"Because it's delicious," said Marina.

"Because we're gluttonous creatures." Lydia pushed out her chair and picked up the turkey platter.

"It's a mystery to me." June shrugged, following Lydia into the kitchen. "I always swear that I won't, but I always do."

Peter turned to Marina. "Are you coming into town this weekend?"

"I have a hair appointment on Saturday. Why?"

"Good. Will you come by the shop? There's something I want to show you."

"What?"

"You'll see. It's a surprise." When Marina frowned, he chuckled and added, "Don't worry, it's something nice."

Marina had been in Peter's shop many times for his annual Christmas party, but it was the first time he'd ever asked her specifically to visit, and she wasn't sure what to make of it.

Peter's shop was located in the center of downtown Hudson where the shops had been renovated and now formed an upscale antiques district. Marina stood in front of the plate glass window as if admiring the antique maps on display. She liked what she saw, the freshly styled hair, crisp white shirt, and her favorite camel blazer. The one that made her feel put together regardless of the loose ends hanging from her life. She shifted her gaze from her image to the framed maps of ancient Africa that hung on a backdrop of charcoal gray suede. Below them in a glass display case lined with pale gray velvet, loose unfurled maps were held down with small glass weights in each corner. The one directly in front of her, of New England, had an elaborate, gilded cartouche around the edges.

All at once, she became aware of someone standing at her side. She stepped away as she turned her head. Peter stood with knitted brow and pursed lips, imitating her contemplation of the window.

"Oh, it's you." She blushed, hoping he hadn't seen her admiring herself.

"It didn't seem you were ever coming in, so I thought I'd better come out and get you."

"The maps are so beautiful, I got caught up in them."

"I could see that. What were you thinking?"

"Oh, nothing really, it's silly. . . ."

"No, really, I want to know."

"I was thinking about how much easier life might be if we were all given maps at birth."

"Hmm, maybe." Peter nodded thoughtfully. "But there

would always be unexpected things, things you couldn't see beyond the borders."

"You're probably right. Maybe a really, really big map? Do you sell anything like that?"

Peter smiled. "I'm not sure. Why don't you come in and we'll look."

Before her first visit to Peter's shop a number of years ago, she had imagined a dark, musty space with heavily carved woodwork covered in dust. But the interior, like the display window, was decorated in shades of gray, golden wood tones, classic lines, and soft lighting. It felt like a cross between an art gallery and a library. A recording of Vivaldi's "Four Seasons" played overhead. She felt Peter watching her as she moved from case to case, running her fingers lightly along the edges of the cabinets, careful not to touch the glass. She was just beginning to feel awkward when he said, "Come. Let me show you what I found."

She followed him into a small sitting room, then through a doorway into a dimly lit vault, where the air felt cooler.

"I hope it's not too chilly for you. We have a climate-control system in here to help preserve the older maps." A wooden table with a slick, polished surface took up the center of the room, and cabinets with wide, shallow drawers lined the walls. Peter put on a pair of white cotton gloves from a box on the countertop, opened a drawer that slid out with a sigh, and withdrew a large cellophane folder.

"I thought you'd enjoy seeing this. It's from the estate 'of a gentleman.' We're working on the provenance now."

Hand drawn on heavy, discolored parchment was a primitive version of the city she had known and loved. A city that had grown in the few hundred years since the map had been set down, but whose heart remained the same: the Arno, the Duomo, the hills beyond—they were all there, lovingly rendered in colored inks muted with age. "It's lovely," Marina breathed, her eyes following familiar streets.

Peter looked pleased. "I have others from the same collection, not of Florence, but they're quite beautiful."

He shifted the maps and bent over to explain their features, but Marina found she was more interested in the nape of his neck where a crescent-shaped birthmark showed itself just above his collar. Again, she caught the scent of his cologne and was shocked by the yearning it evoked in her. What was it that kept her from reaching out, not just to Peter but to anyone?

Peter lingered over the maps for a few moments, then glanced at Marina. "I'm sorry. Here I am going on and on like a kid showing off his toys. How about a coffee? We can go across the street."

Marina stepped away. "No, no, it's okay, really. I love the maps. They're beautiful. But I do have to go. I have things to do. I'm leaving for Florence in a couple of days, and I need to spend some time with Zoe."

Peter nodded. "Lydia mentioned that she was having some difficulties."

Marina stiffened. "She did?"

"She wasn't specific," he assured her. "Just teenage angst, I assume."

"Yes, well . . . I think she's fine right now."

"Is there anything I can do to help?"

Marina shook her head. "No, but thanks. I have some things to straighten out. Everything will be okay. Anyway, I've got to get going." Marina moved toward the door.

Peter followed her. "Are you nervous about your lecture?"

Marina nodded. "Among other things."

"You'll be great. I have no doubt." He opened the front door and walked out onto the sidewalk with her. "But promise me something."

"What's that?"

"You'll send me a postcard."

Marina blushed. "I'll do my best."

* * *

Marina lay on the couch where an hour before, after taking Sasha home, she'd sat down to have a quick cup of tea and flip though a magazine. She'd spent the morning finishing her packing while Zoe and Sasha slept in, then made them waffles. After breakfast she left them to clean up the kitchen and get on with their project, whatever it was, while she went out to clean her studio. Aretha set the tone, and Marina shimmied around the studio to "Jump" and "Freeway of Love" while she put things in order so she could get right to work upon her return. Christmas gifts needed finishing and time would be short. When she went back to the house in the late afternoon to take Sasha home, the girls protested that they hadn't finished their research, but Marina was firm—they'd had plenty of time together and Zoe still had her homework to do.

She knew she should get up off the couch and check on Zoe, who, judging by the walloping beat that traveled down through the walls from her stereo, was unlikely to be getting much work done. But she wasn't ready to move from her supine reverie. The last rays of sunlight slanted across the living room, imbuing the room with a tawny glow, and for the umpteenth time in the last twenty-four hours, her mind drifted to the nape of Peter's neck. What if . . .

A movement nearby pulled her from her stupor. She opened her eyes. Zoe stood just inside the living room, her face blanched of color, the skin around her eyes blotched and red. She looked tiny within the baggy jeans and oversized flannel shirt, as if her body had pulled away from its wrapping like a shriveled seed in a pod left out in the sun.

Marina sat up, swinging her feet to the floor. "Zoe, what is it?"

Zoe walked toward her on rigid legs, a small packet of crumpled papers in her fist. Her mouth was open, but she made no sound. She stopped a few feet from the couch and threw her arm forward as if she meant to fling the papers at her mother, but her hand didn't release them.

"Zoe, what is it?" Marina repeated, reaching for her, but Zoe backed away, waving the papers in front of her. Marina wasn't sure if she was showing them to her or warding her off.

"Zoe, stop!" Fear sharpened her words as she grabbed Zoe's wrist, prying her fingers gently from around the papers.

"You lied to me," Zoe said in a monotone.

"Zoe, sweetie," Marina murmured, smoothing the papers on her lap. She recognized the newspaper clippings. One of them had a small photograph of Thomas with a camera slung around his neck.

"Zoe, where did you get these?" Her mind scrambled as she skimmed the articles, but she could not think what it was she was looking for. "These are about the accident, you already know this."

Zoe was quiet, very still. Marina looked up from her frantic search. She watched as Zoe moved her hands to either side of her face, pressing her fingertips into her cheeks, dragging them slowly down her face, leaving streaks of pink on white, like war paint. She began to speak, emphasizing the words as if pressing each one into Marina's flesh.

"It says he was killed in December . . . *1983!*"

Marina nodded.

"That's five years *after* I was born."

Marina felt the words stick to her heart like leeches in search of blood.

"You told me he died *before* I was born."

Marina watched, speechless, as Zoe's eyes filled and overflowed.

"Why did you tell me he died before I was born?"

Marina stared at her daughter's crumpled face.

"He was never coming to be with us! He didn't want me, did he?" Zoe's voice rose to a wail. Marina moved closer, taking Zoe's hands into hers.

"No, no, Zoe, it wasn't at all like that."

"He hated me. He didn't want me," Zoe moaned.

"No, Zoe, he *didn't* hate you." Marina squeezed Zoe's hands, willing her to believe. "He didn't hate you, sweetie." She hesitated and then stepped off the ledge. "He didn't even know about you. I never told him."

Zoe's sharp intake of breath seemed to suck all the air from the room, leaving only silence. Marina held her own breath, as she had countless nights long ago, waiting for the sound of her baby girl's next breath. And then it came in a whisper.

"You never told him? He didn't know about me?" Each word was torn from her lips, sucked into the silence.

"Sweetie, it was complicated. . . ."

"How complicated can it be?" Zoe wrenched her hands from Marina's. Her voice rose to a mock falsetto. "Hi, honey, I'm home. Guess what? We're having a baby!"

"Zoe, it wasn't like that." Marina's words were firm.

"Well, what the fuck was it like then?" The note of hysteria remained in Zoe's voice.

"That's enough, Zoe!" Marina moved back, putting a little distance between them.

"No, Mom, it's not fucking enough. You *stole* those years from me. *Five years!* I could have had a father, I could have had some memories." The hysteria turned back onto itself and into sobbing.

Marina looked at her daughter as if her love could wrap her, cradle her, protecting her from the truth. She softened her voice.

"No, Zoe, you couldn't have."

"Why not?"

Marina looked away.

"Because he was married. He had another life. He had a wife."

"You screwed around with a married man?" Zoe's face twisted in disgust.

"We were only together that one time. We were good friends. We got confused. I only wish it could have been different . . . for you."

"Why couldn't you tell him? Maybe he *would* have wanted to be with me. Maybe he would have left his wife for us."

"No, he wouldn't have. There was no question of that. His wife wanted children, but couldn't have them. It would have hurt her too much to know about you."

"So what?"

"I didn't want to hurt her. I cared about her."

"Why?"

Marina looked down at her hands and then into Zoe's eyes. "Because his wife was Sarah."

"Sarah! Your best friend Sarah?"

Marina nodded.

"Mom, that's disgusting!" Zoe began to cry again. "How could you do that?"

Marina wasn't sure if Zoe meant, "How could you do that to Sarah?" or "How could you do that to me?" She couldn't tell her that Thomas had taken advantage of her or that she was drunk, or have Zoe think that her conception was sordid in any way. "Like I said, Zoe, it's complicated. Thomas and I were friends, we worked together, and maybe we had more feeling for each other than we thought. We just got carried away one day. . . ." She didn't think Zoe would want to get any closer to the topic of sex than that.

Zoe sniffed and wiped her eyes with the heel of her hand. "But you still could have told him about me."

"I tried, really I did, but I was young and afraid, and . . ."

Zoe stood up and shouted, "So it was easier to lie, and you've lied and lied and lied to me all these years! You're a horrible person and I hate you!" She turned and ran from the room, pounded up the stairs, and slammed her door.

Marina slumped on the couch. She *had* tried. She was certain she had. She'd gone to Thomas's studio to ask for his help—and found out more than she wanted to know about his relationship with the contessa. She had wanted to be honest with Sarah but just couldn't find a way into the truth. It wasn't that she didn't care. God knows, she'd agonized about what to do from the very first moment she knew she was pregnant and through the entire first year of Zoe's life. It was over Zoe's first birthday cake that she had the realization there was no going back. She was leaning over the cake, encouraging Zoe to blow on the candles, when she looked into her daughter's eyes and recognized that she alone was responsible for Zoe's well-being, for protecting her from harm, and that going back would only hurt them both. Now she wasn't so sure. Zoe was in pain beyond anything Marina could have imagined.

The phone rang somewhere near Marina's ear, jolting her from sleep. She felt for it, her hand patting the bedside table, almost knocking her water glass over.

Lydia's voice was soft in her ear. "Sorry to wake you. I just wanted to let you know that Zoe's here."

"What? How?" Marina pushed herself up on one elbow and looked at the clock, which blinked six eleven into the dark room.

"Evidently Sasha let her in a couple of hours ago."

"How did she get there?"

"I assume she walked."

"In the dark? My God, what was she thinking?"

"I really don't think she was thinking very clearly. She was pretty upset. But she's okay now. June gave her half a sleeping pill. I hope you don't mind, but she wouldn't let us call you and we needed to get her calmed down. She's asleep now."

Marina leaned back against the headboard and stared at the ceiling. "Oh Christ. Did she tell you anything? I was going to call you last night, but quite honestly I didn't have the energy to talk."

"She wasn't making a whole lot of sense. Why don't you come over here and we can talk."

Marina pulled on a pair of sweatpants and a flannel shirt over her T-shirt and panties, and headed downstairs, pausing to look in Zoe's room. It was in its usual state of disarray and she didn't see any sign of a note. She turned a lamp on in the living room, but saw no sign of a note. Nothing in the kitchen either. She ran her fingers through her hair, then grabbing a clump on either side of her head, she pulled hard until tears came to her eyes. What had she done to Zoe?

By now the sky was light, the grass along the side of the road covered in frost. Marina hoped that Zoe had at least had the good sense to dress warmly. She couldn't imagine how she had managed to creep out of the house without waking her. The stairs creaked and the back door squeaked, and she was a light sleeper. The evening before, when she'd gone upstairs to try to talk to Zoe, she found that Zoe had wedged her desk chair under the doorknob, and after a round of pleading with her to open the door, Marina had left her alone for the rest of the evening hoping she'd come around.

"So, now what?" Lydia asked, stirring cream into her coffee. She had explained to Marina that, according to Sasha, the girls had decided to make NED scrapbooks, gathering whatever information they could about their nonexistent fathers. Evidently Zoe thought there might be more information about Thomas in some boxes in the attic. Sasha hadn't known what Zoe found because Marina was giving her a ride home when Zoe went up to the attic.

Marina picked at a muffin while she listened to Lydia, then outlined what had happened with Zoe the previous evening. "I didn't know what to do, what to say. I guess I never expected her to find out. I'd forgotten about the stuff in the attic. I meant to get rid of it years ago."

"So she knows that Thomas was married to Sarah, that

Sarah was your best friend, and that you never told either of them."

Marina nodded but didn't look up from the muffin that was fast becoming a pile of crumbs.

"Did she give any indication of understanding your predicament?" Lydia asked.

"God, no. All she cares about is that I deprived her of having a father. All she sees is that I've lied to her over and over and over. The more time that goes by, the more lies she's going to uncover. Little things that I made up." Marina put her head in her hands and began to cry. "It's just going to hurt her again and again."

Lydia reached over and patted Marina's hand. "Don't get ahead of yourself. Just wait until she wakes up and you have a chance to talk to her."

Marina nodded into her hands, then reached for a paper napkin from a stack in the center of the table. She and Lydia had an ongoing debate about the merits of paper napkins versus cloth napkins, with Marina favoring the aesthetics of cloth while Lydia voted for expediency. At this moment Marina was just grateful to have something to blow her nose into.

"I'm going to have to call Josh and cancel my trip. There's no way I can leave Zoe like this."

Lydia nodded, but said, "You've still got a couple of days before you leave. Why don't you wait and see how she is when she wakes up?"

"I suppose. But there's no way I can just go off and leave her like this."

"Of course not." Lydia pushed her chair back. "Why don't we go and check on her. That pill should be wearing off."

Sasha's room, although larger than Zoe's, was in a similar slovenly state. Zoe lay supine on the bed, staring at the ceiling.

"Zoe, sweetie," Marina called softly from the doorway, but at the sound of her mother's voice, Zoe rolled over and pulled the comforter over her head. Lydia gave Marina's shoulder a squeeze, then closed the door behind her. Marina made her way across the room, not sure what to do or say. She stood beside the bed for a moment, then sat gingerly on the edge. She couldn't begin to explain her transgression with Thomas all those years ago. The only thing she knew for sure was that she was grateful Zoe was the result, and while she regretted the web of lies she'd woven, she had no idea how to untangle it.

Marina rested her hand on Zoe's back. "Sweetheart, I know you're really angry and upset, but you can't go running off in the night like that. What if something had happened to you?" Marina's throat tightened at the thought. "I'm sorry I lied to you about Thomas, but it's much more complicated than you can understand. I was so young and I made some mistakes. And then I didn't know how to undo them. I wish I'd done things differently, really I do, but . . . Zoe, please talk to me." Marina didn't know what else to say. When no response was forthcoming, she simply enveloped the mound of bedding in her arms and whispered, "I'm so sorry, Zoe. I love you. Call me when you're ready to talk."

In the kitchen Lydia had cleaned up the table and brewed a fresh pot of coffee.

"Can I make you some eggs? You should eat. You look shattered."

Marina pulled out a chair and flopped into it. "Shattered. Now there's a perfect word."

"I just meant you look tired."

Marina nodded. "I know you did, but 'shattered' is what Zoe's life is right now. Our life."

"How's she doing? Did she talk?"

Marina shook her head, taking the mug Lydia held out. "Now what do I do?"

Lydia sat down with her coffee. "Maybe just leave her alone for now. I'm here all day. I'll keep an eye on her."

"I just feel so helpless. How can I help her if she won't talk to me?"

"She needs some time. Leave her here and call me later. You must have so much to do."

"I do, but it's all for the trip. If I'm not going . . ." Marina shrugged.

"Look, you don't know how Zoe will be doing a couple of days from now. Just give her another day before you decide anything."

Marina sat behind the wheel of her car with the motor running, raising her hand every now and then in salute to other mothers picking up their children. Mothers who somehow managed to navigate the murky waters of marriage and relationship without casting their children onto the rocks. If only . . . But she stopped herself. She'd spent the last day and a half speculating on paths not taken. If only she'd told Thomas, if only she'd had an abortion, if only she'd told Sarah, if only she'd found a mate, had more children, made a happy family. If only she'd told Zoe the truth in the beginning. Around and around she'd gone until she couldn't think about it anymore. Finally, desperate to silence her thoughts, she'd put on Patsy Cline at full blast and sung along to the brokenhearted melodies as she clipped and watered every plant in the house. When she'd checked in with Lydia the previous evening, Zoe was still refusing to come out of Sasha's room, but she'd eaten and Lydia had heard the girls talking.

"So we know she's not in shock. June just went in to see her and says she looks fine, has good color, but doesn't want to talk to anyone right now except Sasha and . . . she doesn't want to go home. I'm sorry."

"That's no surprise. I'll be surprised if she ever wants to come home."

Marina had spoken briefly with June, who reassured her

that Zoe was all right, and the three of them had come to a consensus that Zoe would stay another night with the proviso that she went to school in the morning.

Marina's hand gripped the wheel as she watched for Zoe in the throng of gangly limbs, pimply faces, and shrieking animation. She couldn't remember the last time she'd waited for Zoe after school. Somewhere along the line, the school bus and extracurricular activities had taken her place. Then she saw her, coat unzipped, no hat, walking toward the bus with Sasha and two other girls. She was laughing. Laughing! Marina scrambled from the car and called out, waving her arm. "Zoe!" All four faces looked in her direction—three with surprise, one with a scowl. The girls gathered rank around Zoe, looking nervously over their shoulders at Marina, who had stopped in front of her car, unsure whether to proceed. After a moment, Sasha broke away from the group and walked over to where Marina was standing, and without preamble said, "Zoe says she will call you tonight." Then she turned and walked back to her friends.

Marina drove out of the school parking lot, but instead of turning south toward home, she turned north in the direction of Hudson. The sun was low in the sky, just kissing the treetops on the far side of the river, and by the time she reached the city outskirts, it had dissolved into a lavender dusk. Porch lights were just coming on over rickety wooden porches and cracked walkways. As she turned onto the main street, the buildings straightened out, with brick façades and refurbished accents. She looked around in surprise. What was she doing here? She slowed down as she approached Peter's shop, then put her foot to the accelerator at the sight of the dark windows. What was she thinking? Peter wouldn't be able to help her. He didn't even know half her story. She looked at her watch and turned toward home. She'd have a bath, fix a nice dinner, and wait for Zoe to call.

The drive home through the dark soothed Marina's nerves, and she felt almost peaceful as she walked into the house, but at the sight of the message light flashing, a rush of adrenaline set them on edge again.

Zoe's voice filled the kitchen. Her voice was hard. "Mom, it's me. I'm glad you aren't there. I don't want to talk to you. I'm staying here at Sasha's. You should go to Florence because I'm not coming home anytime soon." There was a pause. "Besides, don't you think you have something to tell your *good friend* Sarah?"

The following morning, Marina made her way to Lydia's as soon as she saw the school bus go by. She had talked to Lydia the previous night, but neither she nor June could induce Zoe to come to the phone.

"She says she has nothing more to say to you. I'm sorry, Marina," Lydia had said. "Why don't you come over first thing, after the girls have left for school, and we'll try and figure things out."

Over their first cup of coffee, Marina told Lydia that Zoe wanted her to go to Florence.

Lydia put a plate of cinnamon toast on the table between them. "Maybe she has a point."

"What! Go off and leave her here? You're kidding!"

"I think Zoe's serious about not going home right now, and I don't think you'll achieve anything by forcing her, if that's even possible. I think she just needs more time. She was going to be staying with us anyway. So why not go to Florence and do the conference. It's a huge honor. You're only away five days, and maybe the time away will help you, too."

Marina nodded. "It is an honor, and I'd hate to miss it." Her nod became a shake. "But I don't know if I could even focus enough to deliver my talk. Besides, what kind of mother leaves her child during a crisis?"

"It's not as if you're abandoning her. She'll be with us, we're her family, and you can trust us to do the right thing."

"I know I can. Thank you. I don't know, I'll think about it. Maybe she'll talk to me tonight." Marina pushed herself away from the table and walked over to the French doors, where she stood with her arms crossed, looking out into the garden. Lydia had large perennial beds on either side of the yard that in early summer were the talk of the county but which now lay dormant, bedded down with hay. Without turning around, Marina said, "You know what else she said? She told me to tell Sarah the truth."

Lydia had just put a piece of toast in her mouth and choked a little. "She said *that?*"

Marina turned around and walked to the end of the table. "Actually, she didn't say it that nicely."

Lydia finished her piece of toast. "I know you don't want to hear this, but maybe you don't have a choice, maybe you won't be able to move on with Zoe if you don't resolve things with Sarah."

"How will telling Sarah change anything for Zoe? What happened, happened. Besides, Zoe is still going to go on hating me for depriving her of the time with her father."

"You'll figure that out as you go along, but telling Sarah is not just for Zoe. Are you even aware of how much your guilt eats you up? For God's sake, Marina, you won't even let yourself have a relationship."

"I have relationships." Marina glared at Lydia.

"No, you don't. You're a serial dater. As soon as someone gets too close, you break it off. You use your work and Zoe as a shield. Anyway, you haven't even dated in a couple of years."

Marina smacked the flat of her hand on the table. "Why are you saying this? Don't I have enough on my plate right now?"

Lydia leaned forward in her chair, her hands on the table. "I'm saying this because I care about you. It makes me sad to see you stuck in this half lie—half life."

Marina threw her hands in the air. "Who the hell are you to pass judgment on my life? You think *you* have the model family?"

"I'm not saying that. I'm just calling it like I see it. Maybe you could have gone on like this and Zoe would have been none the wiser, but the fact is, it's all fallen apart." Lydia's voice rose and she jabbed her finger in Marina's direction. "And you have to fix it."

"So I should tell Sarah? I should hurt her just to clear my conscience?"

"This isn't about Sarah's feelings. You have to put Zoe first. Sarah will handle it in her own way."

Marina shook her head from side to side. "She'll never forgive me."

"Maybe, maybe not. There's nothing you can do about that." When Marina didn't respond, Lydia went on. "Think about it. It's bad enough that you have to carry this lie, but if you don't tell Sarah, then you're asking Zoe to carry it, too."

CHAPTER 13

The plane was full, the cabin dark except where narrow circles of light illuminated those too restless to sleep. Marina shuffled the papers in her lap, put them back in the manila folder, and tucked them into the seat pocket. She couldn't concentrate on her presentation with every thought finding its way back to Zoe. After leaving Lydia's, she'd driven down to the river to a clearing she and Zoe had found years ago while out on a walk. At the center of the clearing, a fallen tree trunk was shielded by low-lying bushes, which allowed the person in the clearing the advantage of seeing without being seen. She sat on the tree trunk, wrestling with her resistance until the sun was high, and she'd come to the conclusion that Lydia was right. It wasn't fair to ask Zoe to carry her lies. She would have to tell Sarah the truth.

Marina switched off the reading light, raised the window shade, and looked out into the bruised purple night sky. There were no stars in sight, not a single one to guide her or wish upon. Zoe had refused to see her before she left, but Marina asked Lydia to extract a promise from Zoe that she would sit down and talk to her mother upon her return. At the Albany airport, she'd hugged Lydia tight, then handed her a note, asking her to make sure that Zoe read it. She'd labored over it for almost two hours, distilling two pages of rambling down to a few lines of essential information.

> *My darling Zoe,*
> *There is no way you can know how utterly devastated and sorry I am to have hurt you so deeply. Just know that you are the best thing that ever happened to me, that I love you more than anything in the world, and that I will find a way for us to get through this. Please call me if you want to talk while I'm away. Lydia has the number. XXXXXX, MOM*

Marina adjusted the pillow behind her neck. Clearly, the only way out of this mess was to move forward, and the only way forward seemed to be back. She closed her eyes and asked herself the question she'd never been able to answer: Why hadn't she stopped Thomas that afternoon? She *should* have, absolutely. There was no doubt. But *could* she have stopped him? She'd gone over and over this point and always came to the same conclusion, that she'd been too drunk to resist. But there remained a tiny voice somewhere in the recesses of her mind that whispered doubt. She couldn't shake the uncertainty any more than she could remember what happened after finishing in the tub, other than being on the daybed, at first cold, then warm, then confused. She imagined sitting across from Sarah at a café, a wasteland of coffee-stained cups and crumbled biscotti between them, trying to explain that she had been drunk and confused, that it was *she,* Sarah, not Thomas, she had been in love with. But did that make any difference? It didn't change what she'd done.

She shifted in her seat and rested her forehead on the icy window. One giant eye stared back at her. She took a deep breath and exhaled and, closing her eyes, focused on the numbing sensation as it spread across her skull.

*   *   *

Marina scanned the hotel lobby, an austere expanse of marble punctuated by clusters of oddly designed, oversized armchairs. She would have preferred a small *pensione,* something reminiscent of her first weeks in Florence sixteen years earlier, but Josh had booked the rooms for the entire American contingent, and evidently they rated five-star treatment. In the far corner, sitting under a lush palm, a young woman in jeans and a bulky red sweater stared at her. What did she see? A middle-aged woman in a gray pantsuit and camel-hair coat, a tourist perhaps? Marina smiled at the girl, hoping to convey that once she had been just like her—young, carefree, on the brink of an adventure—but the girl looked away.

"Signora?"

Marina turned to the receptionist, who indicated where to sign the registration card. "Signora"? When had she ceased being a "signorina"? She accepted the large brass key with a silk tassel and followed the bellman to her room. Josh had gone all out. The room was sumptuous, with a plush burgundy carpet and gold brocade draperies. The heavy door muffled the sounds of the hotel around her. She crossed to the window and peered down into the street, where shops were just opening up for the evening hours. She looked at the bed longingly but decided it might be better to stay up and get in sync with the local time. If she took a nap now, she might be up all night. She checked the phone to see if there were any messages, hoping against hope for a call from Zoe, but there were none. She had told Lydia to have Zoe call her any time of the day or night, whenever she wanted to talk. But what if she didn't ever want to talk to her? What if Zoe refused to see her when she returned? What if Zoe decided she'd rather live with June and Lydia? Marina picked up the phone, asked for an outside line, and dialed Lydia's number, only to reach the answering machine. She left a short message, saying that she'd arrived safely, sent her love, and would call the next day. She walked back to the window and looked out just as the young woman from the lobby exited the hotel. Marina grabbed her coat and bag and hurried from the room.

Outside, traffic buzzed, kicking up exhaust and pigeons. Marina stopped short, familiar sights, sounds, and sensations jostling her as pedestrians flowed toward the end of their day. Her eyes smarted, whether from fatigue, fumes, or emotion, she wasn't sure. Just ahead, the girl from the hotel crossed the road and disappeared down a side street. The next wave of foot traffic uprooted Marina, carrying her forward on its current in the direction the girl had taken. She followed, dodging motorbikes and dog excrement, her eyes seeking out glimpses of denim and red. The narrow streets, lined with cafés and shops, redolent with memories, distracted her until she found herself at the river just in time to see the girl disappear over the crest of the bridge. Marina quickened her pace, but halfway across the bridge, she slowed down and stopped. What was she doing? Who was she chasing? What was she after? She looked upriver toward the Ponte Vecchio, where the tiny cantilevered shops still clung to the old bridge, the same flat-faced ocher buildings stood sentinel along either side of the river, and stone towers rose above rooftops as they had sixteen years ago and for centuries before that. How was it possible that so much in her world had changed while everything here had remained the same? She looked over the side of the bridge, where a large, gnarled root-ball was caught on one of the footings, the water flowing smoothly, heedlessly, around it, and all at once she felt bone weary and in need of food and sleep.

She retraced her steps to the hotel and kept her eyes forward, allowing only fragments of familiar images—shiny brass name plates and door knockers, multicolored fruit tarts, hand-hewn stone—to penetrate her peripheral vision. It was all she could handle for the moment. There would be time enough tomorrow to take it all in.

How odd it felt to stay in a luxury hotel, somehow disloyal to the simple student she'd once been. Hadn't she walked past pricey restaurants and hotels like this and looked disdainfully at the tourists, the invaders of her city? But the fourth-floor hallway, with its thick carpet and flocked wallpaper, was a welcome relief from the world outside, where the past and present converged in a maelstrom of sensations that left her wrung out.

She took the room key from her bag and let herself in. The bed beckoned. Sleep. She needed sleep. A glass of Chianti and a plate of pasta from room service might be just the right sleep aid. She shed her coat, pulled off her boots, and was reaching for the phone when she noticed the flashing message button, mute but insistent, and her heart lifted at the thought of hearing Zoe's voice.

It was Sarah's voice, though, that filled the room. "Hi, it's me. I can't believe you're here. Where are you? Maybe you're with the Uffizi people. Anyway, meet me for lunch tomorrow if you can. I'll be in Piazza Santa Croce at twelve thirty. Can't wait to see you. Ciao." Marina played the message twice more, trying to figure out why Sarah's voice sounded so strange, not at all the way she remembered, then she realized she'd never heard her voice over the phone. Thomas hadn't liked the intrusiveness of the telephone.

Marina curled up on the satin comforter and pulled a pillow over her head, giving up on thoughts of food or drink as she realized that a part of her, a big part, had hoped her letter would go missing and Sarah would never know she was here.

Marina woke feeling rested just after dawn, and following a long, hot shower, decided to eschew room service for a walk and coffee at a café. Outside, pint-sized sanitation vehicles scurried along the curbs and spewed water as Marina crossed into the Piazza della Repubblica and stopped in front of the Gilli café. The lights were on inside and a waiter in a yellow jacket and black tie swept the sidewalk out front. When he saw her, he bowed slightly and said, *"Buongiorno."* Marina smiled but turned away, not ready for an exchange in

Italian or the price of their coffee. Instead she walked in the opposite direction, toward the river again, stopping for a cappuccino and pastry at a small bar on a side street. In the old days, she'd have stood at the bar as she had every morning at the café on the corner of Via Luna, but she felt self-conscious in her tailored trousers and long wool coat, and sat instead at a small table and watched the bartender banter with his patrons over their morning shots of espresso. When she was finished, there was still an hour before the opening presentation of the conference, and she decided to get some exercise.

As she walked along the river in the direction of the Cascina Park, familiar landmarks drifted peripherally in and out. Across the river, the small cupola of Santo Spirito was just visible over the rooftops, the tower of Bellosguardo on the hill beyond that, and just up ahead, the Stars and Stripes fluttered above the entrance to the embassy. Memories assailed her, and she felt herself in a sort of purgatory, no longer belonging to the past but not yet fully in the present. In front of the Grand Hotel, a group of well-heeled tourists boarded a luxury sightseeing bus, and she had the sudden urge to climb aboard and join their adventure, one she imagined might be far simpler and much less stressful than hers promised to be.

When she reached the gates of the Cascina, Marina stopped and looked down the majestic, tree-lined avenue that led into the heart of the park, once a vast Medici estate and game reserve. On their first outing together, Sarah had brought her here to experience the Festival of the Cricket. It had been an inordinately beautiful spring day and the park had been overflowing with families who'd come to enjoy the festivities that marked the celebration of Ascension Day. The avenue had been lined with stalls selling food and sweets, and Marina had heard music coming from some other part of the park. Sarah had taken her hand as if Marina were one of the children begging for a cricket, and pulled her to a display of small, brightly painted cages, each housing a chirping cricket. Sarah had explained that thousands of "lucky crickets" were sold on that day and were believed to bring good fortune to anyone who received one. Marina now wondered if she should have accepted Sarah's offer to buy her one that day, but at the time, with her new life in Florence stretched out before her, she could not have imagined feeling any luckier.

Marina found her way to the conference site at the Palazzo Vecchio, in the Salone dei Cinquecento, on the second floor. It was an enormous room, and forty rows of twenty chairs across barely covered a third of the vast floor space. Marina settled into the last row of chairs and looked up at the coffered ceiling some thirty feet above her head. It was made up of panels painted by Giorgio Vasari that depicted significant events in Florentine history. On the walls to her left and right, colossal paintings, again by Vasari, illustrated the wars against Siena and Pisa, while marble statues of naked Greek wrestlers lined the wall below them. On the dais in front of her, Josh sat with other dignitaries at a long table covered in red damask. Just behind them, a row of men in red and white medieval tunics, tights, and stocking caps lifted their trumpets, signaling the arrival of the mayor, who sported a green, red, and white sash across his chest.

Marina was surprised by the sense of pride that welled up in her and filled her eyes. Perhaps she had done some things in her life that were worthy of commendation rather than condemnation. Up until that moment, with all the chaos of the past weeks, she hadn't allowed herself to fully absorb the honor implicit in the invitation to participate in an event of this caliber. But her moment of self-congratulation was short-lived as a wave of panic washed over her at the thought of the speech she would be giving on the last day of the conference. Just the idea of standing at the podium and looking out on this great hall made her doubt that she had anything of value to share. She had the camouflage of technical language to hide behind when she talked about her craft, but would anyone be interested in the evolution of one woman's career? Josh had specifically asked her to talk about her work and life as encouragement for the neophytes in the audience, but looking around now, she wasn't so sure. The audience seemed to be made up of mostly middle-aged people who were probably well established in their careers and not in need of inspiration.

At the end of the morning, she tried to get Josh's attention, but he was whisked off to an anteroom from where he would most likely go on to a VIP luncheon, so she didn't linger. She headed toward Santa Croce, taking Via de' Neri, the street where Amir had had his apartment, at number fifteen, if she remembered correctly, but standing across from it, she couldn't be sure if it was the right doorway or not. She had often wondered what had become of him after the expulsion of the Shah and the rise of the ayatollahs. She didn't imagine he'd fled the country, since he'd only just returned to care for his aging parents, but neither could she envision him living under such an oppressive regime.

It was just before noon when Marina stepped inside the church of Santa Croce, the vast interior opening before her, its graceful Gothic arches reaching heavenward. In contrast to the mild day outside, the church was icy cold and damp. She hesitated, then moved forward, stopping at the first supine figure in the floor. Her breath came in frosty puffs. She stared down at the form pushing up through the marble floor until the memory of milky water against her skin made her shiver. She moved on toward the front of the church, past Michelangelo's tomb, then Galileo's, carefully watching where she stepped. The altar had not changed, although a more substantial wooden barrier now stood in place of the velvet ropes—perhaps an effort to keep greasy fingerprints off the gilding. While Florence had much grander, more ornate examples of gilding, this one held a special place in her heart.

She stood for a moment recalling that early morning, stocking-footed visit, the cool gilded patina beneath her fingers, the beating of her heart, and for the second time that day, her pride swelled and she allowed herself a moment of recognition for all her hard work. Today, however, she wanted to see the Cimabue crucifix, which had finally been restored and reinstalled in the church museum in her absence. She'd first seen it at age fourteen in two photographs—one of six mud-covered men carrying it from the church, and another showing it receiving a blessing from the Pope after it had been all but destroyed by the flood.

She found the massive crucifix in the last gallery of the museum, where it hung suspended from cables that she assumed could raise it up in the event of flooding. While the concept of sin and redemption as handed down by the Church in the name of an almighty male entity kept her from identifying herself as a Christian, she was drawn in by the rounded hips and belly of this Christ, the feminine, almost coy, positioning of the legs, and the subdued coloring and spare gilding. It appealed to her sense of simplicity. She stood admiring the work, then, remembering why she was there, hurried back through the church.

Standing at the top of the steps, Marina looked across to the piazza, its stone surface pitted and polished from centuries of footsteps, her own included. A group of ragtag boys in dirty sweatshirts played soccer, scattering pigeons as they ran. Marina surveyed the piazza, her hand shading her eyes against the midday sun. Then she saw her.

Sarah sat on a stone bench at the edge of the square, her hair brilliant against the bright green of a small three-wheeled truck parked behind her. If it hadn't been for the red hair, Marina might have missed her in the quiet beige coat and leather boots. She was talking to an elderly man, who, with his neatly clipped goatee, tweed jacket, and felt hat, looked like a character from a Bertolucci film. Stooped by age or in an effort to hear her, he leaned with both hands on a cane, nodding his head at Sarah's words. She sat with her back erect, one hand on the old man's arm. Even from a distance, Marina sensed something different about her friend, something beyond the surprisingly staid ensemble or the elegant handbag on the bench beside her. Apprehension uncoiled in her belly, at first hot, then cold, as the Sarah she'd held in her mind for so long, the Sarah of carefree colors and bright baubles and beads, disintegrated. How could she not have anticipated this? After all, Sarah was a woman whose world had been shattered, who had had to create a new life for herself, and evidently, a new image. But rather than compassion, Marina felt outrage. Was she supposed to expose herself, her shame, her regret to this stranger—this middle-aged, middle-class woman?

Marina turned back toward the church, looking for a place to hide. Wasn't there a rear exit through the gift shop? She couldn't remember. She glanced back just as Sarah shook her head in that old, familiar, futile attempt to rearrange her hair. Marina froze, one foot in the past, one in the future. The old man turned and moved slowly away as Sarah waved to him in that funny, beckoning gesture that had once so confounded Marina. Then, as if she sensed Marina's presence, Sarah turned and looked directly at her.

Marina was never able to say how she made it down the steps and across the square into Sarah's arms.

"My God, you smell exactly the same!" she exclaimed with some relief into Sarah's tangle of hair as they hugged.

Sarah held her at arm's length. "And you *look* exactly the same. I can't believe it." She pulled Marina over to the bench. "Come, sit for a moment."

Marina sat down beside her and found herself suddenly at a loss for words. Her heart squeezed. It seemed only yesterday that they had sat in this spot deciding where to go for lunch, inevitably ending up at Anita's. But within that compression of time lay an expanse Marina was not sure how to cross.

"Look at you. All grown up but without a wrinkle in sight." Sarah laughed the familiar, throaty laugh that had always seemed to belong to a person much older, more serious, but which now seemed, finally, to fit. At fifty, she was as beautiful as ever in spite of, or perhaps because of, the lines around her mouth and eyes that in sixteen years had matured from finely etched to engraved. Sitting next to her, Marina felt very young, and any illusions she might have had about this meeting, about her ability to control its outcome, faded into uncertainty.

"Are you hungry?" Sarah asked.

Marina nodded.

"Shall we go to Anita's? She's excited to see you."

Marina knew she'd end up at Anita's sooner or later but wasn't ready for it quite so soon. "Do you mind if we don't just yet. I mean, I want to, but . . ." She wasn't sure how to put it, not knowing exactly what her reluctance was.

"Too much, too soon?"

"Maybe. It just feels so strange to be here. Everything looks the same, but I'm . . . not." She smiled. "Not that I want to be twenty-three again."

"It *must* be strange after all this time. Now you're an adult, a mother, a successful businesswoman." Sarah paused and looked out across the piazza. "I know what you mean about Anita's. After Thomas was killed, I didn't go back there either, not for a long time. But Anita's like family to me, and in the end, I had to, and it wasn't as bad as I thought it would be. It was sad, of course, but comforting, too. You may feel the same way."

Marina wasn't too sure about finding it comforting, but replied, "Of course I want to go. Maybe tomorrow."

Sarah stood up. "Okay, it's a date. Right now, how about we grab a *panino* and go for a walk."

After choosing mozzarella and tomato sandwiches from a nearby bar, Marina suggested they walk by Sauro's old workshop even though it no longer existed. She knew from Josh, who still consulted with Sauro from time to time, that he'd moved his workshop to the suburbs after his father and grandfather died. Sarah confirmed that rents had gone up astronomically and the new traffic regulations that restricted access to the historic center made it difficult for artisans who needed to move furniture or worked with bulky supplies.

They turned down the street Marina had walked daily during her apprenticeship, but after a few yards, she stopped. "Wait a minute." She looked at Sarah. "Wasn't it right here?"

Sarah nodded.

Marina stared at the sign that filled the space above the door. Stylized soap bubbles foamed up around the name Wash and Dri. At least, she thought, they could have given it some snappy Italian name, one they could spell correctly.

She peered in the window at the rows of shiny washers and dryers. "Wow, I used to have to drag my bag of clothes to the *lavanderia* around the corner from Via Luna and pray that those old ladies wouldn't shrink the hell out of everything."

"These Laundromats have sprouted up all over town in the last year or so. It's actually a good thing. We needed them."

Marina stood for another minute, her mind in another time, the scent of wood shavings, lacquer, and wax filling her nostrils, the light percussion of a hammer and chisel echoing through the workshop, Sauro's reassuring hand on her shoulder.

Sarah interrupted her reminiscence. "Do you want to go by Via Luna?"

Marina had imagined she might go by the apartment at some point, if time permitted, but it was the place that held the most memories, and she wasn't sure she wanted Sarah with her. "Who's living there?" she asked in an effort to avoid the question.

Sarah shrugged. "I don't know. Marcella's parents sold it a number of years ago."

"How is Marcello?" Marina asked, following Sarah down the street.

"Well, he's a she, and her name is now Marcella, with an A."

"Oh my God, he went through with it?"

"No, not exactly, not all the way. He was going to though. He did the hormone therapy and the psychotherapy in preparation for a complete sexual makeover, but Carlo, the man he's involved with, didn't want him to go through with the operation. And really, you'd never know he wasn't a woman. He has breasts and soft skin. I don't know the intimate details of their relationship, but he's very happy, and I'm happy for him . . . her. She has a thriving business as a seamstress/ dress designer. She made this."

Sarah indicated her elegant outfit, beautifully draped trousers and a matching topcoat the color of sand, with cream trim and buttons.

"What's the fabric? It's beautiful," said Marina, rubbing it between her fingers.

"Silk and cashmere, I think. I don't ask. She makes it, I wear it."

Sarah recounted how it was Marcella who finally rousted her out of her mourning bed in the months after Thomas's death, and how when she'd refused to get dressed, complaining that all her clothes were too wild and colorful and made her feel crazy, it was Marcella who created a wardrobe of loose-fitting pants and tunic tops in a muted palette of solid colors. This uniform had served her well in her mourning period, providing a soothing cocoon in which to come back to life. To a new life.

"And as you see, all these years later, she's still dressing me."

Marina realized they were following a route similar to the one they had taken on their first visit to Via Luna so many years ago, and decided to let go of her reservations. She was enjoying her time with Sarah, and it seemed only fitting that they revisit the old neighborhood together. When they passed the flea market, Marina glanced at Sarah's left hand, but the strange ring she'd bought there and worn as a wedding band was gone.

"One man's junk, another man's treasure," murmured Sarah, slowing her pace as they threaded their way through the stalls.

"Thomas used to say that about the things he found in the street," Marina said without looking at Sarah. She had consciously been avoiding saying Thomas's name for fear it might unleash some torrent of confessional language, a Tourette's seizure of truth, but the joy she felt at being with Sarah again made her want to give something in return.

"Yes, he loved his nights of foraging. But I'll tell you, I was glad to see that junk go. I can't believe I lived with all his crap for as long as I did."

Marina didn't know if she was referring to something more than just his junk, but she'd never heard Sarah sound so bitter. Clearly more had changed than just her wardrobe. She stopped walking when Sarah wandered over to look in a window filled with costume jewelry, and watched as the Sarah on the sidewalk and the Sarah reflected in the glass tossed their hair in unison. She might have changed in many ways, ways that Marina couldn't yet see, but the Sarah she had known and loved was still very much there, as was the luminescence that had so attracted her in the first place.

As they walked on, Sarah asked about her life, her work, and of course, Zoe. "I have to say that you send me the worst photos of Zoe. I still don't really know what she looks like. Either she's in a Halloween costume, or the picture is out of focus, or overexposed. I guess you didn't learn as much from Thomas as I thought."

The mention of Zoe and Thomas in the same breath caught Marina off guard, as did the reference to her ploy with the photographs. "I . . . I guess I've just gotten sloppy."

Just then, someone called to Sarah from a shop doorway,

and when the conversation resumed, Marina changed the subject to Sarah's sculpting.

Sarah's face lit up and her gestures grew animated as she talked about her work. Again, it was Marcello (he changed his name to Marcell*a* after he grew breasts, Sarah offered as a sidebar) who had come to her rescue. In an attempt to draw her out of her melancholy, he began buying her art supplies, and for months they accumulated in piles around her apartment, until one day she picked up a piece of charcoal and began to draw.

"It was partly out of desperation to make him stop spending his money and partly because I couldn't resist. Everything was so beautiful! The pastels and pencils. He even bought me wax crayons. And there was paper stacked up all over the place in every size and texture you can imagine." Sarah sketched the invisible stacks with her hands. "It was all so luscious, irresistible. Thank God for Marcello! I don't know what would have become of me. *Really,* I don't."

It wasn't long before she was taking a sketchpad with her everywhere she went, then found herself spending more and more time sitting in the parks drawing the children. This soon led to drawing lessons at a small, private studio, until she felt ready to move on to sculpting, which was ultimately where she realized her full potential.

"I always knew that I wanted to sculpt. I think I told you that years ago. But I never dreamed it would take me so far, or that I'd end up with predominantly children as my subject. Maybe because I never had any of my own." Then she smiled. "But now I have more children in my life than I know what to do with."

Marina wasn't sure if she meant real children, the ones she used as models, or the sculptures themselves. Either way, the reference to children made her insides squirm.

They crossed the boulevard and made their way over to Marina's old neighborhood. The post office was still there, and the little department store, but the cheese shop had become an office supply store with all sorts of electronic gadgets in the window, and the wine shop was now a toy store. As they turned in under the archway that led to Via Luna, Marina glanced into the corner bar to see if there were any familiar faces, but nothing and no one looked the same.

Rounding the corner, she half expected to see her bike propped up against the wall where she'd left it. When she'd finally written Sarah to say she wasn't coming back, that she was pregnant, she'd asked her to get rid of everything in her apartment except her tools, which she wanted Sauro to have.

"Did I ever thank you for dealing with all the stuff I left behind? I'm sorry, it never occurred to me how much I was asking. It must have been a pain to get rid of all that stuff."

Sarah touched her arm. "I think you were probably overwhelmed with the pregnancy at the time. Besides, I asked Marcello to deal with it. I was too upset that you weren't coming back. It made my head spin how quickly everything changed, first you left so suddenly, then you weren't coming back."

The exterior of the apartment looked the same, with the exception of the old painted door, which had been replaced by a new one with a natural stain. Marina was disappointed to see flowered curtains in the kitchen window that blocked the only view they might have had of the interior. No one seemed to be around. They were standing in the spot where she'd first met Marcello, but it wasn't her first days there that Marina was thinking about; it was her final days.

Sarah had come to Marina's the day before she left to help her pack for her trip home. The apartment had been in complete disarray, not because any packing was going on, but because Marina hadn't picked up for days. It was all she could do to fulfill her obligations to Sauro. The rest of the time, if she wasn't crying, she was sleeping. The kitchen sink was full of dishes, crumbs littered the table and floor, a sour smell filled the air, and in the living room, the bed was unmade and clothes were strewn across the floor. The only semblance of order was in her workshop. If Sarah noticed anything amiss, she didn't comment. She knew Marina was upset about her father's illness. Sarah's visit put Marina into a panic, sure her friend would stumble upon some piece of incriminating evidence, something that might clue her in to Marina's disgraceful state, but of course, there was nothing to find. Sarah had simply set about doing the dishes while Marina made an attempt to create order, if not in her mind, then in her living room.

Sarah's help that day had turned out to be a blessing. Her tranquil demeanor had a calming effect on Marina, who was finally able to locate her passport and decide what she would need for a two-week trip home.

Now Sarah asked, "Do you remember your last morning here, before the cab arrived?"

Marina shook her head. "No, not really."

"I came to say good-bye. I wasn't going to. We'd said good-bye the night before. But something made me come again, and of course, now I'm glad I did. You cried and cried. I kept telling you that your father was going to be fine and that you'd be back in a flash."

Marina nodded. Of course she remembered. Of course she'd cried—she was twenty-three and pregnant by her best friend's husband.

Sarah looked up at the sky. "It's strange how things turned out. It never occurred to me that you wouldn't come back, that it would be the last time I'd see you."

"I know. I thought I'd be back. Then . . ." Marina's voice trailed off. *Now! Tell her the truth now!*

Sarah finished her thought. "Life happened."

Marina hesitated, then replied, "Yes, life happened. I'm sorry."

"Don't be sorry. It's not your fault. And look how beautifully it turned out with Zoe and your gilding business."

Marina shook her head, but Sarah had already turned and

was heading back down the street. What better segue into telling Sarah the truth about why she hadn't come back, and what better place than on the threshold of where it all began. But she'd only just found Sarah again—couldn't she have just a little more time with her?

Marina took a sip of wine, lay back in the tub, and looked around the hotel bathroom, every inch of it, including the Kleenex box, clad in white marble. She studied the glass chandelier overhead and wondered if she could get away with such an elegant fixture in her bathroom at home. She slid a little farther into the delicious water. Her time with Sarah that afternoon had felt so familiar, as if they'd seen each other just the week before. She hadn't imagined it would be so easy, so exhilarating. Certainly Sarah had changed, but for the better. She was now engaged with a much larger world than when she'd been married to Thomas, and she had the freedom to be whoever she wanted to be. She had a confidence that showed in the way she talked and carried herself, yet she'd managed to retain the soft hazy edges she'd always had. On their walk back to the center of town, Sarah told Marina a bit about her relationship with Sergio, who owned the gallery in Milan. It had been love at first sight on his part, and when Sarah balked at his attentions he'd waited patiently for Sarah to find her way back to love again. They took turns visiting each other, which seemed to work for them both. Sarah said she wasn't interested in marriage but liked having someone somewhere in the world who cared about her. She asked Marina about her love life and was confounded when she had nothing to report.

"I can't believe there's no one, Marina. You're a beautiful woman in the prime of her life!"

"I date. I've had a few relationships over the years." Marina didn't want to sound defensive, but she could hear it in her voice.

"You should move back here. The men would be lined up at your door." When Marina just laughed, Sarah said, "I'm serious. You should be married, having babies. Don't you think Zoe needs a father?"

Marina hated it when people started saying that Zoe needed a father, as if she was somehow lacking. Having a father wouldn't make Zoe any more brilliant or beautiful than she already was.

"She has a father figure in Peter. He's been around since she was a baby."

"That's your friend's brother, right?"

Marina nodded. "Lydia's brother."

"Any prospects there?"

"Actually, Zoe would love that. But he and I have been friends forever and I'd hate to jeopardize that."

Sarah had spent the rest of the walk grilling her about Peter and encouraging her to test the waters with him, and was so engrossed in the subject that she didn't turn off at her street, and ended up walking Marina all the way back to her hotel.

Marina finished off her wine and let the water out of the tub. She'd never understood why people insisted on playing matchmaker, which in her experience never turned out well. Or why they got so excited when people "found each other." Aside from Lydia and June, she hadn't seen too many healthy relationships or even unions where both people were happy and fulfilled. Right now she'd be happy and fulfilled if she found an outfit to wear to the reception.

Forty-five minutes later, she was dressed and ready for her evening. Except for shoes. Her outfit, black wool pants and an ivory silk shirt, left her two choices for footwear: elegant black suede mules, which she loved and rarely had an opportunity to wear, or her black boots with the low heel and pointed toe. If she wore the mules, she'd have to take a taxi, since she was barely able to keep them on just walking across a room, and she wanted to walk to the reception at the Accademia. There was nothing she loved more than the early evening hours in this city, when housewives finished up their suppertime shopping, workmen stopped for a coffee or *aperativo* on their way home, and shopkeepers hauled in their wares from the sidewalks in front of their shops. She took one last look at herself in the mules, then kicked them off and pulled on the boots.

It was just as she remembered—the smell of exhaust, the hubbub of cars and pedestrians, buses disgorging people into the dusk—and for a moment, she tasted the bittersweetness she sometimes experienced watching people head home to warm hearths and loving arms. Perhaps Lydia was right, maybe she *should* be more open to having a relationship. And what if Zoe was right about Peter? Everyone seemed to know more about what was right for her these days than she did.

She made her way around the Duomo, craning her neck to take in every inch of its pink and green grandeur, its overwhelming mass still confounding her. She headed toward Piazza San Marco and found the entrance of the Accademia di Belle Arti, home to Michelangelo's *David*. The guard at the door inspected her invitation, then directed her to the main gallery, where the reception was just getting under way. She wished Lydia could see this—people milling around, chatting, holding glasses of champagne under the youthful gaze of a giant, stark-naked man holding a slingshot. Lydia might not be into men, but she'd appreciate the humor in it. Marina spied Josh in a small cluster of people on the other side of the room and made her way over to him.

"There you are! How wonderful to see you, my dear." Josh gave her a warm hug.

Marina smiled and squeezed him in return. The way he spoke made her want to belong to another era, one where women wore dresses during the day, handbags and shoes that matched, and didn't consider themselves dressed without hats and gloves—a time when women knew what was expected of them.

"This is quite the setting you have for your cocktail party," Marina said, looking around the room.

Josh chuckled and held up his glass in a toast. "It pays to know the right people."

Josh stayed at her side for almost an hour, introducing her to other presenters and conference patrons, whose names she recognized from trade journals and many of whom seemed to know each other from other events or projects, and it made her realize how isolated she was in her work. She really must take Josh's advice and get out more, go to other conferences. If it weren't for him, she never would have been invited to this one. Once again she wondered if her presentation would make the grade. She'd be both devastated and embarrassed if she disappointed him. She imagined herself at the podium, terrified, mute, her mind blank. Panic uncoiled itself in her belly, and Marina excused herself to search for a bathroom. She could see the fatigue in her face as she reapplied her lipstick, and knew that if she didn't get some sleep, her fears would get the better of her and self-doubt would overwhelm her.

As she made her way back down the great hall in search of Josh, she caught sight of a familiar silhouette. With her heart pounding, she circled around to get a better look. Yes, there was no mistaking the haughty stance of the contessa. Marina observed her from the shadow of a pillar and realized that the wretched woman must be well into her sixties, although she still had that sexy, predator air about her. Thin as a rail, she wore her hair, which was now more platinum than blond, in a French twist. As before, she was loaded with jewelry. Marina watched, fascinated. The last time she'd seen the contessa, she'd been brandishing a riding crop.

"What are you doing hiding over here?"

Marina jumped. "Josh, you startled me."

"Are you all right, my dear? You look a little pale."

"I'm fine. I just think the jet lag has caught up to me."

"Have you eaten anything? The *crostini* are delicious."

Marina shook her head. "I'm really not hungry. I think I need to go to bed and start fresh tomorrow."

"I was hoping you'd join me for dinner. A few of us are going to Leonardo's in a bit."

Marina knew what that meant. They'd be sitting down at nine thirty or ten o'clock, and she'd be lucky to get to bed by midnight. "I'm sorry, I have to beg off, Josh. I'll catch up with you tomorrow. Can we have lunch after the morning session?"

Josh pursed his lips and thought for a minute. "I'm afraid I can't manage lunch, but let's meet for tea after your corridor tour."

"My what?"

"The Vasari Corridor, the tour. It's on your itinerary."

Marina ran her fingers through her hair, pushing it off her forehead. "I'm sorry, Josh, I've just skimmed the itinerary. I . . ."

He patted her shoulder. "I understand, not to worry. But you mustn't miss a chance to tour the Vasari Corridor. It's rarely open to the public, and then only by appointment. You know of it, I'm certain."

Marina nodded. Thomas had told her about it. "Yes, of course."

"We've arranged a tour exclusively for those presenting at the conference. A perk, if you will."

They agreed to meet at Café Rivoire after the tour, then Marina kissed him on both cheeks and said good night.

Marina made herself stay up until ten o'clock in hopes of catching Zoe as soon as she got back from school.

Lydia picked up the phone on the second ring. "It's a great connection. You sound like you're calling from next door. But Zoe isn't home yet. She has photography club until six."

"Photography club?" This was news to Marina.

"She seemed really excited about it."

"Like father, like daughter. I suppose that's the point."

"Maybe."

"Do you think she'll talk to me? She'll be home for dinner, right? I could set the alarm for one A.M."

The line was quiet for a moment, and then Lydia said, "Why don't you wait another day? I think she's still pretty riled up. And you sound tired. You probably need a good night's sleep."

Marina sighed. "What's she been saying?"

"It's not what she's saying. It's just her attitude. I don't think she's ready to talk. But you need to do what's right for you, Marina." She paused. "So, tell me how you are. How is it being there? Have you seen Sarah yet?"

"It's all so strange." Marina lay back on the pillows and stretched her legs out. "It's weird staying in a hotel. And it's unsettling not being who I used to be, not having my old life. It's like being in a time warp. I can't seem to connect."

"You've been gone a long time. You're a different person now."

"I am, and I'm not. I realized that today when I saw Sarah. We took a walk past where I used to work and ended up at my old apartment. It feels like the old part of me, the person I was sixteen years ago, is still *here*."

"Maybe you left so abruptly you left a part of yourself there."

"Well, it's not a part I'm feeling very proud of right now." Marina suddenly felt close to tears.

"Don't be so hard on yourself, Marina. You were young, and your circumstance was dire. Now, maybe you can find a way to make it right. How was Sarah?"

"The same, different but the same. We spent the afternoon together. It felt like we'd never been apart."

"How did you feel about her?"

Marina smiled into the phone. "You mean, did I fall madly in love with her?"

"Well . . ."

"Lydia, you are such a lezzie. No, I didn't fall in love with her, but I bet I could if I hung around long enough. She's still beautiful, and kind, and generous, and . . ."

Lydia laughed. "Okay, okay. Just checking."

"Look, I've got to get some sleep. I'm not going to set the alarm, but if I wake up in the night, I might call, if it's not too late over there. But I'll definitely call tomorrow night. So see if you can prime Zoe for me, okay?"

CHAPTER 14

The next morning Marina woke to find that she had over-
slept and scarcely had enough time to shower, dress, and
make it to the Palazzo Vecchio before the first presentation.
She slipped into the back row just as the first speaker was introduced. Even with a screen full of colorful flow charts, the
topic of budgeting for conservation was a dull one, important but dull, and it wasn't long before she regretted skipping
her morning coffee. She barely made it to the midmorning
break without falling asleep and was the first one to reach the
refreshments at the back of the hall, where a long table
draped in white damask was laden with tumblers of bloodred
orange juice, shots of dark espresso, and an array of glistening pastries. Two cups of coffee and a pastry later, Marina
settled in for the next speaker and a much more promising
topic: new developments in underpainting for both canvas
and wood. Although it wasn't her field of expertise, experience had taught her that when it came to conservation, there
was always something to be learned from the other disci-
plines, and she often picked up ideas on tools or techniques
she could apply to gilding.

During the next break between speakers, Marina stretched

her legs by walking along the perimeter of the room and taking a closer look at the statuary. Each sculpture incorporated two naked men wrestling, limbs intertwined, muscles bulging. She looked at the placard on one of the pedestals that mentioned Hercules and the name of an artist she didn't recognize. Clearly, Hercules was the one who seemed to have the upper hand in each configuration, save one, where his opponent had him by the balls—literally. She cocked her head to one side and contemplated the men, one upside down, locked in Hercules' massive arms and about to be thrown headfirst to the ground, except that Hercules (who was standing upright) was in a bit of a fix. What can you do when someone has a viselike grip on your genitals? She couldn't tell if these were just boyish antics—after all, the ancient Greeks were known for liking all manner of male sport—or if it was a fight to the death.

She sat back down for the final presentation on stone inlay, and wondered what the room looked like from the vantage point of the podium. Would the size of the room be intimidating? Would she be able to concentrate on her talk with naked men wrestling at her feet? The final hour flew by, and just as Marina was beginning to feel the gnawing of hunger, the speaker finished and they were released for lunch.

She found a café behind the Uffizi Gallery and, not wanting to sit another minute, stood at the bar to eat her prosciutto and arugula *panino,* washing it down with a glass of sparkling Pellegrino. She then left the burble of lunchtime conversations behind and headed toward the river embankment. Once there, Marina rested her elbows on the wall and looked out at the opposite bank, where the cluster of ocher buildings stood out in sharp relief against the blue sky. Twenty feet below her, a grassy embankment sloped down to the river, where a group of young men were preparing rowing sculls for launch. A stone ramp led from the dock, up the embankment, then disappeared below her. She leaned out as far as she could, craning her neck until she saw an opening below her, which, considering the number of boats being hauled in and out, must house an extensive storage area. Thomas had often said there were more surprises under the city than one might imagine. Thomas . . . Since the day she arrived, whenever his ghost rode by on a moped or waved to her from a doorway, she'd turned her mind away and focused her thoughts on something else, something that didn't have to do with him. But it wasn't easy, woven as he was into the fabric of the city, of her history there, and whether she wanted to admit it or not, her life with Zoe. Closing her eyes, she turned her face to the sun and let him in.

Marina had not seen Thomas since the dinner with Sarah shortly after the bathtub shoot, and as the opening of his show approached, she steeled herself for another encounter. There was no way around it. Only hospitalization or death would excuse her attending. Her only hope was to make a quick appearance and pray that Thomas would be just as happy to keep his distance from her as she from him.

She dressed carefully in the same outfit she'd worn on Christmas, although the skirt was slightly snug in the waist and she had to let the belt out a notch. Turning sideways to the mirror, she tried to decide if her belly looked any fatter. She didn't think so but pulled on a long cardigan just in case.

Sarah was at the front door of the gallery and gave Marina a hug when she saw her. "You look gorgeous, you're glowing. This is your big night!" She waved her hand at the fateful bathtub image, now a full-sized poster set up on an easel by the door. "Everyone's commenting on it."

Marina shook her head as if to ward off any attention that might come her way. The smaller posters had been in shop windows around town, and she'd felt exposed all over again each time she saw one. She was relieved when two couples came in behind her and Sarah sent her off to have a drink and admire the exhibition. With her head down, she headed to the bar, where she gulped half a glass of wine before turning to look at the scene. It was much the same as the year before: the crowd, the smoke, the wine; only the photographs were different. At the back of the gallery, Thomas, surrounded by the usual entourage of admirers and hangers-on, stood with the contessa. The only nod he'd given to the fact that this was a special occasion was the crumpled corduroy blazer he'd added to his usual ensemble of open-collared shirt and jeans. It didn't surprise Marina that Sarah wasn't able to get Thomas into better clothes, but she wondered why the contessa didn't exert her influence in this area. The contessa, on the other hand, looked as elegant as before, in a bloodred pantsuit perfectly fitted to her narrow frame, from the wide padded shoulders to the flared pant leg. The same cascade of blond hair fell down her back, this time held in place by a wide black headband.

All week, in anticipation of this night, Marina had fantasized about confronting Thomas, of shaming him in front of his fans, maybe even exposing his pornographic exploits with the contessa. But looking at him now, she knew he had no shame. It was right there in the arch of his brow, the set of his jaw, the purse of his lips, and she could just imagine the contessa's throaty laugh dismissing her as easily as she might throw a cigarette butt from a car window. Marina's stomach churned. She looked away and moved to a wall of photographs, which she stared at but didn't see, the rise and fall of conversation and laughter at her back. What was she doing here? She blinked back tears and forced herself to look at the photographs. All of them involved images of stone, either people painted to look like stone or actual statuary from around the city. They were clever and beautiful, but nowhere near the caliber of the bathtub photograph. Before moving to the next wall of photographs, she again scanned the crowd. Sarah was still busy at the door, but when she looked to the rear of the room, Thomas was staring straight at her as if he'd been biding his time, waiting for her to look his way. His face didn't register the slightest emotion—he neither smiled nor frowned, but raised his wineglass to her in a silent, expressionless toast. Marina turned away in a sudden panic and bumped smack into Marcello, whose red wine splashed across the front of her skirt.

He grabbed Marina's shoulder to steady her. "Marina, I'm so sorry. Please excuse me."

"No, no, it's nothing. It was my fault." Marina brushed the front of her skirt with her hand.

"Your beautiful skirt. Come with me." He took her arm and guided her to the bar, where he asked for a wet cloth and proceeded to blot Marina's skirt in spite of her protestations. Finally he stood up. "There, that's much better."

Marina smiled. "Thank you, Marcello. It's fine. It was my fault."

Marcello was not in drag this time, but with his porcelain skin, long eyelashes, and lustrous hair pulled back into a low ponytail, he could almost pass as a woman. He wore a fitted white shirt tucked into skintight, burgundy velvet jeans. He smiled back at her. "Thomas has made you famous. Everyone is talking about your photograph."

Marina laughed nervously. "I hope people don't know it's me."

"You should be proud."

Proud was the last thing that Marina felt. She chatted with Marcello about some of the other photographs before she excused herself and made her way over to Sarah, who was just finishing a conversation with an elegant, older couple. She tapped Sarah on the shoulder.

Sarah's face was flushed and the hair around her face stood out in damp ringlets. "Whew, who knew greeting people was such hard work. I must be out of practice. But I think I'm about done. Everyone's here, more or less." She glanced around the room. "I see the contessa still has Thomas in her clutches."

Marina didn't follow Sarah's gaze. "Sarah, I don't . . ."

At the same time, Sarah asked, "Isn't the show great?"

Marina nodded. "It looks like it's a big hit." She touched Sarah's arm. "Look, I'm sorry, but I can't stay."

"What? Why not? I was hoping you'd join us for dinner."

"I know, I'm sorry. But I called my mother this afternoon and I have to go."

"Oh my God." Sarah put her hand over her mouth. "I'm so sorry. I forgot to ask how your father was."

When Marina had realized she couldn't turn to either Thomas or Sarah for help, she'd fabricated a tale about her father needing an operation that might require her to make an emergency trip home. Her plan was to visit her parents, have an abortion, and then return to Florence and pick up where she'd left off.

"He's doing fine, but my mom wants me home. She's bought me a ticket for the day after tomorrow. I really need to get going, I have so much to do before then, and I haven't even told Sauro yet."

"But you have to eat. Come out with us and I'll come and help you pack tomorrow."

"No, really, I'm not feeling that great. I don't think I'd be good company right now."

Sarah put her arm around Marina's shoulder. "You're always good company. But I understand. I'm just being selfish. Of course you should go and do what you need to and I'll check in with you tomorrow."

Marina looked over Sarah's shoulder as they hugged good-bye, but Thomas was nowhere in sight.

For years she'd thought back on that night and wondered what would have happened if she had confronted Thomas, but in the end, it always came down to the same thing—not hurting Sarah.

The sculls were now gracefully skimming back and forth on the river, each rower balanced and in perfect unison with the others. How did they do that, remain perfectly balanced on something that looked so unstable? She checked her watch and, seeing it was almost time for the tour, headed back toward the Palazzo Vecchio.

Vasari himself met their small group in the courtyard of the Palazzo Vecchio. He was dressed in full fourteenth-century garb made up of a tunic, tights, and a black velvet hat set at a rakish angle on his head. Marina groaned inwardly but dutifully followed along as he shepherded them next door to the Uffizi Gallery and through its west wing, passing the works of Botticelli, Caravaggio, da Vinci, Titian, Filippo Lippi, and others. When they reached the second floor, he led them to an impressive doorway through which they descended a wide, stone stairway, thus entering the Corridor proper. The Corridor was surprisingly wide, which, according to Mr. Vasari, was to accommodate the horses that the resident nobility rode through the passageway rather than mingle with commoners at street level. As they went along, he gave a running commentary on the paintings that lined the Corridor, predominantly from the Medici collection and rarely seen by the public. They traversed the top of the arcade that ran parallel to the river, then took a sharp left over the Ponte Vecchio.

When they reached the midpoint over the apex of the bridge, they stopped in front of a large window. Mr. Vasari began a story about how Mussolini had used this window to keep an eye on things during his occupancy, but Marina was drawn to the opposite window, where she looked upriver to see the rowers still hard at work. The sound of the tourists on the bridge down below, as well as cars, buses, and mopeds traveling along the embankments, was barely audible through the stone and glass. How nice, she thought, to live so far removed from the confusion of everyday life. She'd worked hard to keep her life tidy, and in the process had created more chaos than she could ever have imagined. Behind her, the group began to move again.

At the end of the bridge, the Corridor narrowed, twisting its way around a tower, then continued along the front end of

Santa Felicita. Here it was possible to look down into the chapel from the Medici's private box (again, avoiding contact with the unwashed masses). From here they continued a short distance to where the Corridor ended, and exited through a small door into the Boboli Gardens. Marina stepped into the chilly shadow of the looming Pitti Palace and pulled her coat closer. She stood with the group as they milled around, gravel crunching underfoot, each waiting their turn to thank their guide for his time.

Marina checked her watch and saw that she still had time before her rendezvous with Josh to take a quick spin through the gardens. Now, barely a few weeks before Christmas, nature had stripped itself back to the bare essentials but remained starkly beautiful even without the embellishment of bright hues and textures. She chose a path at random and followed it to the amphitheater, its grass center still brilliant green against tiers of pewter stone. In spite of the sun, it was too chilly to sit, and she continued her meandering, past boxwood hedges, mammoth terra-cotta pots, elaborate fountains, and balustrades. For a moment, she imagined bringing Zoe here and the pleasure it would give her to share this magical city, but like a cloud moving across the sun, a question presented itself: Would she *want* to bring Zoe here when all was said and done? She couldn't imagine Sarah taking her news other than badly, leaving Florence forever an exquisite wound that would need to be left alone if it was ever to heal. She had not yet decided how or when to tell Sarah the truth, and had mixed emotions about their upcoming dinner at Anita's. She couldn't imagine laying it out on the table during dinner. As well, she wanted to catch up a bit more before risking a confrontation. Perhaps if they took a walk after dinner, she might broach the subject—a subject that might better be tackled under the cover of night.

Rivoire, the grande dame of Florentine cafés, rivaled only by the Caffè Gilli in Piazza della Repubblica, occupied the corner of Piazza della Signoria directly opposite the Palazzo Vecchio. The rich, warm scent of baked sugar greeted Marina as she stepped into the clatter of teacups and silver. Josh waved to her from the tearoom at the back of the café, where he'd secured a table by the window. Once he'd taken her coat and settled her into a chair with a view of the square, they ordered tea and cakes and relaxed into a discussion about the Corridor and, eventually, the conference itself. Josh was pleased with its progress and was eager to hear Marina's impressions.

She assured him that she was both impressed and enjoying every minute of it, but admitted to having a few nerves about her own presentation.

"I'm not sure that I should say too much about my career. I know you said it would be inspirational, but quite frankly, I haven't seen very many women in the audience who look like they need inspiration. Everyone seems so accomplished."

"Certainly there are many accomplished craftsmen in attendance, but there are fledglings in the audience, too. You are speaking on the fifteenth-century techniques as well, yes?"

Marina had just taken a bit of cake and nodded vigorously as she chewed, then swallowed. "Yes, absolutely. I will talk extensively about the evolution of the techniques, and I have slides to illustrate them. As I have it now, my own story brackets that information, and I was thinking that I could leave it off entirely."

"Absolutely not, my dear. You see, I've invited students from the Pitti and a number of the smaller studios to come and hear your talk. I dare say that for them your story will be the more inspiring part of your lecture."

Marina was dumbfounded. It never ceased to amaze her how much confidence Josh had in her abilities and to what extent he would go to support her. When she'd first opened her own workshop, he brought her work on a regular basis, and she'd always suspected that he sacrificed some of his own business for hers.

"Josh, I don't know what to say. You are too sweet for words. Thank you."

She could tell he was pleased, but he brushed her thanks aside. "Just give your talk as you wrote it, and I'm sure you'll be fine."

"I'll do my best. I just wish I'd ended up earlier on the roster so I'd have it behind me instead of ahead. The more presentations I hear, the more impressed I am, and the more insecure I feel."

Josh patted her hand. "I understand. It's difficult having to wait until the final day, but just try and let all that go and enjoy yourself. I know you'll do a splendid job. Are you staying on after it's over? Do you have friends to visit?"

"No." She hesitated. "No one. Actually, I'm leaving for the airport immediately after my presentation. I have a late-afternoon flight home. I need to get back to Zoe."

"That's a shame, but perhaps you'll bring her here some day. She's old enough to appreciate it, don't you think?"

By the time they left the café, twilight was settling over the city. Marina walked slowly in the direction of her hotel, admiring shop windows along the way, and was surprised to see so many she remembered from years ago. But what was sixteen years for a business that had been around for a hundred or so? She stopped at a window filled with gloves in more styles and colors than she could have imagined: plum suede, turquoise leather, red leopard, mink trimmed, hand stitched. Mesmerized, she entered the tiny shop, no wider than the window itself, the walls lined floor to ceiling with shallow drawers. For half an hour, she immersed herself in color and texture, coming away with gloves for everyone at home: black leather with fox trim for Lydia, tan cashmere-lined for June, dark brown kid for Ben, purple suede for Sasha, and bright blue suede for Zoe. At the last minute, she chose a pair of black fur-lined gloves for Peter to make up for not sending a postcard. The shopping spree finished, she hurried back to the hotel, where she had just enough time to freshen up before her dinner with Sarah.

Marina stood just inside the door wondering if she had made a mistake in agreeing to come to Anita's, but before she could reconsider, Anita was embracing her, then pulling her face down to kiss her firmly on both cheeks. The top of Anita's head, even in heels, barely reached Marina's chin.

"*Cara mia!*" Anita exclaimed, pinching Marina's cheeks and spewing high-speed exclamations and questions.

"See, it's not so bad being here," Sarah whispered as Anita led them to a table in the small back dining room that looked out on a deserted terrace where a few determined geraniums clung to gangly stalks in large terra-cotta pots.

"Are you all right?" Sarah touched Marina's arm. "Sit down."

Marina sat. "I can't quite take it all in. It's overwhelming. I mean, to be here where you and Thomas and I . . . I had such happy memories of this place. Isn't it hard for you to be here?"

"It was hard, of course it was, but it's been more than ten years. In the beginning, I didn't come at all. God, it must have been a year, at least, before I stepped foot in here again. But it's like what I said yesterday—Anita is family, and partly I came back for her. It helped her to see me here, and in the end, it helped me, too."

Marina looked out at the terrace. She saw the three of them at a table on a mild autumn night, drinking, laughing, Thomas with his head thrown back, nostrils wide. When she turned her attention back to Sarah, she asked, "Can you tell me what happened? I read the clippings you sent, but it's hard to imagine what really happened."

Sarah was quiet for a moment. She sipped her water, then took a roll from the breadbasket and broke it open.

"It had been raining all day," she began. "It was right before his show. He'd been working really hard and had gotten into the habit of going to the studio at night, more than ever. Actually, I realized later . . . after he was gone . . . that he'd been out at night increasingly in the year or so before that. I'd brought it up a couple of times, but he always blamed his insomnia, saying that it was worse than ever. I tried to get him to see a doctor, but you know how pigheaded he was."

Marina nodded.

"Anyway, it was around three in the morning, and Giovanni, you remember, from upstairs, pounded on the door until I woke up. We still didn't have a phone, but he did, and somehow the hospital found him. Maybe Thomas was conscious at some point and gave them the number or his name. I don't know, I can't remember the details now."

Anita came to the table, took their order quickly, and retreated. Sarah tore another piece from the roll.

"He was gone before I could get there. A head injury. The EMTs were still there when I arrived. They said the car must have been going pretty fast. He was hit with such force that he landed a good half block away from where his moped went down."

"How *awful* for you."

"It was awful. For years I relived those moments over and over again, imagining the impact, what it was like for him to lie in the street. But that's faded. I don't experience it in that visceral way anymore. Now I can actually tell the story without falling apart." She looked up and smiled at Marina. "It's true, time does heal all things, in one way or another."

Anita arrived with tortellini in a cream sauce laced with black truffles, which they ate in silence before Sarah finished her story. Evidently no one had witnessed the hit-and-run, which made sense since it happened in the dead of night, but it was inconceivable to Sarah that the driver hadn't stopped. "And what are the odds of a car going down the very same little street over behind Thomas's studio at that time of night. Plus, you'd never drive down a street like that at high speed."

It didn't seem so far-fetched to Marina—a drunk, wending his way home, out of control. "What are you saying? That it was intentional?"

Sarah nodded solemnly as she finished her mouthful.

Marina continued. "Why would anyone want to hurt Thomas?" She didn't miss the irony of her words, but she pushed it aside. This was about Sarah, not her.

"It didn't occur to me right away. I was in shock. But about a month later, Thomas's studio was broken into and badly ransacked. It was odd. When I went there with the police to identify what had been stolen, I realized that they hadn't taken anything. At least not anything significant. All the cameras and lenses were accounted for. It would have been so easy, just throw them in a couple of boxes and walk off with a small fortune."

"So it was just vandalism?"

"No. I think the burglar was looking for something specific, and I think he found it."

"What was it?"

Sarah put down her fork and wiped her mouth. "You have to see it to believe it. I'll show you after dinner. Come back to the apartment."

It was hard to believe it was the same apartment. Marina didn't see a single thing she recognized. Gone were the brightly woven rugs, the tastefully mismatched furniture, the ornate chandeliers, the paintings and photographs. Now the cavernous room was furnished in a palette of beige, wheat, and gray. The furniture was sleek and low-slung, and huge abstract canvases filled the walls. It was the lighting, however, that brought the room together and saved it from looking like a showroom of expensive, very expensive, modern furniture. Lights hidden behind valences and along the floor washed the walls and ceiling with soft shadows, while pinpoint spots illuminated the artwork.

"Wow. This is amazing!" It seemed so unlike the Sarah she had known, but somehow absolutely perfect for the Sarah who now stood next to her.

Sarah linked her arm through Marina's and led her into the room. "I know, it's quite different than you probably remember." There was no mistaking the pride in her voice.

"That's an understatement," Marina murmured, running her hand along the back of a chair covered in butter-soft, ecru leather.

"It was a gradual evolution, but once I started, there was no turning back. Not just this room, but me as well. Everything changed when I started sculpting. I don't know how to describe it. I just kept discovering parts of myself that I didn't know were there. And then I started showing my work and people started buying it, and then Sergio saw my work. . . ." She laughed in a way Marina remembered, as if she were clapping her hands together with pure joy. "I guess the rest is history." She reached for Marina's arm again. "Speaking of history, come and look at this."

Marina followed her through the archway to the bedroom, where a low bed was piled with soft cushions and pillows.

"Marcella made me this." Sarah pointed at a patchwork coverlet folded at the foot of the bed. She stroked it lovingly. "I didn't know it, but she saved all my old clothes, and a few years ago, she gave me this." She pointed to a square of celadon fabric. "Do you remember this? It was from that dress I had when I first met you. I think I wore it to death."

Marina stared at the quilt, recalling the day she'd worn the dress around the apartment as she watered the plants, and contemplated the kind of woman she'd turn out to be. She ran her hand over the quilt. *A liar, that's the kind of woman I've turned out to be.*

"I know it doesn't really go with the new décor, but it was such a sweet thing for her to do for me. I think she was afraid that I'd eradicated myself, that she was partly responsible with the new clothing. And, of course, she helped with the decorating, too."

"Have you?" asked Marina in an effort to quiet her self-accusations.

"What? Erased my past?"

Marina nodded, running her hand over the quilt.

Sarah moved toward the living room and motioned Marina to follow. "Not at all. I think I've just grown into myself. I didn't realize until Thomas died how much I was living his life." She took two glasses and a bottle of wine from the blond sideboard. "Unfortunately, I don't think that's unusual. I think women do it all the time. I know, too, that you were trying to point that out when you encouraged me to get back to my drawing. I just couldn't see it at the time."

Marina accepted the glass of wine Sarah offered and took a seat on the couch.

Sarah sat down next to her. "Since we're talking about the past, there's something I need to tell you that I should have told you a long time ago. I tried putting it in a letter, but it never sounded quite right." She took a sip of wine. "Besides, I'm awful about writing, as you well know."

Marina sat immobilized, her wineglass halfway to her mouth.

Sarah had put her glass down and was twisting her gold bracelet around and around her wrist. "I've always felt badly about how I led you on. You know, all those years ago. I flirted with you shamelessly, passing it off as some sort of bohemian, bon vivant behavior. And I did love you, of course I did, and I loved having you as my friend, but I wasn't looking for a lover, and I think that's how it came across."

Marina felt her face flush but didn't speak.

"It's just that Thomas always took everything for himself, and I was afraid that if I didn't secure you as *my* friend that he would take you, too. He liked it that you liked him and worked with him, but there was a part of him that couldn't stand that you liked me better, or that I spent so much time with you. Please, don't look so stricken. It makes me feel terrible."

"No, it's okay. I'm just trying to understand," Marina croaked. She sipped her wine without tasting it. Was this the moment to tell Sarah that Thomas had, in fact, *taken* her, that she had allowed him to, and now had a gray-eyed, brown-haired memento?

Sarah went on. "And I'm ashamed to admit it, but I think partly I was getting back at Thomas for his relationship with the contessa."

"Oh my God, the contessa. I forgot to tell you. I saw her last night."

"What? Where?"

"She was at the reception at the Accademia."

"Did she see you? You didn't talk to her, did you?"

"No, I hid behind a pillar and watched her weaving her evil web."

A shadow crossed Sarah's face. "It's her fault Thomas was murdered."

"Murdered? What do you mean *murdered?*" Marina was genuinely shocked.

Sarah stood up. "Let me show you." She crossed to an Asian desk, the most ornate object in the room, inlaid with mother-of-pearl and ivory, and withdrew a folder from the top drawer, then returned to the couch and sat down next to Marina. "You're not going to believe this." She began handing the photographs to Marina one by one.

Marina was stunned. Not because she didn't believe it—she'd seen it with her own eyes—but because it was here in Sarah's lap. And there was so much of it! She didn't see a shot of the scenario she'd observed that night, but the sado-masochistic theme was prevalent. Each photograph featured one couple, either homosexual or heterosexual, and many included the contessa in the directorial mode. There were a number with transvestites, but she wasn't sure in which category they belonged, straight or gay.

"Evidently, Thomas had a career I didn't know anything about." Sarah's words were bitter, brittle.

"But how does this relate to his death?"

Sarah stood up abruptly and began to pace. "I knew that bitch had some hold over Thomas. He never would have done anything like this on his own. He wasn't a pervert. Maybe he had a mother-fixation thing with her. I know he had a weird relationship with his own mother. I don't mean sexual, but she was one of those women who couldn't get her husband's attention so she made Thomas into her little companion and confidant." Sarah tapped her forefinger against her temple. "Very fucked up."

Marina picked up a few of the photographs that had fallen to the floor when Sarah stood up. "Are you saying you think she killed him?"

"No, no." Sarah came back to the couch and picked up the stack of photographs. "Look at these people." She slapped the photographs onto the coffee table side by side.

Marina had never seen Sarah this angry, even the time Thomas went off with the contessa during their summer holiday. She was like a woman possessed as she covered the table with sordid images. It gave Marina a few moments to really examine the collection as a whole. She was pretty sure they'd all been taken in Thomas's studio, on the same Oriental rug she'd seen that night, although there were a few that involved chains and straps attached to a wall she couldn't place.

Sarah had finished creating her montage. "Look."

Marina looked but didn't understand.

"I *know* these people. Not personally, but I've seen them around over the years. They are all pals of the contessa, and most of them are bigwigs, city officials, the local aristocracy, captains of industry. Can you imagine the power this gave her, the blackmail potential?"

It all sounded a bit far-fetched to Marina. "Why would the contessa need to blackmail anyone?"

"She probably didn't. With her, it was all about control. That was her drug of choice. They were all just puppets on a string, victims of their own perversions."

"I can see that one of these . . . clients . . . might get nervous about having this kind of stuff floating around, but *murder?* Besides, wouldn't they want to get rid of the contessa? She was potentially the biggest threat, wasn't she?"

"You can't just eliminate someone like the contessa. She's too well connected. It makes more sense to get rid of the person who's actually manufacturing the photos, which would send a pretty clear message to that bitch." Sarah shook her head. "Maybe they just wanted to scare Thomas, and when it went too far, they decided to get rid of anything that might tie them to him."

Marina wanted to take Sarah seriously but was beginning to feel like she was in a Mickey Spillane novel. "Did you take all this to the police?"

Sarah slumped back onto the couch. "No, I didn't see any point. I didn't even find these until four or five years after Thomas's death. It would just have been embarrassing."

"Where did you find them?"

Sarah was putting the pictures back into the folder. "They were taped to the underside of a drawer in the bedroom. I only found them because I was redecorating. Whoever ransacked his studio must have found a set there; otherwise, they probably would have come looking here."

"Did you ever confront the contessa?"

"No, I figured she'd just sneer at me. I did something much better." She shuffled through the photographs and withdrew one with the contessa in it. Oddly enough, it was quite similar to the one Marina had seen in progress, except this one involved a middle-aged woman and man in the horse and rider position. The contessa wore a tight skirt, fishnets, four-inch heels, and stood behind them with glasses perched on the end of her nose and a nasty-looking metal ruler in her hand. "I took one like this and wrote 'murderer' across her forehead with a marker, then sent it to her in the mail."

"God! That must have given her a shock." Marina was feeling a little shocked herself. It was becoming more and more difficult to reconcile this new Sarah with the mild-mannered one of old.

Sarah closed the folder. "I felt a little bad after I sent it. She was crushed, absolutely devastated by Thomas's death. But still . . . she deserved it."

"Wow, that's quite a story. I'm so sorry you had to go through all that."

"I know I must sound like a crazy woman, but I wanted you to have the whole story. I haven't talked about it in a long time. I didn't realize how angry I still am. Anyway, it's water under the bridge. Maybe I'll burn these photos some day. I don't know why I keep them."

Marina felt suddenly exhausted. "It's late, I should go."

At the door, Sarah gave her a hug. "I just want to say again how sorry I am about playing with your feelings all those years ago. I really did cherish our friendship. Can you forgive me?"

Marina moved out of her embrace. "There's nothing to forgive."

Outside, the temperature had dropped and Marina welcomed the cold slap to her face. She turned up the collar of her coat, jammed her hands into the pockets, and decided to take the long way back to the hotel. Her thoughts bounced back and forth between Sarah's murder theory and the strange confession about exploiting their relationship. Their friendship had begun so long ago and the memories were now so distorted that she didn't really know how to think about any of it. Should she feel foolish? She might have fallen in love with Sarah without the flirtation. Should she be angry? She tried on indignation, wondering if it would qualify as justification for sleeping with Thomas. What if Sarah's manipulations had made her vulnerable to him? Perhaps she wasn't to blame after all. No, she couldn't stretch it that far. She'd behaved badly, betrayed her friend, and would continue to do so until she told her the truth. However, the thought of adding another layer to Sarah's surfeit of pain gave her pause. It seemed cruel to lay yet more betrayal at her feet.

In Piazza della Signoria, a group of young people in various stages of embrace sat on the edge of Neptune's Fountain as a lone guitar player strummed and sang softly from the stoop of a café. She turned toward the Duomo, noticing that Christmas lights had appeared on some of the side streets. She'd forgotten that the holidays were not far off and couldn't imagine how she'd traverse the slippery slope that lay between here and home. Not that home was looking too much like a safe haven these days. The thought of Zoe prompted her to quicken her steps back to the hotel.

To Marina's utter relief, Zoe came to the phone. She asked Zoe about the photography club, but it only opened an avenue she'd hoped to avoid.

"Is it true that my dad was a really good photographer, or is that something you made up, too?"

Marina was so pleased that Zoe was talking to her that she let the barb go. "Yes, he was. He was quite well known in Italy and made a good living at it."

"Did he, like, take pictures of people for money or was it all art stuff?"

Marina tried not to think of the pictures she'd seen that evening. "Sometimes he'd do some commercial work, if it was for someone he knew and liked, but mostly he did his own work."

"Did you really work with him?"

"Yes, sweetie, I really did work with him. I helped him in

his darkroom and I went with him a few times when he was scouting ideas for a show." There was a long silence. "Zoe, are you there?"

"Yeah, I'm here."

Marina could hear the beginning of tears in Zoe's voice. "Sweetie . . ."

Zoe sniffed. "I was just wondering if you know where he is. What happened to him after he died?"

The thought had never crossed Marina's mind. "You mean, where is he buried?"

Zoe was crying hard but managed a few words. "Yes, I . . . I thought maybe you could . . . could visit him for me."

"Sweetheart, I don't know where he is, but I'll find out, okay?" Again there was silence, and she imagined Zoe nodding at the other end of the phone the way children do before they understand that the person at the other end can't see them.

"Zoe?" Marina could still hear her crying.

Lydia came on the line. "I'm sorry, Marina, I don't think she wants to talk anymore."

"I shouldn't have asked about the photography. It just set her off."

"It's not your fault. She's been wound up since she came home from Shutterbugs, yesterday."

"Shutterbugs?"

"That's the name of the club. Cute, huh?"

"Yeah. But what do you mean 'wound up'?"

"She started talking about how she could have had a father, you know, while Thomas was alive. I tried to tell her that wouldn't necessarily have been the case, but she wouldn't hear it. Anyway, what do I know? Do you think he would have wanted to be involved, if he'd known about her?"

"I don't believe Thomas would have wanted anything to do with her, and even if he had, I don't know that I would have wanted him in her life."

"You're probably right."

"Remember me telling you about that porn session I stumbled across at Thomas's studio when he was there with the contessa?"

"God, I'd forgotten all about that."

Marina twisted the telephone cord around her finger as she spoke. "Well, it turns out that the two of them had some sort of a little business going on. Not necessarily for money, but it was an ongoing thing. A few years ago, Sarah found a stack of photographs from those sessions."

"Was it all porno?"

"I guess you'd call it soft porn. There was no penetration of any kind, at least not in the photos. It was *weird*. I got the feeling that it was like adults dressing up, then acting like children . . . with some genitalia thrown in."

"Now there's a good reason to have kept Thomas away from Zoe."

Marina sighed. "Yeah, but we both know that that wasn't the reason I never told him about Zoe."

"I know." Lydia waited for Marina to go on, but there was nothing but a faint buzz on the line. After another moment, she asked, "Marina, are you there?"

"Yes, sorry, I was just thinking."

"Go on."

"It's true that I didn't want to hurt Sarah or jeopardize our relationship, at least it started out that way. But I think, in the end, I just got buried in the lies and it became too complicated to undo. As long as I could ignore it, I didn't have to deal with it."

"You were young, Marina. You did the best you could under the circumstances."

"I don't know that I did. And the age defense is lame— plenty of young people make intelligent, morally upstanding choices. Besides, now I'm pushing forty. I need to stop acting like a scared twenty-three-year-old."

"Have you decided what you're going to do?"

"I don't see that I have a choice if I want to get all of this behind me. But I feel awful about putting another piece of shit on Sarah's plate just to clean up *my* life. She's had to deal with a lot more than I imagined. The photographs were a real blow to her."

"How did she handle it?"

"She still seems pretty angry, and she thinks that it had something to do with his death."

"What do you mean? I thought he was knocked off his motorbike."

"He was, but it was a hit-and-run that was never solved. Then his studio was ransacked, and Sarah thinks they were looking for the photographs."

"Some disgruntled customer?"

"Yeah, I know it sounds far-fetched. But according to Sarah, there were some pretty important high-roller types involved who might have wanted to get rid of the evidence."

"Doesn't murder seem a little extreme to you?"

"Yeah, very extreme. But maybe someone was just trying to threaten Thomas, or lay him up for a few days so they could have access to the studio. I don't know. Maybe it was just an accident, like the police said, and no one wanted to fess up." Marina yawned. "The thing is, it's what Sarah believes, and I don't see any point in debunking her theory. Maybe it gives her comfort to think that there was a reason behind his death, rather than just a senseless act of fate."

"I suppose. Listen, you sound tired. I should let you go. When are you going to tell her about Zoe?"

"It'll have to be tomorrow. I only have one day after that, and I should really use that to get ready for my presentation. I said I'd meet her for lunch tomorrow, then I'm going to her studio to see her work. After that, I guess."

"Don't you think it's a bit strange that she's using Thomas's studio after all the weird things that went on there?"

Marina yawned again and stretched out on the bed. "I guess so, but she seems very settled and happy there. But any way you look at it, it's going to be strange for me to be back there."

CHAPTER 15

Marina noticed that she wasn't the only one who chose the same seat each day. The gray-haired man with the large mole on his neck was exactly two rows up and three seats to her left, and the woman who cleared her throat every few minutes until Marina wanted to scream was on the aisle a few seats to her right. Any number of people were in the same spot as on the two previous days. Human nature, she supposed. She'd considered moving to the front for a change, but after the disturbing dream she'd had in the night, she didn't relish anyone at her back. In the dream, she'd been standing at the podium about to give her speech, when she felt a sharp pain in her back. Behind her, Sarah stood with a jagged-tipped lance, her face distorted in anger. "Go ahead," she hissed, "say it. Say it." When Marina didn't respond, she jabbed her with the lance again, repeating, "Say it. Say it." She thought Sarah meant she should begin the speech, but when she looked down at her notes, the pages were blank. Another jab of the lance had woken her, her arms wrapped around her ribs. It took a few minutes before the dread drained from her body and she was able to get out of the bed and retrieve the folder from the top of the dresser. For a moment, she convinced herself that she'd find nothing but blank sheets of paper where her speech should be, but it was all there, neatly typed, double-spaced, black and white.

She had a hard time focusing on the morning's lectures. One was a talk on creating a universal protocol for museums in the event of a catastrophe, and the other was on the history of French polish. It wasn't just the dream that was distracting her. Time was running out, and she still hadn't figured out where, when, or how she was going to say what she had to say to Sarah. She wanted to tell the truth, to take responsibility for her actions, but in a way that was as painless as possible for Sarah. It wasn't realistic to think that it would be pain-free, but she didn't want to exacerbate the hurt with a clumsy delivery. Today they would meet for lunch and then go to the studio, after which Sarah had an appointment. If Marina wasn't able to bring it up at the studio, perhaps she'd suggest a walk the following day. She didn't dare leave it for any later than that. Yes—out in the open, yet private. Sarah could just walk away, if that was what she needed to do.

They met just after noon at a *gastronomia* on Via Torna-buoni that was part bar, part delicatessen. According to Sarah, they made the best *panini* in town. Sure enough, a few elegantly dressed patrons stood on the sidewalk out front with sandwiches in their hands, an unusual sight in Italy, where people took their meals sitting down and at great leisure. Inside, the crowd was three deep at the counter, with people waiting patiently to place their orders. They took their places at the back of the crowd as Sarah translated the menu on the chalkboard. When it was their turn, Sarah ordered a plate of cold cuts, pecorino cheese, black olives, crusty bread, and two glasses of the house red.

They settled themselves at a small table on the perimeter of the room and ate in silence, watching the crowd, which showed no sign of letting up. Marina had forgotten how good simple food could taste.

Sarah sliced herself a piece of cheese and said, "I feel bad about throwing all that information at you last night. I thought about it after you left and realized that it must have been a bit much on top of everything else you have on your plate right now with the conference and jet lag and all."

Marina finished her mouthful. "I'm all right. It must have been a terrible shock for you, though, finding the photos, especially after all those years."

Sarah nodded. "Actually, I think it was better that way. If I'd found them right after he died, I think it would have been too much for me. I'd probably have killed that woman with my bare hands."

"Do you suppose they were doing it for the money?" Marina asked, draining her glass.

"God, no. That woman has more money than she knows what to do with."

"Really? I didn't know that. Maybe that was part of the hold she had on Thomas."

"No." Sarah was adamant. "He was not interested in money. It didn't motivate him at all. I really think it was that weird mother fixation. I think he was just doing what she wanted." She shuddered. "I can't even think about it."

Sarah went to the bar and came back with an espresso for each of them. "You know"—her voice was quiet and Marina had to lean forward to hear her—"he wasn't a bad man. I know he seemed selfish and egocentric and controlling . . . and he was all those things, but he was also generous in ways that people didn't know about." She looked at Marina. "You remember the gypsies?"

Marina nodded. "Yes, of course."

"Some people said that he exploited them with his photographs. And maybe he did, a little, but he was really good to them, too. He helped them in all sorts of ways. He paid their doctor bills at times, got the children out of trouble with the police . . . you know how they were always getting picked up for begging. He was wonderful with the old people."

Marina thought of Zoe and how her teacher had once reported that she had been amazing with the old folks on an outing to a senior center.

"I just don't want you to think he was all bad after everything I said last night."

"No, of course not. But there was something I wanted to ask you."

Sarah looked at her. "Sure, what?"

Marina hesitated. "I don't want to upset you, but I was wondering where Thomas was . . . laid to rest."

"It wasn't something we'd planned for, but Thomas once told me that he wanted to be sprinkled from the top of the Duomo, so he'd blow out over the city."

"The top of the Duomo?"

"I know. It's weird."

"Not really. People seem to get sprinkled from hilltops all the time."

Sarah gave her a level look. "It gets weirder."

Marina raised her eyebrows. "And . . . ?"

"I couldn't do that. I'm sure it's against the law. But I did sprinkle his ashes all over the city."

"What do you mean? How?"

"First, I had to ask Marcello to sift them for me."

Marina couldn't believe she'd heard correctly. *"What?"*

"I know it sounds gross, but I wanted to sprinkle his ashes, and I couldn't bear to deal with all the . . . bits and pieces."

Marina nodded, wondering where this was going.

"This was months after he died, after I finally got out of bed. Marcello was a rock. I don't know what he did." She closed her eyes and shook her head as if to ward off any unwanted images. "He just gave me a shopping bag and said it was ready to go."

"So the ashes were in the shopping bag?"

Sarah nodded. "Yes, and it was heavy. So one night, quite late, like when Thomas used to go out in the streets, I took the bag and cut a small hole in the bottom and just walked. I went to all his favorite places, just letting the ashes sprinkle out. I finished up at the English Cemetery, which he loved and had photographed quite a bit at one time. I knew he'd be pleased to be among all those famous people."

Sarah excused herself to use the restroom, and while Marina waited on the sidewalk in front of the shop, she began to have doubts about confessing. Sarah had worked so hard to put her life back together and seemed to have found a balance between seeing Thomas for what he was and honoring his memory. Who was she to take that away from Sarah? Maybe she could find another way around all this without telling Sarah about Zoe.

As the two women crossed the river, Marina realized that she was on the same bridge as the first evening she'd arrived, the evening she followed the girl in the red sweater. Only three days ago? It seemed that she'd relived a lifetime, and she felt suddenly weary as they walked silently through the lavender shadows of narrow streets.

Sarah pointed to a doorway with a faded black door. "Do you remember the night we walked here looking for transvestites? It was after Thomas's opening. There was one right there in that doorway."

Marina smiled, happy to be distracted from her thoughts. "I remember. That was quite the eye-opening night for me."

Sarah laughed. "The look on your face that night, when you saw Marcello at the opening, it was priceless. I don't think you'd even heard the word 'transvestite' before."

"Of course I had."

"Had not."

"Had so." Marina laughed, then realized that they'd arrived in Piazza Santo Spirito. "Wow, they've sure cleaned this up. I used to have to step over junkies whenever I came here," she said, looking at the neatly swept sidewalks, freshly painted doorways, and carpets airing over balcony railings.

Sarah nodded. "It was quite a campaign, getting the city to step in and do something about it." She stopped in front of a building and said, "Here we are." Its ocher façade was mottled with patches. "I managed to get the owner to repair the front of the building, but it's like pulling teeth to get him to paint it."

Marina raked her fingers through her hair, pushing it off her face as she looked up at shuttered windows.

Sarah put her key in the lock. "Come on, you'll be amazed at how different the studio looks filled with my stuff."

The cold, gray scent of stone enveloped Marina as she stepped around the shadowy shapes of the baby carriages and bicycles that filled the small vestibule. Sarah pressed the illuminated light switch at the bottom of the stairs, and the electric meter jumped to life with an urgent ticking. Marina held tight to the iron railing as she followed Sarah up the stairs, the past and present bumping edges and corners, looking for a place to settle.

The studio was at once the same yet different. Shapes, colors, and smells assaulted Marina's senses, colliding with memories and jockeying for the position of reality, of truth. The room was the same lofty, narrow shape, with tall windows at one end, the darkroom crouched at the other. But now, the windows were draped with a sheer, diaphanous scrim and the wall of shelving was gone, as were the photographs. A long workbench extended the full length of one wall, its surface a jumble of cans and jars stuffed with sculpting tools—plastic spray bottles covered with dried, rusty fingerprints, and mounds of clay covered with damp rags. The storage shelf below held scraps of wood, spools of heavy gauge wire, and half-assembled armatures. In the center of the room, pedestals of varying heights supported shapes cloaked in sheets.

"Would you like a cup of tea?" Sarah asked, heading toward the darkroom door.

Marina stared after her. "Is that still a darkroom?"

Sarah opened the door. "No, it's just filled with my junk, but I kept one of the big sinks for cleaning my tools. I have a little hot plate for heating soup, and an electric kettle for tea." Her voice was muffled inside the darkroom. "You want tea?"

"Sure." Marina stood in the center of the room amidst the crowd of shrouded forms. Her eyes shifted to the partially opened bathroom door. She could just see the end of the bathtub, and for a moment, she felt the chill of the milky water, the flame from the heater, the nest of velvet, and the soft patter of rain on glass. Drawing her coat closer, she turned her attention to the form immediately next to her. She reached for the edge of the sheet and pulled it tentatively until it slid off the sculpture. She knew enough about Sarah's work to expect the figure of a child, but not the quality of the work. The girl's face was exquisite. With a compassionate and delicate touch, Sarah had captured the essence of innocence and wonderment. The next form, small and low to the ground, was a boy squatting down, delicate fingers holding his shoelace, his face upturned. Marina imagined if she were to uncover all of them, it would be like standing at a children's birthday party, figures frozen in time.

"Do you mind that I'm peeking?" Marina called in the direction of the darkroom.

"Peek away. This kettle takes forever."

Marina moved about the room, an invited guest, fascinated and awed by the work. As she worked her way closer to the end of the room, she could hear Sarah rummaging about in the darkroom, and called to her again.

"Your work is beautiful; I'm dumbstruck."

"Thanks. I'm so glad you like it. I should have listened to

you all those years ago when you told me to get back to work."

Marina glanced beyond the darkroom door where the daybed had once been and where now a stack of dusty boxes obscured that corner of the room. She turned away but then felt herself drawn to look. Skirting the boxes, she found the daybed covered in a dust sheet and piled with books, papers, empty frames, and a couple of tattered lampshades. At the foot of the bed, on a low pedestal, a small sculpture was covered with a dust-laden cloth. She lifted the cloth carefully so as to disrupt as little of the dust as possible, and looked, at first with incomprehension, and then with disbelief, at the bronze bust that stared back at her. It couldn't be! It was impossible. But there was no mistaking the shape of the eyes, the full lips, and the rounded cheeks of her daughter. Hearing a sound behind her, she turned.

"Oh, I forgot that was there," Sarah said, blushing, a mug of tea in each hand.

"I . . . I don't understand. How did you know?" Panic and confusion choked Marina's voice.

"I did that after Thomas died. It was supposed to be him. . . ."

All Marina heard was the word "Thomas." "How did Thomas know? Did he tell you?"

". . . but I was missing you, too. You kept creeping into it. . . ."

"You've known all these years?"

Sarah looked at Marina blankly, and then her face changed as she digested Marina's words. "Did Thomas tell me what? Did I know what?"

In that moment, Marina realized they'd been talking at cross-purposes, but it was too late to turn back—the force behind the truth was more than she could fend off. She pointed at the bust. "About Zoe. About us."

It seemed to Marina that Sarah moved in slow motion.

Very carefully, she put the mugs down on one of the boxes, then turned to face Marina. In almost a whisper, she asked, "What are you saying?"

"It was a mistake, Sarah. You have to believe me." Marina clasped her hands together in front of her with such a grip that her fingernails blushed purple.

"What mistake?" Sarah emphasized each word, her voice hard.

"We were doing the bathtub shoot. I drank too much wine. I didn't know what I was doing. Thomas was . . . he . . ."

"You're telling me that Thomas seduced you?"

"He . . . I . . ."

"You fucked him?" Sarah's voice rose.

Marina shook her head. She had to make Sarah understand. "It wasn't like that. You have to . . ."

"I don't have to anything. Did you or did you not have sex with Thomas?"

Marina looked at the floor and nodded. When she heard Sarah move away, she looked up and began to follow her into the middle of the room but stopped when Sarah whirled around.

"You and Thomas had sex here? In this studio?" Sarah covered her face with her hands and shook her head. "And to think that I encouraged you to work with him."

"Sarah, it wasn't what you think. It was you I loved."

"For Christ's sake, Marina. You loved me so much you had an affair with my husband?"

The look of disgust on Sarah's face crushed Marina. She *had* loved Sarah. Perhaps it had been a naïve and misguided love, but her feelings had been pure. She'd been attracted to and fallen in love with the essence of who Sarah was, and the intimacy she offered. She looked at Sarah and began to cry. "It wasn't an affair. It was just that once. I told you, it was a mistake, a mistake I've had to live with all these years. I've never forgiven myself."

As if just remembering the bust, Sarah's eyes opened wide and she covered her mouth with her hand. "You got pregnant. Oh my God! You got pregnant."

Sarah spit the word with such force that Marina winced, and the shame she thought she'd put behind her now scorched every inch of her body, making her wish she'd combust right there on the spot and have it all over and done with.

Sarah turned her back and walked toward the darkroom.

"Sarah, I'm not asking you to forgive me, but *try* and understand. I was young. I was way out of my league. I was in love with you and I didn't know what to do. You even admitted that you led me on."

Sarah turned around. "Oh, so that gives you the right to sleep with my husband and have his child." Her voice was shrill.

"No, of course not. I'm just trying to make you understand how confused I was. I wasn't thinking straight."

Sarah held up her hands as if to ward off Marina's words, then covered her face with them and slid to the floor, her back to the darkroom door. Her body shook with sobs. Marina went to her and squatted down but didn't dare touch her. Her heart broke in the face of Sarah's devastation, and she cursed herself for creating exactly what she'd wanted to avoid. She should have left well enough alone and stayed away from Sarah.

Marina spoke softly. "Sarah, I didn't know what to do. I couldn't tell you. How could I tell you something like that? I wasn't even going to tell you now, after everything you've been through. But I saw the bust. I thought it was Zoe. I thought you knew."

Sarah dropped her hands; her face was ashen. "How would I know? Did Thomas know? Did you tell him?" Her voice broke on the question.

"No, I swear, he never knew. No one knew."

"I cannot believe him!" Sarah smacked the palm of her hand on the floor. "It wasn't enough to have the contessa. He had to have you, too. It didn't matter that I never knew. He knew. He knew he'd taken you from me. He couldn't stand me having something of my own, something he wasn't a part of."

"He never took me away from you, Sarah, never." Marina put her hand on Sarah's arm, but she shook it off.

"He thought he had and that's all that counts. I can't believe I've been such a fool." Sarah dropped her head to her knees and continued shaking it, mumbling. "Such a fool . . . such a fool." Suddenly, she lifted her head again. "Don't think for a minute that he wanted you. He just didn't want me to have anyone but him."

Marina nodded, afraid to speak.

Sarah's face was wet with tears. "I can believe he got you drunk. I wouldn't put that past him, not with what I know now. But why didn't *you* stop him?"

"I don't know, Sarah. I honestly don't think I could have. I was too out of it. It was all hazy like a dream. I'm sorry." Marina knew it sounded lame, but it was the truth. For once, it was the truth, it had been like a dream, a dream about Sarah, a dream that had cost them all so much.

"But how could you not tell me?"

Marina looked into her face. "How could I tell you something like that? I tried, I really did. I wanted to, but I was afraid of losing you."

"But you left me."

Marina shook her head. "I didn't leave you. I left the situation. I didn't know what else to do. I had to go."

"You kept the baby."

"I wasn't going to, Sarah, honest. I went home to have an abortion. . . . I don't know what happened. I just never did. And then it was too late." Marina wiped at her own tears and sniffed. "I don't expect you to accept any of this. I can barely live with what I've done. But it stops here. I can't lie anymore." She realized it was true; as much as she hated hurting Sarah, she couldn't lie anymore.

Sarah stood up. "If you can't live with what you've done, how the hell am I supposed to?"

Marina didn't have any more answers.

"I hope you don't expect me to forgive you?"

Marina shook her head.

"Damn right." Sarah pointed toward the door. "Now, get out!"

The streets were quiet as Marina retraced her steps back to the hotel, the city not quite ready to wrest itself from the siesta. She walked blindly until she found herself once again in the middle of the bridge. She stopped and looked down-river, the Ponte Vecchio at her back. There were no rowers in sight, just the endless flow of water. How could everything have gone so wrong? For a moment, she considered going back to the studio, but what could she say to Sarah beyond excuses? Her confession had been a shock to them both. She'd always imagined that she'd preface her admission with a cautionary statement like, "I'm really sorry to have to tell you this," or "This is really hard to say," or "You're going to find this really upsetting," something to give warning, to soften the blow. Instead, she'd just blurted it out and then babbled excuses. No, she'd give Sarah some time, go back to the hotel and regroup, maybe call Lydia, then try to talk to Sarah again later.

By the time she reached the hotel, the city had come back to life with a vengeance, and she was glad to take refuge in her room. The message light was flashing insistently. She pushed the button, hoping to hear that Sarah wanted to talk, but it was Zoe's voice that she heard. "Mom, it's me. I just wanted to let you know that I'm okay. I'm sorry about yesterday. I want you to come home." Marina played the message three times, relief stinging her eyes. Zoe must have left the message before she left for school, but Marina dialed Lydia's number anyway, and when there was no answer, left a message that she'd try again later.

There remained a full day before her departure, but not knowing what else to do with herself, Marina began to pack. She folded her clothes methodically, stacking them in neat piles on the bed as she tried to make sense of her thoughts. It was impossible not to feel relieved now that everything was out in the open, but at the same time, she felt guilty about feeling relieved, knowing that Sarah was suffering. Certainly they wouldn't be having dinner together now, but maybe she could find Sarah later and they could talk things through. She couldn't leave things as they were.

Marina changed into her jeans and a black cashmere turtleneck before sitting down at the desk to write her note.

Sarah, I'm devastated and sorrier than I can say to know that I've hurt you so deeply. I can't bear the thought of leaving things as they are and am hoping we can talk before I leave the day after tomorrow. That morning I will give my presentation and then leave directly for the airport, but tomorrow I am free. Please call or leave a note at the hotel and I will come to you. There is still so much to say. M.

Sarah's apartment would be her first stop. If she wasn't there, Marina would leave a note and move on to Anita's. If Sarah wasn't at Anita's, she'd go back to Sarah's studio. She thought for a minute, then took another piece of stationery from the desk drawer and wrote a note identical to the first. She'd leave the second note at the studio, if she had to, and hope that Sarah would contact her. What more could she do?

The most direct route to Sarah's apartment took her past the Caffè Gilli, its windows resplendent with igloos made out of marshmallow and spun sugar, marzipan penguins, glitter and gold leaf transforming the North Pole scene into a shimmering fantasyland. However, Marina gave them barely a glance as she hurried down a side street strung with white lights and shop windows filled with Christmas decorations and brightly wrapped packages. Her mouth watered as she passed a pizzeria, the air redolent with garlic and olive oil, but she hurried on until she came to Sarah's street. It was dimly lit by the ambient light from a bar and too few street lamps. No one was on the street. Her heart pounded as she approached the building and her finger shook slightly as she reached out to press the bell. She waited, and when there was no response, pressed it again. Nothing. There was no way to leave the note without gaining access to the mailboxes in the foyer. She rang the bell just above Sarah's, and then the one above that. Where was everyone? Just then the door opened and a young woman appeared with a baby in a stroller. Marina helped her maneuver the stroller over the stoop, and then stepped into the foyer.

Once inside, she decided to go up to the apartment and slip the note under the door so Sarah would see it sooner rather than later. Adrenaline made a knot of her stomach as she climbed the flight of stairs to the first floor. When she reached Sarah's front door, she debated whether to knock or simply slip the note under it. After a moment's hesitation, she rapped her knuckles against the dark wood. Silence. She knocked again and called out as loudly as she dared, her mouth close to the doorjamb. "Sarah, it's me, Marina. We need to talk." When there was still no answer, she slipped the note under the door and made her way back to the street. Her heart thumped against her spine as she leaned her sweat-soaked back against the building to catch her breath. She hadn't given much, if any, thought to what she'd say once she found Sarah. She just wanted her to understand that she had never acted out of malice. Fear, cowardice, and immaturity may have had a hand in some of her choices, but never malevolence.

When Marina reached Piazza Santa Croce, she sat down on a bench and thought back on her confrontation with Sarah in the studio. Sarah had asked that fateful question—why hadn't she stopped Thomas. And, while she sensed that

Sarah accepted inebriation as her excuse, Marina knew better. Finally, the nagging uncertainty at the back of her mind had found its voice. The fact was, she hadn't stopped Thomas because she hadn't tried. Yes, the wine had played its role, but she now realized that a part of her that day had imagined that allowing Thomas to be intimate somehow brought her closer to Sarah. On the face of it, this insight sounded ridiculous, but she recognized it as the truth of a young, confused girl, one of the few truths to have survived the journey of lies. It didn't, by any means, excuse her behavior, but it did help make sense of it, if only to her. Suddenly, a terrible thought gripped her. Had she tried on Thomas the same way she'd tried on Sarah's dress? Marina squeezed her eyes shut, forcing back the tears. No! She had not pursued Thomas, nor had she been frivolous about any aspect of what had happened. She inhaled this truth and allowed it to spread through her body, relaxing muscle and nerve. She wiped her eyes and looked up at the church's beautiful façade. Could she possibly explain any of this to Sarah without sounding arrogant or delusional? Marina stood up and crossed the piazza in the direction of Anita's.

Across from the restaurant, a small parking area overflowed with mopeds of every make, model, and color, the lights from the restaurant reflecting off shiny new fenders and illuminating rusty ones. Marina crossed the street and squeezed between two large terra-cotta pots on the terrace and peered into the rear dining room. It was empty. According to her watch it was still too early for dinner, but Sarah might have come in search of Anita's counsel. Marina wasn't sure she wanted to face the two of them together, but it was too late to turn back. She followed the sidewalk around to the front window just in time to see Anita disappear into the kitchen. There was no sign of Sarah. Marina hesitated a moment, then pushed the door open to the faint sound of a buzzer back in the kitchen. As she crossed the threshold, it occurred to her that she would have to explain herself in

Anita's mother tongue, and her Italian was not what it had once been. The refresher courses she took every couple of years when the urge seized her never seemed to refresh anything but her bad grammar.

Anita came out of the kitchen with a dishtowel in her hands and a scowl on her face, but much to Marina's relief, she smiled and opened her arms at the sight of her. Marina allowed herself the embrace, then followed Anita into the kitchen, where she introduced her to two heavyset women who, if Marina understood correctly, were her sisters-in-law. Following smiles and handshakes, the two women turned back to their chopping and stirring while Anita opened a bottle of wine and filled two glasses. The last thing Marina wanted at that point was a round of polite chitchat, but there was no gracious way to extract herself without a few sips of wine. Anita wanted to know if she was enjoying her time in Florence, did she think it had changed, how was the conference going, and so on, and while Marina had little trouble understanding her, forming a response was another matter, however encouragingly Anita nodded and smiled. After ten minutes of questions and answers and two photographs of Zoe, Marina was able to ask if Anita had seen Sarah, to which she replied that she had not but surely would sooner or later.

Finally, Marina excused herself and headed in the direction of the river, wishing she had a bicycle. It was a twenty-minute walk to Sarah's studio, and the sooner she got there, the sooner it would be over—one way or the other. Her determination was now tinged with anger. After all these years, would there be no resolution? She had always imagined that some sort of conciliatory scene would follow her confession. Perhaps not immediate forgiveness, but she'd make Sarah see that she hadn't meant any of this to happen, convince her of how impossible it had been for her to come forth with the truth after it happened, and how it only became more impossible with each passing year. But the closer she got to the studio, the more her conviction flagged. What exactly was she hoping to accomplish? If Sarah was willing to talk to her, it would probably be only to rake her over the coals. Did she really need to submit herself to that? She could flagellate herself quite nicely without anyone's help.

In the lull between the end of the workday and the dinner hour, the streets around Piazza Santo Spirito were deserted. Light from apartment windows cast sharp-toothed shadows through the trees, creating a jagged, chiaroscuro path across the piazza. Marina made her way to the pockmarked building and was spared the routine with the doorbells when she found the street door ajar. For the second time that day, she climbed to the top floor. There were no sounds coming from the studio; even with her ear against the door, she heard nothing. She knocked, and since no other apartments shared that floor, she called out loudly. Finally, after a few minutes of no response, she pounded on the door with her fist, then burst into tears. Putting her back to the door, she slid down until cold stone met the seat of her pants. She hugged her legs, resting her forehead on her knees, and sobbed. Here she was back where it had all begun, almost sixteen years ago. How could she have come so far only to find herself weeping at the door of a previous lifetime? What did her accomplishments mean if the people she loved were in pain? For the first time in a long time, she wanted her mother. She wanted her in a way she'd never been allowed to want her—as the nurturing, forgiving mother who would hold her and tell her she wasn't the awful creature that she imagined herself to be, who would reassure her that life went on, that people healed, that mistakes were made, and it was never too late to make amends. But the mother she had would say: "If it doesn't kill you, it will make you strong." Marina wiped her face with her hands, took the note from her bag, and slipped it under the door. Sarah could be anywhere. If not here ignoring her knocks, she might be with Marcello, or even sitting in Anita's kitchen, telling her a story of deceit and betrayal. What was there to do now but make her presentation and go home?

Marina had lost track of how many times she'd crossed the river in the last couple of days, but this was the first time she'd seen it so still. Downriver, where the black ribbon of water turned and disappeared from sight, the sunset had faded to pale pink. At the crest of the bridge Marina stopped, and breathing in the sight, her heart uncurled from the crumpled knot it had been all afternoon and the tension in her chest and neck eased. She glanced one last time toward Santo Spirito, then turned her back and made her way toward the heart of the city.

CHAPTER 16

Marina lay on the bed in her pajamas, the telephone resting on her belly. A half-empty bottle of wine and the remnants of her supper sat on the table by the window. She'd been exhausted by the time she arrived back at the hotel, but was determined to stay up to call Zoe. She'd eaten dinner, taken a long bath, shaved her legs, and washed her hair in an effort both at renewal and to pass the time. She watched the phone rise and fall on her stomach, and when she couldn't wait a moment longer, dialed Lydia's number, only to find that Zoe and Sasha had gone to a movie and sleepover.

"I'm so sorry, Marina. If I'd known you'd call again I'd have kept Zoe home, but after last night . . ." Lydia sounded truly distressed.

"Zoe didn't tell you she left me a message this morning?"

"At your hotel? No, she didn't say a thing."

"She left a message saying she was sorry and wanted me to come home."

"She did? That's wonderful! I thought there was something lighter about her today, but I didn't want to read anything into it. You must be thrilled."

Marina smiled. "I am. I cannot wait to get all this behind me, and come home. Today . . ."

"Listen," Lydia interrupted, "I need to give you a heads-up. About Peter."

"Peter?" Marina shifted the phone to the bed and wriggled into a seated position. "What's up with Peter? Is he okay?"

"He's been mooning around our house again. You know how he gets when he's falling for someone."

At another time in her life, Marina would have rolled her eyes and said something like, "What's the current flavor, blonde or brunette?" And she and Lydia would commiserate about how he needed to settle down with a good woman. But now she was surprised and a little disappointed. She'd just seen him. How could he have fallen for someone so quickly?

"Is it serious?" Marina asked.

"I think it might be."

Marina sighed. "I don't think I'm ready for another chapter of Peter's love life."

"Well, you better get ready . . . because it's you he's mooning over."

"Me! You must be joking!"

"Come on, Marina. This has been a long time coming and you know it."

"I do not know it. Just because you like playing matchmaker doesn't make it fact. We're friends, we love each other, but like family."

"Here's a fact for you, Marina. When Peter comes over here and he's alone with me, all he wants to talk about is you. I finally told him to shit or get off the pot, that I wasn't going to listen to him anymore."

"What did he say?"

"Nothing. Now when he's here, instead of talking, he just sits around staring off into space. Actually, he tried to talk to Zoe about you the other day, but she practically bit his head off."

"You didn't tell him anything about what's going on, did you?"

"No. It's not my place to get into that with him."

Marina couldn't imagine telling Peter her story, and wondered how Zoe would feel about keeping it just between them once all was said and done.

Lydia's voice interrupted her thoughts. "Marina?"

"Sorry. I'm here. I need to go to sleep. It's really late."

"Of course. But do me a favor and don't get all freaked out about Peter. Don't shut the door before you even know what's on the other side, okay? Promise me."

"Okay, fine. I promise."

Marina hung up the phone and stared at the ceiling. Today she'd had one of the most important doors of her life slammed in her face, and didn't think she could risk opening another one, even a crack.

The following morning, Marina woke on top of the blanket with the bedspread wound around her like a mummy's shroud. Her head ached, with wine or words she wasn't sure, maybe a combination of both. Between her altercation with Sarah and Lydia's pronouncement, her mind hadn't stopped all night, and she'd hardly slept until, finally, around dawn, she succumbed to a murky slumber. If she'd been able to tell Lydia about finding the bust and everything that ensued, she might have had a more restful night, but Lydia had been so intent on telling her about Peter that she'd been reluctant to interrupt. Besides, she hadn't had time to fully digest it herself.

Marina wrestled herself out of the bedspread, put it over her shoulders, and walked to the window. On the table, pale streaks of winter sunlight played across the congealed pasta and wilted greens from the night before. Across the street, a gypsy woman dressed in voluminous rags sat on the sidewalk, a paper cup in front of her. She was the first gypsy Ma-

rina had seen since her arrival, and it made her think of
Thomas and the first exhibit she'd seen of his work. She recalled the uneasiness she'd felt looking at some of his pur-
loined shots, and how easily she'd shrugged it off in the face
of a new life with exciting, sophisticated friends. With the
thought of Thomas, her mind turned to Zoe. It was Zoe she
wanted to think about, not Thomas, not Sarah, not even
Peter. Zoe, who wanted her back. Marina glanced at the
clock radio on the bedside table, but it was too early to call.
The girls wouldn't be back at Lydia's until midafternoon.
She'd have to wait until evening and pray that Zoe would
still want to talk to her. But would Zoe ever be able to forgive
her for depriving her of her father? If only there was a way to
make Zoe see that she'd been better off not having Thomas
in her life. But it seemed unlikely to Marina that she'd be able
to achieve that without tarnishing the glossy image that Zoe
had of her father, and she didn't want to take that away from
her. Perhaps if she gave Zoe some of what was good about
Thomas, it might be easier for her to let go of what she'd
never had. With this in mind, Marina formulated a plan for
the day.

After a quick shower, Marina dressed in the same clothes
she'd worn the night before and went down to the front desk
for a map of the city. On her way to Piazza della Repubblica,
she walked under the long portico in front of the central post
office, where a flower market was doing a brisk business and
the souvenir stalls seemed to be selling the same trinkets they
had years ago. At Caffè Gilli, Marina allowed herself a pricey
cappuccino and pastry in the company of a few well-heeled
Florentines having their midmorning coffee. She studied her
face in the mirror behind the bar, and for the first time in a
long time, liked what she saw. Her hair was as lustrous as it
had been the night she arrived in this city with a pack on her
back and hope in her heart, and her skin glowed in spite of
the stress she was under. She turned her head from side to
side, examining her jaw and neck, until she realized she'd

caught the barman's eye. She returned his smile before hastily choosing a gift for Zoe, a small box of chocolates with an etching of the Duomo on the lid. She paid the cashier and, with map in hand, set out on her mission. She hoped that Josh wouldn't notice her truancy, but in the face of her daughter's well-being, the conference had to take a backseat. Having decided to start at the top, literally, and work her way down, she hailed a cab to take her up to the Piazzale Michelangelo.

That well-known view of the city with the massive Duomo at its center had not changed except for where construction cranes imposed themselves on the panorama. In the center of the square, yet another copy of Michelangelo's *David* stood on a plinth keeping watch over the city. The statues *Night, Day, Dawn,* and *Dusk* stood guard at its base. Thomas had brought her here on one of their reconnaissance missions for his show, *Flesh in Stone.* She had enjoyed those outings with Thomas, and in Zoe's honor, would retrace their steps as best she could, steps that, if she didn't think about where they'd ultimately led, had been happy and exciting ones. On that particular day, she'd kept notes as Thomas dictated light readings, angles, aperture settings, and any number of details that pertained to the preliminary shots he took for what turned out to be some of the more striking photographs in the show. From there they had climbed a set of steep steps to the little church of San Miniato, arriving just in time to hear the resident monks intone Gregorian chants at vespers.

Marina followed their route up to San Miniato, and once she'd caught her breath, entered the intimate interior where she easily located the pulpit at the entrance to the choir enclosure. Thomas had all but strained his back trying to get just the right shot of the dwarf-like figure with an eagle on his head that held up the lectern, their laughter earning them a reprimand from an elderly priest. She stepped into the choir enclosure, which was empty save her memory of sitting with Thomas as wave after wave of glorious chanting washed over them. Perhaps someday she'd sit here with Zoe and tell her how Thomas had first brought her there, but for the time being, these pleasant memories were the gift she would bring her daughter.

Her next stop was the Loggia della Signoria, but its proximity to the Palazzo Vecchio and the conference made it a little risky. She'd hate to get caught loitering outside instead of listening attentively from her seat in the audience, but the loggia had been a pivotal location when she'd worked on the show with Thomas and a happy time for her, a time she could share with Zoe. Marina skirted the piazza, staying in the shadows as much as possible as she approached the loggia. Many of the photographs in the show had originated there, where plenty of flesh was in evidence, many of the figures wearing little more than a helmet. *The Rape of the Sabine Women* was probably the most famous sculpture in the loggia, but the most beautiful was *The Rape of Polyxena,* and Marina surprised herself by remembering its name. She recalled Thomas telling her the history of each sculpture, but she hadn't remembered the extent of the violence they depicted. In addition to the two rapes, there was Perseus holding a severed head, Hercules clubbing a centaur, and a Greek soldier holding a dead comrade. Marina stood for a long time studying *The Rape of Polyxena,* wondering how an act so ugly could be portrayed in so beautiful a piece of art, or conversely, how so beautiful a piece of art could depict such an awful crime without losing its beauty. A naked soldier (Roman, she surmised by the look of his helmet) held a struggling woman in one arm and a lance in the other while a second woman knelt at his feet imploring him to release his prey, while yet a third female lay dead at his feet. The unity of the women depicted in the flow of the figures struck Marina as beautiful and hopeful as it was tragic.

It was close to noon by the time she left Piazza della Signoria. Once again the sky was clear and the sun filled the square with heat more reminiscent of early fall than Decem-

ber. The cafés on the sunny side of the square had set out tables and chairs, and although she was hungry, she didn't
want to risk running into Josh, who would be leaving the
conference momentarily in search of his own lunch.

A group of Japanese tourists laden with shopping bags
snaked past her as they followed a small orange flag on a
stick. She had been warned that Florence had become increasingly touristy, but she hadn't anticipated seeing so many
at this time of the year, nor had she expected to see the wide
cross-section of countries represented. She couldn't remember ever seeing even one Asian tourist when she worked on
the leather stall all those years ago. Up ahead, a cluster of
people, including shop girls in tight skirts and leather boots
and workmen still wearing their *grembiulini,* stood patiently
in front of a tripe cart waiting their turn to order. As she always had, Marina held her breath as she passed by, wondering what made people want to eat a sandwich filled with an
animal's stomach lining.

The hotel lobby was busy with people checking in, and she
had to wait to retrieve her key. This time when she looked to
the far corner, an elderly man in an elegant black overcoat
was sitting in the armchair under the palm, and she felt a
pang of guilt about skipping the conference, especially after
Josh had gone to so much trouble to see that her presentation
would be well attended.

The receptionist greeted Marina and slid an envelope
across the counter with her room key. The envelope was
white with her name written in blue ink. There was no mistaking Sarah's handwriting. Marina stepped into the elevator,
her eyes fixed on her name. How could six plump letters look
so accusatory? She carried the envelope gingerly down the
hall to her room and set it carefully on the end of the bed.
Eyeing it as if it might explode, she changed from her boots
into loafers. Her desire to see Sarah no longer felt as urgent
as it had the night before, and she took a long time washing
her hands and face before sitting down with the envelope.

She turned it over in her hands as she considered her choices. She could read it now, read it later, or never read it. No, she owed Sarah the courtesy of reading it even if the note contained the harshest recriminations. Marina opened it quickly before she could change her mind and was relieved to see that it was short.

Marina, We need to talk. Come to my apartment at 6:00. S.

Marina flopped back on the bed and stared at the ceiling. She'd been summoned. But for what purpose? It could only mean more shame and humiliation. Any hope of forgiveness had been incinerated in the glare of Sarah's hurt and anger. The one thing she'd always feared happening was coming to fruition. Her friendship with Sarah was over. Marina didn't even try to hold back her tears. She rolled onto her stomach and let the sobs shake her into stillness.

Some time later, Marina woke to the sound of a siren in the street. She made her way to the bathroom and washed her face, removing smeared mascara from under her eyes.

She looked at herself in the mirror. "Stop feeling sorry for yourself. You have things to do."

Marina found sustenance at a small *vinaio* that was barely more than a hole in the wall with a counter. She ordered a glass of red wine and two *crostini Toscani*. It was cold standing in the shadow of the narrow street, but Marina was transported by the thick slabs of Tuscan bread spread with hot chicken liver paste. Feeling revived, she licked her fingers and made her way toward Piazzale Donatello.

The English Cemetery sat high on an oval-shaped island in the middle of the Piazzale Donatello, encircled by a wide and busy boulevard. Although Marina had never visited the cemetery, she remembered Thomas speaking of its beauty and its legendary residents, the most famous of which was Elizabeth Barrett Browning. When at last the traffic thinned enough for Marina to safely cross three lanes, she followed the iron fence that cinched the cemetery's circumference until she found the gatehouse. A wide path bordered by a low hedge bisected the half-acre plot of land that held close to a thousand white marble monuments of every shape and size. Narrow, mostly overgrown paths diverged from the main artery into the shadows cast by a perimeter planting of cypress trees. The sun was still warm but a breeze had come up, pushing leaves along the ground and rustling overgrown rosebushes and patches of nettles. Many if not most of the tombstones were in a surprising state of disrepair, along with broken fencing and bushes in need of pruning. Browning's grave, when Marina found it near the center of the burial ground, was no exception, its beautiful marble vault at risk of tumbling from crumbling pillars. In front of the tomb, a single red rose bloomed on a leggy rosebush, defying nature and neglect.

Marina followed the paths at random, imagining Sarah with her bag of ashes laying Thomas to rest amongst the great artists, writers, and statesmen. All in all, the cemetery had the age-worn loveliness of a grande dame whose beauty was faded but not erased by time. She had remembered her camera, stuffing it in her coat pocket as she left the hotel room, and now tried to decide on a few shots for Zoe that might capture the charm of Thomas's final resting place. She knew he was "resting" in a few other places, but there was no need for Zoe to know that parts of him were sprinkled around the city. She snapped a few shots of Browning's tomb before following the narrow gravel path toward the far end of the oval, where she came upon the life-sized sculpture of a woman atop a roughly hewn tomb. The figure knelt at a prayer desk, her head in her hands, and while Marina couldn't ascertain who was buried there, something in the utter despair of the woman's posture suggested a child's death rather than a lover's. A little farther on, she encountered an unusual subject for a monument. This was a life-sized skeleton swathed in a hooded cloak and carrying a long walking staff.

The skull was gruesome. It reminded her of something from *Night of the Living Dead*, and she could only imagine the uproar it must have caused at its unveiling.

On her way out, Marina heard the sound of someone or something scratching in the dirt just behind a low boxwood hedge. Curious to see another sign of life, she skirted the hedge and nearly fell over an elderly man bent over tidying the area around a simple column topped with a marble urn. He reached out to steady her, then tipped his hat and returned to his job. He wasn't a custodian, dressed as he was in a woolen coat and felt hat. Fine, black leather gloves lay on the ground next to him beside a vase of fresh irises. Odd, thought Marina, moving on toward the gatehouse; the cemetery had been closed to burials since the mid-1800s, so he couldn't possibly be visiting the grave of anyone he knew. But it made her think about bringing Zoe here one day to walk the ground where Thomas lay.

Marina arrived back at the hotel with an hour to spare before her appointment with Sarah, enough time to freshen up and call Zoe, who must surely be home from her sleepover. But to her disappointment, Lydia was again the only one home. Marina sat heavily on the edge of the bed and listened while Lydia explained that the girls had called to ask permission to stay at their friend's until evening.

"I'm sorry she's not here, but I'm glad you called. I felt bad that I never asked how things were going for you with Sarah. I shouldn't have been so pushy about Peter. Have I scared you off?"

"No, it's fine, really. I have so much on my mind here, I don't have time to worry about anything else."

"I was sort of hoping that you wouldn't worry about this, that you'd just keep an open mind and see how things unfold."

Marina clenched her jaw. Lydia was like a bulldog when

she got her teeth into something. *She* was the one who would worry it to death.

"Lydia, listen." Marina kicked off her loafers and swung her feet onto the bed. "I told Sarah about Zoe."

"When? How did she take it?"

"I didn't exactly tell her. It's more like we stumbled into it together." Marina gave Lydia a quick sketch of their confrontation the day before, her subsequent search for Sarah, and the note the desk clerk had given her.

"It's good that she wants to talk, don't you think?" Lydia asked. "I mean, she was probably in shock and now she's had some time to think."

"That's what I'm afraid of."

"What do you mean?"

"Yesterday, at the studio, we really only talked about . . . you know . . . what happened with Thomas."

There was a pause before Lydia responded. Her tone was gentle. "I've never said this to you before, Marina, but don't you think that what Thomas did could be considered . . . rape?"

"Oh, my God, Lydia! No! It wasn't like that. Why would you say that?"

"It's always been at the back of my mind, Marina, but I didn't think you'd want to hear it. You've always been so intent on excusing Thomas."

"I do *not* excuse him. But I'd never say that he raped me. Why would you think that?"

"What do you call it when an older man gives a young woman too much to drink and then forces himself on her sexually?"

"Lydia, I never said there was force involved."

Again, Lydia's tone was gentle. "I thought you didn't remember."

"I'd certainly remember if he'd used force. Why are you being so horrible?"

"I'm sorry. I don't mean to be horrible, but when you talk to Sarah, don't let him off so easily. Sarah's instinct is going to be to blame you anyway."

"I am to blame."

"You are only partly to blame. Don't you think she might feel differently about the whole thing if she knew he'd coerced you?"

"I think she already has that impression. But I'm not going to say he used force when he didn't. I've lied enough already."

"I'm not suggesting you lie." Lydia sounded exasperated. "I just think your view of what happened is naïve."

Marina sighed. This was not the conversation she wanted to be having. "Maybe it is, but can we just agree to disagree for now? What I really need right now is some support for the next go-round."

Lydia was all business. "Okay, shoot."

Marina took a breath and gathered her thoughts. "Now that she's had time to think about it, I can only imagine that she'll want to know why I never told her, why I've let her believe that Zoe belonged to someone else. She's got to be feeling completely betrayed."

"You're right, she probably is, but I'm sure you can make her see your dilemma."

"I'm just afraid that when I see her, I'm going to forget everything I want to say, everything I want to make her understand." Marina knew she sounded whiny, infantile, but she couldn't help it.

"I think you need to let go of making her understand anything. She's going to process all this information in her own way, at her own pace."

"I know, but . . ."

"It's not reasonable to expect resolution in two conversations for something that's been going on for fifteen years. All you can do is tell her the truth as you know it."

"My truth is so ugly."

"It's still the truth."

"I'm scared. I'm afraid I'll lie."

"It's a scary thing you're doing, to face your mistakes, to admit you've done wrong, to take responsibility. But it's also incredibly brave, Marina."

Marina put her feet on the floor and fished around for her shoes. "Christ, I feel like I'm twenty-three again."

"Well, you aren't. You are a grown-up, successful woman, and a wonderful mother. You have to hold on to that and stick to the truth as if your life depended on it."

After she hung up, Marina stood by the window watching the lights come on as dusk fell over the city. Lives—her life, Zoe's life, and their life together—did depend on her telling the truth, of finally doing the honorable thing.

At a little before six, Marina stood in the greengrocer's around the corner from Sarah's apartment debating over daffodils, tulips, or hyacinths. She'd already given up on the idea of chocolates after scrutinizing boxes in several windows along the way—candy was a gift for lovers or people in the hospital. The flowers were lovely, but she imagined proffering the bouquet only to have it slapped from her hands. Perhaps it was presumptuous to think that a peace offering of any sort would be welcomed. It might very well be perceived as frivolous. It might be best to go in with head bowed, prepared to receive the blows she deserved. She left the flowers and walked to the back of the shop where a shelf above the root vegetables held a selection of wine. A drink was just what she needed to calm her queasy stomach and steady her shaking hands, and she wished she'd stopped in the hotel bar for a stiff one on the way out. No, she'd go empty-handed.

It was completely dark by the time she pushed the bottommost doorbell on the front of Sarah's building. After all these years, there was still no name on the brass plate next to the bell. It took all her willpower not to run back to the hotel and the safety of her room as she waited for Sarah to buzz her in, and it seemed an eternity before she heard the click of the latch and the front door released. The stairwell light was on, but no one looked down or called out to her. The handrail was icy as she pulled herself up, each step becoming steeper as she climbed, the urge to take flight tugging at her back. When she reached the second-floor landing, she saw that Sarah's door was ajar, and she forced herself forward, knocking lightly on it as she entered. "Sarah?" Her voice snagged on something in her throat, and she wasn't sure she'd actually made a sound. She closed the door behind her, cleared her throat, and called out again as she took the few steps into the living room. This time her voice seemed too loud, an assault on the stillness. A woman who was not Sarah stood up from where she was sitting on the couch.

"You remember Marcella." Sarah's voice came from the shadows, where she was little more than a silhouette against the French doors. The only light in the room came from two sleek glass lamps at either end of the sofa.

Marina stared, confused for a moment, until she saw that it was Marcello! She'd seen him in drag before, but this was different. She could see that being (almost) a woman agreed with him. He had the same flawless beauty he'd had years earlier, but time and hormones had softened his features and given him curves in all the right places. Marina smiled and took a step forward, but when he gave her a curt nod and sat back down, she stopped, unsure what was expected of her. Certainly not hugs and kisses.

Sarah stepped into the light, her arms wrapped across her chest as if she was cold. She was dressed entirely in black, her face a pale oval above the turtleneck, her hair pulled back in a severe knot at the back of her head. "I asked Marcella to be here for me."

Marcello looked up at Marina through his lashes as he crossed his legs and smoothed the tight skirt over his thighs.

Marina looked at Sarah. "I got your note. Thank you."

"Sit if you like." Sarah's voice was quiet and without into-
nation.

Marina sat in the chair closest to the door without taking
off her coat. When no one spoke, she began, "Sarah, I . . ."

Sarah held her hand up, closed her eyes for a beat, and
shook her head slightly before turning away and walking toward the bedroom. She became a shadow again as she
reached the far end of the room, where she stopped, but instead of going into the bedroom as Marina had anticipated,
she turned and walked slowly back toward the circle of light.

Without looking at Marina, she said, "Just give me a moment." Then she turned again and retraced her steps to the
far end of the room. She took two more slow laps before
stopping. Her disembodied voice came from the shadows. "I
have some questions."

Marina didn't dare move from her chair, but she shifted so
that she was facing the dark end of the room. "Yes, of
course." She glanced at Marcello, but he looked down at his
hands. He really did seem to be a "she," but Marina found it
too confusing to think of him as Marcella.

When Sarah emerged from the shadows, she had something in her hands. "And these?" She held up the stack of
photographs that Thomas and the contessa had engineered in
their spare time. "Were you in on this? Was it a cozy three-
some?" Two red spots appeared on Sarah's cheekbones as
she spit the words at Marina.

"God, no! No, Sarah. How could you even think such a
thing?"

"Quite easily at this point." Sarah's face was hard, her
glare unwavering.

Marina looked down at her hands, shaking her head. "No.
I had no part in it."

"But you knew something, didn't you? I could tell the
other night. You were pretending to be shocked."

Marina continued looking at her lap and shaking her

head. There was no way she was going down that road. If she admitted she'd seen something, it would just be one more thing she'd kept from Sarah, one more seedy connection to Thomas. She heard Sarah move away, and when she looked up, Marcello was looking at her intently.

Sarah's voice preceded her into the light. "You say this . . . thing . . . with Thomas wasn't an affair."

Marina wasn't sure if it was a question or a statement, Sarah's tone was so flat, but she couldn't help but respond. "No. No, it wasn't. Nothing ever happened between us . . . until that day."

Sarah stopped for a moment. "And after that day?" Then turned her back on Marina's answer.

"No, nothing. I never saw Thomas again except the one night we all had dinner together. And then at his show, but we didn't even speak that night."

Sarah continued her pacing. "And before that? When you worked together. Were you . . . intimate . . . in any way?"

Marina leaned forward in her chair. "Sarah, it wasn't like that at all. It wasn't Thomas I was interested in, you know that." She lobbed her shot into the dark, but if it hit the mark, Sarah didn't react.

"But he flirted with you?"

"No more than you." It was out of her mouth before she knew it was there, sounding every bit like the accusation it was.

"Touché," came Sarah's soft response from the dark. Now she walked back to the couch and perched on the arm, her back rigid. If there was a crack in her armor, it didn't show. Her arms were still crossed in front of her chest, but now in a posture of judgment rather than defense. Marcello studied Sarah as if taking a reading, but didn't do or say anything.

Sarah cleared her throat. "So, you had sex with Thomas and kept it a secret."

Marina wanted to say that, actually, he'd had sex with her,

but she held her tongue. These were her lashings to take. There was no point in foisting them off on a dead man.

"What did you think would happen? That things would just go on as before?"

Marina shook her head. "I don't know what I thought would happen. I did want to tell you. I was desperate to tell you, but I was terrified that you'd take his side and banish me from your life."

Sarah nodded but didn't respond.

Marina continued, "When I found out I was pregnant, I didn't know what to do. I didn't see how I could tell you, since I hadn't told you what happened in the first place."

"If you'd told me, maybe I could have helped you." Sarah's bitterness was unmistakable.

"Do you honestly think you would have helped me abort Thomas's baby?"

Sarah stood up abruptly and began to pace again.

Marina's voice reached into the shadows after her. "Think about it, Sarah. What was I to do? I went back to the States with every intention of having an abortion so I could come back without anyone knowing anything."

Sarah was back in the light, her hair beginning to come loose, curling around her face. "Things never would have been the same, whether I knew or not. Not after what you did with Thomas. And you *didn't* have the abortion and you *didn't* come back." Sarah's words cracked with tears, and Marcello reached for her hand, but she didn't take it. "You've lied to me all these years. I feel like such a fool."

Marina stood up and took a step forward, but Marcello gave her a look so sharp it sent her back to her seat. She clenched her hands in her lap. "I know. I didn't mean it to be that way. I'm so, so sorry."

Tears ran down Sarah's face, but still, she held herself tall. "How could you do that to me? Every note you wrote, year after year, full of lies."

"It wasn't all lies. It's just that . . . as more time went by, the harder it was to take it all back."

"Did you even try?"

"I almost told you . . . after Thomas died."

Sarah gasped, as if she'd been slapped.

Marina knew she'd taken a wrong turn but couldn't see any way out but through it. "Sarah, listen to me. I thought it might comfort you to know that some part of Thomas, the best of him, everything that was good about him, had lived on. But I wasn't sure you'd take it the way I meant it, and I didn't want to risk hurting you on top of everything else you were going through at the time."

Sarah was sitting on the couch next to Marcello, her face in her hands as he rubbed her back and murmured into her ear.

Marina sat paralyzed, afraid to say another word.

After another moment, Sarah pulled away from Marcello and ran into the bedroom. He rose immediately and his face twisted with anger as he hissed a few words at Marina that she didn't understand, but their sentiment was clear.

CHAPTER 17

Later, Marina could not remember how she'd made it back to the hotel. She'd remained in the chair in Sarah's living room, listening to her sobs until she couldn't stand it another second, but she didn't recall leaving the building or which route she'd taken. On entering her hotel room, the first thing that registered was the clothes she'd laid out on the bed for the following morning. The black pants lay smooth and flat, their lifeless legs dangling off the end of the bed, and the black cashmere sweater was tucked neatly into her camel blazer. She stared at them, uncomprehending. It looked as if she'd lain on the bed with her arms spread in supplication, and then simply disappeared—pulverized, turned to ash and blown away, only her clothes remaining. Then she remembered. Her presentation! It was first on the agenda tomorrow, the final day of the conference. She sat down on the bed next to the insensible form and put her head in her hands. She couldn't do it. There was no way she was getting up on that stage in front of God only knew how many people to talk about what an inspired life she'd led. The only thing in her life that even hinted of inspiration was the multitude of lies she'd told. She would call Josh and tell him she was deathly ill. Marina lay back and stared at the plaster rosette on the ceiling. Get a grip! If only she could cry, scream, tear her hair out, anything would be better than the tension that pulled on every muscle until she thought her bones might pop from their sockets. She took a deep breath and visualized the pond she hadn't seen since Zoe's birth.

After about ten minutes of deep breathing, the pain left her body and Marina began to feel as if she might survive. As her mind cleared, she realized that for the first time in almost sixteen years, she was free. There was no longer any need to lie, pretend, deny. She felt at once liberated and exposed. If she had nothing to hide, then she no longer needed anything to hide behind—not Zoe, not her work, not her professed penchant for solitude. A familiar tingle of fear stirred at the base of her spine, but before it could become a full-blown shiver, the phone rang. She sat up. It couldn't be Sarah, could it? She vacillated for five rings, then grabbed it, praying it was Zoe or Lydia, but it was Josh calling to explain why he'd missed that morning's session. Evidently he'd been invited to tour the Villa I Tatti, once Bernard Berenson's estate, now Harvard's Center for Italian Renaissance Studies, and it was an opportunity he simply couldn't pass up, not even for his own conference. Marina gave him half an ear as he waxed lyrical about the grounds designed by some famous English landscape architect, the library filled with rare books, and the collection of Renaissance and Asian art, grateful that she didn't have to make excuses for not being at the conference herself, but unsure if it was a lie to let him assume that she'd been in attendance. He asked if she had plans for the evening and invited her to join his group for dinner, but Marina made a convincing case for needing her beauty rest and agreed to meet him in the morning for a coffee at Rivoire.

The idea of food held no interest for Marina, but she thought a glass of Chianti and a bath might be just what her battered soul needed. After that, she'd call Zoe. Lydia had as-

sured her that the girls would be home for dinner. Then she'd
go over her notes one last time and try and get some sleep.

When Zoe came to the phone eager to talk, Marina vowed
that if there was a goddess of small miracles, she would become a devotee. Zoe was excited about the photography club
and wanted to know what kinds of cameras "Dad" had used.
Marina did her best to sound as natural as possible, but having Zoe talk about Thomas as if he'd been an accepted, ongoing presence in her life since birth was unnerving.

"Did you find out where my dad is buried? Did you visit
him for me?"

Marina sat down on the edge of the bed and pictured the
cemetery. "I did, sweetie. But he wasn't buried. He was cre-
mated. And his ashes were sprinkled in the most beautiful
cemetery I've ever seen."

"What does it say on his stone? Does it say he was a photographer?"

"Sweetie, there is no headstone because his ashes weren't
put in the ground. No one's allowed to be buried there anymore. Sarah sprinkled him all over, so he's a part of the
whole thing. The cemetery is full of famous artists and writers, just the sort of people he'd want to be with." Marina pictured the Grim Reaper.

"Have you told Sarah about me?" The challenge was evident in Zoe's tone.

Marina nodded. "Yes . . . yes, I did."

"Did she want to know what I'm like? Or was she too
mad?"

What had happened to make Zoe so willing to go where
Marina had never dared? "I told her all about you a couple
of days ago."

"Is she mad at you now?"

Marina hesitated, then said, "She's pretty upset."

"Now she probably hates me."

"Zoe, sweetheart, she doesn't hate you. How could she

hate you? You are everything that was good about Thomas. It's me she's mad at, not you. None of this is your fault."

"So, you aren't friends anymore?"

"Not right now, we're not."

"She might forgive you, Mom."

Marina didn't think that was likely. How could anyone forgive a betrayal of such magnitude? What Marina wanted to know was if Zoe would ever be able to forgive her, but it was a question she would save until they were face-to-face. Although she was thrilled that Zoe was talking to her again and seemed eager for her to come home, Marina had no illusions about everything being forgiven. She recalled a conversation they'd had when Zoe was eight or nine, after Sasha had broken Zoe's favorite china doll. Marina had tried to make Zoe understand that it was okay to be angry and sad, but if she didn't forgive Sasha and kept holding on to her angry feelings every time she saw her, she, not Sasha, would be the one who suffered. It was a hard concept for anyone to grasp, let alone a child who wanted revenge, but Zoe had found a way to forgive her friend, and Marina hoped that she would somehow, someday, find a way to forgive her mother.

Marina woke at dawn and lay in bed watching the windowpanes turn from gray to lavender to pink. She felt surprisingly calm and well rested. After ordering coffee, she got out of bed to retrieve her lecture notes from the dresser. The room was chilly and she pulled on the plush hotel robe before getting back in the bed and setting the folder on her lap. Her dream that the pages were blank came back to her in a flash, but her words were right where she'd left them. She began to read about the history of gilding and the fifteenth-century techniques that had been passed down through the generations, and which she had been fortunate enough to learn from Sauro. She wondered if Josh had invited Sauro but wasn't sure they'd stayed in touch after Josh stopped coming to Italy on business. She could have tracked him down herself, but with everything that had gone on in the past few days, she hadn't given him a thought until now. Shortly after her return to the States, Marina had written a note to Sauro to let him know that she wouldn't be returning, and she wasn't surprised when she received no reply. He was a simple man whose life revolved around his family and his work, and she'd never known him to express any interest in a world beyond Florence.

The coffee arrived, and Marina read through her lecture one last time, pleased to see it was better than she remembered and relieved it would soon be over. Even though she'd written the speech herself, when she read about the evolution of her career, she was genuinely surprised by all she'd accomplished, and allowed herself a moment's pride. There had been people along the way, mainly Josh and Lydia, who reminded her from time to time of her achievements, but for the most part, she had simply kept her head down and done the next task in front of her. She'd approached single-parenthood in much the same way, and couldn't remember ever feeling sorry for herself or complaining about the work and responsibility of raising a child alone. Even in the early days after Zoe's birth, when she fantasized about a life with Sarah, it had not been because she was afraid to go it alone. The thought of Sarah pierced her reminiscence, and like an arrow to the heart, she felt a sharp stab of regret. How could something that had once been so fresh and exciting have gone so terribly wrong? She gathered her papers together. No, now was not the time to go down that road. She had the rest of her life to look back on what had happened. Right now she needed to keep moving forward.

An hour later, she was showered, coiffed, made-up, and dressed. Her bags were packed, and after she left them with the porter, she'd be ready to meet Josh for breakfast. At the front desk, the receptionist took her key and handed her a copy of the bill, then asked her to wait while he retrieved an envelope from his desk. Marina's heart stopped as he walked toward her with the white envelope. Her hand shook slightly as she took it from him, and she turned her back before looking at it. Her full name was typed across the front, and the logo of the car service that would take her to the airport was stamped in the upper-left corner. Her heartbeat returned to normal, and as she crossed the lobby, she glanced one last time at the chair under the palm, but it was empty.

Outside, people were heading to work or their second cup of coffee while children trudged toward school, the hems of their blue smocks peeking from beneath their jackets. Marina inhaled the morning scent of the city, with its undertone of wet stone and exhaust, and overtones of sweet yeast and dark coffee. She turned toward the Ponte Vecchio, wanting one more glimpse of the Arno before she met Josh at Rivoire. When the conference ended at midday, there would be just enough time to get back to the hotel before the car arrived to take her to the airport.

The day was gray, like so many during the winter she'd lived there. The Arno's ashen waters barely reflected the storm clouds overhead, and Marina was sorry not to have a sunnier memory to take away with her. She walked along the bridge past the little shops, their gems and jewels hidden behind shutters and padlocks, and wondered when she might return. No doubt Florence would be high on her daughter's list of places to go, as it had been on hers when she was Zoe's age. When she thought about being in Florence with Zoe, she imagined it would mean showing her Thomas's world, and realized that in order to do justice to his memory, which was part of Zoe's history, she would have to find a way to forgive him. She looked upriver in the direction from where the floodwaters had tumbled all those years ago, precipitating her journey that was now coming to a close. Crossing to the other side of the bridge, Marina watched the water flow downriver, away from her and toward its uncertain but inevitable fate.

* * *

The half-hour Marina spent with Josh over a cappuccino and brioche at Café Rivoire held her in good stead as she waited her turn at the podium. Josh had been both reassuring and encouraging, talking to her in a soft, rhythmic voice until, by the end of their breakfast, she felt focused and calm. He had walked her across the piazza, his hand on her elbow, and guided her into the Palazzo Vecchio and up the stairs to the Salone dei Cinquecento. She listened attentively from the front row as he gave her an eloquent introduction, and was surprised when he referred to her as courageous.

Marina had never thought of herself as courageous, but if what he said was true, she hoped it would surface in time to get her through her lecture. It was difficult not to feel insignificant, considering the grandeur of the room and the amazing artwork that surrounded her. She looked at the massive painting on the wall to her right, where a melee of charging horses, tangled bodies, and sharp weapons illustrated brave men defending their history. Marina thought about her own history and the mistake she'd made that had changed her life forever and hurt two people she cared about deeply. But must she continue on a path determined by five minutes sixteen years ago? Hadn't she now changed the course of her future? Perhaps she couldn't expect Sarah, or even Zoe, to forgive her, but couldn't she choose to forgive herself and move on? She wasn't sure exactly how she would accomplish this, but as Josh had said in his introduction, she wasn't one to shy away from a challenge. For the first time in a long time, Marina felt the thrill she'd felt so many years ago upon her arrival in Florence, the thrill of possibility, the possibility of a new life.

At Josh's signal, Marina approached the podium, looked out over the audience, and was surprised to find that the dimensions of the hall inspired her. She squared her shoulders and heard her voice ring strong and clear as she thanked her hosts for their kind invitation and began her story.

"My thanks would not be complete without thanking my

eighth-grade teacher, Mrs. Casey, for assigning the term paper 'An International Catastrophe,' and my mother for handing me the *Life* magazine with its coverage of the 1966 flood that devastated this city. From that point on, my sights were set on one thing and one thing only: coming to Florence. Little did I know where it would lead, or that I would one day have the honor of recounting my story in this great hall."

Any lingering doubts Marina might have had were dislodged and washed away in her flow of words.

CHAPTER 18

Marina gave the small frame one final caress with the polishing cloth and set it on her workbench. She'd purchased the engraving for Zoe on her dash back to the hotel following her presentation. The final morning of the conference had gone like clockwork, and she had more than enough time to retrieve her bags from the hotel and make it to the airport in time for her flight, but with her lecture behind her, her only thoughts were of getting home to Zoe. The engraving of the Piazzale Donatello had caught her eye in a shop window as she hurried by, and she'd been at the counter asking to see it before she had time to hesitate. The store was empty, and the saleswoman had been quick and efficient in packaging it when Marina explained she had a plane to catch.

It felt good to be home. Billie Holiday wound her voice around the refrain of "Easy Living" as Marina stretched her back, then moved to look out the window. A snowfall during the night had transformed the garden into a glittering reminder of the windows at Caffè Gilli and the fact that Christmas was only a breath away. In spite of the jet lag, which after a week had only just relinquished its grip on her, she had managed to complete the two restorations she'd started before her trip and the frame for Zoe's engraving. She'd unearthed the frame years ago in a junk shop but hadn't found a suitable mate for it, until now. She considered it a stroke of pure serendipity to find a print that not only fit the frame but had special meaning for Zoe. She hadn't wavered a moment in buying it, but when she unpacked it a few days after her return, she wondered if it might be a bit macabre to give Zoe a reminder of her father's final resting place. Undecided, she proceeded with the cleaning and regilding of the simple frame. Now that it was finished and the print safely under its glass, there seemed nothing morbid about it. Zoe would be thrilled.

Although Zoe had not thrown herself into Marina's arms at the airport, she had clearly been happy to have her mother back, slipping her arms around Marina and squeezing her tight for a long few moments without saying a word. She'd remained silent as Lydia drove them home, and once there, had escaped the car and gone straight to her room while Marina brought in the bags.

Marina had found Zoe on her bed, hugging a stuffed penguin. "Hey, sweetie." She sat on the edge of the bed and stroked the animal's soft fur, frayed and dingy at the edges. "I haven't seen Opus in a long time."

Zoe hugged the toy tighter. "I dug him out while you were gone," she said softly without looking at her mother.

The stuffed animal had been her daughter's constant companion for the first seven years of her life, until he'd been accidentally left behind at a Disney World hotel. Zoe had cried for days before the toy was found and shipped home, after which it was decided that Opus would spend the remainder of his days safely in the house.

Marina put her hand on Zoe's leg. "I know we have a lot to talk about, and we will . . . in time . . . But for now I just want you to know how very much I love you."

Zoe was quiet for a moment before she spoke. "I know, Mom. And I know you were doing what you thought was best for me." She paused, then lifted her head to meet her mother's gaze. "And, I am still mad that I didn't get to meet my dad." Her eyes filled. "But I love you more than I'm mad."

Zoe began to cry, and Marina drew her close and rocked her. The joy that came with holding her child in her arms was bittersweet, tainted by the understanding that this love Zoe proffered was about survival, not forgiveness. What she had done in depriving Zoe of her father, whether for better or worse, was unforgivable, but it made sense that Zoe might tamp down her anger for fear of losing the only parent she had.

Marina kissed Zoe's head. "It's okay for you to be mad at me, sweetie. You should be. What I did was . . . not okay. And it's okay if sometimes you are too mad to talk to me or spend time with me. I understand that." Marina disentangled herself and looked into Zoe's face. "But it's *not* okay to run off in the night and put yourself in danger."

Zoe rolled her eyes and leaned back against the headboard. "It's not exactly dangerous around here, Mom."

"I know, but you could have fallen, stumbling around in the dark, or been hit by a car, or been picked up by some random creep driving by. You just don't know."

"Yeah, I guess."

"Zoe, I need you to promise me that you won't run away again, that you'll come and talk to me. Or talk to someone else. But no running away." Marina blinked against the threatening tears. "Promise me."

Zoe didn't respond immediately, but then a smile twitched at the corners of her lips. "Okay, I'll promise . . . If you promise to answer *all* the questions I have about my dad."

Marina hesitated, then nodded. She would be as honest as she could and find a way to finesse the questions that were better left unanswered. "Yes, we'll work on that."

"*And*, promise you'll take me to Florence. Soon."

Marina looked at her daughter's determined face and

thought of her own mother's broken promise. Perhaps if her mother had taken her to Florence, she wouldn't have had to go on her own and she wouldn't have met Sarah and Thomas and . . . she wouldn't have Zoe.

"Yes, I promise I'll take you."

"Soon!"

"We'll talk about what soon means." Marina put her finger gently on Zoe's lips, silencing her protest. "But not tonight."

Marina now studied the engraving, her eyes tracing the path she'd taken in her quest to follow the trail of ashes. How could she possibly honor her promise to answer Zoe's questions about her father when there were things no daughter should ever know? She would just have to come as close as she could to the truth and leave some things out. It was all such a tangled mess. As a surgeon might view a mass of intertwined veins and arteries where one false move might cause the life to bleed out of it, she envisioned the life she created. Could she undo her mistakes without damaging the whole? Could she be ruthless with herself but delicate with Zoe? She didn't imagine Zoe would want to know about the night of her conception—adolescent denial of a parent's sexuality would see to that—but at some point she might wonder. Marina prayed it would be when she was old enough to understand that a couple of drinks could loosen your inhibitions, or to understand casual sex, or that sometimes sex was a mistake. Then she might see how these things could happen. If she was lucky, Zoe would never want to know. A knock on the studio door rescued Marina from her quandary.

"Knock, knock." Peter stood in the doorway, paper bag in his hands. "I've got lunch."

Peter had called Marina a couple of days after her return to ask how her trip had gone, but she'd been in the daze of reentry and didn't recall much about their conversation except that it had been brief. Now she remembered she had accepted his lunch offer. She looked at her watch to buy a moment's composure, then moved toward him. "Hey, you, is it that time already?" She allowed him to draw her into a hug.

He tightened his grip, rocking her back and forth. "Hey, you, relax. You're home."

She *was* home, and it was delicious to be held and let everything else fall away, if only for a minute. She returned his squeeze. "It's great to see you," she said. It was great to see him, it had always been great to see him, but until Lydia's revelation about his feelings for her, she'd taken his place in her life for granted. He was Lydia's brother, father figure to her children, kind uncle to Zoe, gravy-making partner, generous, thoughtful, always there when he was needed. He was, she realized, one of the touchstones in her life. Zoe, their home, the studio, Lydia and June and the kids, they were all part and parcel of her existence, and Peter, too; without them, she might simply drift away. Marina extricated herself from his embrace and turned her flushed face away. She cleared a space on her desk, then collected glasses and paper napkins from a shelf while Peter unwrapped the sandwiches.

"Extra pickles for you, madame. No mayo for me." He indicated the sandwiches with a flourish.

"Thank you, kind sir." Marina's attempt at nonchalance sounded hollow. How did he manage to be so relaxed and at ease? He couldn't possibly know that Lydia had shared his confidence with her, could he? She picked up the framed engraving. "Look what I found for Zoe." She realized too late that she would now have to explain the significance of her choice.

Peter studied it carefully. "Very nice. A talented hand." He tapped the glass. "I've been to that cemetery."

"You have?" Marina had forgotten that Peter had been to Florence more than once.

"Sure. It's beautiful. Why did you choose that for Zoe?"

She had no idea how much of her story Peter knew. She trusted that Lydia hadn't told him things she shouldn't, but over the years, she herself must have made casual references to her past. But which? She was shamed by the realization that after all the years of watching Peter live his life and share his loves and heartbreaks, she really had no idea what she'd shared with him, or how much of it was true.

But it was no secret that Zoe had a father. "You know Zoe's father lived in Florence?"

Peter nodded.

"And that he died a long time ago?"

Again Peter nodded. "Before she was born," he said as he took a bite of his sandwich.

How was it that the most damaging of all her lies could be proffered so artlessly? Her chest tightened and her heart raced. It had never occurred to the people close to her, the people who loved her, that she might be anything but honest with them, that she could betray their trust. She'd been so concerned about Sarah's feelings that she hadn't given any thought to how Peter might feel. Or her parents for that matter, she suddenly thought. She'd sold them the one-night-stand story a long time ago, and they accepted the fact that Zoe's father didn't want to be involved. And there was June, and behind her a long line of people for whom Marina had altered the truth, sometimes vaguely, sometimes specifically. The magnitude of the task ahead, the making right of so many wrongs, was more than she could think about with Peter standing in front of her. Would he understand? She looked at him as he took another bite of his sandwich. Yes, he probably would, but this was not the moment. It was all too much, too soon.

She took a deep breath. "His ashes were scattered in this cemetery, and I thought Zoe might . . . like to have this." In light of all she left out, this meager piece of the truth seemed a shabby offering. Peter looked at her intently. Could he see the word "liar" emblazoned across her forehead? She swallowed hard. "Do you think that's too weird?"

"No, not at all. It's very thoughtful. And from the way

Zoe has been talking about Florence, I think she'd love anything that had to do with that city."

Marina willed herself to relax. "She's been bugging me about taking her there."

Peter crumpled his sandwich wrapper. "You should. She'd love it."

"I'd like to, but . . . it's complicated."

Peter seemed about to say something, but stopped, took her by the arm, and led her to the desk, where he pushed her gently into the chair. He moved the sandwich in front of her. "Eat."

Marina complied as Peter filled the glasses with water and set one in front of her. He took the other and stood at the window looking out. All Marina could hear in the sticky silence that filled the studio was the static buzz of her mind. She looked at Peter's back and wished she could break free, reach out and touch his shoulder, tell him everything.

"I haven't been completely honest with you," Peter said.

The bread stuck in her throat. Wasn't that what she should be saying? She tried to swallow but couldn't.

Peter pulled out the chair across from her, sat down, and put his hand over hers. "I haven't been honest because I didn't know the truth, not until you were away." Marina took shallow breaths through her nose. She couldn't move, couldn't swallow. She stared at Peter.

Peter kept his hand on hers. "I have no doubt my sister has filled you in." He smiled. "If she didn't call you in Florence, she's certainly talked to you since you got back." He held up his hand. "No, don't say anything, just nod if I'm right."

Marina swallowed hard, managing at last to clear her throat, but she did not speak. She wanted to deny that she knew anything. She wasn't ready to hear his words, but her head nodded.

"I did not confide in Lydia with the idea that she would tell you. In fact, I hadn't intended to confide in her at all, but you know how she is."

Marina managed a wry smile. "She beat it out of you."

"Exactly. But it didn't take a heavy stick. I think my behavior was pretty self-explanatory."

Marina sat back in her chair, once again willing herself to relax. "'Mooning and moping about,' I believe was the description."

Peter removed his hand from hers and scraped it through his hair. "Oh God, she told you gory details."

"Peter, it's fine. I was so preoccupied with everything I was dealing with at the time, I barely remember a word she said." She made what she hoped was an apologetic smile. She couldn't tell if Peter looked relieved or disappointed.

"I don't know any of the details, Marina, but it seems you were dealing with more than just the conference over there, and I get the impression that whatever it is, is upsetting you."

Marina folded the remains of her sandwich into the wrapper and looked toward the window as if an answer might rise up from a snowbank. Did she want to hear about Peter's feelings or talk about her complicated life? After a long moment, she looked at Peter and said, "It's complicated. I hate to keep saying that. And it *is* upsetting. I have a lot to figure out."

"Can I help? Be a sounding board or something?"

Marina shook her head. "Thanks, but I have to sort some things out with Zoe before I can talk with anyone else. It's all a bit much."

"The last thing I want to do is add to your burden. . . ."

"Oh, Peter, no . . . you aren't, really, it's okay. I just want to make things right with Zoe and get through the holidays."

"Is she okay? I saw her while you were gone and she seemed fine, excited about this new photography club, always out and about with Sasha."

Marina had seen that look so often over the years, a simultaneous tightening and softening of the face that conveyed concern, compassion, and she liked it that Peter seemed to feel as protective toward Zoe as his own niece and nephew. "She'll be fine, she's having some . . . growing pains. It's . . ."

"Complicated." Peter smiled. "Look, what I have to say can wait, but you have to promise me we will talk long and hard in the new year."

Marina's reflexive response was to demur, but in that moment, she knew without a doubt that, eventually, she would tell him everything—and she would be safe.

"Good," Peter said, standing up. "And when I say the new year, I mean January one."

CHAPTER 19

Marina's breath came in short gasps as she struggled to keep up with Lydia. There had been a brief thaw, followed by freezing temperatures that had turned the path by the railroad tracks into a slick chute of ice.

Marina slipped and fell to one knee. "Ow! Shit! Slow down, you beast. I thought this was a walk, not a race to the summit."

Lydia shaded her eyes from the sun and called to her friend. "Are you okay? Come on, there's a wall here. We can sit for a minute."

In spite of her throbbing knee, Marina was happy to be out, getting some exercise and having some quality time with Lydia. They'd talked every day the week of her return, mostly by phone or over quick cups of coffee on the way to or from picking up kids and running errands. They'd discussed her confrontation with Sarah from every possible angle until Marina couldn't think about it anymore—she was ready to move on. Then Peter had come to see her, and it was almost another week before Marina felt ready to face Lydia, who would probably want to know every detail. In fact, she was surprised that Lydia hadn't been on the phone to her directly.

Marina hoisted herself onto the crumbling stone wall that marked the perimeter of what had once been a grand estate. Through the trees, she could just make out the bulky shape of a mansion overlooking the Hudson River.

"It's great to be out and to have some uninterrupted time with you," said Lydia. "Are you okay? I didn't realize it would be so slippery out here."

Marina rubbed her knee. "I'm fine, maybe a little bruised. At least my knee hurts more than my heart right now."

Lydia put her arm around Marina's shoulder and chuckled. "Nothing like a little pain therapy. But seriously, are you feeling any better? You were so exhausted last week. How are you doing?"

Marina inhaled the crisp air and turned her face to the sun. "I'm fine, much better. The jet lag's gone. God, it seemed to drag on forever. And it really helped to talk the Sarah thing to death, thank you. I feel like I can lay that to rest and concentrate on giving Zoe what she needs, try to answer her questions."

"How's Zoe? Is she driving you crazy with questions?"

Marina looked at Lydia. "The funny thing is, she isn't. We're in our usual routine, coming and going, eating together, talking . . . about nothing." Marina shrugged. "I don't know."

"Maybe she needs more time just having you back. I think she was pretty shaken up by everything, especially her own anger. Running away like that, then you being away . . . Don't get me wrong, I think you did the right thing to go when you did, but I think having you gone underscored how important you are to her. Maybe it made her think twice about how she treated you."

"But she's right to be mad at me, really mad, and running away makes sense . . . in that crazy, out-of-control, teenage way. I don't think it was a smart thing to do, and it scared the hell out of me, but it helped me *get* the intensity of what she was feeling. But what's she doing with those feelings? I don't want her to stuff her feelings because she's afraid of losing me."

Lydia hopped off the wall. "Come on, I'm getting cold. Let's try walking between the rails, maybe it won't be as slippery." The two women walked side by side, leaving fresh tracks in their wake. "I agree, it is appropriate for Zoe to be mad, but I don't think you can make her unafraid of losing you. The reality is, you are the only parent she has."

Marina sighed. "I know. I guess I can only encourage her to have her feelings and reassure her that I'm not going anywhere."

They walked on in silence, the snow crunching underfoot, until Lydia bumped Marina with her hip. "June told me not to ask, but I have to. How was your lunch with my brother?"

"What did June say?" Marina was surprised. While June was a loving and compassionate person, she had a strict sense of boundaries to which she adhered with a tenacity that sometimes made it seem as if she wasn't interested or didn't care.

Lydia grinned. "The usual, that I should mind my own business. However, she did have a good point, something I hadn't thought of. What if you two got together and then had a fight or broke up, how would I be able to pick sides? What if you broke his heart?"

"Or he broke mine." The words slipped out as easily as any bit of friendly banter might, but the instant they crystallized in front of Marina, captive in her frosted breath, there was no denying their truth.

"Then I'd have to kill him." When Marina didn't laugh Lydia bumped her again. "Hey, I'm just kidding. I would never choose sides. We're all adults here."

Marina put her hand on Lydia's arm and brought them both to a standstill. "I . . . can't." Her eyes filled with tears.

"Honey, what is it? What can't you do?" A tear ran down

Marina's cheek. Lydia drew her into her arms. "What is it?" As Marina sobbed, Lydia rubbed her back. "Hey, hey, it's okay. We'll work it out, whatever it is."

Marina pulled away and wiped her face with a mittened hand. "It's not okay." She put her hands to her chest and pressed into the layer of down. "It hurts too much. It's bro—" Her sobs choked off the words.

Lydia gathered her back into her embrace. "Honey, I know. It's broken. Your heart is broken." She spoke softly into Marina's ear. "It's been broken for a long time, but now it's going to mend, you'll see. Trust me. It's going to be okay."

Marina lay on the couch, too exhausted to move. Choosing a Christmas tree with Zoe had always been a production, but this year it had seemed they might never find one that suited her daughter's criteria. They were all either "gross" or "lame." After an hour of torment, the poor salesman showed them a tree he was holding for someone else. Zoe promptly pronounced it *"perfectissimo,"* and they tied it to the roof of their car. Marina turned her head to where it stood in the corner of the living room. She had to admit that it was perfect in every way, but she felt sorry for the wrath the tree salesman would incur once his customer discovered his tree had been hijacked.

She sighed. Truth be told, she was feeling a bit sorry for herself as well. In the aftermath of her breakdown with Lydia the day before, she'd felt drained, her mind foggy, her heart numb, and her body sluggish as if weighted with lead. Was it any wonder she rarely allowed herself to cry—the aftereffects were more excruciating than the release. As well, the outburst had unnerved her. She hadn't seen it coming. She'd felt fine after Peter's visit. They'd agreed to talk in the new year. No big deal, right? Clearly it was a bigger deal than she realized, but she couldn't think about it yet. She needed to focus on Zoe.

She listened to the thumping from overhead as Zoe wrestled boxes of Christmas decorations from the attic. Marina had spent a restless night and, as the day dawned pink, had come to the conclusion that she wouldn't be able to help Zoe mend *her* broken heart if she didn't first come to terms with her own. And there was no denying it was broken. Yesterday's unrelenting tears and the lingering pain in her chest were irrefutable. She wanted to blame Sarah, but hadn't she actually broken her own heart by believing in fantasies, then cracked it a little more each time she lied to cover her mistakes? And now she'd broken her daughter's heart as well. How could she possibly come to terms with that? Lydia's words came back to her: "Only love can mend a broken heart." Had she meant she should love herself, love Zoe, or let Peter love her? Zoe's voice calling from above pierced her thoughts.

"Hey, Mom, I need your help. I can't do this by myself."

A few hours later, Marina and Zoe stood back to admire their handiwork. They had a system that had evolved over the years. First, Marina thinned the tree by clipping branches close to the trunk, creating space for ornaments to hang inside the tree rather than solely on the tips of the branches. Next was threading tiny white lights through the branches, which they did together, making short work of an aggravating task. Then Zoe decided on which branch each decoration would hang while Marina stood by with clippers to ensure each ornament hung free and clear of other branches. All in all, it was a laborious process, but the result was stunning.

"Wow, Mom, I think it's the best one we've ever had." Zoe turned to her mother with shining eyes and cheeks flushed. "Don't you?"

Marina put her arm around Zoe's waist and hugged her. "I think you're right, but it still needs the tinsel. Why don't you start that while I make us some cocoa?"

For some unfathomable reason, Zoe loved putting on the

tinsel. This suited Marina just fine, as the patience she counted on in the studio deserted her when it came to hanging two or three strands of staticky plastic strips on the end of each tree branch, a task that seemed to put Zoe into a Zen state.

Marina rummaged through the cupboard for a tin of cocoa powder, then gathered sugar, milk, and a saucepan.

"Hey, Mom," Zoe called from the living room, "can I sleep under the tree on Christmas Eve? You know, like you did once. How old were you? What did Gram and Gramps think?"

Marina stirred the milk, the grit of sugar grating against the bottom of the pan. "Sure," she called back. Was it a lie to let Zoe think it was something she'd done in childhood when in actuality the only time she'd done it had been the Christmas she spent with Sarah and Thomas? Marina tucked an errant curl behind her ear. Christ, Zoe seemed to remember everything she'd ever told her. Marina would just have to figure out a way to untangle the mess, lie by lie, and honor the promise she'd made to answer all Zoe's questions about her father. What sort of backlash would there be when Zoe came to realize just how much she had made up? How would it be for her to have her childhood fantasies disassembled piece by piece? Thankfully, she hadn't asked any questions so far, but Marina knew it was only a matter of time.

"That looks great, sweetie. Here, take a break and have your cocoa."

Zoe came down from the stepladder and took the mug from her mother while eyeing the tree. She pointed. "I think that red one there is too close to the gold star. What do you think?"

Marina smiled. This was the final phase, rearranging wayward ornaments as the tinsel was being put on. The tree looked fine to Marina but, too tired to argue, she sipped her cocoa and nodded in agreement.

Zoe removed the red ball and stood with it in her hand as

she scrutinized the tree. "I think it's sad that Peter's not coming to Christmas. Did he tell you why?"

Marina lowered herself onto the couch. "He's not coming? He didn't say anything. I didn't know he wasn't going to be here."

Zoe found a place for the ornament. "Sasha said he's going skiing."

Marina put her head back and closed her eyes, willing the knot in her chest to release.

The sea of crumpled wrapping paper and tangled ribbon that spread from the base of the tree to the foot of the couch was the only sign of the three adolescents who had spent the previous two hours sorting, passing, and unwrapping gifts with great whoops of glee. The pungent aroma of New Zealand lamb drifted in from Marina's kitchen, where June stood at the sink washing the breakfast dishes. Lydia lay on the couch in the living room, flipping through a new cookbook, while Marina set the table for a late lunch. Early that morning, Lydia and June had opened stockings with Sasha and Ben at their house and then loaded all the gifts from under their tree into the car and delivered them to Marina and Zoe's tree, a system that was reversed on alternate years and never questioned. From the very beginning, the two families had taken turns hosting the holidays, transporting food, baking dishes, and gifts from one house to the other, and now that the children were older, the secret middle-of-the-night Santa runs were, thankfully, no longer necessary.

Marina held up champagne flutes. "Champagne with the oysters?"

Lydia looked up from her book. "You don't have to ask me twice, and you know you don't have to ask June at all. Too bad Peter's not here. We could have made him spring for the bubbly."

Marina glanced at the small pile of unopened gifts under the tree and went back to setting her table. Had she imagined it, or was there an edge to Lydia's comment about Peter? Was it Marina's fault that he decided to go skiing with friends instead of join them for Christmas? He'd called her a few days after their lunch and was contrite when he heard she already knew he was going away; he'd wanted to tell her himself. Friends of his had a ski house out west, and none of them had kids, so it would be adults only.

"Not that I have anything against kids. You know that. I'll miss you all."

"Zoe will miss you," Marina managed, hoping he couldn't hear the disappointment and irritation she felt.

"I hope you will miss me, too."

"Of course I will." She wasn't sure if she was angry with him for deserting them or angry with herself for caring.

"Do you think you can handle the gravy without me?"

Marina smiled. "It'll be hard, but I'll manage somehow."

"I'll see you in the new year. Remember, January one."

"I'll be here."

"I'm counting on it."

He told her he'd left a gift for her with Zoe, something they'd collaborated on, and that she should open it on Christmas and not wait for him. Marina glanced at the pretty package leaning against the wall near the tree. It looked like something in a frame. Zoe had wanted her to open it earlier, but not wanting to open it in front of Lydia and June, Marina had begged off, using the excuse of attending the roast. Nor had she given Zoe the etching of the English Cemetery, deciding at the last minute to hold it back until they were alone. She would surprise Zoe later, and they could open their packages together.

"Do you like it, Mom? It was Peter's first choice all along, but I made him show me some other maps before I gave him the go-ahead."

The day had wound down to its inevitable conclusion of overstuffed bellies and foggy heads. The house was in a state of disarray, but Zoe couldn't wait another minute and in-sisted Marina open her gift from Peter. Marina stared at the map of Florence, the one Peter had shown her that day in the shop, which was even more beautiful framed and matted. She looked at Zoe. "I can't accept this. It's much too valuable."

"You have to. He was so excited to give it to you."

It suddenly struck Marina that Zoe had spent time with Peter while she was gone, just the two of them on their own. It felt odd to think of Zoe having a secret with Peter. Not an unpleasant thought, just different. It occurred to her that if she ever hoped to share her life with someone, she'd have to get used to the idea of sharing Zoe. Perhaps it wasn't such a bad thing to get involved with someone who already knew her daughter, like starting in the middle of a story rather than at the beginning.

"Earth to Mom." Zoe waved her hand in front of her mother's face.

Marina looked at the map, remembering her conversation with Peter that day at his shop and her wish for a map that would show her the way. Perhaps she was looking at it. She looked at her daughter's expectant face. "Yes, of course I'll keep it. I love it."

For a while the two of them sat side by side with their heads bent, studying the map, Zoe tracing the streets with her finger as Marina pointed out landmarks.

"Where's the English Cemetery? Where Dad is."

Marina clenched her jaw at the reference to Thomas as "Dad." "It's not on this map, sweetie. But that reminds me. I have one more gift for you."

Zoe unwrapped the small package and held the framed en-graving for so long without saying anything that Marina began to doubt her choice. Finally Zoe whispered, "It's the best gift you've ever given me."

Marina turned off the car and turned to Zoe, who was still pink from her afternoon of ice-skating with Sasha. "What do you say we take the tree down on New Year's Eve instead of waiting until after the new year?"

Zoe gathered her hat and mittens from the floor of the car. "Why would we do that?"

"I just thought it might be nice to start next year with . . . a clean slate."

"It's a dumb idea." Zoe got out of the car and headed for the house.

Marina watched her cross the lawn and pick up a large box from the front porch on her way into the house. It probably was a dumb idea. But in the days following Christmas, Marina found herself unable to settle into her work. Instead, she sorted drawers, organized closets, and made great piles of things to be taken to the Salvation Army. On several occasions, she'd tried to entice herself into relaxing in front of the fire with a glass of wine and a new novel, but whenever she sat still, her mind began to speculate on the conversation she and Peter were to have on the first day of the year—what he might say, how she might feel, would they fall in love, was she already falling—and before too long, she found herself dragging boxes out from underneath a bed or folding napkins she hadn't used in years.

Marina shrugged off her coat in the front hall and tossed her hat and gloves into a basket under the Shaker bench. She found Zoe in the kitchen, staring at a large box on the table. "What is it? Did we order something?" Marina picked up the kettle from the stove and filled it at the kitchen sink. "Sorry, what did you say?" She adjusted the flame under the kettle.

"It's for me." Zoe's statement sounded like a question.

"Would you like some tea, I'm having some?" Marina pulled two mugs from the cupboard.

"Mom, I think it's from Italy."

"What?" Heat flooded Marina's body, followed by a flash of icy cold that prickled the hairs on her head and down her arms. "Let me see." The return address confirmed her fear. She placed her hands on either side of the box as if she could divine its contents, calculating the harm it might do her daughter.

"It's from Sarah, isn't it?" Zoe already had the kitchen shears in her hand and began slicing through the tape and cutting the string.

Marina stood, unable to move or speak, and of all things, her mind focused on the small lead *piombino* that secured the string just below the knot. She recalled the first time she'd tried to mail a package from Florence and the poor woman at the post office who'd tried to explain that she needed a *piombino,* and how it was Sarah who finally helped her buy the little lead seal and showed her how to thread it on the end of the string before tying the knot, and then flatten it with pliers so that the package could not be opened without cutting the string.

Zoe had the box open. A white envelope with "For Zoe" written in Sarah's loopy script lay on the mass of shredded paper. Zoe reached for the envelope, but Marina grabbed her wrist.

"Ow, Mom, you're hurting me."

Marina let go and gently took the envelope from Zoe. The envelope was stiff and felt surprisingly heavy in her hand. Looking down at it, she found she was unable to think, not one thought formed in her brain, but as her heart rate slowed, she realized the futility of her action and handed the envelope back to Zoe.

Zoe hesitated a moment, then opened the envelope and read the note. "Wow! Look at this."

Marina scanned the note for signs of danger and, finding none, read it slowly to herself.

> *Dear Zoe,*
> *Your mother told me that, like your father, you have some interest in photography, and I thought you might like to have one of his cameras. This was his favorite. He was a wonderful*

photographer with a great eye for people, and I
wonder if perhaps you have inherited his talent.
Best regards, Sarah

Zoe extracted a familiar black camera case from the nest of paper. She looked at her mother. "What's 'Hasselblad'?"

Marina swallowed. "It's one of the best cameras in the world."

Zoe put the camera on the table and removed it from the case with great care. She ran her fingers over its black and silver casing. "It's so beautiful. Look, Mom."

It was beautiful, but no more lovely than her daughter's shining face. Marina realized she'd been holding her breath, and now let it out slowly. She couldn't remember telling Sarah that Zoe knew Thomas was her father, or even who Sarah was. Perhaps Sarah had just assumed that Zoe knew, although it seemed like a dangerous assumption, considering the damage it might have done if Zoe had not known. Marina pushed the thought away; she had enough to handle without dreaming up worse scenarios. She watched Zoe handle the camera. It looked natural in her hands, and Marina sensed that before long she would be able to think of it as Zoe's camera without the ghost of Thomas attached to it.

Zoe placed the camera back on the table and looked at her mother. "Why did you decide to tell me that my father was dead?"

The care with which Zoe asked the question touched Marina deeply, the use of the word "decide" changing what might have been an accusation into a question that showed a new maturity. It was the question that went to the heart of the wound, about the lie that could never be undone—there was no father, no Thomas, to make up for lost time. There was only the truth.

Marina pulled out a chair and sat down. "It's complicated, Zoe, but let me try and explain."

Please turn the page
for a very special Q&A
with Kathryn Kay.

I understand you once lived in Florence and I'm wondering how much of this story comes from your own experience living there?

Yes, like Marina, I did live in Florence when I was in my early twenties, but I stayed for five years. And like her, I did take a restoration course, but I specialized in fifteenth-century inlay techniques, although gilding was a component of the course. I had a friend there, a man, who apprenticed with a master gilder, and I found it fascinating. I did live in Via Luna and my landlord was a poultry broker, but as far as I know, his son was not a transvestite. I do remember seeing the transvestites in the doorways, as I described them the night Sarah and Thomas take Marina for a walk, but I didn't know any personally. The list goes on and on. As in any fiction, there are bits and pieces of me, my experiences, the people I know, mixed in with the fantasy. Just to set the record straight, I was not seduced by my best friend's husband nor did I have his baby. In fact, it was something I worried about regularly while I was writing the book—what if readers, especially people who know me, imagine I did these terrible things?

The relationships between the female characters in the novel are quite complex. Can you say something about that?

Yes, I think relationships between women can be quite complex, and I found that I had to be careful not to go off in too many directions since I had not only the central relationship between Marina and Sarah, but also the lesbian relationship of Lydia and June, their relationship with Marina, and the question of her sexual preference, and then there was Sarah's deep friendship with Marcello/Marcella the transvestite.

The original inspiration for Marina falling in love with Sarah came from a story that a good friend of mine (an older woman) once related to me. She told me that when her children were young, she'd had a good friend, someone she'd known for years, a woman with whom she'd raised her children, who one day confessed that she had "feelings" for my friend and wondered if there was any possibility of a more intimate relationship. My friend did not share these feelings and, while not offended, their friendship was never the same. I qualify that she was older only to point out that women having crushes on or falling in love with their female friends is not peculiar to contemporary generations. The more I delved into this subject with women, the more I realized how common it is and how little it is spoken about, and so I wanted to bring it out into the light and see what would happen. It's a very particular type of relationship. It's not about becoming a lesbian; it's about straight women and what they do with these feelings. I created the lesbian relationship between Lydia and June to better help Marina (and the reader) understand her own sexual orientation. What can I say? It's a complex topic with amorphous boundaries.

The other major relationship, of course, is between Marina and her daughter, Zoe. I understand that you were a single parent who raised a daughter. How much did that inform your characters?

Although my daughter did have a relationship with her father, whom she saw regularly, I raised her predominantly on my own and with very little financial support. She and I had (and still have) a lovely and very close relationship, but I did not hide behind it the way Marina did to avoid intimate relationships. Certainly, the love and emotion Marina feels toward Zoe are informed by the feelings I have for my daughter, and I can imagine the fear she feels when Zoe runs away and the terror at the thought that she may have lost her daughter's love. I know other women who are single parents, and I'm sure bits and pieces of them have crept into Marina's story.

Many if not most of the characters in your book are artists or are creative in some way. Is that because it's set in Florence, or is there another reason?

Florence does lend itself to art—that goes without saying—but my life has always been filled with creative people. My father, who was a businessman, was very creative and could paint and draw and make just about anything you might imagine, and was a good storyteller, too. There are six children in my family, and every one of us is artistic in some way.

When I lived in Florence, most everyone I knew was an artist of some sort, and I continue to be surrounded by creative people today. My husband is a businessman (who says we don't marry our parents?), but he's also a musician, and he paints and writes beautifully as well. I suppose it's true that we do write about what we know.

Your main character, Marina, struggles with forgiveness. Is this a concept you chose to explore for a reason?

Actually, I was about three-quarters of the way through writing the book before I realized that forgiveness had become a predominant theme. The concept of forgiveness is something I'm curious about. Intellectually, I understand the theory that if we do not forgive (give back) the injustice that is done to us, we are the one who suffers, not the one at which we direct our silent rage. But it's a concept I struggle with in spite of having had some modest success in that arena. Once I realized the theme was there, I began to work with it on various levels with each character. It makes sense to me that Marina might be able to find a way to forgive herself for her transgressions against Sarah, but perhaps find it more difficult to forgive herself for hurting her daughter. I could imagine Zoe forgiving her mother but perhaps only as a means to survive. After all, she's only fifteen and Marina is the only parent she has. Although I couldn't imagine how Sarah might find a way to forgive Marina, it's not beyond the realm of possibility, and I chose to leave that in the reader's hands.

Was there a particular, specific inspiration for writing this book?

There were a number, including the topics we've already touched on, but I also wanted to explore what happens when a good person makes a bad mistake. I wanted to create a sympathetic character who did something so bad it was unforgivable . . . and, yet, was it? In Marina, I created a character who made a terrible mistake when she was very young and then chose, out of fear and naïveté, to cover it up. Very quickly, it took on a life of its own, and before she knew it, she'd built a life on a foundation of lies. The thing is, she's not a bad person, but how does she survive a life like that and what can she do when it begins to unravel? I'll be very interested to know if the readers will forgive her.

Can you tell us about your writing practice?

Hmm, "practice," of course, is the operative word here. You have to practice if you are going to turn out good work . . . or any work at all. To be honest, I have to say that my writing practice is sporadic. I have a busy family life and a lot of other things I like to do. I enjoy teaching my workshops and coaching other writers, I'm a passionate gardener, I love to sail, I'm involved in community service, I love to travel, and my friends and extended family are spread around the world. But I'm not happy for long if I'm not writing. What works best for me is to write first thing in my day, and the only place I really produce work is in my office, which is over the garage and removed from the house. I spent many years beating myself up when I wasn't writing, until I realized that for me there is an ebb and flow, and that returning to my practice is just a part of the process. And I'm always grateful when I do.

THE GILDER

Kathryn Kay

ABOUT THIS GUIDE

The suggested questions are included to enhance
your group's reading of Kathryn Kay's *The Gilder*.

Discussion Questions

1. The novel's title, *The Gilder*, refers to Marina's profession. In what ways does the concept of "gilding" become a subtext of the story?

2. In what ways does Marina's youth influence her attraction to Sarah and Thomas and her initial experience in Florence? Did her upbringing make her more sophisticated or more naïve?

3. What does Marina learn about Thomas when she first attends his photography show? How do you think she feels about what she discovers?

4. To what extent was Marina culpable in being seduced by Thomas? At what point in the story did the seduction begin?

5. Marina did not tell Sarah about being seduced by Thomas for fear it would damage their friendship irreparably. When she discovered she was pregnant, do you think she should have told Sarah and Thomas? Was there another point in time at which she could have told them about Zoe?

6. What was the basis for Marina's attraction to Sarah? Did Sarah play with Marina's feelings intentionally? Was Marina a lesbian/bisexual or simply a woman who fell in love with her best friend? Do you think Sarah loved Marina in a way she was unable to accept?

7. Was Marina right not to tell Zoe the truth about her father's identity? How much of the truth should she have shared with Zoe?

8. To what extent does Marina use her work and her daughter as an excuse for not allowing herself a personal life?

9. After Zoe's birth, Marina's life is closely linked with that of Lydia and June. Why did the author create a lesbian couple to befriend Marina?

10. Marina vacillated greatly about whether to tell Sarah the truth when she returned to Florence as a grown woman. If Marina had not stumbled upon the bust in Sarah's studio, do you think she would have told Sarah the truth?

11. Do you think that Sarah sending the camera to Zoe at the end of the book indicates she will forgive Marina? Is it conceivable that a person might be able to forgive such a betrayal?